CORRODE

FOUR HORSEMEN
BOOK THREE

SARAH BAILEY

Published by Twisted Tree Publications
www.twistedtreepublications.com
info@twistedtreepublications.com

Paperback ISBN: 978-1-913217-25-9

To all the ladies with dark little hearts
craving violence, passion and lust

ONE

SCARLETT

TEN YEARS AGO

T he number of times I'd tried to convince myself I shouldn't go after them couldn't be quantified. Ever since Francis told me what they intended to do, I'd told myself it was okay. But a part of me couldn't stomach the idea of them being only sixteen and going this far. Doing something they couldn't ever take back. The boys and I had done so many reckless things together over the years, but there were lines you didn't cross. Things no teenager or adult, for that matter, should ever consider doing.

This... this was one of them.

It was why I'd followed them despite Francis warning me to stay away. They didn't want me involved, even though this affected me too. They were doing it for me. And I didn't want them to.

The night sky was cloudless, making it cold as hell. The chill seeped into my bones as I made my way through the gap in the fence of the silent building site. A couple of developers were putting up some new blocks of flats in the area. Some of the local residents had contested it, but the council had granted planning permission anyway. We needed new housing.

The boys and I came out here at night to hang out and drink despite the fact we were underage, so I knew my way around. My feet crunched along the gravel as I weaved through the JCB diggers and excavators and made my way over to the skeleton of the first block. The plastic sheeting flapped in the wind. Otherwise, it was eerily quiet.

It didn't feel right being here without my four protectors. The boys and I had been friends since primary school. We were a close-knit group and rarely kept secrets from each other. It's why Francis had told me. He didn't feel right about not including me, even though they'd agreed to this plan of theirs behind my back.

I walked into the ground floor of the skeleton building. None of the outer walls had been built yet. No one was around. I climbed the first set of concrete stairs and found the floor I arrived on empty too. I knew exactly where they'd be if they weren't here. I mounted two more sets of stairs and walked towards the other side of the third floor, where a lone figure stood staring out at the night's sky.

"West?"

I would recognise his bulk anywhere. The boy I knew on an intimate level. The one I'd fallen irrevocably in love with from the moment I'd laid eyes on him and had only confessed the truth to recently. It was only because of what almost happened to me I'd had the courage to tell him how I felt. And that almost event was part of the reason the boys had come out here tonight to do something nefarious.

West turned and stared at me across the expanse of the floor.

"You shouldn't be here, Little Nyx."

My heart lurched as it always did when he called me that. It had been my nickname for as long as I could remember. Drake had started it by winding me up about my height compared to them. Little Scarlett Nyx, their best friend and the only girl any of them ever hung out with.

I approached him, not wanting to listen to his warning. West's warm amber eyes came into view the closer I got. No matter what he did, he couldn't hide the way he felt about me. His eyes gave him away. When I stood before him, I could see the tension lining his face.

"Where are the others?"

West reached up and stroked his fingers along my jaw.

"Around."

I swallowed. Something about his demeanour was off. I had a feeling I was too late. Much too late.

"Frankie told me. Did… did you do it?"

West's eyes turned dark.

"He shouldn't have said anything to you. We didn't want you involved."

"West, did you do it?"

His hand slid along my face and into my hair. He tugged me closer to him, wrapping his other hand around my waist.

"Do you really want to know?"

His face lowered to mine. I couldn't stop myself from reacting. The way my body heated from being so close to his had me trembling with need. It reminded me of when we'd been together last week. When he'd made love to me for the first time. His gentleness. The way he'd watched me, cared for me and made me feel special. He'd erased the pain and gave me a new memory to hold on to. This boy had given me everything I'd ever asked for. And I appreciated him more than words could ever express.

West kissed me before I could respond, parting my lips with his tongue and taking my ability to think straight from me. My hands curled around his body, one wrapping around his neck to get even closer.

"Scar," he murmured against my lips, "remember I love you."

Then he released me. I rested my cheek on his chest, breathing him in as he held me.

"I love you too."

West and I had always shared this deep-seated bond with each other. We were connected on a level I couldn't explain. The five of us were, but the attraction between West and me was different. We wanted each other on a physical level. A desperate gnawing urge to be as close as possible. To be one.

"What did you do?" I whispered.

I needed to know the truth. Needed to hear the words from his mouth.

He held me against him as if he never wanted me to leave his body again.

"What we had to."

"West—"

"They tried to hurt you. They were going to rape you."

The anger and hatred in his voice made me flinch. I hadn't forgotten what the twins had tried to do to me. Ryan and Ray were two years older than us. They were sick, twisted and enjoyed hurting people. West, Drake, Francis, and Prescott had been trying to get them to stop harassing the girls in our class for months. Not to mention the things they'd got away with. The twins thought they were all-powerful because of who their father was, but everyone hated them.

"What did you do?"

He let out a long sigh, nuzzled my hair with his nose, and rested his chin on the top of my head.

"We shoved them into the foundations on the other site."

The builders had only recently started to lay the foundations for the second block. It was being built by a different developer and had a separate crew on site. They were months behind the first building. The one we were standing in.

"And?" I whispered, scared of what he would say next. Terrified of what the boys I'd grown up with were capable of. I knew the four of them like the back of my hand, but we were sixteen. None of us should be even considering this.

"We poured concrete over them."

I swallowed the bile rising in my throat. My worst fears had come true.

"You killed them."

"Yeah, Scar, we did. They can't hurt you or anyone else again."

While I wanted to stay in West's arms and pretend he hadn't just admitted to me he'd murdered two people with our three other best friends, I couldn't. The boy I loved was a killer at fucking sixteen years old.

Extracting myself from his grasp, I stared up into West's amber eyes. The ones that had the power to rip me to shreds.

"You drowned them in concrete?"

"We knocked them out first, so they couldn't struggle."

His statement was so matter of fact like there was nothing wrong with murder. They had planned to murder two people tonight. They'd carried it out.

"What the hell, West? That's not okay. You killed two people. The four of you. How could you?"

His eyes darkened.

"We did it to protect you and everyone else from them, considering Daddy is constantly covering up their shit for them. They raped Gillian, Becca, and Yvette and got away with it. You could have been next. If Drake hadn't been there, I fucking dread to think what they'd have done to you, Scar." He stabbed a finger towards where the other building would be constructed in the distance. "They're dead and the world is a better place for it."

I waved a hand around, feeling frustrated by his answer.

"How the hell do you think they aren't going to tie this back to you when their bodies are found, huh? Their parents know who you are. They know you hate the twins."

West took a step back and stared out at the night's sky.

"Their bodies won't be found. Who is going to check? We barely disturbed the equipment and they literally just started pouring that area today. All we did was make it a little higher than it had been before. They aren't going to notice."

I shook my head. The four of them were crazy. How could they think they wouldn't get caught? We weren't criminal masterminds, we were kids. Teenagers.

"They're going to investigate it. You can't kill the kids of a man like Stuart Carver and not expect him to do something about it! The man is famous. Did you lot even think this through?"

"Of course we fucking well did. We're not stupid. Nothing is ever foolproof, but this is the safest place to hide a body. When the building is finished, no one will ever know."

I paced away. I couldn't even look at him any longer. By insisting he tell me, I'd made myself a part of this when they hadn't wanted me to be here. They'd wanted to protect me. My four guardians had done this for me. And I hated myself for it. What the twins had done wasn't my fault, but I bore the responsibility of their deaths alongside the boys.

"I can't believe you did this. I can't... this is wrong, West. I know they were crazy, but you didn't have to kill them. No one needed to take it this far."

I felt him approach me, and when his hand landed on my shoulder, I shoved him off. Turning around, I could see the hurt in his eyes. I'd never once stopped him from touching me.

"Scar, we did it to protect everyone."

I shook my head and took a step back.

"How is this protecting people? You've put a target on all of our backs. They're going to find out and you'll all go to prison. I can't... I can't live without you. I can't. You are my world. All of you are. How can I ever live without you by my side?"

West stepped closer, but he didn't reach for me.

7

"No one is going to find out."

"They will! When they realise the twins are missing, they'll know."

"Scar—"

His hand came up. I took another step back to avoid him.

"No! Don't touch me!"

"Scarlett!"

Another step and my foot slipped. I looked back, finding I'd got way too close to the edge. My eyes went to West just as I fell. He lunged forward, grabbing my arm. I screamed. My arm was almost wrenched out of its socket when West slammed himself down on the floor and held on to me. I was dangling off the fucking third floor of the building with only my boyfriend keeping me from falling.

"West!"

"I've got you, Scar. I've got you, just reach up and grab the edge."

He sounded calm, even though I could see the frantic panic in his eyes. I was frozen in place, terrified by the drop below me. And scared he wouldn't be able to pull me back up.

"I can't."

"You can. I can't pull you up otherwise."

His other hand was braced on the floor to keep himself from sliding off too. West was trying to be brave for both of us. The least I could do was try back. I reached up with my free hand, but I couldn't stretch far enough.

"I can't!"

"God-fucking-damn-it, Scarlett."

He let go of the floor and tried to grab my other hand, but I was now swinging. Another scream erupted from my lips as we helplessly tried to grasp each other.

"West, I'm going to fall."

"No! You're not going to. I won't let you."

The problem was my grip on him was slipping. Tears blurred my vision. My breathing was out of control, along with my heart.

"West, I love you. Remember I love you, okay? Never forget that."

He shook his head, still trying to grasp me with his other hand.

"No, don't say stuff like that, Scar. I'm going to get you back up."

My hand slipped down his arm a fraction. He couldn't lean further out or we'd both fall. This was an impossible situation.

"I can't hold on."

"You have to. I need you. I can't live without you, please. I love you."

Tears fell down my cheeks. I knew it was too late. There was no one else around to save us. Whether the others had heard me scream was immaterial. They couldn't get here in time.

My hand slid from his arm. He tried to keep a hold of me, but he couldn't. Gravity dragged me lower. The last thing I felt from the boy I love was his fingertips grazing mine as I fell to my doom. The scream from my lips echoed around my skull, as did his shout.

"NO! Scarlett!"

It felt like it took forever for me to fall, even though it must have only been seconds. I stared up at West's horrified face, taking in every one of his features to brand them into my memory. And when I hit the ground with an almighty thud, all I could see was him.

"I love you, West, forever," I whispered before the pain sunk in and the world went black.

TWO

WEST

TEN YEARS AGO

My entire world shattered into a tiny million pieces. The girl I loved lay there on the ground, unmoving. I stared at her in complete and utter disbelief. She'd fallen three storeys. I hadn't been able to keep her safe. She'd fucking slipped and I couldn't get her back up.

"Scarlett!"

I had to get to her. And I needed the others.

Scrambling up to my feet, I ran like the fucking wind towards the stairs. My hand went to my pocket, digging out my phone. I mindlessly dialled Drake's number. I should call an ambulance, but I needed the boys more.

My feet carried me down the first set of stairs. I jumped down the last few steps in my haste to get to Scarlett.

"West?"

"Scarlett fell. Get the fuck over here."

"What do you mean, she fell? Is that why we heard screaming?"

"She fucking fell off the third floor. I'm scared she's fucking dead, okay? Get here. Now!"

I hung up. I was halfway down the third lot of stairs. I leapt down the rest of the way and ran towards her body. My heart raced at a hundred miles an hour.

You have to be alive, Scarlett. You have to be. I need you. I can't live without you.

My knees slammed down in the dirt when I reached her. Her body was at an odd angle. There was no escaping the fact she'd likely broken a leg. I couldn't deal with that right now. The only thing I could do was touch my fingers to her chest and see if she was breathing. I didn't want to move her, scared of injuring her further.

I let out a hoarse cry of pain when I felt her chest moving. It was sluggish, but she was breathing.

"Scar, I'm sorry. I'm so fucking sorry."

Tears I didn't want to fall started welling in my eyes as I felt for her pulse at her neck next. It was there. She was alive. But for how long? She'd fallen so fucking far. How could she be okay after this?

My hands went to the back of her head and came away slightly sticky. Oh fuck, she was bleeding. This could not be good. This was the worst fucking thing to have ever happened to us. To her. She shouldn't have come here. Francis shouldn't have told her what we planned to do.

"Scarlett," I whispered, stroking her face, "you're okay. You're going to be okay."

I didn't know that, but I had to reassure myself. I needed her to be okay.

Footsteps sounded, followed by a shout. I looked up, finding Prescott, Drake and Francis running towards us. They looked horrified.

"What happened?" Prescott said, reaching us first.

"She slipped… I couldn't hold on to her. I couldn't. She's hurt. She's fucking bleeding! You need to phone an ambulance."

Drake was already pulling his phone out when he got to us. Prescott knelt down beside Scarlett and looked her over, his face pale as he stared at our best friend. Francis joined us a moment later, his face stricken.

"How bad is it?"

"I don't fucking know!"

He knelt beside me and checked her visible injuries. The blood at the back of her head worried me the most. Had she cracked her skull? Fuck, there were too many possibilities. Too many options. And none of them were good.

Scar, please, you have to make it. I can't live without you in my life.

I couldn't stop stroking her cheek, reassuring myself she was still here. Her eyes were closed and her breathing was laboured, but she was alive.

"Scar, please, you have to live. You have to make it."

Drake put his hand over the phone.

"Where did she fall from, West?"

"The third floor."

He resumed talking to the emergency services, his voice too low for me to make out the words. All I could focus on was

Scarlett. Leaning closer, I stared down at her unconscious face, the most beautiful face I'd ever beheld.

"You have to make it," I whispered to her. "You have to."

I couldn't imagine my world without her in it. She was the thing keeping me going. The one person who brought light into my life. Fuck knows I had enough shit to deal with. My parents were cunts who didn't give a shit about me. Not when they saw me as one big fuck up. I couldn't help the way I was.

Tears fell down my cheeks. I didn't care if I was crying in front of the boys. They had no idea what had happened between me and her.

"Why the fuck was she here?" Prescott asked.

"You can direct that question towards him." I jerked my thumb at Francis. "He told her what we were doing here."

"What the fuck, Francis?"

Our friend looked between us before concentrating back on Scarlett.

"She deserved to know. We killed them for her, so don't act like this had nothing to do with Little Nyx."

Rationally, I knew he was right, but I couldn't think like a sane person right now. The girl I loved had life-threatening injuries. She was all I could see and feel. I needed her to be okay.

Drake moved closer.

"They'll be here soon, okay?" he said to the three of us before getting back to the operator.

Tonight had already been fucking taxing enough without this. It's not like any of us had wanted to kill Ray and Ryan, but they were rapist scum. They didn't give a shit about who they hurt. We'd had far too many run-ins with them. And no doubt it's why they'd tried something with Scarlett. They hated the four of us with a passion, but we never took any of their shit. So they'd gone after our best friend to prove a point. To show us they were untouchable. Well, they weren't. We'd proven that tonight.

"How did she fall?" Francis asked.

"We were arguing over what the four of us did. She's not happy we killed the twins. Kept going on about us getting caught."

Our argument was a blur in my mind. All I could think about was how she'd fallen. How I hadn't been able to hold on to her.

"She kept backing away and got too close to the edge. I tried to stop her, but it was too late. And fucking trust me, I tried to get her back up, but she slipped out of my grasp. I couldn't stop her, she... she fucking fell before my eyes and her fucking body lay there motionless. I... oh fuck, I can't."

I gasped and more tears fell. Francis reached out and put a hand on my arm as I dissolved into a mess. The tears dripped down on Scarlett, but I wouldn't move. I wouldn't leave her.

You can't leave me, Scar. You just can't!

In the distance, I could hear sirens. It didn't fill me with relief. If anything, I dreaded the moment they got here. We were going to get asked questions about why we'd been trespassing on the site.

"We need to get our story straight," Francis said, breaking the silence between us.

"We were out here messing around. That's all they need to know," Prescott said. "We're teenagers. They're not going to know what we really came here for."

They looked at each other before eyeing Drake. He could hear us and he gave them a sharp nod. There was no way he would give anything away. I could see the worry in his eyes as they flicked down to Scarlett.

"No one mentions the twins under any circumstances, okay?"

"I'm not fucking mentioning them. As if I want any of us to get into shit. Fuck, Francis, we're not stupid."

I'd left not long after Drake had hit the button to pour the concrete because I couldn't handle it. A part of me wanted to hurt the twins more. I couldn't stay and watch it without feeling rage building inside me. The others would deal with the rest. It's why I'd gone up to the other building to calm down. And then she found me there. Now everything had gone to utter shit.

I was trying not to lose it. I had to be strong for Scarlett. She'd need me when she woke up... if she woke up. No, I couldn't think like that. She had to wake up. She had to. The doctors would save her. I had to believe in them. Had to believe they would keep her alive.

"We should be worrying more about him, anyway," Prescott continued, pointing at me.

Francis looked at me. My tears had soaked Scarlett's cheek. My eyes were on her chest, watching for signs she was still breathing. I needed her alive.

The sirens were close now. They were almost here. I couldn't leave her. I needed to stay by her side so she'd know she wasn't alone. My hand went to her face again, stroking my tears away from her cheek.

"Stay alive for me, Scar, please."

The other two got up to go direct the emergency services, but I stayed with her. Kept staring at my beautiful girl who was so broken right now.

"Come back to me… please. I love you, Scarlett Nyx. You're my one, remember? My only one."

My voice was barely audible, but she had to know I was talking to her. Deep in her heart, she could feel me.

The next thing I knew, I was being pulled away by Prescott as the ambulance crew arrived. For a moment, I protested, trying to stay by her side. I didn't want to leave her, but I knew they needed to work, so I relented.

The four of us huddled together, watching them. Prescott had his arm wrapped around my shoulder as if he thought I might fall to my knees or something. To be honest, I might well do at this rate. My body was trembling all over and I couldn't control my thoughts. They were chaotic. I kept replaying the moment she fell over and over in my mind.

I didn't save you, Scar. I didn't fucking save you!

They worked quickly, assessing her injuries and strapping her up to lift her onto the gurney. Their faces betrayed the seriousness of the situation. One of them came over to us and asked what happened. I explained it again. Somehow I managed to, despite the fact I was a mess on the inside. Then he told us they were taking her to the hospital where it was likely she'd have to have surgery given her condition.

Scarlett had a suspected fractured pelvis, broken leg and arm. The thing they were most concerned about was her head injury.

"Can I come with you? Please, I need to be with her." My voice sounded desperate and needy. "She's our best friend."

Not like I could tell them she was my girlfriend because Prescott, Drake, and Francis didn't know about our relationship.

The guy gave me a sympathetic look but refused to relent, as I was underage and not family. At the very least, he told us where she was being taken.

I was going to lose my fucking mind as the police approached to ask us what happened. I needed to be with Scarlett. They asked us all sorts of questions and got Scarlett's mother's number from Drake, who was in a far more rational state of mind than I was. Lylah was going to lose her shit when she found out what happened to her daughter. Scarlett was the only thing she had in this world. Scarlett's father died before she was born, leaving Lylah alone to raise their daughter.

By the time the police were done talking to us, I was completely at my wit's end. A cold sweat beaded all over my body. Scarlett had been taken away in the ambulance. None of us knew if she was going to be okay. We stood together, not talking, not saying a word.

What if she didn't survive? What if her injuries killed her?

Drake put his arm around me, pulling us all closer together. I would have collapsed if he didn't have a hold of me.

"She's going to be okay. She has to be."

"You don't know that," I replied, my voice shaking on all of my words.

"I know our girl is strong as fuck."

Scarlett was the strongest girl I knew. But none of us could predict what would happen next, nor whether she would survive the fall. And my heart was breaking into a tiny million pieces, knowing I was the one who couldn't keep her safe.

CORRODE

She'd fallen because of me.

THREE

WEST

"I remember!"

Her words echoed around my brain. Did she? Had Scarlett truly remembered who I was? Who we were? Did she remember the night she'd fallen? How this was almost the exact situation we'd been in, only this time I wouldn't let her go. Scarlett was mine for life.

"I fucking remember, okay? Please, don't let me fall again. Please!"

Her voice was desperate now. Scarlett's eyes were wide with terror.

She knew.

She fucking knew.

I didn't hesitate, gripping the pillar tighter and dragging her back up. I almost fell backwards as she hurtled towards me. Letting go of the pillar, I caught her up in both my arms and took several steps back. Scarlett clung to me, her breathing erratic and her little fists clutching my coat. A sob erupted from her lips.

"I've got you, my little Scar. I'm never letting you go again. I promise. I fucking promise," I murmured in her ear.

There was nothing on this earth that would stop me from getting to my girl. My woman. No one would stand in my way.

The way she trembled had me holding onto her tighter, keeping her against my body so she could regain her equilibrium. I'd keep her upright until she could stand on her own two feet again.

A minute later, she released my coat and slapped my back with her hand.

"I can't believe you fucking did that to me. What the hell is wrong with you!"

Her words came out all shaky and her body was still trembling. The fact she'd told me off even when she was terrified had me smiling. There was my strong, vibrant girl who never cowered in the face of fear. Who always gave the four of us hell when she didn't approve of our actions.

"I've done a lot of things to you, Scar. Not sure how this is the worst."

She hit me again.

"Fuck you. You're the worst."

My smile grew wider.

"So you do remember me?"

She struggled in my grasp, but I wouldn't let her go. I couldn't. My Scarlett was here. My beautiful girl. The one who held my damn heart in her hands.

"Let me go!"

"Not until you answer me."

"Jesus fucking Christ, I remember you, West Greer." She stopped struggling and let out a shaky breath. "I remember that night."

I released her. Scarlett stared up at me. Then she clutched her head as if she was in pain. I wrapped an arm around her and drew her further away from the edge, scared of the same thing happening again. A moment later she shoved me off, then she was leaning down and throwing up the contents of her stomach. I gathered up her hair, keeping it from getting splashed by the sick. She moaned and threw up again, putting her hands on her knees.

I rubbed her back with my other hand, wanting to soothe her. I'd known forcing her to remember would cause her pain, but we couldn't go on like this. None of us could. It was killing me. I knew it was destroying Prescott. Even Francis hated it. Drake was just being a little bitch. He knew we needed her to remember us. He didn't want to face up to the consequences. Me? I was done hiding.

"Fuck," she hissed, straightening and wiping her mouth with the back of her hand.

"You done?"

She gave me a quick nod, so I helped her step over the sick and drew her away from it. Neither of us needed to stand too close. Not when I was worried she might throw up all over again. Her body was still trembling. My hand stayed on her arm, making sure she didn't fall over.

Scarlett tipped her head up to mine, staring at me with recognition in her hazel-green eyes. Finally, after all this time, she knew who I was. And when she reached up and touched my face, I shuddered under her fingertips. It was as if she was reminding herself of the boy I'd been. But that boy was dead. He'd fallen off the edge of the building alongside her. And he'd died the day she was taken away from us.

"West." Her voice was shaky and full of emotion. "I... I can't believe I forgot who you are."

I swallowed, trying to hold back from crushing her to me. From reminding her exactly how much I fucking well loved her. I didn't want to scare her away. I needed her to keep seeing me, even if it was only for a minute. Even if it was only for one more second.

Her fingers fell from my face and touched the space over my heart. It hammered away in my chest. The heart belonging to her. She knew it did. My girl knew. And it fucking hurt beyond belief, because then she dropped her hand and frowned. Her whole demeanour turned sour. I almost told her no. Told her she had to keep seeing me. But it was much too late.

My little Scar, please don't hate me for this. I tried to save you. I tried so fucking hard.

"You lied to me," she whispered before her eyes darkened. "You all lied to me."

There wasn't anything I could say. We had lied to her. It was for her own fucking good and ours. We couldn't trust her. Not after those fucks had stolen her from us and brainwashed her. They'd sent her here to get rid of us, but we were smarter than that. We weren't going to allow Stuart Carver to take us down.

"You... you, oh god, you did it. All of you... you did what... fuck."

She shook her head as if she was trying to remember more. As if her memories hadn't yet completely returned. I was sure it would take time.

"But they're not... how did I... oh god, I don't understand."

She took a step back from me, her hand going to her mouth. Her eyes were wide and full of shock. For the first time in a long time, I felt like a selfish piece of shit. I'd forced this on her. Made her remember the worst night of our lives. I didn't regret it even if I'd gone about it in the most unorthodox way I could think of. It wasn't exactly smart to make her relive the experience. It was the only thing capable of breaking through the barrier in her mind. The one keeping her from remembering everything.

I'd done what I did best. Taken a sledgehammer to the situation. Smashed through the glass ceiling and now the shards were raining down hell upon us all.

"I've always known they're not my real parents, but how... what... I..."

How could I explain it to her? Tell her the Carvers had taken her to punish us. To use her against us because they suspected we killed their sons. I mean, we had, but they didn't know for sure it was us. The bodies had never been found. They were missing, presumed dead. No one except the four of us knew what happened the night they died. And her. But Scarlett couldn't remember... until now.

She shook her head again. I could see the horror in her eyes. It was as if that night was playing out in her mind over and over. The realisation we'd destroyed everything because we were trying to keep her safe. We were trying to protect her and instead, she'd got into an accident and lost who she was.

"Why… why did you lie to me?"

What a fucking question. I took a step towards her, but she backed away.

"I should take you back to Fortuity."

I needed the others. They would help me explain it. We'd made these decisions together. We should tell her together. Besides, I was scarcely holding it together right now. Seeing the look in her eyes, knowing she recognised me, but her mind was too full of the past. Too full of memories. She was hurt and afraid. I'd already fucked it up by forcing her into remembering. If I did any further damage to Scarlett's mind, I might never forgive myself. I already felt far too guilty for not being able to save her in the first place.

"No! I don't want to go back there. You all lied! You're liars!"

"Scar…"

"No. Don't you come near me. You just fucking well dangled me off the building."

If this had been any other time, I would have grabbed her and taken her against her will. Right now, I couldn't stop replaying the night she fell over and over in my mind. I'd blocked it out when I'd made her relive it, but I couldn't any longer. We were both lost in that fucking night and it killed me. Fucking crippled me.

"I needed you to remember."

"By putting my life in danger again? You are crazy, you know that? Absolutely fucking insane."

26

She'd told me I was crazy before, but this time it hurt to hear it. Her remembering me and still feeling that way? It broke something inside me. And I was already broken enough as it was.

"You're no son of mine."

His words echoed around my skull, making me bleed on the inside. My cunt of a father had sent me off to a fucking psychiatrist a year after Scarlett disappeared. After I broke. They slapped me with an antisocial personality disorder when I turned eighteen. And that was it. They didn't want a son who was as fucked in the head as they thought I was.

Well, fuck him. Fuck his bullshit. I wanted to kill the cunt. I wanted him dead. Didn't care if he was my father. I didn't even care about my mother either. She could burn with him. They weren't worth my fucking time. The only people in my life who cared about me unconditionally, no matter how much I pissed them off, were Prescott, Drake and Francis. That number had included Scarlett once upon a time, but the way she was looking at me... it spoke volumes. She couldn't see me the same way she did when we were teenagers.

"Yeah, I am fucking crazy." I took a step towards her. "Doesn't change the fact you're coming with me. You're coming home, Scar. You're coming because you're mine."

"Home? I don't have a home. I don't belong to you." She waved a hand around. "I don't belong anywhere."

I gritted my teeth. It was the shock and anger talking. She knew she was mine. It hadn't changed. It would never fucking change. Scarlett had been mine since the day she was born. She was our fucking destiny. Fate had brought us together from the beginning of our lives and it would keep us together until the end.

"You are mine, Scarlett Nyx. You will always be mine. And you know why."

For a long moment, she looked at me as if she was trying to work out what I meant. Maybe she hadn't remembered everything yet. Maybe it's why she didn't understand, but she would. Eventually, she'd know why we all belonged to each other. There was no fighting it.

"I. Am. Not. Yours."

Then she turned and ran towards the stairs. It took me a second too long to react. She was almost at the stairs when I started after her. Scarlett didn't get to run from me now. I wouldn't let her.

"Scarlett!"

"No, you stay the fuck away from me."

She disappeared into the stairwell. I cursed, chasing after her. Down the stairs we both went, me calling her name and her not answering. She was determined to get away from me, but I wouldn't let her. I couldn't lose Scarlett again. I wouldn't survive it. Not after the last time she disappeared. It would annihilate me.

By the time I reached the ground floor, I could see her running into the crowd surrounding the boxers, who were a different set to the ones who'd been fighting when we'd arrived.

"Don't you fucking dare, Scarlett!"

I pushed through the crowd, trying to follow her light brown head of wavy hair, but there were too many fucking people. More had arrived in the intervening period. By the time

I'd got to the other side of them, she was nowhere to be seen. I dragged my hands through my hair, desperately searching for her with my eyes.

"Fuck!" I dragged my hands down my face. "FUCK!"

I wanted to kick the shit out of something, but finding Scarlett was far too important. If I had to search this entire site, I would. I'd go to the ends of the earth to find my girl. Didn't matter if she couldn't see me the way she had all those years ago. I would track that damn woman down.

Scarlett Nyx belonged with us. And I was never allowing her to disappear from our lives again.

FOUR

SCARLETT

uddling inside the cab of the abandoned digger, I tried to make myself as small as possible. I could hear him calling my name, and it fucking terrified me. What if he found me? What if he took me back there with them?

I couldn't face it. None of it. It was too much for me to handle. The memory of the night of my accident had slammed into me like a ton of bricks. It was all I could do to keep upright.

A tear slid down my cheek, knowing I'd run away from West. The boy who'd been my best friend as a teenager. The problem was, the man West was a full-on psychopath. He did whatever the hell he wanted. He went from normal to crazy in the blink of an eye. He fucking well dangled me off the damn building to get me to remember the night I'd almost died. If they weren't the actions of a crazy person, I didn't know what was.

To be honest... I didn't know what was up or down any longer. My whole life felt like one giant lie. Everyone I knew had been dishonest with me. They'd outright fucking told me lie after lie after lie.

I don't know who I am any longer. I don't know anything.

It was too confusing. All of it. My memories were all tangled up in my head. I kept seeing them flash before my eyes. They were far stronger than they were before. And they weren't in order. The only clear thing I could see was that night. The night I'd argued with West and fell off the damn building he'd brought me to this evening. It's why I felt sick being here. Why everything felt so wrong. This was the place where I'd lost all my memories. Where everything had ended and my new life began.

I knew in my heart I shouldn't have run from West. He was my connection to the past. All of them were. And yet they'd lied. They'd pretended we didn't know each other. The four boys who'd protected me as teens had ruined me as adults. The things they'd done since I'd arrived back in their lives made no sense. Why would they treat me with such little care now after everything we'd been to each other?

Another tear fell. I held back a sob. My heart was broken. My mind was shattered. I had nothing. Literally nothing. No family. No friends. Nothing.

Well, I had the Horsemen, but considering the way they'd behaved, I was inclined to stay the hell away from them. But no... they weren't the Horsemen to me. They were my best friends. At least, they had been ten years ago.

Why now? Why did we find each other again now?

The logical answer was I'd been locked away until now. And it only led to more questions. Why did the Carvers have me? How did they get hold of me? What really happened when I was in a coma?

I shook myself. Those were things I couldn't answer on my own. However, there was no way in hell I was going back to my father. But he wasn't my father, was he? I'd spent ten years believing it, but it was another lie. Where did they end and the truth begin? I didn't know any longer.

My goal right now was to escape West. To get away from this building site where I'd had my accident. To attempt to cope with the biggest revelation of my life. And the memories flooding my brain.

Raising myself up, I peered out of the window of the cab. I could see the skeleton building with its occupants, but little else. It'd got dark and the glow of the streetlights didn't penetrate this far. It made me curious why the building never got completed, but the thought was fleeting. The coast looked to be clear, so I needed to get out of here. Who the fuck knew where I would go, only it needed to be away from everyone I knew.

I climbed out of the cab, trying to stay as silent as possible. Then I crept towards where I thought the gap in the fence was. It was almost instinctive, like I'd done this hundreds of times before. And I had. This site had been somewhere we'd hung out many times as teenagers. When it was a wasteland. When they announced they'd be building a new block of flats there. Then when the developers started building works. It was within walking distance from where we all lived, but far enough away, none of our parents knew about it.

I pulled back the fence and slipped through. Instead of going back the way we came, I continued on between the two fences until I reached the end. Things had changed in the intervening years, but I could still jump the fence here and land on another street behind the building site.

I remembered once Drake and me had been running away from this group of boys who lived two streets over. They claimed we looked at them the wrong way. Drake had given me a foot up to get over the fence and I'd had to drag him over too. We'd landed in a heap in the gap between the two fences, our limbs tangled, both of us trying not to piss ourselves laughing. We didn't want to get caught by the boys. I'd clung to him as we heard them go past before we dissolved into a fit of giggles.

My heart burnt. He'd been so full of life and expressive when we'd been kids. And now? Drake was cold and unfeeling. Some of the why was clear to me now. The accident. It was the event he'd told me about last night. The one that changed all of them.

My hand went to my face, wiping away the tears falling. It hurt me so fucking much. The whole thing. The memory. Knowing I'd been torn away from the four boys who promised me we'd be friends forever. This place was a fucking graveyard of my mind, and I needed to be away from it.

Jumping the fence, I landed with a thud and took off toward the nearest bus stop. I'd find somewhere to stay tonight and deal with everything in the morning. Right now, my mind was too erratic. I didn't know how much longer I could keep going. I wanted to collapse into a heap. The flood of the past was threatening to burst through the dam in my mind. The one

West had taken a fucking sledgehammer to. The cracks were wide. The water was leaking through the glass. Soon, it would shatter and I would break.

I jumped on the first bus that arrived, not caring about the direction. Digging a tissue out of my bag, I dabbed my eyes. It was lucky it hadn't fallen off my body when West flung me over the side of the damn building. I looked through the contents. My phone. My purse. I had money. Maybe I should get a hotel room for the night. I could fall apart alone there without anyone knowing where I was. It was the only plan I had. I couldn't think past that. Not when I had lost everything this evening. It forced me to focus and check where I was.

There were a few missed calls on my phone from Francis, Drake, and Prescott. I ignored them and plotted a route to the nearest place I could stay. Then I turned it off so they couldn't contact me again.

By the time I got to the hotel, I was barely hanging on. The dam was breaking. And I had to be alone when it happened. No one could know. I was on my own now.

It was lucky they had rooms available. The place was kind of fancy, but I didn't care about the cost. I had enough money of my own with what they were paying me, considering I had no bills. The thought of using the money I'd earned from them made me sick, but I had no other choice.

It was a relief to get into the room. I shut the door behind me, threw my bag onto a side table, and collapsed on the bed. Then the tears started again. A hoarse wail erupted from my mouth, muffled by the covers, and my hands went to my head. The pain driving through it was far too intense. Like someone had taken an ice pick and dug it into my temple.

The glass shattered. The flood made my vision blur. White-hot pain echoed around my skull. I held my head between my hands and tried not to make a sound. The images were vivid, full of sounds and scents. They passed by too quickly for me to make most of them out. Flashes of the boys and our lives together were the clearest ones. And losing them consumed me. It was all I could do to lie there, tears streaming down my cheeks and let it all wash over me.

When the pain lessened, I undressed, left my clothes in a pile on the floor and curled up under the covers in the foetal position. There was one single memory that kept echoing in my mind over and over as I drifted off from exhaustion. The last time I was truly happy before everything went to shit.

My naked limbs were tangled with his. My hands were in his light brown hair. And his amber eyes were on me, full of love and affection. They held my future and dreams. They were the eyes I could drown in for the rest of my life. And they belonged to the boy I'd promised it to.

"I love you," I whispered. "I love you forever, West Greer."

"I love you too, Scarlett Nyx."

It was the most devastating part of all. I'd loved West my whole life. And I didn't recognise the boy I'd fallen in love with in the man who had forced me to remember the worst night of my life.

FIVE

DRAKE

The moment I stepped out of the lift after I'd finished work, I knew something was wrong. The tension in the atmosphere between Prescott and Francis was palpable. They weren't talking, but neither of them looked particularly happy.

"Dare I even ask what's going on?"

Francis looked at me, his grey eyes full of irritation.

"West is gone."

I frowned, digging my hands in my pockets as I walked into the kitchen to grab a beer.

"What do you mean?"

"He's not here, Drake."

"And?"

I had told West we needed a meeting tonight regarding the memory stick and getting in contact with Penn. He'd not responded, but he rarely did. He usually showed up. I hadn't told him in the message what we would be talking about. Knowing West, he hadn't deemed it as important.

"You did tell him we wanted to talk. He should be here."

"This is West. He does whatever the fuck he wants when he wants. Did you call him?"

Francis and Prescott looked at each other.

"His phone is off."

I didn't know why they were so concerned. West had a tendency to disappear whenever he felt like it. Pulling open the fridge, I extracted a bottle and popped off the cap with the opener before putting it to my lips. I closed the fridge and looked at the boys again. They were both staring at me with expectant expressions on their faces.

"What?"

"Did you forget who else should be here right now?" Prescott said, crossing his arms over his chest.

He and Francis were sitting on one of the sofas together. I scratched my head and set the bottle down on the kitchen island. Then my eyes darted about the place.

"Where's Scarlett?"

"And there we go," Francis muttered, rolling his eyes.

My first thought hadn't been her. Today had been busy, and I didn't have a chance to consider what we were going to do about her and the memory stick. We needed to find out what was on it first before making a plan.

"Where is she?"

"We assume she is with West, but we don't know for sure," Prescott said, raising his eyebrow.

I set my hands on the counter.

"Did you call her?"

CORRODE

"Yes. It went to voicemail."

I pulled out my phone and tried her myself. Letting out a little sigh of frustration when it also went to voicemail, I stuffed my phone back in my pocket. I picked up my bottle and walked over to the living room, taking a seat on the sofa opposite the boys.

"What are we going to do?" Francis asked.

What the fuck could we even do when neither of them were answering?

As much as I wanted to lose my shit, we didn't know what was happening. And I wanted to trust in West to a certain extent. He wouldn't put Scarlett in danger. He loved her even if he'd not admitted it to any of us out loud.

"We're going to assume she is with West."

"Where do you think he took her?"

"I have no fucking idea."

West was a law unto himself. In a way, I was happy he was making an effort to spend time with her. Fuck knows he needed to. We'd all seen what losing her had done to him. He'd kept his distance far too much, except for when he'd carved a damn brand on her skin. My annoyance over the whole thing had lessened with the passing days. Scarlett hadn't complained about it to us. If anything, she'd accepted it. The girl took a lot of things in her stride. Even my shitty behaviour.

I sipped my beer, trying to work out how on earth I would fix all the shit between us. Last night had been a start, but it wasn't enough. When I was alone in my room, all I could think about was her. How I wanted her to see me. The real me. Perhaps her finding me playing on the roof had ignited something in me. I couldn't turn it off.

39

I wanted Scarlett to actually want me back. And it meant I would have to stop being such a dick to her. Stop acting like she wasn't exactly what I needed. Her fiery spirit and tenacious soul were so fucking intoxicating.

I miss the girl you were, little wisp. I miss confiding in you. I miss you so fucking much.

Yet even as I wanted to open up to her, there were so many things holding me back. Too many secrets we were both holding onto. How could I show her me when she didn't even know who I was before? When she didn't understand everything we'd done was to bring her back to us. It didn't change the fact we needed her to destroy Stuart Carver. She was the key to his destruction. She was the only person who had ever been on the inside. And while I was sure Scarlett couldn't tell us much, she had a way in. A way to get to him.

The problem was, everything changed when she came back here. When we all realised, we couldn't look at her as our friend any longer. When we wanted her so fucking badly, we'd gone to extreme lengths to have her. And I wasn't talking about when we'd bided our time until we could return her to us, although it had been extreme too. The desire we all felt towards Scarlett was fucking crazy. It consumed the four of us, making it impossible to do anything but give in.

Perhaps it was always meant to be this way or maybe now we were adults and we'd all changed, things were different. We'd undergone a huge transformation in the time she'd been missing. We'd turned to darkness and depravity without her. But when I thought about it, I knew Scarlett was as fucked up as we were. She was seduced by the corruption. And we'd debased her further. We drew her into our world and made her a part of it. She'd become a member the day she'd killed a man. The day we'd forced her to face her own perverse little soul. And what a kinky little thing she was. Desperate for discipline but with a need to disobey.

My little wisp. Our girl. Our queen. Our everything.

"I don't like this," Francis said, turning to look out of the window at the fading light. "I've felt off all day... like something fucked up is about to happen."

"Same, something isn't right," Prescott muttered.

I don't know why these two were acting so fucking superstitious, but then again, the whole thing with the memory stick and Scarlett finding me last night had thrown me for a loop. Maybe I was ignoring the signs. But what could go wrong between West and Scarlett?

"Well, you two can sit here acting like the world is about to fall apart," I said, raising myself back to my feet. "I'll do dinner."

They watched me walk away. I could feel their eyes on my back. Probably wondering why I was acting so blasé about the situation. The truth was, I couldn't afford to allow it to get to me. My mind was already way too full right now. Things regarding the business. Shit with Scarlett last night. It was occupying far too much space in my brain.

Making dinner helped focus my mind on something else, and it was a relatively silent affair between us. We sat watching TV while we ate rather than getting set up at the table. Prescott and Francis were agitated, and it showed. It was affecting me too.

Who the fuck decided we should put on a thriller show about some psycho guy who'd kidnapped a girl and made her into his sex slave?

41

It made me think of our own situation and hit a little too close to home. I mean, I didn't regret anything we'd done, even so, I had to question what the fuck Prescott and Francis were thinking when they picked this out.

"Are you two serious with this?"

I waved at the TV.

"What do you mean?" Prescott asked, giving me a curious look.

I rolled my eyes and stared at Francis, who also glanced at me with a shrug like he didn't know what I was getting at either. These two were getting on my last fucking nerve right now. I opened my mouth to reply when my eyes went to the lift, watching it light up. My jaw snapped shut as it arrived on our floor and the doors slid open.

I was not expecting West to stumble out of it, his amber eyes full of panic. He looked between us and ran his hand through his hair.

"What's wrong with you?" Prescott asked before I could.

West took another step towards us. A part of me wanted to question whether he was on something, but then my attention went back to the lift. No one else came out. My eyes narrowed.

"Where is Scarlett?"

The tension in the room ratcheted up a notch. The fact West hadn't immediately responded put me on edge and I was already anxious as it was.

"She ran away from me," West finally responded in a quiet voice.

Francis stood up and stepped towards our friend.

"What do you mean, she ran away from you? What the fuck did you do this time?"

West flinched, but he didn't look angry with Francis. It was unusual. In fact, it made me even more concerned as to why he was acting so strangely.

"Do you want the good news or the bad news?"

"Is there any good news?"

He rubbed the back of his neck.

"Kind of."

Francis threw up his hands.

"Just fucking tell us."

West shuffled over to us and took a seat on the free sofa before putting his head in his hands.

"She remembers who we are."

We all went very still, our eyes on West, who looked like his world had just fallen apart. I didn't know what the fuck had gone down this evening, but clearly, it was nothing good. I cleared my throat.

"Dare I ask how she remembered?"

West dropped his hands but didn't look up.

"I took her to the site... we went to go see the bare-knuckle boxing, but I got into a fight and... and then I took her up to the third floor."

Prescott sucked in a breath while Francis sat down again, his silver eyes wide.

"She tried to kiss me and I got agitated by it. I can't kiss her when she doesn't remember who the fuck I am."

He looked up at us then, his amber eyes full of unrepressed fear.

"You don't understand. She kissed me the first time. She... she initiated it and there she was, doing it again. It didn't feel right."

He rubbed his hands along his thighs as if telling us this story was making him crazy. Well, crazier than usual.

"I needed her to remember. I told her we knew each other. I asked her if she'd remembered us. If she'd seen us in her memories... and she had. She fucking well had. All of us when we were younger, but you know, she didn't want to believe it was real. I couldn't take it. She was acting like remembering was impossible."

I don't think I'd seen West this emotional since the day Scarlett fell. In fact, it had been the day we found out she'd disappeared when West had lost it completely.

"What did you do?" I asked, unsure if I wanted to know what the fuck it was.

The fact West had taken her to the site of her accident made me angry as hell. I'd warned him about going back there, even going so far as to get him banned from the fucking fighting ring. But no, West didn't want to listen to me. The idiot just wanted to torture himself because he held himself entirely responsible for her fall. We all knew it wasn't his fault. There was nothing he could have done to change what happened, but the guilt? Well, it ate him up inside.

West's eyes met mine, and I knew what he said next would not be good.

"I reminded her of that night... by dangling her off the building."

SIX

FRANCIS

D rake was up and out of his seat the moment the words left West's lips. He crossed the distance between them before slamming his hands down on the back of the sofa, forcing West to sit back and look at him.

"What the actual fuck, West?"

For once in his life, West didn't give us one of his maniacal smiles. He didn't act like a cocky little shit either. He stared at Drake with abject misery written all over his features.

"She needed to remember," he whispered, his voice laced with pain.

"So what, you decided it was a good fucking idea to put her life in danger? Jesus fucking Christ." He gripped West's shirt in one hand and looked like he wanted to strangle our best friend. "What happened that night was an accident. We all know that, but this… you took her there and fucked with her head."

Drake paused, his voice coming out strained and full of anger. West hadn't moved. He was still staring up at Drake with too many emotions in his eyes.

"I begrudgingly accepted you branding her because of things I don't claim to understand about your relationship. Then you do this."

"Her memories came at a cost."

"A cost? What if you dropped her, West? Did you think about that? What if you fucking well killed her, huh?"

West flinched. The last thing he would ever want was Scarlett's death on his conscience.

"I didn't kill her. I would never. You know how I feel about her."

"How you feel? How you fucking feel?" Drake dropped West's shirt and waved his hand around. "What about the rest of us? Don't you think we feel something for her too?"

West looked absolutely defeated, as if the evening had taxed him heavily. And judging by what he'd told us, it had. Then he steeled himself and glared at Drake.

"I needed her back. We all need her back. Pres wanted it. Frankie did too. You're the only one who was standing in our way. You didn't want to face the consequences of her finding out. And now she has, we all have to fucking face it."

Drake straightened and put the fingers on the bridge of his nose.

West wasn't wrong. Prescott had been adamant about it for weeks. While I hadn't exactly voiced it in the same way, I'd wanted her to remember too. Drake was the one who'd stopped us. He slammed the brakes on it. And it was something we were supposed to be discussing tonight, on top of the damn memory stick. Now, I had no idea when we'd deal with that shit. Didn't matter when Scarlett was missing. She was far more important.

"What happened after you dangled her off the building?"

West didn't immediately answer. He looked out of the window and rubbed his thighs with his hands.

"I didn't drop her, not after she remembered. And she does. The way she looked at me when I hauled her up. She saw me. She recognised who I was. She knew me. And it was everything."

He rose to his feet and shoved Drake away from him before walking to the window. Placing his hand on it above his head, he stared out at the dark city skyline.

"Only she ran away afterwards. She ran from me because we lied to her. Now she's out there all alone without us when she needs us the most."

His words echoed around the room. I glanced at Prescott who looked like he wanted to break. My hand went to my heart, rubbing it absentmindedly as it ached in my chest. Scarlett needed us. And we weren't there for her… again.

Drake sat down heavily in West's vacated place and put his head in his hands.

"You've made a real fucking mess of this," he said in a pained voice.

"That may well be, but I did what I had to. I made her remember us."

And there was the West we all knew. The man who was unapologetic about his actions. To be honest, I wasn't sure I wanted him to apologise for what he'd done, either. Fuck knows, we needed Scarlett back in our lives. The real Scarlett, who wasn't locked behind a glass wall in her mind. We wanted our girl back. The one who completed our family.

"Where would she go?" Prescott asked after a long moment of silence.

"She wouldn't have gone back to Stuart if she remembers that night," I said. "Did you tell her what they did to her?"

"No," West replied. "I didn't get a chance to. She didn't give me one. I couldn't explain."

Even though she remembered the past, there was still a chunk of it missing. After her surgery, she was in a coma, then they kidnapped her and she was never heard from again until she turned up here ten years later, a fully grown woman who didn't remember who we were. Scarlett needed context to understand why the Carvers weren't her family. They weren't who she belonged with.

"We need to find her."

West turned his head, his eyes full of darkness.

"I know that. Why do you think I came back here? I need you three to help me work out where the fuck she would have gone."

If the four of us put our heads together, we could come up with something. Scarlett wouldn't have gone far. She didn't have a ton of options.

"I'm guessing she's going to want to be alone for a while," Prescott said, glancing at me. "It's got to be a lot for her, remembering sixteen years of her life." His eyes turned sad. "I can't even imagine what that would be like." His hand went to his hair. "My poor little lamb."

We all knew Prescott was in love with Scarlett. He was the most affected by her pain. Her sadness. And yet knowing she was suffering made me want to hurl something at the wall. It forced me to admit my feelings for Scarlett ran deep.

The girl I'd known my whole life had dug her way inside me as an adult. She'd shown me her vulnerabilities just as she'd done when we were teenagers. She'd trusted me to keep her safe. Our woman might not have remembered who we were, but it hadn't changed her personality. She was still Scarlett, just not the complete version who knew us.

I got up and paced away, unable to take the emotions swirling in my gut. The image of her lost and alone was like a fucking knife to the chest. Those hazel-green eyes full of confusion and misery. And how she'd be helpless against the tidal wave of her memories.

I didn't know what the fuck to do with myself. My feet carried me into the kitchen and the empty beer bottles sitting on the counter. I picked one up, stared at it before hurtling it halfway across the room. It smashed on the wooden floor, making everyone turn to look at it. Then their eyes went to me. I was too worked up to care about their disapproval. My hand went to the second bottle. I threw it. The sound of it breaking echoed around my skull.

"Francis."

Drake's voice was full of concern, but I ignored him, picking up the third bottle and tossing that one for good measure. I wanted to scream, but my voice was caught in my throat. It was getting hard to breathe. We were meant to be there for her when she remembered. All of us. We'd always taken care of Scarlett.

My hand went to the last bottle. I stared down at it in my hands. If I smashed this one too, would it make me feel better?

Would it take away the agony? Would it stop hurting so fucking much?

For the past ten years, I'd tried to keep my emotions at bay. Tried to shove them down in a box. My denial had only worsened them. All it did was make me want to hurt everyone who'd wronged us. It made me crave violence and destruction the way West did. Yet my conscience was a ticking time bomb. It loved to rear its ugly head and remind me of all the blood on my hands. On all our hands. The stain that would never come off. And if I was honest, I didn't want it to.

I'd battled with my own inner nature my whole life. The two sides of me. The one who was kind and cared about those he loved. And the one who revelled in depriving people of things. Starving them of their last moments. Their dying breaths. I almost laughed. I'd always considered it a sickness inside of me. The part of me that related way too much to the damn name they'd branded us with. The man who wanted to live up to it. It wasn't a sickness or a curse. It was me. I should have accepted it long before now.

They say it's feast or famine… and it's time I embraced the latter.

I put the bottle back on the counter. Then my knees gave way. I slid down it, placing my head in my hands. It wasn't just my acceptance I craved, but hers too. I missed her gentleness. The way she always understood.

The night we'd made her kill someone, she told me in the shower the fact I liked to kill and had no remorse for it didn't scare her. The way she'd stared at me had tipped my world upside down. And yet everything held me back as she didn't recognise me.

If Scarlett truly saw who I was, including the boy she remembered back when we were kids, could she love me?

The very last person I expected approached me and sat beside me, resting his head on my shoulder. I glanced at West, who looked as defeated as I felt. Clearly, he'd noticed I was having an existential crisis.

"I forgive you," he whispered. "For that night... I forgive you for telling her."

"You do?"

He nodded and stared down at his hands.

"Why? You've never wanted to forgive me before."

I had a hard time wrapping my head around it. West had always been angry at me over it. He held me responsible for Scarlett being there.

"Seeing her tonight, going through it again... it made me realise we should never have kept it from her. You were right to tell her, even if it led to this. She deserves the truth. It's why I wanted her to remember. I mean, yeah, I'm not going to lie. I was fucking selfish going about it the way I did. I was desperate, but it's what she wants, isn't it? To remember?"

I nodded.

"More than anything."

She'd basically told me as much. And Prescott, for that matter.

"I just wish she hadn't run."

"Me too."

Prescott peered over the back of the sofa at us. His blue eyes were sad.

"Are you thinking about the day we found out she disappeared? This reminds me of it."

West didn't look up at our friend, but I narrowed my eyes. That day was a breaking point for all of us. It was nothing like what we were experiencing now, but I could see what Prescott meant. The heavy atmosphere between us was suffocating.

"We're going to find her, Pres," I said, not wanting to consider the possibility of her disappearing for good.

"I just don't know where to start. It feels... hopeless."

Drake stood and came closer. He stared at the three of us with a haunted look in his eyes.

"We are never going through that day again, Pres. Never."

The conviction in his voice reminded me of Drake's dogged pursuit of Scarlett after she went missing. He never gave up. He sent us all after lead after lead. And when we found out Stuart Carver had taken her, he devised a plan to get her back. Drake wasn't going to let this faze him. And we shouldn't either.

Drake came closer and squatted down in front of us. West looked at him. While Drake was pissed off with West for what he'd done, he understood why. And he wasn't going to hold it against our friend.

"I promise you, West, we'll find her and bring her back. We need her."

Prescott got up and came over to us. He rested his hand on Drake's shoulder.

"I promise too."

West gave them a nod and stared down at his hands. I had a feeling all of us were now thinking about the day she'd disappeared now Prescott had brought it up. It was a memory I hated almost as much as the night Scarlett fell, because it was the day we all had to face up to the consequences of what we'd done. And how it had ruined everything.

SEVEN

PRESCOTT

TEN YEARS AGO

M y eyes were fixed on the TV, but I wasn't paying attention to it. How could I when our best friend was lying in a hospital bed in a coma because of her head injury, and had been for the past couple of weeks? When she'd been through major surgery to pin her pelvis back together and had suffered a fractured arm and leg. Scarlett wasn't okay. And neither was I.

Not sure I had words to describe what happened that night. My three friends and I had become killers. We'd murdered two people to protect Scarlett. To make sure they never hurt her or anyone else ever again.

For as long as we'd been at secondary school, the Carver twins had terrorised everyone. And hated us. We never took their shit. Ray and Ryan had a vendetta against the five of us. It's why they took Scarlett and tried to hurt her. They were going to rape her. A day hadn't gone by since then when I didn't appreciate Drake's intervention. He'd stopped it before it could go too far. But now… now Scarlett might not wake up. And it hurt too fucking much to think about.

We couldn't lose her. She was our best friend. The person keeping us together. Scarlett was the beating heart of our group. Without her, we were at a loss for what to do next.

Drake, Francis, and West were at my place. Mum was out at work, but as it was the school holidays, none of us had anywhere else to be. A couple of weeks ago we'd been celebrating the end of exams. Now, we were all on edge, worrying about Scarlett's condition and whether she'd wake up.

West had been crashing on my sofa since the night of the accident. Mum didn't mind him being here, especially under the circumstances. Mum had always treated the boys and Scarlett like family.

West sat with his arms crossed over his chest, his amber eyes fixed on the window of my living room. Francis and Drake were next to me, having a quiet conversation about the latest bullshit with Drake's parents. Yesterday they had a shouting match in front of us when we were over at his place. I swear Drake's mum, May, was better off without his dad, Oscar. He had cheated on her and made no apologies for it. Drake was stuck in the middle of the two of them, though at this rate, he'd never want to go near his father again.

"Is it okay if I crash at yours again?" Drake asked, rolling his eyes.

"Yeah, course," Francis replied, giving him a nudge.

Francis and Drake lived next door to each other. May and Francis' mum, Eliza, were best friends, just like their sons. I'd met them at primary school, along with West and Scarlett. We'd become quickly inseparable, spending every moment we could together. There was magnetism between us, coupled with the fact we all shared an unbreakable bond forged long before we even met. Scarlett liked to call it destiny. She said we were meant to be. The thought of her made my chest ache.

West's phone rang, breaking through the tense atmosphere. He grunted and pulled it out of his pocket. I lowered the volume of the TV when his eyes widened and he shoved it against his ear.

"Lylah, how is she?"

His voice sounded gruff and was filled with desperation. West had taken her accident the hardest. He blamed himself for not saving her, but we all knew there was nothing more he could have done.

West's silence made me nervous as he listened to what Lylah had to say. His hand curled into a fist in his lap, the only sign something was wrong.

"Are the police involved?" he asked after a few minutes had gone by.

The way his eyes went black made me swallow.

"Yeah, we're okay, Lylah."

I could tell it was a lie to appease her. West wasn't okay at all. He was hardly coping. None of us had been since that night. It was bad enough we'd killed two people, but Scarlett's accident had taken a huge toll on all of us.

"I'll talk to you soon ... okay ... bye."

The phone dropped into his lap. Then his bottom lip trembled.

"What did she say?" Drake asked.

With slow, laboured movements, West stood up. His phone slid to the floor with a thump. Both his hands balled into fists.

"Someone took her from the hospital."

"They moved her? Why?"

West's head snapped to Drake.

"No, Drake, they took her... someone took her without them authorising it. They kidnapped Scarlett." He sucked in a jagged breath. "The police are involved. Lylah sounded like she was barely holding it together. She's missing... Scarlett's gone."

There was a rushing sound in my ears as his words settled into my bones.

Scarlett is gone. She's gone. Gone.

"She's been kidnapped?" Francis said, his voice shaky.

West nodded. His fists unclenched and clenched again at his sides. I could see the war brewing in his head. The agony and pain.

"Why would anyone do that? She didn't do anything wrong."

None of us spoke. We'd done something wrong, but no one knew about it. At least, they didn't know we'd been involved in the twin's disappearance. Three days after Scarlett's accident, the news broke. Stuart Carver's twins were missing. He was the owner of Rotherhithe United Football Club. We'd met him on a few occasions. We didn't like him because he looked down at us. He sneered at me the most because I came from a single-parent household.

It was two days after the headlines broke when the police turned up on my doorstep to question me. The others had similar experiences. The man who'd interviewed each of us was Detective Inspector Garrett Jones. He creeped me the fuck out. All of us got a bad vibe from him. Not to mention he was the father of the twin's dickhead best friend, Mason. He was older than them and had always been on the twins' side whenever fights broke out between us. Not to mention his creepy as fuck crush on Scarlett. The guy was six years older than us. It was lucky she hadn't noticed Mason watching her whenever he picked up the twins from school. A twenty-two-year-old staring at a schoolgirl was just plain fucked up, in my opinion.

We'd denied any knowledge of what happened to the twins to the police. They had nothing to go on. The four of us had been careful when we lured the twins to the building site. There was nothing to connect us to it other than Scarlett's accident. They didn't know the twins were dead, just missing. And they wouldn't find the bodies. We'd checked the site several times over the past couple of weeks. The foundations had finished being laid. We were in the clear so far.

"I don't fucking know, Frankie," West muttered, then paced away, his back radiating with tension and his hands still fisted at his sides. "But she's gone. I can't fucking believe she's gone."

He opened the patio doors leading out onto the back. Mum had a two-bed council flat on the ground floor. We were lucky to have a back garden even if it was tiny. I got up and followed him, worried about what he was about to do. And I was right to be.

The moment West got outside, he tipped his head back and let out a horrifying wail of pain. The next thing I knew, he was throwing the garden furniture around and kicking it in his frustration. Drake and Francis joined me by the door, watching West wreck the place, but none of us stopped him. How could we? All of us were suffering. All of us were in pain.

When he dropped to his knees and pounded the ground with his fists I moved, running over to him and falling to the floor too. I wrapped my arms around him from behind. West let out a choking sound of pain.

"I've got you," I whispered. "We're here."

Francis and Drake came over, both of them getting on the floor with us. They wrapped themselves around West and me. His body shook with the weight of his misery.

"She's gone," he sobbed, making me aware he was crying. "She's fucking gone."

It sunk in for all of us. I could hear the other two unable to hold it together. Francis was breathing heavily, and Drake let out a choked gasp. I bit my lip to stem the bleeding mess of pain left in the wake of knowing she had disappeared. My face dropped to West's spine. I allowed the tears to flow. There was no use holding back. The four of us had seen each other at our worst. We'd killed together. And none of us would be the same again. Not now we'd lost the one person we'd fought so hard to protect. It turned out none of us could protect her from this. From the unknown.

"We'll get her back," Drake whispered. "We're going to get her back."

"How?" Francis asked. "We don't even know who took her."

"I don't know, but we will. I promise."

It was a crazy promise to make considering we were four sixteen-year-olds who didn't even know where to look, but I felt it deep in my soul. The four of us would find Scarlett.

"She belongs with us," West said, his voice hoarse.

Scarlett did belong with us. She was our best friend. The girl we'd kill for. And we wouldn't let anything keep her from us forever.

"If we stick together, we'll find her, no matter how long it takes," I said.

We all squeezed each other as if we were cementing our promise. No matter what happened, we would stick with each other. We'd make sure we found our best friend if it was the last thing we ever did.

EIGHT

DRAKE

T he weekend had passed by without a word from Scarlett. Without a single fucking trace of her. And all four of us were on edge. I didn't know who was worse. West spending the entire time spaced out after smoking copious amounts of weed, Francis pacing the place like a caged tiger, or Prescott constantly coming up with very unhelpful suggestions of where she might have gone. The truth was, none of us knew where Scarlett had got to. And we didn't want to alert anyone to her disappearance.

Francis sat on the sofa in my office, his hand propped up on the arm as he stared out of the window. He'd come in here a few minutes ago and hadn't said a word, merely seated himself with a faraway look in his eyes. I didn't comment on it. If he wanted to say something, he would. I continued working, although my concentration was shot to pieces. All I could think about was her.

Scarlett remembered us. She knew who we were. And how we'd spent the past couple of months she'd been with us lying to her.

"What if she goes back to Stuart?"

I looked up. Francis was still staring out the window, but there was a furrow between his brows.

"She wouldn't."

There was one thing I was sure of. Scarlett was terrified of the man. Scared enough, she sought shelter with us when Mason hurt her. She was willing to kill to stay away from him. The power Stuart had over Scarlett concerned me. When she learnt the truth. He'd taken her to punish us for what he thought we'd done. She'd give up her own truths to us. At least, I hoped she would. I didn't know if we could restore her trust in the four of us now.

"You know I'm thinking we should have told her the truth from the start," Francis said after a long moment.

"Have you been in West's drug stash or something? I remember you saying it was imperative she didn't know who we were until we were ready when we devised our plan."

Francis shrugged.

"Maybe I was wrong." His eyes flicked to me. "Maybe I'm realising our plan was flawed and would have never worked."

The only thing we wanted was her back with us. None of us cared how we achieved it. But playing with Scarlett's emotions and head was a heavy price to pay, given our current circumstances. The way we all wanted more from her. I'm not sure how it came to this. Our pull towards her had overtaken our common fucking sense. If we'd stuck to the original plan, then maybe none of this would have happened. If we'd done what we were supposed to and not given into desire. But it was futile thinking like that. Fucking pointless.

"Why? Because you want her?"

"No, Drake, because she's a fucking human being."

I flinched. It was easier to not think of her as a person, rather a tool we could use to take Stuart Carver down. He would never stop. Not when he suspected we'd killed his kids. We had, but there were only five people who knew about it. The four of us and Scarlett. And until now, she didn't remember. The fact she did put us all in danger. It's why we'd decided not to reveal the truth straight away. We needed time to work on her, so when she remembered, we wouldn't be at risk. And yet West had fucked it all up by forcing her to remember. Then she'd run.

"We would have been fucked either way. It's easy to put aside your feelings for someone when they're not right in front of you. But her being right here... it changed everything."

"Is that an admission she fucked with your head from the day she walked in here?"

I gripped the arm of my chair and gritted my teeth.

"Yes."

Lying to Francis would be pointless. He knew me too well.

"She fucked with mine too. She did it to all of us."

"Well, we all knew she would ruin West, but Pres? That was unexpected."

He snorted.

"No, it wasn't. You know as well as I do the only people he cares about outside of himself are Rosie, us and Scarlett."

I smiled despite myself. We'd always been close to Rosie, Prescott's mum. She was the type of person who welcomed anyone who was a friend of her son with open arms.

"Guess Pres had deeper feelings for Scarlett than we thought."

"Pretty sure that applies to all of us, Drake."

I wanted to scowl, but I didn't. Francis was right. I'd never wanted to look at Scarlett that way because she was my friend, but a part of me had always held a torch for our best friend. And as an adult, it had only intensified. My thirst for her was unquenchable.

The things I wanted to do to her sinful little body would make most people raise their eyebrows and think I was some kind of sick deviant. They weren't wrong, of course, but I didn't care about other people's opinions. However, right now, I would settle for having her curl up in my lap with my arms tight around her. I wanted to kiss away her pain and show her I cared.

"Regardless of all that, we need to find her."

"Do you think she might try to find Lylah?"

My stomach roiled in protest at the thought of it.

"Maybe."

None of us had considered she might want to search for her mother.

"It's a strong possibility, Drake. She doesn't know."

"I know she doesn't," I snapped, slamming my hand down on my desk.

Francis raised his eyebrow but didn't comment on my outburst. The very thought of telling Scarlett the truth of

Lylah's fate made me want to throw something at the fucking wall.

"Shouldn't we try—"

A noise from outside the door made my head whip around and Francis shut his mouth. I got to my feet and strode across the room. My hand reached out and gripped a shoulder, pulling whoever was out there into my office. The moment I took in who it was, I gave them a hard look.

"What are you doing, Tonya?"

She looked startled, her eyes going wide.

"N-n-nothing."

"Hmm, and why don't I believe you?"

I had never liked my step-cousin. To be honest, I thought she was a conniving little bitch, but it wasn't something I voiced to anyone else. The only reason I'd given her a job was to keep Fletch from realising I was using him for his fucking money. The guy was a bit of a cunt, not to mention I hated his sister with a passion for breaking up my parents' marriage. Well, I also blamed my father for being a cheating piece of shit, but there we go. I'd gone to extreme lengths to make sure no one realised my true feelings towards my step-family. To be honest, they could all go fuck themselves. Fletch was useful because he was rich, but that was about the extent of my interest in him. I should have got rid of Tonya a long time ago, but she hadn't become a real issue… until now.

"I noticed Scarlett wasn't here today. Is she unwell?"

I glanced at Francis, who was frowning heavily at Tonya. Why the fuck did she care where Scarlett was?

"She's fine," I said a moment later. "Just taking the day off."

"At such short notice?"

"What makes you think her schedule is any of your business?"

Tonya backed away a step.

"It's not, I'm sorry, Drake."

"I told you it's Mr Ackley in the office. Did you forget that all of a sudden?"

She paled but tried to give me a smile. I'd never been harsh with her before. My patience was rather thin today, and she'd just pissed me off. After the way she'd treated Scarlett, the fact she was asking about her made me incredibly suspicious.

"No. My apologies. I'll just go back to work."

"You do that."

Tonya dashed out of the room. I shut the door behind her before turning to Francis.

"Am I the only one who wants to know what the fuck that was about?"

"I'm more concerned about how much she heard."

"I am too, but why does she care where Scarlett is?"

"She's been asking too many questions about her recently."

I took a step towards him.

"What?"

He waved a hand around.

"Ever since West threatened her, she's been far too curious about our girl. I didn't tell Tonya anything, but it's suspicious."

I rubbed my chin. Francis hadn't told me, but then again, I'd been far too focused on other shit to spare a thought for my step-cousin.

"Hold that thought."

I opened my office door and strode out. My steps slowed as I neared the lobby where Tonya's desk was. Peering around the corner, I caught her on the phone, but her voice was low and I could only make out a little of what she said.

"They don't know where she is."

My skin prickled. It confirmed she'd overheard me and Francis talking about Scarlett having gone missing. Who the fuck she was talking to was the more important question. It must be why she was so interested in Scarlett.

I backed away down the hallway towards my office. No way I wanted her to catch me eavesdropping. Francis was still seated when I got back.

"She knows Scarlett is missing, and whoever she is reporting to knows too," I said before he could get a word in.

His eyes went dark.

"Well, that's going to be a problem."

I nodded, sticking my hands in my pockets.

"Perhaps it's one we can use to our advantage. After all, I have access to Fletch's tracker on her phone."

"He keeps tabs on his daughter?"

"No matter what his feelings about his kids are, they're assets to him. Besides, he is probably monitoring me too through her."

Francis raised an eyebrow.

"Why would he do that?"

"It's the only way my father gets any information about me."

"Why the fuck do you allow that?"

I shrugged.

"Oscar can do whatever the fuck he wants. He knows if he comes near me, I will end him."

The last time I'd spoken to my father face to face, I'd told him as much. If he tried to come near me, I wouldn't hesitate in ruining his life.

"And you don't consider this interfering?"

"I find it funny he thinks he can worm his way back into my life without me knowing about it. He's a fool."

Francis snorted.

"He has no idea what you're truly capable of."

I cracked my knuckles and walked back over to my desk, seating myself behind it. It was time to find out what Tonya was really up to. If she left the office, I wanted to know where the fuck she was going.

"I don't think many people do. Pres gave me this mug for a reason."

I tapped the mug on my desk containing the coffee I'd made earlier, given Scarlett wasn't around to do it for me. While the words on the mug weren't the slightest bit amusing, they were apt when I considered what they called us. The Four Horsemen of the Apocalypse. And I was the last one they ever expected when I came for them.

West was the violent one, but me? I was the executioner.

You cannot outrun Death.

No one could outrun me. They shouldn't bother trying. I found Scarlett after years of searching for her. And I would do it again. I would fucking tear down the world to find those who'd wronged me. Then I would end them all, my father included, if he dared try to fuck with me again.

"Is it wrong that I want him to go too far so I can watch you destroy him?"

I grinned as I clicked through my emails to find the link to the tracking site Fletch had sent me a while back.

"He will... eventually, so perhaps you'll get your wish."

Francis' grey eyes glinted with violence. It'd been a long time since I'd seen him look that way. Before everything with Chelsea, something I knew haunted him. Perhaps Scarlett's presence had encouraged Francis to get out of his own head. If so, good. He needed to get over it and be himself again. The fucked up deviant I knew he was inside.

My eyes scanned the screen. The little dot was located in our office building. Tonya was staying put... for now. I didn't trust it would remain so.

"If she leaves the building, I'll go after her with West. You and Pres can stay here and man the fort."

"Are you sure it's a good idea to take West after he threatened Tonya?"

"That's why I'm taking him."

Francis shook his head and gave me a devious smile but didn't comment on it.

"And what do we do about Scarlett?"

"That's why you're staying here with Pres... in case she turns up."

He gave me a nod. I didn't know what else we could do about our girl at this point. The only lead we had was the chance she might go looking for Lylah. And I hoped for Scarlett's sake, she didn't.

NINE

SCARLETT

Two days of hell lay behind me. Two days of memories flooding my brain. Two whole fucking days of tears, agony, and pain. All of it left me exhausted and listless, but I remembered.

I remembered everything.

And nothing about it made me feel any better.

There was no sense of relief knowing who I was. No sense of freedom from the locked cage in my mind having its door blasted open. No, my memories had only afforded me more questions than answers. And it fucking sucked.

Should I be grateful to West for shattering the glass wall in my mind?

Maybe.

In a lot of ways, I was. It might not have been the most orthodox way to go about it, but blunt force had been effective. And it was just his fucking style. The man was violence personified.

It didn't, however, stop me from being pissed as fuck at him.

Dangling me off the side of the building was just about the most screwed up thing he could have done. Especially given it was in the exact same place I'd had my accident, using the same method and having me fucking terrified for my life. But West wouldn't hurt me on purpose. At least, not the boy I'd known all those years ago.

West Greer had loved me.

Did he still love me?

Why did the thought of him not doing so hurt so much?

It made my heart bleed. And I hated myself for it.

Now I knew why the damn heart of mine kept telling me to trust them. It knew them. It recognised the boys I'd grown up with. The four boys who'd promised me we'd be each other's best friends forever. My four guardians. Prescott Ellis, West Greer, Francis Beaufort, and Drake Ackley. They had been my family and me, theirs. But now... I couldn't reconcile the boys they were to the men they'd become. And why they'd treated me the way they had since I'd come back into their lives.

The only way I'd get answers to all the questions flooding my brain about what they'd done and why was by going back to them. By demanding they tell me the truth. And making them give me a fucking explanation for the past ten years.

First, I had something important to do.

I'd checked out of the hotel over an hour ago, having spent far too much money in the three nights I was there. I barely left the room and ordered room service rather than venture down to the restaurant. I couldn't face the world while my mind was all over the place. Having got my shit together, I was ready to do what was needed.

Now, I stood in front of the building I'd grown up in. The block hadn't changed much in the past ten years. All the doors were still painted blue with gold numbering. I saw a flash of me running along the first-floor balcony where all the front doors on that level were. Shaking myself, I walked over to the outdoor stairs and made my way up them. My breath stuttered when I came to number eighteen. My heart twisted painfully in my chest, but I had to do this. I needed to know.

My hand rose, and I knocked. A minute went by with no answer. I stepped back and glanced at the front window. The curtains were drawn, so I had no idea if anyone was home.

This flat had been my mother's ten years ago. It was the place I'd spent the first sixteen years of my life. And had been one level up from Prescott's mum, Rosie's place.

Did she still live here? I couldn't imagine so with how ridiculously wealthy the boys were now. Prescott would have done everything he could to give his mum a comfortable life, especially given how his father had fucked off and left them alone, flitting in and out of their lives every so often. Every time Ezra came back, it was never for long. And he always left Prescott miserable. All he wanted was a father who actually cared, but the only person Ezra Ellis gave a shit about was himself.

The thought of Prescott made my chest hurt worse. The thing was, even though I was angry about the lies and deceit, my heart remained his.

I was completely and utterly in love with Prescott Ellis.

Those feelings weren't going to magically disappear because I'd known him ten years ago. And yes, it was hard to see the boy Prescott and the man Prescott as the same person. But he was still Pres to me. My heart's desire.

I didn't know if I wished it wasn't the case. Right now, I wasn't sure of anything. I wanted to see him. To talk to him. I needed the truth from his fucking mouth before I decided what I was going to do.

I knocked at the door again. No way I was leaving without trying every avenue. I could ask the boys what happened to my mother, but my anger with them was making it hard for me to contemplate going back to Fortuity.

Lylah Nyx was my real mother. I remembered everything about her. How I looked like a younger version of her with the same wavy light brown hair and hazel-green eyes. People had mistaken us for sisters when I was sixteen. And all this time, I hadn't known how much I missed her.

Letting out a sigh when another few minutes went by, I looked around. The place wasn't deserted, but there weren't many people wandering about. The door to my left opened. A man stuck his head out, giving me the once over.

"You looking for who lives there?"

I nodded, digging my hands into my coat pockets. He stepped out and leant against the door frame.

"It's been empty for years."

My heart sank at his words. She wasn't here. I don't know what I was expecting. Maybe for her to welcome me with open arms. For her to tell me why she'd let the Carvers have me. Why had they told me they'd adopted me? Why had they... lied?

"Do you know how long?"

He shrugged.

"Think my mate Danny said it'd been ten years or some shit like that. Why you interested?"

I let out a sigh. Maybe if I told him the truth, he might be inclined to tell me what he knew.

"It was my mother's flat... I grew up here."

Saying the words out loud made it so fucking real to me. Ten years of my life had been stolen from me. I'd not known who I was for all that time. And everything had changed.

"You did? Huh." He tipped his head. "Only lived here a couple of years, but there's someone who comes to visit the place once every six months or so. Think they make sure it's all good or whatever."

"They do?"

"Yeah, last time was months ago. That's all I know, though."

I stared at the door.

"Well, thank you. I should really..." I waved as if I was going to get out of here.

"Sure, sure, you're welcome."

He gave me a nod before disappearing back inside his own flat. I rubbed my face. Waiting around here would be futile, yet knowing what I had to do next made me sick to my stomach. Seeing them would only hurt me. Going back to the men with whom I had an incredibly complicated relationship didn't fill me with anything other than dread.

I'd stood outside this building for almost half an hour before getting the courage to come up here and knock at this door. Now I was no further forward. To be honest, it had only given me more questions, like, where had my mother gone? Why was the place empty after all this time? Who came to look at it regularly? Did they own it?

I took a step towards the stairs when someone appeared at the top of them. My eyes narrowed against the sun, allowing me to see who it was. And it only left me reeling.

"You're here."

I widened my stance and gave her a dark look.

"What are you doing here?"

Tonya stood there with her handbag clutched to her side and her eyes fixed on me. I had no idea how she'd found me or why. How the hell did she even know I'd be here? I hadn't told a soul.

"Making sure you hadn't disappeared completely."

My feet carried me forward before I stopped a couple of feet away from her.

"That doesn't tell me anything. How did you find me? And why?"

She looked away for a moment. The fact she'd turned up here set me on edge.

"I suppose you'll find out soon enough." Her eyes landed on me again, narrowing with irritation. "Mason Jones sent me to find you."

Mason? What the hell is she doing talking to Mason?

"Since when do you and Mason know each other?"

"Since you made West threaten me."

I put my hands up.

"I had nothing to do with him threatening you. That was all him."

"He wouldn't have done it if it wasn't for *you*."

The vindictive note of her voice made me flinch. West's behaviour had nothing to do with me. He was a law unto himself. I had no control over the man.

"That still doesn't explain Mason."

She shrugged.

"He approached me. Asked me to get information about what you're doing. I was happy to oblige him. After all, you're a thorn in my side, Scarlett."

I'd known this woman was a bitch, but now she was showing her true colours.

"Me? A thorn in your side? What did I ever do to you?"

The way her eyes darkened with anger and her hand came up made me take a step back. She stabbed a finger in my direction.

"You turned up and wound them all around your little finger. Even Drake, and I've never known him to care about anyone but himself. They were perfectly easy to work for before, apart from West, but he's always been crazy. Now they're all making my life hell and it's all your fault."

I almost fucking laughed. She was delusional. I had done nothing of the sort. If anything, I was at the mercy of the boys, not the other way around. And if they were making her life hell, it was her own damn fault. She was the one who had been out of line when she spoke to me, not the other way around.

"Are you serious? I'm not responsible for them. If you didn't know what they're truly like, that's not on me."

She shook her head, continuing to glare at me.

"You wouldn't understand. I'm not here for that, anyway. Mason made me an offer I couldn't refuse. And now I'm taking you back to him."

I wasn't going anywhere with her and especially not back to Mason, even though I had a boat load of questions for him. Did he know the truth about what happened to me? And why would he be complicit in keeping me away from everyone I'd known before?

"Excuse me? I am not going with you."

I heard the sound of a car below us and the engine switching off.

"Yes, you are."

The next thing I knew, Tonya had launched forward and grabbed hold of me. Her long nails dug into my forearms, making me wince. I'd rolled up the sleeves of the cropped coat West got me as it was warm out.

"Get off!"

I tried to shove her away, but she held on tighter, backing away towards the stairs.

"I knew you would make this difficult," she ground out. "A little stuck-up bitch like you has no sense of self-preservation."

I had the fucking sense to know going with her would be a mistake. Digging my heels in, I wrenched myself out of her grasp. Her nails left red scratch marks all down my arms, but I didn't care about the pain. Getting away from Tonya was my only goal.

I turned and tried to run, but she caught me by my hair, dragging me back. I yelped, putting my hands up to attempt to pry her off me. My scalp burnt, making my head ache with it.

"What the fuck is wrong with you? Let go!"

And she did. I stood there for a moment, surprised she actually had. Then I turned around and found out why.

Standing there with a murderous expression on his face was West. His hand was wrapped around Tonya's throat, keeping her from going anywhere. I didn't like seeing him touch her. Especially not his hand being around her neck. My own itched to feel his tattooed hand around it. No matter what had gone on between us, my heart told me West belonged to me. She didn't want him touching Tonya in the way he did me.

Stupid traitorous heart.

Next to them stood Drake, his indigo eyes pinning me in place. Seeing him made my body freeze.

"I swear, it was so embarrassing," he said, dropping his chin to his chest. "I don't like rejecting people."

I put a hand on his arm.

"You could have asked me to let her down gently."

Drake looked at me, a small smile playing on his lips.

"My little knight in shining armour, huh?"

"Oh, shut up! You don't need rescuing from Rachel. She's harmless. Now, if it had been Kylie Adams, you're on your own then. I'm not touching that shit."

I leant my head on his shoulder as Drake laughed.

"Not so knightly now. I thought you were brave."

"I'm brave because you four make me that way."

He stroked my knee.

"No, you're strong enough on your own without us, Little Nyx. You choose to stay with us because we're meant to be. One day, you'll see that."

I swallowed. The memory was like cold fucking ice being doused all over me. Drake had been so warm, kind, and funny back then. Now, he was none of those things. I ached to see the man behind his mask. To see if the boy I cared for remained.

My heart twisted in my chest, making me want to rub away the agony building inside it. Seeing him and West had my emotions running riot. They were conflicting. On one hand, I knew these boys, and on the other, as men, they'd done a lot of shit to me I wasn't entirely happy with. How could I trust them when they'd broken it so thoroughly by lying to me all this time?

My eyes went to my arms. The pain registered then. The scratches had grazed my skin in places, leaving angry red marks on my forearms. My eyes darted to West, who was staring at them intently. When he looked at me, I was reminded of a conversation we'd had the night after I'd taken Ecstasy and slept with all of them. And I knew I was in big fucking trouble.

TEN

DRAKE

A fter Tonya left the office, it didn't take us long to work out where the fuck she was going. West and I had taken the car in case we happened to find Tonya with Scarlett. There was no other reason for her to come to this estate other than to seek out Scarlett. The question was, how did she know our girl was here?

Scarlett was staring at West with abject horror on her face. Fuck knew why. All I cared about was her being here. Scarlett was safe. The relief I felt over her being relatively unharmed was palpable. I didn't want anything to happen to her. And I was fucking glad we'd found her before anyone else had the opportunity. Tonya had led us right to her.

"How did you find me?" was the first thing out of her mouth.

"We tracked this bitch's phone," West said, squeezing Tonya's throat. The way Scarlett narrowed her eyes had me thinking she wasn't best pleased about the way he was touching Tonya. Somehow, I didn't think Scarlett would be very happy if one of us touched another woman. There was a certain possessiveness in her eyes. It had me wondering if she'd ever direct it my way.

"Yeah, well, she said Mason sent her, although she didn't tell me how he knew I was here."

I turned to Tonya. She looked about ready to shit herself, but she should be scared. West had a hold of her and he wasn't known for his restraint.

"How did he know?" I asked her, my voice brokering no fucking objections.

Her fearful eyes fell on me.

"He's tracking her phone."

Well, that was just fucking wonderful. And unsurprising. The fucker had got on my last nerve. I was about done with his bullshit. If there was a way we could cover it up without it leading back to us, I would set West on him. The cunt had become a damn problem. We'd need to do something about him tracking her phone. At the same time, we couldn't make him suspicious we were on to him either. I'd fix it somehow.

First things first, we needed to deal with Tonya and get Scarlett back home where she fucking well belonged.

"I see."

West shifted on his feet, his eyes fixed on Scarlett's arms where there were large scratch marks down them.

"Who did that to you?" he asked, his voice low.

"Who do you think?" Scarlett retorted.

West looked at Tonya and his amber eyes turned deadly.

"Well, I was going to go easy on you, Tonya, but now…" He turned his attention back to Scarlett and gave her a maniacal smile. "Now Scar knows exactly what I'm going to do."

Scarlett swallowed. I looked between them, wondering what kind of threat West had made. Then I remembered this was West. No doubt it was fucked up.

"The first thing we're going to do is get in the car," I said. "Whatever you have planned, I'm guessing it's not something we should be engaging in out in the open."

"You would be correct."

Scarlett stepped forward and put her hand up.

"Wait, I need you to answer something first."

I raised an eyebrow and waited for her to elaborate. She looked over towards the door of the flat where she'd grown up.

"Where is she?"

West flinched and I stiffened. I'd known it was coming, but it didn't make it any easier.

"That's something we should discuss at home."

"Home?" She turned back to me. "I don't have a home."

"Your home is with us," West ground out, "you know that."

She threw a hand up.

"How can you say that when you've spent this entire time lying to me! All of you have *lied* so many times, I don't know what the truth is any longer."

West shoved Tonya at me and strode towards Scarlett. He caught her by the arm and pulled her against his chest. She watched his other hand come up and cup her cheek.

"When I promised you forever, Scar, I meant it," he murmured. "That's the truth."

For a long moment, she said nothing. I held onto Tonya's arm, making sure she couldn't escape and waited. We needed to move, but I could allow them this moment. West needed it after everything he'd been through.

"I don't know who you are anymore," she whispered. "You're not my West."

West's expression hardened, but he didn't stop caressing her cheek with a gentle touch.

"He died on that building site when he watched you fall. When he begged you to wake up and you didn't. He died the last night we saw each other."

Tears welled in Scarlett's eyes.

"West…"

He dropped his hand from her face and his expression became shuttered as if he was trying to hide his true feelings about her words. But I knew they'd broken something inside him.

"I told you what would happen if you ran from me, Scar." He pulled her arm up and showed her the scratches. "You ran and got yourself hurt, didn't you. Now I have to punish you."

"I don't want—"

He put his finger over her mouth.

"I don't care what you want. You're going to be a good girl and take what you're given." He glanced at me. "Isn't it fortuitous Drake is here with us, hmm?"

Scarlett's eyes went wide. What on earth had he threatened to do that involved me?

He didn't wait for a response. His hand tightened around Scarlett's arm and he pulled her towards the stairs with him.

"It's time we got this little show on the road."

I followed them down the stairs, dragging a dumbfounded Tonya along with me.

"West, this really isn't necessary," Scarlett protested as he opened the car door on the passenger side and shoved her into it.

He leant into the car slightly to look at her.

"It is entirely necessary, my little Scar. You were warned."

He shut the door and opened the back one for me to force Tonya inside. When he shut it, he looked at me.

"What are you planning?" I asked, tugging the keys out of my pocket.

"Oh, nothing you need be too concerned over. In fact, I think you might enjoy it."

"West."

He put his finger up and dug out his phone.

"Get in the car and drive, Drake. I'll give you the address."

I walked around to the driver's side and got in while West made his phone call. Scarlett turned to me.

"Please don't let him do this."

I don't know why the fuck she was pleading with me.

"Do you think I have control over West's actions?"

Her mouth thinned. Reaching out, I took her arm with the worst scratches on it in my hand. Scarlett watched me stroke my fingers down them before I brought her arm closer to my face. She let out a breath when I pressed my lips to the first scratch.

"I'm sorry we didn't get here sooner," I murmured. "You shouldn't have had to endure this."

"I thought you'd be angry with me for running."

My eyes flicked up to hers.

"Angry? Hmm, perhaps I am. As for you getting hurt, well... that's unacceptable. No one is allowed to hurt you. I don't blame you for these marks, Scarlett. I want to take care of them for you, but don't mistake this for kindness or mercy. I'm relatively sure whatever West has planned will be punishment enough."

She didn't say a word as West got in the back and rattled off an address for me. I let go of Scarlett's hand, turned the engine on, and punched it into the satnav. Turning back to him, I indicated Tonya with my head.

"Give me her phone."

West grabbed hold of her bag, which was sitting between them, and pulled her phone out, slapping it into my hand. I opened the car door, stepped out and walked closer to the front tyre. Squatting down, I placed it right in front of the tyre before straightening and getting back into the car. Releasing the handbrake as my foot hit the accelerator, I felt the slight jolt of the car driving over the phone. I checked in the side mirror, satisfied with the sight of the crushed phone. I stopped the car and got out, walked over to it, and gathered up the pieces. Smiling to myself, I brought them back into the car and dumped them in the cup holder next to the gear stick. Then I set off properly towards the address West had given me.

"Turn your phone off, Scarlett. I'll deal with Mason tracking it later."

She did as I asked, digging out of her bag and switching it off. I'm not sure she wanted to piss me or West off, given she knew when we reached our destination, she would be punished.

No one spoke for the rest of the journey, not that I knew where the fuck we were actually going. I pulled up outside a rather nondescript looking house in a quiet street. West got out first and walked around to drag Tonya from the car.

"Drake."

I glanced at Scarlett as my hand went to the door handle.

"What?"

"He's going to—"

"I'm pretty sure I know what he's going to do with her, Scarlett."

I opened the door and got out of the car, not caring what else she had to say. Right now, I wanted to get this shit over and done with so we could take Scarlett home. Then we would have a conversation between the five of us. A very important conversation. It couldn't wait much longer.

I walked around to the pavement where West stood with Tonya. He gave me a nod as Scarlett got out of the car. Then he led the three of us up to the house and rang the doorbell. A minute later, it opened to reveal Penn with a rather smug smile on his face.

"Well, hello there. I see we have quite the party here."

I glanced at West, who gave me a smile. My suspicion about what would happen next had been confirmed, but I didn't say a word as I followed him and the others into the house when Penn stepped out of the way.

"Basement, yeah?" West asked as Penn shut the door.

"It's all yours."

Penn waved at an open doorway located under the stairs. Tonya struggled then as West dragged her over to it. He ignored her and tugged her through the door.

"Nice to see you again," Penn said to Scarlett, who stood next to me, her face having gone rather pale.

Her eyes darted towards him.

"What did you do with the guy?"

Penn smirked.

"Do you really want to know?"

She nodded. Then, much to my surprise, she reached out and slid her fingers between mine. The gesture made my heart hammer in my chest, but I didn't outwardly show my shock.

"I drove him out to a secluded place, dug a grave, dumped his body in it… then I poured petrol over him, lit a match and waited whilst he burnt before filling in the dirt." He shrugged. "Doubt he'll get found, and even if he does, I scrubbed any traces of what you did to him."

Scarlett stared at him for a long moment before she rubbed her face with her other hand.

"Well, that's… thank you, I guess."

"You're welcome."

Scarlett looked up at me, her hand tightening in mine. I could feel her fear bleeding out of her. And it made me even more curious about what West was going to do.

I tugged her towards the basement door. Even if she tried to tell me to stop this, I wouldn't. Scarlett knew I wasn't the type to give mercy. She didn't try to fight me as we walked down the steps. At the bottom, there were two doors. One was open. I led Scarlett inside, finding a concrete room with a chair in the middle. Along the walls were shelves with various implements on them. West had already sat Tonya down in the chair, tying her arms behind her. He gave us both a grin when we came to a stop just inside the door.

"Nice of you to join us."

I shook my head while Scarlett curled herself into my side as if I was going to save her.

"What are you going to do?" Tonya asked, her eyes going to me.

West turned to look at her. The way he smiled made her flinch.

"Isn't it obvious, Tonya? I made you a promise. If you fucked with our girl again, I would gut you."

Tonya paled, her eyes still fixed on me. What was it with women today and thinking I was their fucking saviour? Honestly, did they not know me at all? Well, Tonya didn't, but I was relatively sure Scarlett had some idea. Then again, the fact she was pressed against me, my hand in hers, was making me feel things. A part of me wanted to soften to her and show her affection in return.

I didn't get a chance to because Tonya opened her fucking mouth.

"Are you going to let him do this to me, Drake?"

Was I going to let West kill her?

You fucking bet I was.

ELEVEN

WEST

I watched Drake let go of Scarlett's hand and curl his arm around her shoulder, holding her closer to him. Perhaps killing Tonya would be a step too far for him, but I highly doubted it. I knew his true nature. Drake was brutal and unforgiving. He wasn't the type of person to show mercy.

"Do you think because you're Fletch's daughter, that will save you?" Drake asked, his voice cold as fucking ice.

"Y-y-yes," Tonya replied, her voice shaky as tears sprang to her eyes.

The way Drake smiled was absolutely chilling.

"We're not family, Tonya. We never have been. Your father was only ever good for one thing. His money." Drake reached up with his other hand and stroked Scarlett's hair, cradling her closer to him. "You, on the other hand, are expendable. Always have been. Let's just say I did him a favour by taking you on. You know who could do a fucking better job in her sleep than you, hmm?"

Tonya didn't respond. A tear slid down her cheek.

"That's right, you have never meant anything to me. When you decided to stage this little campaign of hate towards Scarlett, you sealed your own fate. I protect what's mine. And Scarlett... she's *mine*."

Drake's declaration made Scarlett look up at him with wide eyes. He didn't spare her a glance, but I could see it took a lot for him to admit it out loud when she was right there.

"So yes, Tonya, I am going to let West do whatever the fuck he wants to you. And I'm going to enjoy watching you bleed."

His eyes turned to me and he gave me a nod as if to say go ahead. I winked and strolled over to the shelves on the wall, checking out Penn's collection. He'd been more than willing to let us have use of his basement. This was the room he used to 'fix' people. The other was where he tattooed. Normally, I wouldn't have asked him for a favour like this, but we needed to get rid of Tonya cleanly. Well, her death wouldn't be clean. The cover-up would be, though. It was the least I could do for Drake. His step-cousin turning up dead would raise a few eyebrows after all.

While I could gut her with my knife, I was in the mood for something bigger. I had promised Scarlett a trophy from the kill. And I was going to deliver.

The whimpering erupting from Tonya's mouth was ignored by me and Drake as I looked the knives over. Penn had a large collection of torture implements, but my weapon of choice was a knife... or a sledgehammer. He had one of those resting against the wall. She would die too quickly if I used it. I wanted to torture the bitch. She deserved no less.

I selected a meat cleaver, testing it in my hand before swinging it around. I had to think big, considering the threat I'd issued to Scarlett. She needed to know I was serious.

"Drake," came Scarlett's small voice. "Is he really going to do this?"

I eyed the two of them. Drake stroked her cheek as soothing a frightened lamb, but his face remained impassive.

"Yes. And I'm going to make you watch him."

Before she could say a word, he turned her towards Tonya and stood at her back, his hand resting on her shoulder. I knew if she looked away, he would hold her chin in place.

I set the cleaver down on a small table next to Tonya's chair and pulled out my knife. Drake and I had changed before we left Fortuity, knowing if things went south, it might get messy. We were both all in black.

"Now, I think I made you a promise, didn't I, Tonya?" I crooned, dragging the knife down her cheek as I stared at her. "This knife and you have a date with each other. And it starts now."

I didn't hesitate in whipping it down and planting it in her stomach. She let out a wail a moment later as I dragged it upwards. Blood pooled around the wound, soaking her white blouse. I ripped the knife from her and wiped it on her sleeve. Then I took a step back, letting Scarlett see what I'd done. Her hazel-green eyes were wide, but she didn't move from the spot Drake held her in. She didn't close her eyes or make a sound.

My warrior. You're so fucking brave.

Sliding my knife back into my pocket, I gave Tonya a smile. She was still screaming, but no one would hear her. Penn had his basement thoroughly soundproofed.

"It hurts, doesn't it? Well, this won't kill you just yet."

My hand went to the cleaver and my fist wrapped around the handle.

"When I told my little Scar what would happen if she ran from me and got herself hurt, I made her a few promises. Since you decided to inflict pain on my woman, I'm collecting your debt to her. Your limbs come first. And then your heart. Perhaps I'll take your head too, I haven't quite decided yet."

The incomprehensible blubbering out of Tonya's mouth made me laugh. She should have stayed in her fucking lane.

"It wouldn't matter who hurt her, Tonya. My promise is my fucking word."

This was for Scarlett. Proving to her when I said forever, I meant it. She was going to watch me kill for her. I'd destroy the universe if it meant I had Scarlett. She was my beating heart and soul.

I backed up from Tonya, letting the meat cleaver hang in my hand by my side. Turning when I reached Drake, I met Scarlett's eyes. I switched out my hands so the right one, which was covered in blood, touched her face, smearing red across her cheek.

"Which would you like first, hmm? Her arms or her legs? Or do you want me to cut her heart out, give her a quick death?"

Tonya was already bleeding. If I hacked into her limbs, she probably wouldn't survive too long.

Scarlett said nothing for a long moment. Her eyes were fixed on mine. Her bottom lip got caught between her teeth as she contemplated my words. The fact she wasn't screaming and telling me to stop just went to show she was as fucked up and depraved as we were. I'd always known Scarlett had darkness lurking inside her.

"Give me her heart."

Her voice was barely audible, only meant for me. I smiled, stroking more blood across her cheek.

"As my little Scar wishes."

I turned away and approached Tonya.

"It's your lucky day. Scar wants to give you a quick death, but it doesn't mean it won't hurt."

I lifted the meat cleaver and brought it down hard in the centre of her chest. Tonya let out a horrific scream as metal cut through flesh and bone but I didn't care. Ripping the cleaver from her chest, I brought it down again, making room for me to rip out her fucking heart.

I dropped the cleaver on the table when I was satisfied I could gain access to what I needed. Tonya passed out sometime during the ordeal. There was blood everywhere, but I'd placed one of Penn's plastic sheets down underneath us for an easy clean up.

My hands went to her ribcage, prying it open with my bare hands. I'd cracked them enough, so I had easy access. My hand dived into her chest cavity and wrapped around the still-beating organ in her chest. I tore it out and stared at it. It was fucking beautiful. The perfect trophy for my woman.

I spun on my feet and presented it in my hand to Scarlett and Drake. She stared at me with a haunted expression on her face. Drake had a devious but satisfied look in his eyes. The blood did it for him.

"I promised you a trophy, my little Scar."

Drake let go of her shoulder. She took a step forward and reached out for it. I smiled as I placed it in her hand.

"Thank you," she whispered, her voice full of hesitancy as if her appreciation of my gift was something she had trouble with.

Scarlett stared at the heart for a long time. Neither Drake nor I spoke while she tried to find her words.

"West, I'm not going to stop you from punishing me, but please, can it not be in front of... her."

I was sure Penn wouldn't mind if we used his tattoo room as long as I cleaned it afterwards. Giving her this was the least I could do.

"As you wish."

I took the heart from her and placed it on the small table with the meat cleaver. My hands were covered in blood, but I'd told Scarlett I wouldn't stop to clean it up.

"Let's go."

Drake hadn't bothered to close the door behind them, so I walked out into the hallway. I pointed at the closed door when they followed me. Drake opened it and stepped in, flipping the light on. Scarlett went in after him as I brought up the rear.

When we were all inside, I pointed at the tattoo chair.

"You can sit there, Drake."

He raised an eyebrow as if asking me why the fuck I kept ordering him about. This was my fucking punishment for Scarlett, so I called the shots. He could deal.

"Listen, if you don't want to join in, that's on you, but I'm pretty sure you're going to enjoy what's about to go down."

Drake didn't say a word, merely shrugged out of his jacket and hung it up on the hooks by the door before he closed it. I watched him take a seat in the tattoo chair, satisfied he wasn't going to object any further.

I walked up behind Scarlett and tucked her hair behind her shoulder, running my bloody fingers down her throat.

"First, I want you to undo your jeans, pull them halfway down your legs along with your knickers. Then I want you to crawl over Drake and get his dick out," I murmured in her ear as I tucked my fingers under her coat to take it off her arms. "I'm sure he's already hard for you. You know how much he likes blood. Maybe you want to run your bloody hand over his face, make him dirty too."

Her harsh breath made me grin. No doubt all the fear rushing through her veins was making her wet and wanting. I knew my little Scar liked to be afraid. It made her horny as fuck. She needed this, even if she didn't want to admit it.

I discarded her coat on the stool Penn sat on to tattoo. Her fingers went to her jeans, undoing the button and unzipping them. As requested, she tugged them and her knickers down her legs. I walked her towards the tattoo chair, making sure she didn't fall. Scarlett knelt on the chair and crawled over Drake's lap. His indigo eyes had darkened. I wasn't sure if he heard what I'd told Scarlett to do. Reaching up, Scarlett ran her finger down his cheek, smearing the blood on her hand over his skin. The sharp intake of his breath and the way his hands curled around the leather chair made me smile harder.

I raised my hand and brought it down on her exposed behind, making her jolt. The second one had her letting out a yelp.

"What did I tell you, Scar? This is not about pleasure. It's a punishment."

Several more strikes came, making her little arse red, not to mention the blood transferring from my hand on it. My fingers caressed her skin next, stroking the redness.

"You going to be a good girl for us, hmm? What else did I tell you to do?"

She braced a hand on Drake's chest while she undid his trousers. He watched her silently. I could tell this was killing him, but he was going to do what I said, just like our girl.

Scarlett got his dick out and stroked it with her bloody hand.

"Mmm, that's right, Scar. Look at how hard he is for you."

"He is," she whispered, her eyes fixed on Drake's.

My fingers went to my own jeans, unzipping them and pulling my cock from my boxers. I'd been hard for what felt like forever. I took my place behind Scarlett, running my hands over her behind and adjusting the angle of her hips so she was lined up with my dick. Fisting it, I rubbed it over her wet little slit. Then I ran my hand up her back and gathered her hair up in my fist.

"Do you want me to fuck you until you scream, hmm? I'm going to use this little pussy. You like it when I hurt you. It feels so fucking good, doesn't it?"

My fist tightened in her hair.

"Punish me. Make it hurt."

It only took one brutal thrust for me to sink my dick inside her wet heat. She cried out from the sudden intrusion. Drake placed his hand over hers on her chest, as if reassuring her she could take it. Pulling back, I gave it to her without letting her adjust to me. I'd warned her she was going to be fucked until she was a mess.

"That's it. Take it like the dirty little girl you are. Your pussy wants it. She belongs to my dick."

"West," she whimpered, "please."

"What's that? You want me to fuck you harder? Well, who am I to deny you."

My fingers tightened further in her hair and I pulled her upright by it, making her neck snap back. I met her eyes and smiled at her.

"You're such a good girl, Scar. Now, open that pretty mouth of yours. Drake's got something for you."

I shoved her back down by her hair. She opened her mouth and wrapped it around Drake's dick. He let out a grunt, his fists going white around the tattoo chair. Using her hair, I directed the strokes of her mouth along his dick. And when I pushed her further down, making her take more, she gagged. My eyes met Drake's.

"Mmm, isn't that the sweetest fucking sound?"

I knew Drake wasn't vocal during sex, but I was determined to make him snap. He needed to let go. Let our girl make him feel good. My fist in her hair forced her lower, making her engulf his entire dick in her mouth and down her throat.

"Fuck," Drake ground out through his teeth.

"You hear that, Scar, he's showing his appreciation for your talented mouth."

"Fuck off, West."

"She likes to know she's being a good girl."

I let her back off his dick a little, giving her room to breathe. Her hands were planted either side of Drake on the chair, keeping her steady while I fucked her from behind and used my hand to make her suck Drake off.

"You can praise her then."

"She wants to hear it from you."

"When she deserves it, she will."

I couldn't help grinning.

"Is that a promise?"

He glared at me, but I shoved Scarlett further down on his dick and his eyes rolled back in their sockets. His hand left the chair and curled around her shoulder. Making him lose control only had me fucking Scarlett harder. She whimpered around his length, but she took it all. She didn't complain or try to escape.

"Mmm, I think Drake's going to paint your sweet little face soon. He likes to make you messy."

Drake didn't even refute my statement. He was too far gone to care what I was saying.

"Scarlett," he muttered. "Fuck, don't stop."

I made her suck him faster, wanting to watch him let go and explode all over her face. Her clean hand left the chair and gripped his shirt. His breath came out in harsh pants. The sight of this was making me fucking crazy. Punishing her for running was a fucking high.

"Fuck!"

I pulled Scarlett from his dick, watching him erupt and it coat her face. She blinked, her mouth still open so some of his cum spurted inside it. It was so fucking hot, I could barely hold back. I let out a grunt as the tingles started at the base of my spine.

"Shit," I ground out. "Fuck, Scar!"

I lost it, my cock spurting wildly inside her hot little pussy. I didn't even try to stop it. Scarlett hadn't come, but this wasn't about her. This was her punishment, not her pleasure. And fuck, it had felt so damn good.

Letting go of her hair, I ran my hand down her spine. The blood had dried on my hands now so it didn't get all over her t-shirt.

"Good girl, such a good girl."

It took a long while before the three of us moved. It was time we cleaned this place up. And made a plan with Penn to get rid of Tonya's body. It was lucky Drake had smashed her phone, so Fletcher couldn't track where she'd got to. Drake would have to deal with the consequences of her going missing, but considering he hated most of his family, I didn't think it would be a hardship for him.

After we'd adjusted all our clothes, I brushed my hand over Scarlett's shoulder.

"I won't ask you to help us with Tonya, little Scar, but you can clean up the mess we left in here. Penn's cleaning supplies are in the cupboard over there."

She gave us a nod. The girl still had cum on her face, but she'd sort herself out.

Drake and I walked out of the room and back into the one with Tonya's dead body.

"Well, what are we going to do about this?"

Drake rubbed his chin and then looked at me with a feral glint in his indigo eyes.

"We're going to make this look like some crazy ritualistic murder and have the police chasing their tails."

"Are you serious?"

He winked.

"Very. You did rip her heart out."

I rubbed my hands together.

"We better make it good then."

The way he smiled made me grin back.

This is going to be so much fucking fun.

TWELVE

PRESCOTT

The moment Francis and I heard the lift doors open, we both sprung off the sofa, our eyes darting to it. Out strolled West, followed by Drake, and then there was my girl. The instant she saw me, her eyes softened with recognition. And it made my whole damn world fucking drop out from underneath me.

She remembers. She truly fucking remembers me.

Scarlett didn't walk over. Her eyes flashed with hurt the next moment before they moved to Francis. Pain lingered in her expression, making him shift on his feet, his hands clenching and unclenching at his sides. We'd hurt her by lying about how we knew each other. We both knew that. We'd been discussing it before they turned up.

It had been fucking hours since West and Drake disappeared to go after Tonya. I'd almost called one of them, but Francis told me to leave it. If they needed to, they would have got in touch with us. Didn't stop me from being concerned, given it was now early evening and they'd left around eleven in the morning.

Scarlett strode over to the stairs the next moment with a determined expression on her face after she stopped looking at Francis.

"Where are you going?" Drake asked.

She paused on the bottom step, glancing back at him.

"To take a fucking shower because you two decided to get blood and cum on me."

West let out a bark of laughter at her words. Scarlett gave him a dark look before walking up the stairs and disappearing along the hallway. Drake frowned slightly, digging his hands into his pockets.

"Dare I even fucking ask what happened?" Francis said with a scowl.

My feet were moving before I registered what I was doing. It wasn't until I was halfway up the stairs when Drake's voice caught up to me.

"Pres, we need to talk."

"She can tell me what happened," I replied and didn't stop to see what else he had to say.

My heart wanted Scarlett. She'd been gone for three days. I missed her so fucking much.

Somehow, I knew where she would be. So when I found her in my bathroom stripping out of her clothes, I couldn't help the way my chest constricted. She turned at the sound of my footsteps, her nearly naked body on show. I stopped in the doorway, afraid to move any closer. Her expression was guarded, but she didn't move to cover herself. I'd seen it all, anyway.

"Little lamb."

"I don't want to talk right now."

I took a step towards her, putting my hand out, but she stepped back.

"Don't."

Her rejection made my chest hurt worse. Her eyes filled with sadness and heartache.

"I can't, Pres. I just can't."

Then she burst into tears. I didn't care what she said. I wasn't going to stand there and let her cry on her own. My legs closed the distance. My arms went around her, tugging my woman against my chest and stroking her hair.

"Shh, sweetness, shh. It's okay. I'm here, my sweet little lamb. I've got you."

Her tiny hands fisted my shirt at my sides.

"He killed Tonya," she sobbed. "They made me watch… and… and he ripped out her heart and gave it to me as a trophy… and… they fucked me in Penn's tattoo chair as punishment for running away."

Her words made me pause.

They did what?

"There was so much blood and… and I should have felt disgusted by it, but I didn't. What's wrong with me, Pres? I shouldn't be okay with what they did."

I held her closer and kissed the top of her head.

"There's nothing wrong with you."

And there wasn't. Scarlett was one of us. She didn't belong in the world of morality and goodness. She belonged in the grey where the lines between right and wrong were blurred.

"Why does it feel like there is?"

"No one said living in our world is easy... it's going to make you question yourself."

"I don't understand myself."

"You've had a rough few days, little lamb. It's okay to be overwhelmed."

I didn't know for sure, but I had a feeling Scarlett had suffered the whole time she'd been gone. The way her body shook and her words made me think she'd been through an ordeal. Remembering her past couldn't have been easy.

"I need to wash, please. Let me get clean... and... and then we can talk."

I let her go, only to cup her face in both hands. Those beautiful hazel-green eyes were full of tears, but she'd never looked more beautiful to me.

"If that's what you need."

She nodded, staring up at me with such a heart-breaking expression, I almost suggested I get in the shower with her. But she'd asked me to let her do this herself. Whatever my girl needed, she'd get.

I leant closer, pressing my forehead to hers. Needing the connection between us because I couldn't stand not being close to this woman. The owner of my heart.

"You remember me... don't you?"

"Yes," she whispered. "I remember my best friend who made me laugh and held me when I cried. I remember he called me sweetness and light. And the mischief we got into. I remember you, Pres. I remember it all."

One of my hands left her face and slid down to her chest, pressing against her heart.

"Then you know why you belong with us... Little Nyx."

She bit her lip.

"I do."

I couldn't stop myself from brushing my mouth over hers.

"I love you, Scarlett. That will never change. Even if you hate me for lying to you. Even if you're angry. I will still love you until the end of fucking time. You're mine, little lamb. And I'm never letting you go again."

A tear slid down her cheek.

"God damn it, don't make me cry more. I can't take it."

I pressed my mouth firmly against hers, stealing away her words. Her fists tightened on my shirt as she kissed me back. The longing between us was a blazing inferno. I tried to keep a lid on it for her sake. I didn't want to overwhelm my lamb more than she already was.

Pulling back, I pressed my lips to her forehead.

"Take your shower, sweetness. I'll be here when you're ready."

I let her go completely and walked out of the bathroom, knowing if I didn't leave, I wouldn't be able to stop myself from taking her into the shower and having her up against the damn glass. She did not need to deal with my lack of impulse control right now.

I took a seat in the armchair by my shelves to wait for her, staring out over the darkening city. Whatever Scarlett came at me with, I would take it. I'd known lying to her this whole time was wrong. When I fell in love with her, my guilt over it worsened. She deserved so much more from all of us. Now she knew the truth, there were so many other complications that went along with it. Not least of all the fact she knew what happened the night of her accident. She knew we'd killed

Stuart Carver's twin sons and buried them in the foundations of a building.

The whole fucking reason he'd sent her here was to get the truth and to destroy us. We'd known it from the beginning. And we had planned to do everything in our power to prevent it from happening. Then Scarlett showed up and everything fucking changed. It all went to shit, and we were trying to pick up the pieces as best we could.

I sighed, rubbing my face with both my hands. We had a lot of explaining to do. I just didn't think she needed to hear all of it tonight. What my girl needed was to be fed, tucked up in bed, and allowed to sleep. I would hold her all night if she asked it of me.

When Scarlett came out of the bathroom, she was wearing a little black robe she'd left in there and little else. She'd put her wet hair up in a messy bun. Her feet carried her over to me. I sat back, allowing her to crawl into my lap and wrap herself around me. I stroked my fingers along her collarbone just above where West had carved into her skin. They were angry red lines, reminding me of violence.

"Can I ask where they found you?" I whispered, leaning my cheek on top of her wet head.

Her fingers traced along my shirt collar, where it was hanging open.

"I went looking for my mother."

I tried not to flinch at the mention of Lylah. And judging by the softness of her voice, she had no idea of the truth. West and Drake hadn't told her. I certainly did not want to be the bearer of that news.

"Tonya found me outside the flat. Mason has been tracking my phone, and it turns out she's been spying on me for him."

Scarlett shifted, pulling up the sleeve of her robe. There were scratch marks down her forearm.

"She tried to get me to go with her to Mason, but I refused. Drake and West turned up, took us to Penn's place, and West killed Tonya for hurting me. The reason we took so long is because they had to deal with her body and stage her... murder. I stayed in the car whilst they did whatever the fuck it was with her so you can ask them about it."

Scarlett settled herself back against my chest and placed her hand on my shoulder.

"I don't want to talk about that though. I don't have the energy to be angry. I just want you to tell me what happened to my mother. Drake said we'd talk about it at home, but I don't feel like talking to him or West right now after what they did."

I let out a breath. There was no fucking way I wanted to upset her with this, but she needed to know the truth.

"I don't know how to tell you, little lamb," I admitted.

She pressed her face into my shoulder.

"It's bad, isn't it."

She didn't frame it like a question, but a statement.

"Yeah, it's bad."

"Then just tell me one thing... is she alive?"

I pressed my mouth into her wet hair.

"No, sweetness, she's not."

Scarlett didn't respond. I wrapped my arms around her, wanting to give her the space she needed to process the fact Lylah was dead. She slid her hand beneath my shirt, seeking out my skin. I don't know if I was any comfort to her or not, given she was likely pissed at me, but I was going to try my best to help her through this.

"Pres."

"Mmm?"

"I'm angry at you for lying to me." She didn't sound angry, but she'd told me she was tired. "But right now, I need you more than I want to give you a hard time over it. Just know you're not forgiven."

"I know, sweetness." I stroked her shoulder. "I don't expect you to forgive me. Especially when I've not told you how sorry I am, but that's a conversation for tomorrow."

She shifted again, removing her hand from my shirt so she could undo the buttons. I didn't comment on it, wondering what she wanted. She parted my shirt, exposing my chest to her gaze. Then she was pressing her mouth to my bare skin, peppering kisses across it while her hands travelled down my stomach.

"I love you, Prescott," she whispered. "I'm so in love with you, it hurts. Every time I look at you, my heart aches with longing." Her fingers were at my belt, unbuckling it before she unzipped my trousers. "I'm so fucking angry and hurt and upset, but I don't want to think about those things." Her hand dug into my boxers and wrapped around my cock, making me choke out a breath. "I just want you. I fucking want you so much."

She shifted around to straddle my lap, her lips still trailing along my chest. Her mouth latched onto my shoulder and her teeth closed around my skin. I grunted when she bit me, but I didn't say no. I didn't tell her to stop. How could I? Her fist was wrapped around me, stroking in a maddening way and making all my blood rush to my dick.

"You're mine," she hissed against my skin. "I fucking claim you as mine."

THIRTEEN

SCARLETT

The way he let out another grunt before whispering, "I've always been yours, little lamb," had my heart in knots. There were so many other things I should be doing right now. Things I should be thinking about. But… all I wanted was him. I wanted the man I loved to take my pain away, even though I was angry with him. Even though he'd hurt me and broken my trust again.

I just wanted Prescott.

I needed him like air.

"Touch me. Please. I need you."

His hands went to the belt of my robe, tugging at it to loosen it. Then he parted the sides and his fingers roamed over my skin. His touch made me tremble. Raising my head, I looked into his blue eyes. They were full of possessive heat and need, reflecting my own desire for him.

West and Drake hadn't let me come earlier when they'd punished me. I wanted a release. And I desperately wanted it with Prescott.

"Claim me, Pres," I all but demanded. "Be my Pestilence."

His wicked smile had my pulse skittering. He gripped both my hips, pulling me directly over his dick. I held it for him so he could sink me down on it. I groaned at the sensation of him filling me. Leaning closer, he ran his tongue along my jaw.

"I've infected you," he murmured before he nibbled my skin. "My sacrificial little lamb."

There were no truer words spoken. Prescott had been in my heart my whole life, along with the others. It might never have been sexual, but I'd loved the four of them like they were my family. Now he had more of me. He owned pieces of my fucking soul. And I couldn't tear him out. Not when I knew as well as they did.

We all belonged together.

No one else would understand. They didn't get it. For our whole lives, something had tied us together. It had bound us and made it impossible for one to be without the other. Only I'd been torn from our gang of five, not that I understood why. It was a question for tomorrow.

"I want you to make it hurt. I want to bleed for you."

He growled, his chest vibrating with it. Taking both of my hands, he locked them behind my back with one hand. Then he latched onto my neck with his teeth before thrusting upwards, impaling me the rest of the way on his cock. I cried out from the intrusion and the sharp pricks of pain from his bite. But it felt so fucking good. It was what I needed.

116

I craved the primal side of Prescott. The rough way he handled me. His teeth digging into my skin. I wanted him to lay me down on his altar and fuck me without a care for what I wanted. I needed to be used.

"Mine," he growled, thrusting up again and making spots form in my vision from the exquisite pleasure and pain.

I didn't care if he left bruises. I already had 'war' carved into my skin. What the fuck did it matter if I wore the marks of our passion?

"I'd kill for you, sweetness," he whispered as he kissed his bite. "I'd fucking die for you because I wouldn't want to live in a world where you don't exist. We waited ten years for you, but I would have waited a lifetime. You are everything to me."

This fucking man. I can't deal with him. The things he says to me. The way he cares.

"You're everything to me too."

The words came out without me wanting them to. The moment overwhelmed me. Made me want to spill all my feelings towards him. He was king in my heart. It didn't fully register that he'd told me they'd waited ten years. I was too focused on wanting him to tear my body to pieces with ecstasy.

The next thing I knew, Prescott had let go of my hands and crawled out of the chair with me, pressing me on the floor, where he proceeded to fuck me with vigorous strokes. My body was pinned, with his hands covering mine. He bit down on my shoulder, leaving another mark. I gasped as he trailed his hot mouth down my chest until he met my breast. I bucked when he took my nipple between his teeth. And I cried when he tortured it.

My leg hooked around his hip, drawing him ever closer. His clothes rubbed against my skin with the force of his pounding, but I didn't care. Losing myself to him was the only thing on my mind. Delirious bliss was my focus.

"Don't stop, please. Never stop!"

He bit me again, this time right above my breast. I had told him to claim me. To infect me. And he'd listened.

He raised his head the next moment, his eyes boring holes into mine. I was lost in his gaze. In his possession. In everything Prescott Ellis.

"My beautiful little lamb wearing my marks," he murmured, giving me the most deviant smile I'd ever been graced with from him.

I shivered as he pulled away and rose to his feet. He put his hand out. I clasped it, letting him pull me to my feet. I was barely upright when he backed me up to the window like a hunter with his prey in his sights. Gripping my waist, he turned me around and pressed me against the glass. I didn't get a chance to say a word with him at my back. He tugged up my robe, then he was thrusting inside me. Prescott took my hands and held them against the glass. As my robe was open, my breasts were smashed up against it as he fucked me.

"If only the world could see you right now," he told me, his voice low and seductive. "They'd be in awe. And they'd be jealous of me getting to fuck such a beautiful creature. They can't have you, though. You're mine. I own every part of you."

I pictured everyone being able to see me right now. Watching me get fucked by one of the deviant and infamous Horsemen. It would be even hotter if it was all four.

What the fuck? Where did that come from?

I'd had sex with them all at once before, but both times were under rather dubious circumstances. Maybe I should be the one who got to call the shots next time. Would there be a next time? Did I want there to be?

Yes, you do. It felt good. So very right.

I shoved away those thoughts, wanting to stay in the moment with Prescott. He was giving it to me so hard, I could hardly breathe, especially with the way I was pressed up against the glass.

"Such a dirty little lamb putting yourself on display like this. You want to be watched, don't you? You love it."

"I want you to watch me."

He groaned and fucked me harder in response.

"Mmm, you know how much I like seeing you in the throes of ecstasy."

"I want you to tell them what to do to me."

His hands tightened around mine. Apparently, my mouth was running away with me.

"Tell them how hard to fuck your little pussy, huh? Make them shove their cocks in you until you're crying?"

"Yes!"

"That can be arranged, sweetness."

I shuddered.

"Please, Pres."

His clothes were chafing against my skin as he hadn't bothered to take them off, but it was only making me wilder. I wanted to free-fall into the abyss.

"Anything for you."

"I need to come, please."

He let go of one of my hands and pressed his between me and the glass. I moaned when he rubbed my clit. The desperate note in my cries echoed around the room. It was all I could do to stay pressed up against the glass while Prescott used my body for his own pleasure and drove me towards my end.

I was on fire when I came. Bliss washed over me. The coolness of the glass against my heated body was such a sharp contrast, but it only made it that much sweeter. I moaned Prescott's name, never wanting it to end. This was exactly what I needed to get out of my own fucking head. To just not feel anything but our bodies together.

"Little lamb," he grunted as he erupted inside me, clearly unable to hold back now I was clenching around his cock with my climax.

The two of us were panting and sweaty when we came down. He leant heavily against me, but I didn't mind. It reminded me of how big he was compared to me. And how I was safe with him wrapped around me.

When he caught his breath, he pulled back and picked me up, carrying me over to his bed and setting me down on the covers. I stretched and lay on my back, not caring about closing my robe over just yet. He leant down and kissed me, allowing our tongues to meld together with a rough passion, leaving both of us wanting more. He smiled when he pulled away, stroking my cheek.

"Is that what you needed, hmm? An escape from your thoughts?"

I nodded, not even caring he'd seen right through me. Thinking would only have me angry and upset all over again.

Thinking would allow grief to sink into my bones. And I didn't want it.

You're going to have to deal with the fact your mother is dead, you know.

I told my brain it needed to take a hike. There were a lot of things I had to deal with. Too many. I didn't have the energy for them tonight. Today had been fucking crazy. If I went further down the rabbit hole, I might not be able to dig myself back out. Self-preservation had finally kicked in, protecting me from the horrors awaiting me. The truth wouldn't be pleasant, of that, I was sure.

"Did Drake and West get you dinner?"

I shook my head, making him let out a puff of air as if he was frustrated with the two of them for not looking out for my well-being.

"I will have words with those two."

"You don't—"

He put a finger over my lips.

"No, I do. You are precious to me. I won't accept them not taking care of you."

I stared at him for a long minute before he lifted his finger from my mouth and straightened. Prescott moved away to change, leaving me on the bed with far too many questions running through my mind. Like, could I love this man more than I already did? He was making it very difficult to remain angry with him.

Prescott had always been the most attentive when we'd been kids. While Francis had been one I always confided in, Prescott was the one who made me laugh when I was sad, he always had my back and never failed to be my rock in every aspect of my life. The two of us shared something the others didn't. We were raised by single mothers and it gave us a little extra in common.

"How is Rosie?"

He paused in the process of pulling a t-shirt on, turning his head to meet my eyes. There was a softness to them I hadn't seen since I'd re-entered his life. Prescott loved his mother more than anything.

"She's good. I bought her a house outside of London when we made our fortune. She lives with three dogs, five cats and six chickens. I try to visit every couple of months, but sometimes it doesn't work out that way."

His words made me smile. I was glad he'd moved her outside the city. Rosie had always been a free spirit of sorts.

"Quite the menagerie."

He chuckled.

"Yeah, she loves her animals. She was going on about wanting a duck pond, but I talked her out of it. I'll take you with me next time I go."

When Prescott was growing up, Rosie had a black and white cat named Clevedon, who was the grumpiest little shit. He used to spend all his time sleeping on the windowsill except for when he was meowing to be fed.

"I'd like to see her."

"And she'd love to see you, sweetness. I haven't told her you're back yet, but I will."

He fell silent as he finished changing. I sat up and grabbed the tissues from his bedside table, doing my best to clean myself up. Prescott paused on his way to the door.

"I'll get you some dinner and then you can go to sleep, okay? We'll talk about everything in the morning."

"I think that conversation should include all five of us."

We had work tomorrow. And I had no idea what they were going to do about the fact Tonya was no longer with us.

"You're right. It should, even if it means we're all a little late starting. I'll tell them, sweetness. Don't worry about it now, though. You just rest."

And with that, he walked out of the room.

I wasn't looking forward to the conversation, but there were things we needed to address. Answers they needed to give me. And depending on what they were, I would have to decide what I did next.

Now I knew my father... no... Stuart's theories about what happened to his sons were not unfounded. They were true. The boys had killed them.

But the thing was, they'd done it for me. And it made me complicit in the whole thing too.

FOURTEEN

Francis

I woke up way too early this morning. Staring out the window with a cup of coffee in between my fingers, I'd watched the sunrise across London and wondered how we got into such a fucking mess. The plan we'd so carefully constructed had crumbled the moment Scarlett came back. Perhaps the years separating us had been the driving force behind making us throw caution to the wind to be close to her again. None of us could help ourselves when it came to Scarlett. To the woman who had been our family. Our hopes. Our fucking dreams.

I felt her before I heard the pad of her feet across the wooden floor. My body turned when she paused and our eyes met from across the room. Scarlett was the most stunning woman I'd ever had the fortune of laying eyes on. No one else was comparable. Her beauty wasn't skin deep. It radiated out of her, shining so fucking bright like a beacon in the darkness.

She wore the black blouse with little white horses she'd had on the first day she started working for us along with navy trousers and a little black belt, but her feet were bare. Her hair was up in a bun, with little wisps surrounding her face.

I set my coffee cup down on the side table nearby, but I didn't move away from the window. Her hazel-green eyes were full of conflicting emotions. We hadn't spoken yet. Not since her memories returned. There were so many things I wanted to say to her, but they were all caught in my throat. Knowing she remembered me was all I could think about. All I could see when I looked at her. She knew our history. It rendered me unable to do anything but stare at her.

There was a moment of stillness before she broke out into a run, almost skidding across the floor until she was in front of me. She didn't stop there. No, Scarlett launched herself at me, wrapping her arms around my neck and burying her fists in my hair.

"Frankie," she breathed my name out like it was a fucking prayer.

My arms went around her, cradling her against my body.

"Little Nyx," I whispered into her ear, which was right by my mouth.

She let out a shudder and a sigh, like hearing her nickname from me was all she needed.

"This is not me forgiving you, but I can't help it. It's like a part of me was missing without you."

Her words constricted my chest. Guilt. It's all I could feel. Knowing I'd been complicit in keeping the truth from her. It had all seemed so easy when she wasn't right there in front of us.

126

"I'm so sorry."

"I know."

I kissed the skin right below her ear. She gripped my hair harder in her small fists before pulling away to look into my eyes. The recognition in them had me flipping us around and pressing her against the window. I pinned her there. If she left me right now, I was likely to break in half. My best friend was back. The girl I'd do anything for. The girl I'd fucking well killed for.

"No, Scar, you don't know. You don't even know the half of it. I need you to see me when I tell you I'm sorry for all of it. Every single second you weren't here with us where you belong. Every passing day. All the hurt, anger and pain you must feel at the four of us for keeping it from you. But there's one thing I'm not sorry for…"

She stared up at me, her lips parting on a breath.

"What's that?"

"This."

I took those lips with my own, stealing her breath as my tongue delved between them and curled with hers. Perhaps I shouldn't have kissed her, but I would never be sorry for the intimacies we'd shared. The ones I never expected to have with her. I wanted her to know I wouldn't give them up. I wouldn't give her up for anything. Any-fucking-thing. Not when it felt right to kiss her. To feel her against me. To be inside her.

I held back a groan when all the blood rushed to the place it shouldn't. Releasing her mouth, I leant my forehead against hers, closing my eyes and breathing her in.

"You were supposed to be my safe place," she murmured.

The words almost decimated me. Scarlett had always shared her deepest, darkest secrets with me. She'd confessed how she felt about West years before she'd done something about it. I'd never revealed it to anyone else. It was in my vault, along with many other things we'd spoken about over the years. She always called me her safety. And when she came back, I fell back into the role without thinking about it. Only I hadn't kept her safe this time. I'd dragged her into the dark with us, but she belonged in it even if she didn't realise it.

"I know."

"Sorry isn't going to earn my forgiveness."

I nodded. Sorry was a start, but it was only the beginning.

"I still need the truth."

"You'll get it, Scar, when the others come down."

She rubbed her face against mine as if reminding herself I was here. I was real. I was her Frankie. Not just the man, but the boy too.

"Now I know why you refused to tell me when your birthday is."

I let out a snort.

"Can you blame me?"

"No, it would have had me asking more questions… ones I imagine you didn't want me pestering you with."

Pulling away, I opened my eyes and gave her a look. She was smiling, which put me slightly more at ease.

"You try explaining to the girl who doesn't remember you why you and your friends all share a birthday with her."

Her smile fell slightly and her eyes clouded over.

"Yeah, it's not so funny when you put it like that."

I stepped back, knowing I needed to give her some room. Her gaze fell to the floor, her hands fisting in her trousers.

"What I don't understand is why you kept it from me. Why all the lies? I mean, okay, I get it to an extent because of what happened that night, but it still doesn't make sense to me."

There wasn't anything I could say to her. Not when the rest of them weren't down here yet. I didn't want to do this alone. Besides, when Prescott had come down last night, he may have had a go at Drake and West over their lack of care when it came to Scarlett. West had ignored him, but Drake had been pensive. Gave me the impression something had occurred between him and Scarlett, but knowing Drake, he wouldn't talk about it.

And when they'd told us what they did regarding Tonya... well... I can't say I was entirely surprised West had killed her. But the way they'd staged her body out in the woods with a bunch of cult-like symbols, candles and other paraphernalia surrounding her? It was a new one on me. Apparently, it had been Drake's idea after West had ripped out Tonya's heart. No fucking surprises that Penn had been on board with it. He and West were like two peas in a pod. Both of them were psychotic on some level. Probably why they were friends.

I doubted anyone could tie this shit back to them. We'd always been careful when disposing of bodies. Usually, we got rid of all traces and went about it quietly. With Tonya technically being Drake's family, guess he wanted to draw the heat away from us. If it didn't make the fucking news, I'd be surprised.

"We'll talk about it when those three idiots get downstairs."

Scarlett snorted and looked up at me.

"Idiots, huh?"

I shrugged.

"They have their moments."

I took her hand and pulled her over to the sofa, making her take a seat. I pressed a kiss to her forehead before going into the kitchen to make her some tea. Her eyes were on me. I could feel her stare, making my skin itch in the best way possible.

"Do you like watching me, Scar?" I asked as I poured boiling water into a mug.

I glanced over at her and watched the blush rise up her cheeks.

"Yes," she squeaked, pressing her fingers to her face.

"Oh yeah? Why's that?"

"You know why."

I shook my head and gave her a smile as I stirred her tea.

"No, I don't think I do."

She let out a huff and crossed her arms over her chest.

"Stop fishing for compliments."

"You sure you don't want to tell me?"

She wrinkled her freckled nose.

"You just want me to tell you I think you're hot and I wish you would come over here and take care of my pussy for me."

"I wouldn't say no."

Her cheeks burnt hotter, going the most delicious shade of red.

"You have no shame."

"When it comes to you? None."

"Well, if you want my forgiveness, you better be prepared to make it up to me."

"By putting my tongue in your pussy?"

She shifted in her seat.

"Oh my god, that is not what I meant!"

I finished up making her tea while she stared at me with an adorably embarrassed expression on her face. Given the type of things others said to her, I wasn't sure why me saying I wanted to stick my tongue in her pussy made her react like this, but it was fucking cute.

I carried over her mug and set it down on the table before kneeling at her feet and spreading her legs. Scarlett watched me as her hands dropped to either side of her. My hands ran up her thighs, making her bite her lip.

"You sure you don't want me here, Scar?" I murmured as my fingers drifted between her thighs, stroking close to her crotch. "Because I want my little whore to come on my tongue."

"Frankie," she whispered, clenching the fabric of the sofa below her.

My fingers went to her belt, undoing it and unzipping her trousers. She didn't stop me. She didn't say a word. Just watched me as I peeled her clothes from her body, shoving them far enough down her legs so I could gain access to her pussy. My mouth trailed up her inner thigh. My hands latched onto her thighs to keep them spread wide for me, with her legs resting on my shoulders.

"Your wet little pussy looks so fucking appetising."

And I dived in, making her let out a little cry of pleasure as my tongue met her hard clit. I groaned before sliding two fingers inside her. Clearly, my words had an effect on her, as her pussy was so slick and hot. I slid them out and back in again, making her buck into my face. My mouth latched onto her clit, licking and sucking in the way I knew she liked.

"Oh god," she whined. "Frankie, fuck!"

"I love your pussy. It's my fucking heaven."

And I'm pretty sure I'm falling in love with you too, Scar. I just want you to love me back… so fucking much.

The thought was almost sobering, but I shoved it away, concentrating on driving her wild. Her hands went to my hair, shoving me harder against her pussy.

"Don't stop, Frankie, god… don't stop!"

My fingers moved faster in and out of her wet heat, wanting to push her closer to the edge. A third joined the first two, making her cry louder. I didn't care how much noise she was making. It was music to my ears.

"That's it, scream for me, little whore."

Latching back onto her clit, I grazed it with my teeth, drawing another cry of pleasure from her lips, and more begging for me not to stop. Then I slowed the pace of my thrusts, not wanting her to come just yet. Lifting my head slightly, I met her eyes. Her pupils were blown and her face was flushed with her arousal.

"I'm not your god, Scar," I murmured, "I'm your horseman."

The way she stared at me had me giving her a wink before I dived back in, my tongue circling her clit. And the way she panted out a breath had me sucking on her, making her squirm and try to close her legs. She couldn't. My hand was keeping her from doing so, not to mention my head was jammed between them.

"Well, well, what do we have here?" came a voice from behind me sounding distinctly like West's.

"Oh my god!" Scarlett squealed, then she was trying to wriggle out of my grasp, but I wasn't having any of it. "Frankie!"

I didn't give a shit if the others saw what I was doing. My attention was on my woman. On making her scream with her pleasure.

"Don't mind us," Prescott's voice echoed around the room. "We're quite happy to watch."

I inwardly scoffed. Of course, he would enjoy this.

"Speak for yourself," Drake said with irritation lacing his voice.

"Frankie, please," Scarlett hissed, but I didn't stop. No fucking way.

Her hands gripped my head, trying to tug me away. It only made me want to hold her tighter. Send her higher. Make her fucking cry for me. I wanted her tears.

"Oh, Jesus," she cried out when I thrust my fingers harder and she gave up trying to get me off her, giving into the pleasure I was drawing from her body. "Fuck, oh, oh, I'm going to…"

Her back arched off the sofa, her fingers digging into my scalp as she moaned out my name again. I groaned when she came over my fingers and face. There was nothing like it. No one like her. If the boys hadn't come down, I would have done more than just eat her pussy. I would have pinned her hands down and fucked her until she screamed so loud, her voice got all hoarse. I would have denied her orgasm over and over, depriving her of her self-control until she was desperate for a release. And only when she begged me, when she called me hers, I would have let her fall into fucking oblivion.

Soon. I'll have you soon, little whore. I'll have you in fucking chains for me.

The thought brought me up short as Scarlett slumped on the sofa, breathing heavily. I slid out from under her legs and clothes, setting them back down. Then I leant over her spent body, gripped her chin and kissed her, not caring she could taste herself on me. I reminded myself Scarlett wasn't Chelsea. And I wouldn't take it too far. I could be in control. I would be in fucking control.

If Scarlett was ever going to see the real me, then I had to be honest about myself with her. She knew me because of our history, but I'd kept so much from her. I intended to remedy it as soon as I could.

"If you could stop mauling Scarlett, we need to talk," Drake said, forcing me to pull away from her lips.

"She was enjoying being mauled, weren't you, my little whore?"

She blushed but nodded. Drake let out a huff. Someone was in a fucking mood. Then again, we were about to tell Scarlett the truth. Probably why he was feeling sour.

I helped Scarlett back into her clothes, grabbing some tissues to clean my mouth before I sat next to her. Reaching out, I handed my woman her cup of tea, which she sipped gratefully and leant her head against my shoulder. The others gathered on the sofas after Drake had made himself a coffee.

Guess it was time to have the conversation none of us wanted to. And I was pretty sure Scarlett was going to rain down hell on us when we were done.

FIFTEEN

SCARLETT

I held my mug in my hands and stared at the others from where my head rested on Francis' shoulder. For days, I'd wanted answers and now, when I was about to get them, I was nervous, scared even of what they'd say.

Perhaps I shouldn't have allowed Francis to go down on me this morning when I was pissed off over the lies. Something inside me snapped when I saw him standing by the window, bathed in the early morning light. He looked so young. So damn handsome. He reminded me of my teenaged Frankie, who had always felt like he was in the shadow of the other three. The one who had no idea how attractive he was. Even now, Francis held those same demons. I could tell by the way he never quite believed me when I expressed my admiration.

He was never in their shadow. He was my safety. The person I trusted with my whole self at all times. I might have loved and desired West, but Frankie was the one I told everything to.

Every. Single. Thing.

And I wanted Francis to know he wasn't second best to anyone. He was perfect all on his own.

It was all I could do to run to him and hold him. To remind myself he existed as both my teenage best friend and the man who did the most amazing things to me with his mouth. Even now I could feel the aftereffects of my orgasm washing over my body. His proximity had my heart in overdrive.

And yet... he'd lied to me along with the others.

"I thought we would start by talking about Lylah," Drake announced, rubbing his chin with his fingers.

My chest tightened. The world went dark around me. If there was one thing I didn't want to talk about, it was my mother. The fact she was dead had me holding back a tidal wave of grief threatening to burst through.

"No," I blurted out.

Drake's eyebrow rose.

"No? I thought you wanted to know what happened."

"Pres told me already."

Drake glanced at Prescott.

"I didn't tell her the circumstances, just that, you know, she's..."

My head rose from Francis' shoulder and I leant forward, placing the mug down on the coffee table.

"Dead. My mother is dead."

The silence echoing around the room from my pronouncement made my hands shake. I swallowed hard.

"I don't want to know why or how or anything else. I can't..." I took a breath. "I can't face it. Don't make me... please."

I didn't sound remotely confident, more like pleading. Like a desperate child who didn't want their innocent view of the world shattered. I wasn't ready. Not when the first sixteen years of my life had been shoved back into my consciousness and I had to confront the fact everyone had lied to me.

I don't know why, but my eyes went to West's first. There was a hardness to his expression. It didn't soothe me in the slightest. Perhaps he was thinking about the fact I'd told him yesterday he wasn't my West any longer. While it was the truth, it didn't mean it hurt any less.

The thing was, I could still see parts of Francis and Prescott I'd known as kids in the men they were today. Prescott hadn't stopped being a cheeky little shit. And Francis was still the quieter one who didn't wear his heart on his sleeve. Drake and West were a very different matter. Drake was cold, calculating, and terrifying at times. West was just... I didn't know how to describe it, but he could. He'd told me the boy he'd been had died the night I fell. And I believed him.

"Okay, we won't talk about her," Drake finally said after a few minutes had gone by.

My eyes went to him, finding those indigo blue ones full of sympathy. It took me back slightly, seeing Drake display emotion so freely after all these weeks of coldness. I couldn't allow it to knock me off course. There were questions I had, and I was determined to make them answer me.

"I want you to tell me what happened when I was in a coma."

My voice came out surer this time now we were off the subject of my mother.

Drake looked at the others before he leant forward, resting his arms on his knees, and let his long hands dangle between them. I had to tear my eyes away from them. Why I found his hands so attractive was a mystery to me.

You like it when he wraps them around you and makes you feel as though you're at his mercy. When he uses them to punish you. You like how big he is compared to you. How terrifyingly beautiful he is. You want everything he has to offer.

I pursed my lips, trying to prevent those intrusive thoughts from showing on my face. Didn't matter how attractive he was. It didn't even matter if my feelings were all tangled up and conflicted over the fact I'd known them when we were kids. And it was making me absolutely fucking crazy. The only thing that mattered was getting answers from them.

"We were questioned by the police over the disappearance of Ray and Ryan," Drake started, his voice steady. "And nothing came of it as they couldn't pin anything on us."

It made sense. This was exactly why Stuart had sent me here. He wanted to know what happened to his twin sons. He was sure they were dead. And he was even surer about the Horsemen having had a hand in it.

"You were put into a medically induced coma after your surgeries. They were concerned about the swelling in your brain with your head injury and wanted to give you time to heal. Two days before they were due to bring you out of it, as the swelling had gone down, you were taken from the hospital overnight. You vanished without a trace. None of us knew why you'd been taken. And it…"

He swallowed and bowed his head.

"It broke us."

I didn't say a word. Drake made one thing very clear. I'd been kidnapped. Taken away from my life. And we all knew by whom.

He took a moment to gather his thoughts before his eyes snapped to mine.

"It took us three years to find out who took you, Scarlett. Three years of searching, running down every single lead, doing everything we could to be sure of what happened. And when we discovered it was Stuart Carver... there was nothing we could do. Not when we were nineteen with very little to our names."

He waved a hand around.

"This? We built all of this for one reason."

My fingers knitted together, knowing exactly what he was going to say.

"We did it for you."

"Me?" I whispered, my voice shaky.

For the first time since he'd been a teenager, Drake's indigo eyes softened a fraction. It almost destroyed my anger. Almost.

"Yes. You, Scarlett. We did all of this... for you. To get you back."

I couldn't take the way he was looking at me. The way they were all looking at me. As if I should be grateful to them for going to those lengths. Except I couldn't be grateful. Not after everything they'd done to me since I'd come to Fortuity.

I stood up and paced away to the window, staring out at the city. Looking at them hurt too much. I crossed my arms over my chest, trying to stem the irritation rising inside me. But what was the point? I was angry. I was fucking livid. None of what he'd said explained why they'd treated me like I was a toy. Using me for their sexual gratification. Making me kill someone. Forcing me into an impossible situation where I didn't know what was fucking up or down any longer.

"So what? I'm supposed to say thank you? Am I supposed to express my gratitude for you going to all that trouble, huh?"

I laughed, but it came out hollow and stilted.

"I'm not fucking thankful. In fact, I'm not even sure I'm happy I'm here right now with you because this is all bullshit."

I dropped my hands from my chest, my fists clenching at my sides.

"What you're telling me is I was kidnapped at sixteen years old because of something you four did, right? It's why he took me. Because you killed his children. I mean, you didn't say it, but that's the implication, right? Why all of this happened."

I didn't want to see their faces. I knew the truth would be right there. They couldn't deny it. I'd surmised it pretty well, using what I knew of what Stuart wanted me to do.

"He took you because he thought you could tell him what happened the night of the accident, the night the twins went missing. And when you couldn't... things changed, obviously," came Drake's voice. "And before you ask, yes, we knew what he wanted when he sent you here. We knew everything."

I swallowed. My limbs shook with his words. They knew my reasons for being here. They'd known I was trying to double-cross them.

Fuck. Why didn't I realise this before? It's so fucking obvious now.

"How? How did you know?"

"Phoebe."

I spun around on my bare feet and stared at him, unable to stop the shock racing through my body.

"What?"

"Well, it's not what you're thinking. She doesn't know."

I put my hand up.

"Hold on. Hold on just one fucking minute." I let out a breath. "You mean to tell me you knew about everything because of Mu... Stuart's wife?"

I'd been about to call her Mum. But she wasn't my mother. My mother... my real mother was dead. And I had to shove away the ache starting in my chest. The grief threatening to undo me.

"It was Phoebe and Mason, to be exact."

I didn't know how many more fucking revelations I could take.

"Explain," I gritted out.

Francis stood up and took a step towards me. I flinched. His grey eyes were full of conflicting emotions like he just wanted to hold me and make this go away, but he knew it had to come out. It had to be said.

He wasn't my safety right now. Francis was complicit in this entire thing, and I didn't think I could let it slide. Not with him. And not with the rest of them.

"After we announced our plans to expand, we wanted to know if our bait had worked. The only reason we did that was because we found out where they were holding you. There was no way we could infiltrate their estate to rescue you. We needed another avenue. A different way to get to you. So we had Phoebe followed," he said, taking over from Drake. "Stuart would have noticed, but she is a little more… careless."

I almost scoffed.

More like she turns a blind eye to everything.

"She met with Mason outside of the estate. And the two of them discussed what was going to happen with you."

"Mason? What do you mean, she met with Mason? They barely even tolerate each other."

Francis looked at Drake, who gave him a nod.

"Phoebe has been sleeping with Mason for years."

There were many things I could believe. Many, many things I could take at face value, but this? This was not one of them.

"You have got to be kidding me."

SIXTEEN

SCARLETT

They all gave me a look as if to say, 'why would we lie to you?', but they'd been lying to me for weeks. I didn't know what the fuck to do with myself.

How could Mason be sleeping with Phoebe?

What the actual fuck?

I took a step back, banging into the glass behind me. Nothing about what they'd revealed felt right. And it wasn't even the half of it. There were so many things they hadn't told me. So many things they hadn't said.

"We're not," Francis said.

"We don't have any reason to lie to you," Drake added.

"I think you have every reason to lie to me considering you've been doing it since the day I stepped into this building."

He didn't flinch, but I could see the pain in his eyes. Why the hell did my heart ache at the sight of it? Why did I feel things for them? I hated my stupid feelings. I hated the way these four men had so much fucking power over me. They knew it too. They wielded it with perfect efficiency. And made it impossible for me to stay away.

I couldn't escape destiny. None of us could.

It didn't mean I had to forgive them for the lies. It didn't mean I was going to submit. And it certainly didn't negate my anger. My frustration. My abject fucking misery they were all partially responsible for.

Drake stood and dug his hands into his pockets.

"I understand why you wouldn't believe us."

"Oh well, thank you *so* much for being *so* understanding. I *really* appreciate it."

He looked at me as if he didn't appreciate my sarcasm. Yeah, well, maybe if he wasn't being such a condescending dick, I wouldn't have to sass the shit out of him. Right now, I didn't give a shit if he wanted to take me to task or punish me. I wouldn't let him. Not when he had some explaining to do.

"Fine. If you don't want to believe us, we'll have to show you the truth."

Drake looked at the others, who eyed him with trepidation in all of their expressions.

"Show me?"

"You think we don't have evidence?"

I should have known better. This was where they had me at a disadvantage. I might now know about our past, but there were four weeks I couldn't account for. And ten years separating us.

There were things they didn't know. The torment I'd suffered. The beatings. The long, lonely nights in the concrete cell. The times I'd prayed for freedom. To be let out of my cage. To remember who I was. And to live the life I chose rather than the one everyone else had decided for me.

I couldn't admit those things to them either.

I didn't trust them.

And yet my heart ached. It yearned. It begged me to stop this anger. It asked me to go to them. To let them hold me and chase away my pain by whatever means necessary. Whether it be with gentle caresses, murmurs of reassurance and precious kisses or by brutal but blissful fucking, torturing my body with pleasure and pain, bringing me to the brink of sanity, only to tip me over into madness.

My heart wanted them. All four of them. At once. No holes barred. Just us. Together. And delirious ecstasy.

And my head? Well, she was not on board with those ideas at all.

"Fine. Show me your evidence. And then you are going to tell me why the fuck you all decided it was okay to treat me the way you have done."

None of them said a word. They didn't flinch or act like I'd said something to hurt them. No, Prescott and West stood up and Drake led them towards where their home gym lay. It took me a second to realise they expected me to follow. On very shaky legs, I did, although I kept my distance lest my body betrayed me and my wayward thoughts.

Drake put his hand on a modern white bookcase sitting next to the gym door. The next thing I knew, it had swung back, revealing a hidden door. He punched in a code on a keypad next to it, opened the door, and stepped into the room beyond. West and Francis followed him.

"What's that?" I blurted out just as Prescott stepped up to it.

He paused, his head turning back and his blue eyes assessing me with concern.

"The war room."

Its name didn't reassure me at all.

"Come, little lamb."

I wanted to tell him to stop calling me that. It made me melt and want to give in. But I didn't say it. I was annoyed, sure, but I loved Prescott. Perhaps too much now I recognised every part of him.

I made my way over to him, walking into the room after he did. What I was met with had me frozen to the spot.

One entire wall was filled with photographs, lines of string connecting them, and text written below it. It was like something out of a detective series or a photo board a stalker would create. Or even... a serial killer. I knew the latter wasn't exactly off the cards, but I didn't think they were the type who *needed* the kill. They did it out of their fucked up sense of justice and to protect themselves. West had killed Tonya to fulfil his promise to me. It was his form of retribution. And no matter how much I tried to convince myself otherwise, I understood it.

"What is this?" I pointed at the photographs.

"Look for yourself," Drake said as he leant up against the table in the middle of the room.

I ventured closer, my eyes darting over the pictures to take in everything. It was a timeline of sorts from the day I disappeared to... now. Well, the day I walked back into their lives. The last photo was of me, taken from security footage, walking into Fortuity. Like a lamb to the slaughter. The irony was not lost on me at all.

There were pictures of Stuart, Phoebe, Mason and others in Stuart's employ. There was one of what looked like a high-ranking police officer. I narrowed my eyes. I knew him. Or, at least, I'd seen him at the estate in plain clothes, but I didn't know his name.

"Who is this?"

I pointed at the officer.

"The Met Police Commissioner," Prescott supplied with a dark note to his voice.

"He's friends with Da... Stuart. I saw him at the estate a few times."

"Yes, best friends."

I followed the string connecting him to a picture of the four boys. The text underneath told me he was the one who questioned them regarding the twin's disappearance. And it didn't bode well at all.

The web of connections over the years made my ears ring. Especially the things and people Stuart was linked with. And it made me sick to my stomach.

My eyes traced a path from Mason towards Phoebe. The lines met in the middle. And there it was. A picture of them. It had clearly been taken with one of those long-range cameras. They were in bed together in what looked like a hotel room. There was no denying it. Not when they were embracing each other.

It wasn't the only line connecting Mason. There was one going straight to the police commissioner. Underneath it read: family.

I glanced between the two men, trying to understand what it meant. Mason didn't look like him. At least, the similarities weren't immediately noticeable. The commissioner had lighter coloured hair and blue eyes, but the set of their jawlines were the same.

"Who is the commissioner to Mason?"

"His father."

I swallowed, realising this went far deeper than I expected. It was overwhelming. But it wasn't the final straw. No, it came when I followed the path of Mason to me.

"What does that mean?"

I pointed at a symbol drawn underneath the line. It looked like a small skull. And it left me with the impression they hadn't told me everything about Mason. I mean, I'd just found out his father was the Met Police Commissioner. It was a revelation in itself. I'd never known. Then again, why would I? Mason didn't talk to me about himself. And right now, I was beginning to think I knew nothing about him at all. Not the real Mason, anyway.

"The symbol for death," came Drake's deep and low voice, sending a shiver down my spine.

"And why is it on the line connecting him to me?"

"That's a conversation for another time."

I glanced at Drake. His expression was impassive, but something deadly burnt in his indigo eyes. Something reminding me of a predator. And one I shouldn't provoke. The man may have strict control of himself, but below all of it lay someone who would grant you a long, slow, painful death if you fucked with him.

"Why are you showing me all of this when you say you know why I came here?"

None of them answered. I turned around, facing all four of them.

"Well?"

"You wanted proof," Drake said after a long moment.

"And what, you're banking on the fact that I'm not going to tell him what you did?"

"Yes."

His answer was plain and simple, said with no inflection or trace of emotion. Drake was so sure of himself. They all were by the looks of the expressions on their faces.

I crossed my arms over my chest.

"What on earth makes you so fucking sure?"

Drake's fingers were wrapped around the table. I could see them whitening. The only sign my question had rattled him.

"If you were going to tell him, you would have done it by now."

"You don't know that."

"I do." He lifted one of his hands from the table and held it out as if offering me his words of fucking wisdom. "You're scared of him."

He said it so matter of fact, like there was no question in his mind. I was terrified of the man who'd told me he was my adopted father. It made me ball up my fist behind my back. Drake was right. He saw through me. And I didn't know if I hated him for it or not.

"You're so scared of what he might do, you ran to us when Mason hurt you. You came here and begged Pres to keep you safe. Not to mention the way I heard him talking to you that

149

night I found you alone on the phone to him. And let's not forget what he asked you to do the night of the match."

I flinched. There was confirmation he had the memory stick Stuart had given me.

"So, Scarlett, are you going to stand there and tell me you're going to take what you know to him? To the man who kidnapped you to punish us. Who kept you from your family all because of a theory he can't prove? Because I don't think you are. In fact, I am more than sure you won't for several reasons."

He dropped his hand straightened, levelling me with cold eyes, void of all traces of affection for me. It cut me far worse than anything else he'd ever done. Even when he'd used sex to punish me. I didn't know who he was then. I didn't know the boy he'd been. The one who used to treat me like I was the most precious fucking thing in the world. Who had rescued me from the twin boys who'd tried to rape me. And who'd, along with my three other best friends, had killed said boys to protect me.

Seeing Drake like this made me want to cry. For him. And for myself.

"You must know the first reason, and if you don't, well... it's because of love. You go to Stuart and confess, how do you think that's going to make him feel, huh?"

Drake was referring to Prescott, who looked away at his words.

"You aren't going to throw that away. And before you object or ask me how I know, you forget, I grew up by your side. I know you. We all know you. Ten years hasn't changed who you fundamentally are inside. It didn't take away your heart and crush it into a thousand tiny little pieces, destroying the girl we knew."

Tears welled in my eyes. I didn't try to blink them back. His words hurt. They hurt so fucking much. Because the truth… the truth has the power to shred you to pieces.

"Ten years is nothing when you know we all belong together."

He took a breath. The only sign of the way his own words had affected him.

"We were born together. And we will die together."

And there it was. The one thing I'd been avoiding talking about. The one thing making it impossible for me to walk away from them. The one thing connecting all five of us to each other.

Twenty-six years ago, we entered this world on the same day, in the same hospital with a few rooms separating us. We'd taken our first breaths within hours of the other. And we'd come together five years later. Drawn to each other like moths to the flame. Like we knew we were linked. We were meant to be. It was a thing we shared. Something no one could take away from us.

Fate had brought us back together.

And fate wouldn't allow us any room to escape it again.

SEVENTEEN

FRANCIS

A fter Drake's words, Scarlett's bottom lip trembled, her hazel-green eyes wide with tears gathering in them. She wasn't the only one they'd knocked the fucking wind out of. Prescott, me, and even West were visibly affected by his pronouncement.

It wasn't a lie. We'd been brought into this world at the same time. And I had a feeling we would leave it as one. While it might be crazy to leave things up to shit like destiny and fate, this was something none of us could escape.

"You say that like it's a curse. Like we're all fucking cursed to be bound to each other for life."

"Maybe it is," Drake said, his voice cracking on the words. "It sure feels like one."

She sucked in a breath as tears spilt down her cheeks.

"Is that why you've been so fucking cruel to me, Drake? You hate the fact you can't stay away from me? Is that why you've become so cold?"

He didn't respond, and the longer the silence went on, the more her tears flowed. The worse the atmosphere between the five of us became. The tension was utterly suffocating.

"I have my answer then," she whispered on a sob. "I bet none of you wants this, do you? None of you wanted it to happen like this." She wiped her face, but it didn't stop her tears. "Fuck fate. What the hell does it even matter? Us being born at the same time means nothing if it's the only reason you want me. If it's the only fucking reason, you found me. Right now, I wish you hadn't bothered if you don't care about me beyond that."

She wrapped her arms around herself like she couldn't contain her feelings any longer. They were written all over her face. The way this had broken her. Being forced to remember everything. Realising she'd been kidnapped. How the last ten years had been a lie. The way we'd treated her after all the promises we'd made of protecting her for life as kids. Now, confronting the fact we'd all become so tangled up in a web of lies, desire, hate, lust, longing and need.

We hadn't meant for it to happen like this. It wasn't a part of the plan. We weren't meant to fall for our best friend, but I was pretty sure all of us had. Even Drake.

When no one responded, Scarlett dropped to her knees and buried her hands in her face. The sobs echoing around the room made me flinch. And the way she couldn't catch her breath had me fucking concerned.

What the hell are you doing standing there like a fucking lemon? Do something!

I crossed the room in four long strides and squatted down next to her. Tentatively, I reached out and stroked her shoulder. Her hands dropped from her face, planting on the floor in front of her.

"I... I... I can't breathe," she choked out. "I can't."

I could feel the tremors running through her body. The last time I'd seen her so shaken was the night of the killing. When she'd woken up after a nightmare. Knowing exactly what I needed to do, I shifted closer and wrapped myself around her body, holding her so she wouldn't fall apart.

"Shh, Scar, I've got you," I whispered into her hair. Then I turned my head and looked up at the others. "One of you is going to get me a rope. Right now."

"Why?" Prescott asked, looking at us rather helplessly.

"Because she needs it and if you love her, you'll fucking do it."

For a second he hesitated, then he walked out of the room to do what I asked. I turned back to Scarlett, who had gripped my arm around her with her tiny hands and held onto me.

"I can't," she gasped, choking on her own tears. "I can't. It hurts."

My arms locked tighter around her chest. It wouldn't be enough to settle her, but it was all I could do until Prescott got back. And I was glad she hadn't pushed me away.

"I'm right here. I'm going to make it go away for you, Scar, I promise."

I could feel West and Drake staring at me, but I didn't give a shit. Drake didn't need to say the things he had. He'd made this shit infinitely worse than it needed to be. While I knew he cared about Scarlett, he also had to stop taking his own shit out on her. He had to stop blaming her for the things she'd had no control over.

Scarlett hadn't asked us to kill for her. She hadn't asked to lose her memories in an unfortunate accident. She hadn't asked to be kidnapped and taken away from her life. She wasn't at fault. And while she'd come here with ill intentions, she knew the truth now.

Prescott was back in short order with a couple of my ropes. He brought them over and dropped them at our feet. I extracted myself from Scarlett's grasp and held onto her face with both hands, forcing her to look at me. Her tear-stained face made my chest ache so fucking much.

"I'm going to wrap you in these, okay? Just like last time. Do you want me to do it over your clothes or do you need to feel the rope against your skin?"

The way her body shook was almost more than I could take. I had to remain calm for her. Scarlett didn't need me freaking out over this whole thing. She needed me to be in control so she could fall apart.

"S-s-s-skin."

I nodded before my hands dropped to her face and went to her blouse, my fingers working to unbutton it. She kept crying, gasping for air, but she didn't stop me from removing her clothes. I left her underwear on, knowing she probably didn't want or need to be completely exposed to the others. It surprised me they hadn't left, but maybe they realised this concerned all of us. Her well-being and safety did.

I picked up the first rope and used it to bind her wrists together. The rope coiled down her arms, pressing them close before I put them to her chest. She shuddered as I wrapped the rope around her back, securing her just right. This time, I made everything tighter. Scarlett could handle it. I had a feeling she needed it to calm down. After I'd finished with her torso, I bound her legs, bringing her knees up so she was completely secured and unable to escape. It wasn't about that, though. It was the comfort and peace being constricted would bring.

Scarlett let out a shuddering breath as I shifted behind her, seating myself at her back. I leant against the wall, pulling her with me so she could rest there against my chest. My arms looped around her, making sure she knew I wasn't going anywhere.

"I've got you, Scar," I murmured in her ear. "There's nothing to be afraid of. You can let go. Breathe for me."

Her little sobs echoed around the room as she turned her face into me, resting it against my shoulder. I watched her eyes close as she continued to cry and shake in my arms.

"Is this really going to help her?" Prescott asked in a low voice after a minute had gone by.

"She'll be okay, Pres," I replied, stroking Scarlett's skin. "She needs this."

Scarlett let out another choked breath, but her body was starting to relax against the bindings. This would work. It had to. I'd recognised it in her the first time. Her need to feel safe. And being surrounded by something helped her in ways nothing else could.

"Frankie," she whispered.

I kissed her hair.

"What do you need?"

"You."

"You have me, Scar. Always. I'm never leaving you. It has nothing to do with fate. I want you because you're you."

"P-p-promise?"

I smiled and rubbed my face against her hair.

"I promise."

It was clear to me she needed reassurance. And it was the truth. I cared about her because she was Scarlett to me. The strong, fierce and kind girl with a big heart who did everything in her power to be there for us when we were younger. Who never backed down and always gave as good as she got. Fate had brought us together, but what kept us together was each other.

Her crying subsided after a few minutes, but she was breathing heavily. Or as far as she could with the way I'd bound her. Her eyes were still closed and her face pressed against me as if my presence gave her the peace she needed on top of the bindings.

I looked up when West walked over and squatted down next to us. He reached out and stroked the wisps of her hair back from where it'd been plastered to her cheek by her tears. I didn't stop him when he leant closer, pressing his lips to her ear.

"You know fate isn't why you belong to me, little Scar," he murmured before stroking his finger down her cheek. "It never has been."

She let out a breath but didn't say a word to him.

"I can't be the boy you knew, but I can be the one who protects you... even from him."

Scarlett's eyes flicked open as West pulled away. His eyes flashed with emotion before he rose to his feet. Scarlett's head turned to watch him walk over to Drake.

"You. Me. Outside. Now."

West strode away towards the door without waiting for Drake to say yes. Drake hesitated, staring at Scarlett with an unreadable expression, but I knew what was going on in his head. He hadn't meant to hurt her. Something had broken inside of him the day she was ripped from our lives. Something he couldn't fix. But I had a feeling she could... if he let her.

He strode away a moment later. If he didn't go after West, the fucker would only drag him out of here.

"I shouldn't let them talk by themselves," Prescott muttered, rubbing his face.

"No. It will end in fists," I replied. "And we don't want that."

He let out a long sigh before making his way over to the door. He paused there, gripping the frame.

"The way I love you, little lamb... it consumes me. It's not destiny. It's you. You consume me. And I will prove it to you if I have to."

Scarlett's lip trembled as she turned her face back to me and met my eyes. I nodded at her.

"I love you too, Pres," she choked out, her voice gravelly.

His shoulders sagged in relief. Then he walked out.

For a moment, Scarlett did nothing but look at me as if she was memorising my features. It was almost unnerving. I'd never had anyone scrutinise me the way she did.

"I didn't mean what I said before," she whispered.

"About what?"

"When I implied you were no longer my safe place."

My heart squeezed.

"You'll always be that for me. No one else can take your place, Frankie. Only you can give that to me."

I bit the inside of my cheek. There were so many things bubbling up inside me at her words. She knew my insecurities. They hadn't disappeared over the past ten years. It had always been me standing behind the others. But Scarlett telling me I was the only person who could provide her with a place she could feel safe in? It was everything to me. And it gave me the final fucking push I needed to be honest with her about a lot of things. I was going to tell her about Chelsea. Tell her about my real desire to chain her up and how doing it terrified me because of what happened before. But not right this second. Scarlett had been through enough today. I would take care of her and when she was feeling more like herself, I'd broach the subject.

"Can I kiss you?" I whispered, wanting her permission after the emotional upheaval she'd been through.

"Only if you call me…"

She licked her bottom lip, leaving the words unsaid because she wanted them from my lips.

My hand left her arm and rose to her face. Gripping her jaw between my fingers, I kept her in place as I dropped my face towards hers.

"Can I kiss you, my little whore?"

"Yes… please."

I pressed my mouth to hers, kissing her with tentativeness and care. Reassuring her I wasn't going anywhere. She responded by kissing me harder, her tongue snaking between my lips to dance with mine. I smiled as I let her. I'd give her anything she needed.

When I released her, she opened her eyes and blinked.

"Do you like it when I call you that?"

She nodded.

"I like being yours."

"I like being yours too."

She rested her head back on my shoulder, her mouth turning up at the sides.

"Can we stay like this a little longer?"

"We can stay like this for as long as you want."

"Thank you."

I pressed my lips to her forehead and didn't say a word, letting the peacefulness and silence of the moment wash over the two of us. Thoughts of work had gone out the window. Didn't matter when Scarlett needed me to care for her. Besides, there was a lot of shit waiting for us to deal with. And right now, I just wanted to be with her.

EIGHTEEN

WEST

Seeing the way Scarlett had broken down fucking decimated me. While I didn't outwardly show my feelings, it was ripping me apart inside to know how upset she was. This wasn't how we were meant to deal with the situation. Drake had let it escalate, and I was pissed off with him for it. I couldn't say I was the best at broaching difficult subjects, but he didn't have to be cruel to her. None of us did.

I waited for him in the living room, pacing the wooden floor with my agitation. When he walked out of the war room, his expression was impassive. He dug his hands into his pockets before approaching me.

"What is wrong with you?" I ground out the moment he came to a standstill by one of the sofas.

"Nothing is wrong with me, West."

The way he said it only fuelled my ire. Like he couldn't understand why I was questioning him.

"Oh, really now? You think you put up with a lot of shit from me." I pointed at my chest. "But the truth is we put up with way more from you."

His lip curled up in irritation, his indigo eyes betraying his incredulity. Drake could hide behind his emotionless mask all he wanted with other people, but not with me. I saw right through him because he suffered the same fucking affliction I did. The pain and suffering caused by Scarlett being ripped from our lives, compounded by the problems we had with our parents. While I had turned violent, he'd turned cold, but Drake and I? We were far more similar than he liked to admit.

And he could be mad at me all he wanted. He didn't have a fucking leg to stand on after what he'd said to Scarlett.

"That in there." I waved my hand at the war room. "That was bullshit, Drake, and you fucking know it."

I dropped my hand when he didn't respond.

"You act like I'm the one who causes all these fucking problems, but you're the one who stopped us from giving her the truth. And now she knows, you make her think you don't care? What the fuck is that, huh? There was no need to hurt her. None. Not when she's already suffering. Do you think this is easy for her? It's not. It's not easy for any of us. It was cruelty for no fucking reason, and you know it."

He let out a tut before he drew his hands from his pockets.

"Funny you're accusing me of being cruel after yesterday."

I tilted my head.

"Yesterday. You want to talk about yesterday. I see. You're going to tell me what I did was cruel." I licked my lip. "Scarlett knew the consequences of her actions. I warned her what

164

would happen if she ran from me and got hurt. She didn't walk into that situation yesterday blind."

He was about to open his mouth when Prescott walked out and looked between us with a doubtful expression on his face. Rather than letting Drake railroad me, I went on the offensive.

"Fate, destiny and all that other bullshit are all very well, but it's not why we stayed with each other, Drake. We stay because it feels right. We've been with each other through thick and thin. We have her back and now you want to ruin it. I'm not going to let you. I won't let you hurt her until she breaks. I won't let you destroy the woman I..." I faltered, finding it hard to get the words out.

His eyes narrowed on me.

"You can't even say it, can you? You can't admit how you feel about her."

"Neither can you. That's why you're taking it out on her."

He flinched and looked away. Prescott came closer as if he was concerned this might turn violent. I didn't want to hit Drake. I wanted him to tell Scarlett the truth. And not about everything we'd done, but his fucking own truth. The one he didn't think any of us knew about.

"What feelings are you referring to, West?"

I let out a sharp laugh before licking my lip again.

"The ones both you and I feel about her but can't say out loud."

His eyes narrowed.

"I don't—"

"You do."

Prescott stared at Drake as if he was seeing him for the first time.

"And I don't hate you for feeling that way, Drake. I never have. Why the fuck do you think I've never once given you lot any shit for being with her when she was with me first, huh? Do you see me punching Prescott's lights out for being in love with her? Do you think it hurt me to hear she loves him?" I paused, taking in Drake's cold, hard gaze. "You all like to see me as a fuck up, but I've never begrudged any of you. What Scarlett needs is more important. She needs all of us. I understand that. I know Pres takes care of her and Frankie too, but you? All you've done is cause her more pain."

He needed to hear the truth. All of it. I wasn't going to hold back any longer.

"You love her, Drake. You love Scarlett and you hate that she never loved you back the way you wanted because now you know she loved me."

And there was the chink in his armour. The one that made him put a hand to his chest and rub it as if my words had hurt him. Then he dropped his hand and walked away into the kitchen, placing both his hands down on the counter as he leant over it.

"I don't want to hurt her," he said after a long moment. "I don't."

"Then why do you keep doing it?"

"I don't fucking know."

"You do."

He gripped the counter harder.

"She wasn't there when I needed her."

And there we had it. His real reason.

"But you're torturing her for not being here too, West, so don't put this all on me."

I clenched my fist, hating him for being right, but this wasn't about me.

"Stop deflecting. My relationship with her might be fucked up, but I know I have to fix it. You don't seem to get that about your own one with her."

Drake released the counter and turned to me. The haunted look in his eyes almost made me flinch.

"I fucking know I have to fix it. I just don't know how… I don't know how to be the person she knew before."

"You and me both."

A loud clapping noise startled both of us. Our heads whipped around to Prescott who was applauding us for some unknown reason.

"What the fuck, Pres?" I ground out.

Prescott dropped his hands and gave us a grin.

"It's nice to see you've both finally realised what the problem is."

I crossed my arms over my chest and glared at him.

"And what's that?"

"Your stubborn, idiotic nature getting in the way of doing what's right."

"Fuck you."

He shrugged.

"I'm merely stating the truth. You two get in your own way all the fucking time and it's exhausting for me and Francis to deal with. The problem isn't Scarlett, it's you two."

"I should plant my fist in your face."

"Go ahead if it'll make you feel better, but it won't fix what you broke."

This little shit was getting on my last nerve already, even though he wasn't wrong.

"And how do you think we should fix it?"

"You can both start by apologising to her. Then Drake can give her the whole truth, including why we lured her here and what we were going to do until everything went to shit. She isn't to blame, so stop acting like it. We should be directing our anger at Stuart, not Scarlett. And you, West, you can tell her the truth about how you feel. But if you can't do that, you can start by saying it to us."

The thought of saying the words *I love you* out loud to her made my stomach twist in knots.

"What? You expect me to tell you that I..."

The words caught in my throat like I knew they would. Why the fuck was this so hard?

"That you love her? Yes."

I wanted to say, "What about Drake?" but what fucking good would it do? He had his own shit to deal with. And I had to take responsibility for mine. Not to mention my history with Scarlett was way more fucked up than anyone else's. We needed to deal with it. The night of her accident. Because the guilt was eating me up inside.

"I do."

"I know you do. Now say it."

I swallowed, dropping my arms from my chest and looking away.

"I can't."

"You can. Stop being a fucking coward, West."

I gritted my teeth. Why was he making me do this? My fingers itched to lash out at something but hitting Prescott wouldn't make me feel any better. Punching Drake might, since he was being a dick. Then again, getting into a fistfight with him wouldn't end well. Not sure Scarlett would appreciate us fighting over her, either.

Scarlett. You're doing this for her. You need to admit it out loud so you can say it to her.

"No. I'm not going to give you those words because none of you fucking well deserve them. The only person who does is her."

I didn't care what Prescott was saying. This wasn't helping me.

"West—"

"Just shut up, Pres. You don't get it. She doesn't see me the way she used to. She told me I'm not her West any longer."

"You don't need to be him. You need to be you. She wants you."

"You don't know that."

Prescott smirked, the fucker.

"I do. She's all messed up right now, as the past has clashed with the present, but she wants this version of you. She *needs* this version of you."

I fixed my gaze on him, not understanding what the fuck he was saying. What did he mean, she needed me this way? She called me crazy. She didn't want my crazy. She wanted the West she had before. The one who wasn't... psychotic. Who hadn't been slapped with an antisocial personality disorder. She didn't know that part, but she had seen my behaviour. She knew who I was. I hated the diagnosis. Hated how it defined me in the eyes of other people. They didn't get it. I wasn't mindless or an animal or anything else. I was me and I didn't need a fucking diagnosis to know there were things about me most people found abhorrent.

I didn't care what anyone else thought, but I cared about her. Scarlett's opinion mattered to me. And she'd made it very clear. She wanted the boy West, not the man West.

"No, she doesn't."

"Yes, she does. You give her something none of us can." He waved a hand at me. "I'll leave you to work out what that is. In the meantime, I'm going to make breakfast."

He walked over to the kitchen, ignoring my stare. What the fuck was Prescott on about? What did I give her they couldn't?

Drake was watching Prescott with suspicion in his eyes like he couldn't understand what the hell our friend was going on about either. I was glad I wasn't the only one who thought he was off his rocker.

"Now, have you two put some thought into what we're going to say when they find Tonya?"

Drake let out a huff.

"We're not going to say anything because we don't know anything."

We'd agreed to keep our mouths shut. Penn, Drake, and I had done our best work and made sure it couldn't be tied to us. The police would be led on a merry trail to a dead end. No doubt they'd want to speak to us as her employers and Drake being her step-cousin, but we weren't worried about them finding out I'd killed her.

"You sure about that? Aren't you meeting Fletcher for lunch on Thursday?"

"I'll deal with Fletch. You don't have to worry about him."

170

Prescott raised an eyebrow but didn't say anything further. I was sure Drake could handle his step-uncle. After all, he'd been dealing with his family for years, pretending to give a shit about them when really he wanted them all dead. Well, except for his mother. She was the innocent party in the mess of his parents' divorce.

I turned away and stared out of the window. Was Prescott right? Did Scarlett want me this way? How could she? While I never apologised for the way I was, it didn't mean I was unaware of my... faults. I'd never let Scarlett go, that much I was sure of, but as for her loving me like this? I didn't know how when I couldn't be the boy she'd known.

Can you love me, my little Scar? And if you can't... then how will I survive? You are who I live for.

NINETEEN

PRESCOTT

The rest of the day passed quietly with no further incidents. Francis had remained upstairs with Scarlett while Drake, West, and I went downstairs to work. We couldn't afford to act like anything was wrong to the outside world. No doubt, when the police found Tonya, things would be fucked up. It wasn't the only issue we had. There was still the matter of the memory stick and Stuart. I hadn't asked Drake if he'd spoken to Penn about getting it looked at, but I would. We needed to deal with it.

What I hadn't been expecting when I was done for the day was to find Scarlett in my doorway. She had on a blue summery dress. It fell to her knees paired with white trainers. Her hair was still up in a bun, making her look far younger than she was. Her bright smile lit up all her features.

Fuck, she is stunning.

I rose from behind my desk, watching her carefully. While she'd told me she loved me earlier, things were tense between us after Drake had gone and brought up the circumstances of our birth. I hadn't been very impressed with what he'd said to Scarlett, but West had laid into him enough for all of us. I hoped it would actually get through to him. I was getting tired of picking up after him when it came to our girl.

"Hi," she said in a shy voice.

"Hey, how are you feeling?"

She swept her toe across the carpet.

"I'm okay. Frankie took care of me, so I'm feeling a lot better."

"Did he now?"

Her cheeks went red at my suggestive tone.

"Not like that! He ran me a bath after we had breakfast and we cuddled in his bed."

"All day cuddles? Look at you getting spoiled."

She scowled.

"Shut up!"

I walked over to her, stopping by her feet and giving her a smile.

"You deserve to be spoiled, sweetness."

"Is that so? Are you offering to spoil me too?"

"If you want me to."

She reached out and fiddled with my tie. I had a feeling she had come down with the intention of asking me for something.

"I would like you to take me out on a date."

"Is that why you're all dressed up?"

She looked down at her outfit, then back up at me.

"This? I thought you'd like it if I looked a little... innocent."

I raised an eyebrow.

174

"What kind of date are you asking for?"

She rubbed her fingertips against my chest.

"The kind where I'm your sacrificial lamb."

I swear my heart just about stopped in my chest. After everything she'd been through today, the very last thing I was expecting her to ask for was… this.

"Are you sure you want that?"

"I wouldn't ask if I didn't, Pres."

I didn't want to deny her anything, but a part of me was concerned this wasn't what we should be doing right now. Even so, my body was on board with the idea. What she was wearing was perfect. I wanted to dirty her up in all the ways I'd been imagining since I'd told her I wanted to chase her down and fuck her.

"I just worry about you."

She reached up and cupped my cheek.

"Do you trust me?"

I nodded.

"Then trust that I'm telling you what I want." Going up on her tiptoes, she pressed a kiss to my mouth. "I love you, Pres. And I need you to do this. I want you to show me no mercy."

My fingers went to her neck, cupping the back of it and running my thumb along her skin.

"Okay, but first I need to change and we should eat something. You're going to need it."

She grinned, dropping back down to her feet and taking my other hand in hers, linking our fingers together.

"Frankie is making an early dinner."

I followed her along the corridor as she dragged me down it to the lift.

"Did you tell him about this?"

"Yes, and he encouraged me to ask you for what I want."

I would have to thank him later. Scarlett and I had talked about doing this before, but I hadn't broached the subject since then. We'd been so caught up in everything else going on. Perhaps it was exactly why she needed this. Kinky fuckery was her way of getting out of her own head for a while. She liked to be used and shown no mercy. It grounded her.

The two of us made our way upstairs to my room. Scarlett watched me change from her seat on my bed. It was something she enjoyed doing every morning she spent with me, watching me dress for the day. I couldn't deny having her full attention fed me. The way she fit into my routine was effortless. The two of us had found an equilibrium together despite all the lies and secrets. Love tethered me to her and her to me.

When I was done, we shared a quiet meal with Francis. Fuck knew where Drake and West had got to. After this morning, those two needed to handle their shit, and fast. I'd already shared my opinion on the matter. It was up to them now.

Scarlett held my hand in the car as I drove after we'd made our way down to the basement carpark. It took some time for us to get outside of London, but Scarlett didn't mind. We listened to music and talked about our childhood, reminiscing on the mischief the five of us had got into regularly. We didn't bring up what was said earlier today. And we didn't talk about the past ten years either. If she wanted to ask me about it, she could. I wasn't going to press the subject with her.

Dusk had well and truly fallen by the time we reached our destination, just north of London in a nature reserve. I took her hand after I'd locked the car, pulling her into the woods. We walked for a while before veering off the path deeper into the woods, using the fading light to guide us through the trees.

When I thought we were far enough in, I stopped and turned to her. Scarlett was bouncing on the balls of her feet. I could feel the anticipation and excitement leaking out of her.

"We need to set a few ground rules before we do this."

Her hazel-green eyes met mine before she gave me a nod.

"If at any point it's too much or we need to stop..."

"You want a safe word. I have one with Frankie. Red."

"We'll use that, then you don't have to remember another one."

Her smile was her agreement.

"When I'm chasing you, I won't pounce unless it's safe and away from too many trees. I don't want you to be afraid I'll do anything to seriously harm you. Don't run in a straight line either. I don't want you to make it easy for me to catch you. I need the hunt, little lamb. Make me work for you."

She squeezed my hand.

"I trust you not to harm me, Pres."

"Is there anything you specifically want me to do, or don't want for that matter?"

Her blush made me cup her face with my other hand.

"I want you to fuck me from behind and to push my face into the dirt. I want to feel like I am trapped by you, at your mercy and under your control. Be rough with me. Bite me... spank me. I want to be treated like I'm a bad girl for running when you know I want it."

Her words had me shifting on my feet.

"My bad little lamb?"

SARAH BAILEY

"I don't want to be your good girl tonight."

"I'm going to punish you thoroughly for running."

Her eyes twinkled.

"I want you to." She shifted on her feet. "Is that everything we need to go over?"

"Mmm, yes."

Leaning down, I kissed her, wanting one last tender moment between us before the hunt began. She wrapped her hand around my neck, pressing her body into mine and groaning when she felt how hard I was already. The mere thought of chasing her aroused me beyond belief. I wanted her so badly, my need was palpable, coursing through my veins like an inferno.

When I released her, she backed away slightly, giving me a rather salacious look.

"Little lamb…"

"Chase me, my big bad wolf."

With that, she turned and ran. I shook myself, giving her a little head start before I gave chase. I didn't want to lose her in the trees. My feet pounded the dirt as I darted around the trees, following the blue sundress streaming behind her.

"Little lamb," I called after her. "You're not going to get away from me."

"You can't catch me," she shouted back, causing some birds to scatter above us.

I grinned, keeping my pace even and steady. If I caught her too quickly, it would ruin the game. I wanted her out of breath, her pulse racing and her body trembling from the effort of trying to escape.

She veered off to the right, forcing me to change direction to follow her. We didn't want to run out of woods or encounter anyone else who might be out here this evening. And I really didn't want her to make it easy for me.

She darted behind some trees, making it harder for me to see her. I picked up the pace. Running to me was like second nature. I spent most of my time on the treadmill in our home gym, but I also got out at least twice a month to do cross-country. This was me in my element, chasing after my prey, who had no idea of the stamina I possessed. She would run out of her own long before I did.

I noticed an incline ahead of us and a figure scrambling up it. My lips turned up as I watched her make it to the top and turn to look for me.

"You think I won't get you up there, little lamb?" I asked as I drew closer, slowing my pace down.

Instead of answering, she gave me a wink and stuck her tongue out at me. A low growl sounded in the back of my throat at the sight of it. Then she was running again. I shook my head, chasing her up the incline.

"Don't think you're going to get away with that. I'll make you pay for taunting me."

"You can try!"

I chuckled as I got to the top and looked left and right. She was running along the line of the incline as opposed to further into the woods. I turned to the left and ran after her, watching my little lamb pick her way through the trees. My eyes darted around, looking for a good spot to pounce on her, but I couldn't yet see anywhere. By the time my attention was back on my lamb, she was almost tumbling down the incline to get away from me. When she reached the bottom, she ran faster, her breathing laboured as she disappeared into the trees. I growled again and chased her down the hill.

"Oh, big bad wolf, can't you keep up?" I heard her voice echoing through the wood.

"You're playing with fire, my lamb."

"Maybe I want you to burn me."

I was going to burn her all right. Make her pay for all of her words. Scarlett would not come out this unscathed. My girl would be marked and claimed. I'd make her messy. I wanted her tears and pain. Scarlett was going to bleed for me.

I saw her dress in the distance. Her pace was slowing, so I picked mine up. She could hear me chasing her through the undergrowth. Her head turned back, catching sight of me. She tried to run faster, but I wasn't going to let her get away. No, now was the time to catch her and make her take everything.

There was a slight clearing filled with ferns she was running towards. I smiled, ready to make my move.

Oh, little lamb, you've found the perfect place for me to dirty you up.

My hands reached out as I caught up to her. They latched on to her body, tugging her backwards into my chest. She let out a yelp when I slowed to walk and backed away into a tree. My arm wrapped around her torso and my hand went to her mouth. Her body trembled and her heart pounded in her chest. I could feel her breathing heavily as fear coursed through her like wildfire. She wanted to be scared. She liked it. Fear fed my little lamb unlike anything else.

It was time she met the big bad wolf in the flesh. The wolf who wouldn't grant her any mercy.

Leaning closer, my lips brushed across her ear.

CORRODE

"I've got you, little lamb, and now... now I'm going to make you pay for running from me."

TWENTY

SCARLETT

I don't think I'd been so scared and excited at the same time in my life, but something about Prescott chasing me through the woods made my heart sing. I'd wanted it for a long time. To be honest, ever since I had the dream about being chased, I'd been desperate for it. And now it'd come true. He'd chased me down and caught me.

I trembled in his hold, his arm pinned across my torso, holding my arms at my sides and his hand covering my mouth. His hot breath was against my ear, making me fear him even more. The way his voice sounded animalistic had my own breath coming faster.

It might be crazy for me to want an experience like this with him after everything that happened today with the others. The thing about love was you didn't get to control who you felt it for. No matter the lies and secrets, I loved Prescott with every inch of me. I couldn't live without this man behind me. And I needed this with him. To let go of my emotions and dark thoughts. Running from him had given me a sense of freedom I never thought I'd ever feel. Now, I craved the brutality he was about to deliver.

He licked my ear, making me shudder as he walked us a few steps forward. Then he was pushing me down into the dirt on my hands and knees. His body covered mine, his hand pressing against the back of my head as he shoved me face-first into the ground, just like I'd asked for. The dirt was cold against my skin. I turned my face to the left, gasping for breath as he held me down, his fingers twined in the bun on top of my head.

"Bad girls deserve to get fucked in the dirt," he told me, his voice full of menace. He wasn't my Prescott right now. He was my wolf. My punishment. Prescott was my Pestilence. And I was his innocent, sacrificial little lamb.

"You've been a very bad little girl, haven't you, little lamb?"

"Yes," I moaned, feeling him start to undo the little buttons at the back of my dress with one hand.

My body arched into his, wanting him so badly it hurt all over. I ached with my need to feel him using me for his own pleasure.

"What's this, hmm?" He chuckled. "Are you wet for your wolf? Is this pussy dripping for me?"

I shifted in his grasp, not to escape, but to rub myself against him. The next moment, I felt the sharp sting of his palm hitting my flesh over my dress.

"Stay still," he growled, making me freeze.

He leant closer and ran his lips over my shoulder, where he'd bared it after finishing with the buttons. Then he bit me, making me cry out with the pain of his teeth.

"Answer me, little lamb," he demanded around my skin.

"Yes," I gasped, "I'm so wet for you."

His free hand slid my dress up, exposing me to him. Fingers ran over my behind while another low growl sounded in the back of his throat.

"Only bad girls are bare and ready for their wolves."

"I'm a very bad girl."

"Mmm, yes you are."

He spanked me again, making me jolt, and my face pressed harder into the dirt. I could feel it digging into my skin, but it only made my need worse. I whimpered as he continued to pepper my behind with strikes, no doubt thoroughly reddening it. It made me ache to feel more of him. I wanted him to fuck me so hard, I cried.

My hands scrabbled at the dirt as his strikes got worse. It stung so fucking bad, but I'd asked for this. I wanted it. The pain made me needier. I couldn't help wriggling in his grasp. It only earnt me a harder slap and another warning growl from him. I didn't realise how hot it would be when he made that noise, more animal than man.

When he stopped, there was a moment of stillness before he pulled me upright by my hair, making my scalp burn. With his other hand, he shoved the front of my dress off my arms, leaving it bunched up against my waist. He peeled down one of the cups of my bralette and pinched my nipple between his fingers. And then he bit down on the side of my neck.

"Pres!" I cried out, gripping his hand with both of mine.

He said nothing, his teeth digging in harder. I rocked back against him where he'd pressed me to his chest. I could feel him hard against my behind. Fuck, how I wanted his cock in me. If I begged, would he give it to me? Would he punish me with his dick until I couldn't take it anymore?

"Please," I choked out. "Please, I want you."

"Bad girls don't get what they want, little lamb. They get what's given."

He shoved me back down, planting me face-first in the dirt again. The next thing I knew, he'd spanked my pussy, making me yelp with the pain. Then he slid his fingers between my lips, dragging them through my arousal.

"My dirty lamb is so desperate for me. Does this soaking wet little pussy need punishment, hmm?"

"Yes, yes, please, please."

The high-pitched note of my voice betrayed my desperation as my body pressed back against his exploring fingers. He swiftly removed them. I almost complained but felt him shift behind me. Then hot flesh rubbed against my raw behind.

"Do you feel that?" he ground out through his teeth, pressing his cock against me. "Your wolf wants to fuck your wet little hole and make it all his."

"Please!"

He didn't give me any warning. One second he was rubbing against my behind, then next, his cock slid inside me with one brutal and unforgiving thrust. I lurched forward, letting out a cry of shock. My fingers dug into the dirt as he pulled out and shoved himself back in. The pace he set was unlike anything else. I was hard-pressed to keep up with the way his body was pounding into mine. Each thrust made my behind throb with pain as his skin slapped against me.

"Fuck," he grunted, "so wet, fuck, you're soaking."

I wasn't remotely embarrassed by the sucking noises of him fucking me. It was evidence of how much fear and pain turned me on. Made me wild with need.

Prescott leant over me, pressing his body into mine before his teeth found my ear and tugged on the lobe.

"You're not innocent," he taunted. "You're a corrupt little lamb. And you're mine."

"Yours."

He pulled me upright the next moment, planting me in his lap and forcing his dick deeper inside me. His arm wrapped around my body, pressing me down into him. I squirmed in his hold, but he didn't let me go. No, he thrust upwards and I cried. Tears ran down my cheeks at the catharsis of this experience. I let go of everything and allowed Prescott to drown me.

His other hand snaked down between my legs, his fingers gripping my clit between them and pinching. I bucked and whimpered as he tortured it while he fucked me, his dick hitting just the right spot.

"That's it. Come for me, dirty girl. You're covered in it. It's all over your face."

I had no control over myself. The pressure was too intense. Too fucking much. I writhed in his embrace, my hands gripping his body behind me as I exploded on him. My body shook, my nails digging into his t-shirt. Prescott had changed into athletic clothing earlier, making it easier for him to run after me. He looked fucking hot in it, but I had been too busy wanting him to fuck me to tell him earlier.

"Pres," I whined as I came on his dick.

I could feel him breathing heavily against my back, but otherwise, he continued to fuck me, drawing out my climax until I went limp in his hold. His fingers left my clit and hooked into my mouth instead.

"Open wide," he demanded, shoving them deep.

I spluttered, but obeyed him, letting him fuck my mouth with them. Then he tugged me off his dick and forced me to turn around. He fisted my bun and dragged my head down.

"Lick your cum off my dick. Taste yourself on me."

My tongue snaked out, flicking over his crown, but it wasn't good enough for him. He shoved me on his cock, making me take him in my mouth. I could taste the tang of my arousal all over him.

"That's it, clean me up real good."

My tongue skated across his dick. The pressure of his hand on the back of my head forced me into taking more. His dick slid into my throat and I gagged on it. My hands curled around his thighs, giving me something to hold on to while he continued to feed me his cock. My nose pressed up right against him the next minute, leaving me almost unable to breathe. He held me there for a long moment before pulling me off. I choked, spit dribbling out of my mouth, but before I could take more than a few breaths, he pulled me up and claimed my lips. It was a messy and unyielding kiss, but it didn't last very long.

Prescott released my mouth and pulled me into his lap, shoving me back down on his dick. He groaned at the feeling of my pussy wrapped around his cock, and I shivered at the intrusion. His hand went to my chest, shoving me backwards until my head hit the dirt. He rose up on his knees and drove into me, holding me down with his palm flat on my chest. I could see the dark glint in his blue eyes. The danger radiating off him was intoxicating. My predator had a hold of me and I never wanted him to let go.

"This pussy is mine, lamb. Fucking mine."

He let go of my chest and tore down the other cup of my bralette. Then he was leaning over me and taking my nipple between his teeth. My fingers threaded in his hair, wanting to keep him there even as it hurt. My other hand remained against the dirt, my fingers digging into the cool ground.

"Mine," he growled, biting down on my chest to mark me. "You belong to me forever, little lamb."

"Yours," I cried as he bit harder. "Forever, Pres."

It wasn't a lie. I wanted forever with him. It felt like an impossible task when our lives were so fucked up and crazy right now. When there were so many things left unsaid and secrets remaining. But we could fight this together. All of us could... couldn't we?

"Touch yourself. Make yourself come. Your climax belongs to me."

My hand left his hair as he straightened. It snaked between my legs, finding my clit and stroking it. He gripped my hips and fucked me harder, forcing me down on his dick over and over. He watched me touch myself for him. Showing him how much I wanted to obey his commands. To be his lamb. He'd laid me down on his altar. This was his sacrifice and mine.

"That's it. Give it to me, lamb."

I rubbed harder, my body grinding back against him with his thrusts. He shifted to change the angle. I was fucking lost when he hammered into me again. I was done. This was too much. Too fucking everything.

"Fuck, Prescott!"

I swear I shouted it, but I didn't know what was up or down any longer. This second orgasm was more intense than the first. It drove into me, knocking me for fucking six. I was shaking, clawing at the dirt as it claimed me. But my eyes were locked on his. Watching the way his blue orbs were full of satisfaction from seeing me this way. The longer it went on, the more out of control I got. My body was fighting against the tide of pleasure, wanting it to end but needing it to go on. It was all I could do to give into it.

The moment I settled, he pulled me off him and set me on my hands and knees again. I could barely hold myself up, but he didn't care. He slammed into me, leaving me breathless. His hands were around my hips, pressing my dress into my skin with his ruthless demands on my body. I was whimpering as he fucked me, using me for his own end.

"Take my cum, little lamb," he growled before he emptied himself into me, his body twitching against mine. I felt utterly claimed by him right then. Like he'd branded himself inside me.

Both of us were breathless and panting when he stilled. Prescott pulled me down with him in the dirt, circling my back with his body and keeping himself inside me. He pressed a kiss to the shell of my ear before settling next to me. We lay there in silence for a long time, letting the experience sink in. It was everything I'd needed and so much more.

"I love you," he whispered against the back of my sweaty neck, pressing his lips against me. "And I'm sorry for the lies.

I'm sorry for everything, little lamb, but it doesn't stop me from loving you and hoping you'll find it in your heart to forgive me for the way I treated you. I can't live without you. You're my world. And my soul."

A tear leaked out of my eye. His gentle caress was the balm to my aching and satisfied body. He'd given me exactly what I'd asked for. And I didn't think I could adore this man more than I did now. My heart was his. My whole being belonged next to him. But forgiveness? It would come when I knew the whole truth. He knew that and he wasn't asking for it now, just when I was ready.

I pressed myself further back into his embrace, needing him to hold me tight and never let go.

"I love you too."

TWENTY ONE

DRAKE

Thursday had rolled around, and I was in an absolutely foul mood. Yesterday afternoon, the news broke about Tonya's death after her body was found late on Tuesday evening. The headlines had dubbed it a *'ritualistic sex murder'*, which amused the fuck out of West, but I wasn't in the mood to laugh about anything after the last few days of hell. Not sure where they got the sex part from, given we hadn't touched her like that, but whatever. I didn't care what the tabloids said. It was what the police did that mattered the most. And so far, we hadn't been questioned, but no doubt it would happen.

I thought Fletch might cancel our lunch today, but no such fucking luck. It was time for me to suck it up. I stood up, buttoning up my suit jacket before starting towards the door. My feet came to a halt when someone appeared in the doorway. Scarlett had her hair down today, giving her that innocent appearance I hated. Well, I didn't hate it. More like it drove me fucking crazy. Not to mention the indigo dress she was wearing. It was all floaty in the skirt and cinched in at the waist. It had a high neckline and little sheer capped sleeves. My eyes narrowed. She rarely wore dresses at work. I'd come down early this morning so hadn't seen her until now. And it did not escape my notice she'd picked something to match my eyes.

What is she playing at?

"Can we talk?" she asked when I said nothing.

There was no timidness to her. She straight up asked me with all the confidence she possessed, staring me down like she was on a mission. I didn't know what to make of it.

"I have a meeting, Scarlett. You know this."

Her eyebrow curled up.

"Didn't your step-uncle cancel?"

I tried not to scowl.

"No, and don't call him that. He's Mr Sinclair to you."

She rolled her eyes, making my hand twitch with the need to punish her for it, but I knew I couldn't. Our relationship was in the gutter right now after what I'd said to her on Tuesday.

"Okay, so you're still going?"

"I just said I was."

"Well, I'll come with you and we can talk on the way."

If she thought I was letting her go to lunch with Fletch and me, she was crazy.

"No, you absolutely cannot come with me."

The way she looked at me as if I was the crazy one had my hand involuntarily clenching into a fist.

"No? You afraid of what I'm going to say?"

"I am not scared of speaking to you, Scarlett."

"Then I don't see the problem."

"This isn't a negotiation."

"I wasn't aware we were negotiating. I need to talk to you and it can't wait."

I let out a huff. I'd never allowed my emotions to get the better of me, but with Scarlett, it happened all the fucking time.

"I don't have time for this."

I walked towards her, meaning to remove her from the doorway. Scarlett stood her ground, crossing her arms over her chest and staring up at me when I stood before her.

"I think you'll find you have ample time if I come with you."

"You are trying my patience," I muttered.

"Good. Maybe you'll stop being an emotionless robot then."

I blinked. What the fuck was this? Her attitude was pissing me off, and I'd meant what I said. I did not have time to deal with her.

"Excuse me?"

"You heard what I said, Drake. Now, come along, you don't want to be late."

She took my hand and pulled me out of the office. For some reason, I didn't extract my hand from her grasp, nor did I object to her taking me down to the lifts. I couldn't form a response. Scarlett reminded me far too much of the way she'd been when we were younger. Headstrong and stubborn. I don't know what happened between Tuesday and now, but something had shifted in her. It's as if she'd joined together the pieces of her past to her present self. And now she was whole.

It was only when we were in the lift riding down to the ground floor when she broke the silence. I stared down at our clasped hands, wondering why she was okay with this when I'd said some fucked up stuff to her. Stuff I'd yet to apologise for. And after the way West had a go at me about it, I knew I had a lot to make up for.

"Now we're alone, there are some things I need to say to you."

"Okay," I replied, unsure of how this conversation was about to go, given the way she'd manhandled me into this lift and didn't want to listen when I told her she couldn't come to lunch.

"First of all, I'm done fighting with you. Literally done, Drake. I refuse to do it anymore." She looked up at me, her hazel-green eyes full of determination. "We share too much history with each other and I will not let you throw me or that away."

Her words made my chest ache. I didn't want to throw her away. I wouldn't have searched for her if that was the case. I wouldn't have tracked her down and got her back. She was important to me, even if I hadn't made her feel like she was.

"Secondly, you owe me an apology for the things you've said to me. You were mean and I don't think it's okay to take out whatever shit you've been going through on me."

I bit the inside of my cheek. She was right. It wasn't okay.

"And lastly, you are going to finish explaining everything to me because I deserve the truth."

I waited a moment to see if she was going to say anything else, but she didn't.

"Is that everything you want from me?"

"For now? Yes, yes it is."

"I see."

Her eyebrow curled up.

"Is that all you have to say?"

"We will talk about this after lunch."

I almost smacked my hand into my face, realising I'd insinuated it was okay for her to come with me. The conversation I was going to have with Fletch wouldn't be easy, considering he'd just lost his daughter. Even if I didn't care about Tonya, I wasn't about to drive the knife in further.

You have gone and fucked this right up.

"Okay, after lunch it is."

She gave me a smile as the lift doors opened. I didn't say another word as we walked into the lobby and out the front door. The restaurant I was meeting him at was a short walk from the office, so I didn't bother getting on public transport. I didn't enjoy going on it in the first place. The tube was always stuffy, and I'd rather be stuck in traffic in a car than on a fucking bus.

When we got there, I had to explain to the maître d' that I needed an extra place setting at the table. He didn't bat an eyelid thankfully as he led us over to where Fletch was already seated and waved at one of the waiters.

My step-uncle was a short man with blonde hair and brown eyes. He wore a rather bland black suit and a pale yellow shirt with one of those ridiculous cartoon ties. I almost rolled my eyes when he stood up. He didn't look remotely upset, which would be odd considering his daughter had just been found brutally murdered but Fletch wasn't known for being a caring father. In fact, I think he liked me more than his own flesh and blood. Fuck knows why when I didn't talk much and refused to bullshit him. Actually, it was probably the exact reason.

"Fletcher," I said, putting my hand out and shaking his.

"Drake, it's nice to see you." His eyes flicked to Scarlett, who was still clutching my other hand and wouldn't let go. "And who is this lovely lady I see here?"

Scarlett immediately stuck her free hand out to him.

"Hello, Mr Sinclair. I'm Scarlett, Drake's girlfriend."

Fletch raised an eyebrow as he shook her hand. I gritted my teeth, wanting to ask her what the hell she was playing at announcing that to him. If anything, she should have told him she was my PA.

"Girlfriend? Well, you kept that quiet, Drake." He gave Scarlett a smile. "He's never introduced me to a woman before. You must be something special."

Scarlett blushed and dropped his hand.

Wonderful. Now my father is going to find out about this. No doubt he'll tell my mother and then I'll have her on the phone asking me who Scarlett is. She's not meant to know Scarlett is back yet. This is a fucking nightmare.

To say I disliked the fact my parents still spoke to each other after the things Oscar had put her through was an understatement. It wasn't my place to tell my mother what she could and couldn't do, so I kept my mouth shut.

"She is," I said, knowing I had to keep up this fucking charade. "Very special."

It wasn't a lie. Scarlett was more than just special. She owned a piece of me. Something I wasn't best pleased about West or Prescott having knowledge of. No doubt one of them had told Francis. Those three were always ganging up on me.

The way Scarlett looked up at me after I uttered those words with such strong affection in her eyes made my stupid heart tighten.

"Well, sit down, sit down," Fletcher said, eyeing me with curiosity.

I pulled out a chair for Scarlett as he sat, trying to be a gentleman even though she knew very well I wasn't one. While we'd been talking, the waiters had set a place for her. I sat down to her right and she placed her hand on my thigh. I stared at it, trying not to screw my face up with disbelief. It took a supreme effort on my part not to ask what the hell she was playing at.

She gave me a brief smile before turning to Fletch.

"I hope you don't mind me bringing this up, but I'm very sorry to hear about your daughter. It must have come as a shock."

The genuine note in her voice almost made me narrow my eyes. This was the father of the woman she'd watched West kill. She'd held his daughter's heart in her hand. Not sure why she was being so pleasant, but then again, Scarlett was far more compassionate than the rest of us.

"Thank you, Scarlett. It is… a very difficult time for us, especially T's mother."

Fletch did, to his credit, give Scarlett a sad smile.

I'd already spoken to him about this earlier this morning when he called to ask if I was still coming to lunch. Despite me saying it wasn't necessary and we could reschedule, he'd insisted. Now, I was stuck pretending Scarlett was my girlfriend, and this wasn't awkward as fuck.

She kind of is your girlfriend, you know.

I wanted to tear my stupid thoughts out of my head and stamp on them. Girlfriend, indeed. I didn't even know what the fuck we were at this point. It certainly wasn't normal. But me, Scarlett, and the boys had never been normal. Not sure why I was surprised we'd found ourselves in this situation. Whatever the fuck this whole thing was.

Scarlett carried the conversation while we ordered and waited for our meals to arrive. I sat in silence, watching her animated face as she told Fletcher about her now-deceased horse, Chocolate. I didn't know she could ride. Then again, I hadn't bothered to ask her anything about her life at Stuart's. It reminded me of how much of a mess our relationship was.

I rubbed my face. How the fuck would I fix this shit between us? She'd given me an opening. I had to take it. I had to make things right. Scarlett deserved that from me.

"I just need to nip to the ladies," Scarlett said, rising from her seat.

I gave her a nod, not expecting her to lean over, squeeze my shoulder and press a kiss to my cheek. My eyes followed her path towards the toilets as she weaved through the tables.

"She's quite something."

My head whipped back around to Fletcher, who was staring at Scarlett's arse. My hand clenched under the table.

"Yes. And I would hasten to add she's too young for you, not to mention she's *mine*."

"All right, Drake, hold your damn horses. I was only looking."

"Well don't. She's not on the fucking menu."

Fletch's eyebrows shot up.

"What's got into you?"

200

I leant back in my chair, trying to appear relaxed. I didn't need him questioning my behaviour.

"Nothing."

"Possessiveness is an unattractive trait according to most women."

"She knows who she belongs to."

"Well, I never. Didn't peg you as the type, but I see I was wrong."

I levelled my gaze at him.

"We're not here to talk about my relationship with Scarlett."

I wasn't going to tell him she'd insisted on coming with me and I'd had no intention of introducing her to anyone in my so-called family.

He let out a sigh.

"No, we aren't."

"Then spit it out. I'd rather you tell me before she gets back."

He fiddled with his cutlery.

"Your father wants to see you."

And there was the fucking kicker.

Good one, Oscar. Send your fucking brother-in-law to do your fucking bidding.

TWENTY TWO

DRAKE

As if I didn't have enough on my plate, now my fucking father wanted in on the action. I'd already told him to stay away from me. I don't know why he kept trying after all these years. It's not like I was interested in having a relationship with him. To be honest, I should cut all of my family out of my life. Well, not my mother, but everyone else. They were all cunts, including the man in front of me.

"I don't want to see him."

"Listen, I know how you feel about Oscar, but—"

"But nothing, Fletcher. He burnt his bridges."

He had the fucking audacity to tut.

"You really like to hold grudges."

"If you want to be added to the list of people I've removed from my life, then by all means, keep talking."

He leant back in his chair and eyed me warily. I wasn't going to sit here and listen to him go on about all the reasons why I needed to speak to Oscar.

"And you can tell him if he tries this shit again, he knows what will happen."

"You should tell him that yourself."

"Why would I when I can just go through you like he has."

I had him there. He let out a breath and looked away. Thankfully, that was the moment Scarlett returned. She looked between us as she sat down, resting her hand on the table. I immediately placed mine over hers, curling my fingers around her small ones. Both she and Fletcher watched the movement. Scarlett looked startled while Fletch's expression turned to amusement. Apparently, seeing me be possessive over a woman was quite something. I didn't have girlfriends. In fact, I think my mother despaired over me ever finding someone to settle down with. I'd had enough lectures from her over it.

I didn't want anyone but the woman sitting next to me. I had to admit it to myself, even if I couldn't do it to her yet.

"Is everything okay?" Scarlett asked, her eyes wide as she stared at me.

"Yes."

She gave me a disbelieving look. I wasn't going to talk about my father to her right now.

"Are you sure?"

"Come here."

"I'm already right next to you," she said, lowering her voice and giving me a weird look like I was asking for something crazy.

"I want you closer."

She glanced at Fletcher with a worried expression on her face.

"Are you asking me to sit in your lap or something? Because I'm not going to do that in a restaurant," she hissed as she met my eyes again.

"No."

"Then what do you want, Drake?"

You. I just want you. I don't know why the fuck I can't say it.

"Just sit closer to me."

She huffed but shifted her chair until it was right next to mine.

"Better?"

I let go of her hand and tucked her hair behind her ear, stroking my fingers along the lobe. Her thigh was pressed against mine. I don't know why it made me feel better, but it did.

"Yes."

The waiters arrived with our meals, but it didn't stop Scarlett muttering, "bossy," under her breath. I pinched her ear between my fingers to let her know I heard. She merely fluttered her eyelashes and gave me a smile, as if she wasn't acting like a fucking brat.

You like it when she pushes your buttons.

I didn't want to like it… but the truth was, I did. I liked it too fucking much.

While Fletcher made a start on his meal when the waiter left, Scarlett continued to look at me, pressing her thigh harder against mine.

"Do you want something?" I asked in a low voice.

"You know what I want from you."

"I mean, right now."

The rather deviant look in her eyes made me suspicious, but she turned away and picked up her knife and fork.

"No. I'm pretty sure you don't do PDA."

It took a second too long for what she said to register. By that time, she'd already started eating. And I was left wondering if she wanted me to kiss her or if she was just saying it to get to me.

I turned to my own meal, picking up my fork with a small smile playing on my lips as I leant a little closer to her.

"The type of PDA I'd want to engage in with you would get us thrown out of this place," I murmured.

The blush rising to her cheeks had me hard-pressed not to smile wider. That was until she laid her knife down and wrapped her hand around my thigh.

"Don't threaten me with a good time."

"You've been hanging out with Prescott too much."

She smirked and squeezed my leg before going back to her food.

"Or you've just forgotten I remember everything about you... including how to make you smile."

I tried really hard not to, but I couldn't help it. My lips curved up. Fuck. I was utterly screwed. The quick-witted and no fucks given Scarlett was back. And she was on a mission involving me. I wasn't entirely sure how I felt about it.

The rest of the meal passed with Fletcher asking me about how the business was going and all of us avoiding the topic of Tonya. I could only be glad he didn't suspect us of having anything to do with her death. Not that he would have any reason to, but we couldn't be too careful.

Fletcher told Scarlett it was lovely to meet her when we were saying goodbye and hoped we could do this again. I refrained from commenting but took her hand and led her out of the restaurant.

"Am I in trouble?" she asked after we'd been walking for a couple of minutes.

"Why would you be in trouble?"

"I told him I'm your girlfriend."

I glanced down at her, noting she wasn't letting go of my hand… again.

"We'll talk about *that* when we're at home."

She was about to open her mouth when my phone rang. I fished it out of my pocket, almost groaning when I saw who it was.

"Hello, Mum."

"I have a bone to pick with you."

Oh, Jesus Christ.

"Why do I have to find out everything about your life last, Drake?"

I'd known this was going to happen, and I still wasn't prepared for it.

"What are you talking about?"

"You introduced your girlfriend to Fletcher and not me. That's what I'm talking about. You are always hiding things from me and I'm sick of it."

I gritted my teeth. Scarlett's eyebrow was raised, but she couldn't hear what my mother was saying. She'd known exactly what May Ackley was like when we were younger, and she hadn't changed. Always up in everyone else's business and never letting me get away with anything. Mum hadn't bothered to change her last name after the divorce. I wished I didn't have the same fucking last name as my father, but it couldn't be helped.

"I didn't keep anything from you. It's... new."

"I don't care if it's new. I'm your mother. You should be introducing her to me first, not Fletcher."

"Okay, I'm sorry I didn't."

There was no use telling her I hadn't meant to introduce Scarlett to anyone at all because she wasn't actually my girlfriend. And the only reason Fletcher had met her was because the damn woman wouldn't take no for an answer.

"Who is she? Your father said her name is Scarlett and all I could think about was little Scarlett who used to hang off your arm when you were kids. It's such a pity she disappeared. You always had time and a smile for her. I was hoping one of you boys would end up marrying the girl."

Did she really have to bring that up? For fuck's sake. I don't need to be reminded of that shit when she's right next to me, reminding me every single fucking day.

Fletcher had worked fast if he'd already told my father and he'd rung my mother. Honestly, I swear nothing was kept secret in my family. It's why I never told them anything.

I sighed. I couldn't exactly tell her the truth, but she would give me hell for lying. What would I even say, anyway? Oh yeah, by the way, we're all fucking her, so your hopes for us ending up with Scarlett came true? That would go down so well.

"I don't have time to discuss who she is right now."

"You never have time for anything, Drake. Why can't you make time for me, hmm? I just want to know what's going on in your life."

"Mum—"

"Is it serious? Are you in love with her? I want you to bring her around to dinner and I won't take no for an answer."

My fingers tightened around Scarlett's, making her let out a yelp as we walked through the doors of Fortuity. My mother was getting on my last fucking nerve.

"What was that? Is she there?"

"Jesus, Mum, are you going to let me speak?"

"Well?"

"I'm back at the office and I have to go."

"Drake Ackley!"

"Bye, Mum."

I hung up and stuffed my phone back in my pocket. Scarlett raised her eyebrow as I practically dragged her across the lobby to the lift, not even stopping to say hello to the receptionist.

"You know, I didn't think you'd turn out bossy like your mother."

"What?"

"May liked to keep you in order. I see where you get it from now."

"Are you quite done pushing my buttons today, Scarlett?"

"Oh, come on, Drake, you need to relax."

I stabbed the lift button several times. Relax? Was she fucking kidding? She'd made my day infinitely worse. My mother was going to give me absolute hell for hanging up on her.

I tried to extract my hand from hers, but Scarlett laced her fingers with mine to keep them trapped. My other hand clenched. Did she have any idea how much I wanted to punish her? Actually, she likely did, and it pissed me off even more.

The lift arrived. I tugged her inside and hit the button for the office floor. As soon as the lift doors closed on us, I backed her up into the corner and stared at her defiant little mouth.

"You are giving me a fucking headache, Scarlett."

She didn't bat an eyelid. Instead, she traced the fingers of her free hand down my torso.

"Am I? Well, I'll just have to help you with that."

"Help me? More like put me in an early fucking grave."

She smiled, which was unnerving. I didn't trust the look in her eyes.

"I would never."

I gritted my teeth and paced away from her.

"You drive me insane," I muttered.

"I know I do."

I didn't respond. What I needed was to get the hell out of this enclosed space with her before I did something stupid like kiss the damn look off her face.

"Drake…"

"What? What is it now?"

"I meant what I said. I want to help you relax."

"You have helped more than enough already, thank you very much."

She came over to me and wrapped herself around my arm. I didn't shake her off me, but I didn't look at her either. She wasn't making it easy for me. And I didn't expect her to.

The lift finally arrived on the office floor. I tried to walk towards my office, but I found myself tugged towards the stairwell by a very determined little wisp of a woman.

"What are you doing? I have to get back to work."

"No, you don't. I know for a fact you have nothing scheduled this afternoon and work can wait."

"I'm your boss, Scarlett, not the other way around."

She smirked and continued dragging me into the stairwell.

"As your PA, it's my job to see to your needs."

"I don't recall telling you I need to go upstairs."

"And to anticipate needs you might not know you have," she continued as if she hadn't heard what I'd said.

I had no idea what I could say to make her stop, so I didn't. I allowed Scarlett to pull me up two flights of stairs and open the roof door, securing it so it wouldn't close over and lock us out. Not that it mattered, as I would have called Francis or Prescott to come to open it.

"Why are we up here?"

"Stop asking questions and come with me."

She took me across the roof to my glass house and opened the door, ushering me inside. The next thing I knew, she was unbuttoning my suit jacket and sliding it off my shoulders. I was so dumbstruck by the whole thing, I let her undo my tie and place both on the sofa along with her handbag. Then she pulled me over to my armchair and sat me down in it.

Scarlett leant over me, undid the first few buttons of my shirt and took out my cufflinks, rolling my sleeves up slightly. She kicked off her heels and dropped to her knees at my feet. I was about to protest her taking off my shoes and socks until she gave me a look that spoke volumes. She set them aside and looked up at me from where she was kneeling between my spread legs.

"Now, are you going to apologise to me or not?"

"Why are you kneeling?"

She let out a puff of air.

"Are you going to sit there and tell me you don't want me at your feet? I know you like this and I told you, I'm giving you what you need... sir."

I swallowed. Denying it would be futile. She looked so beautiful kneeling there in a dress the same colour as my eyes, waiting for me to give her what she needed in return. Even though she'd frustrated the hell out of me and got me in trouble with my family, I couldn't help but lean forward and take one of her hands, pulling it up towards my face. All I could think about was her mouth and the need to make things right about her.

I pressed a kiss to the heel of her palm.

"I'm sorry."

"For what exactly?"

Everything.

"The things I said, the lies... and for being a dick."

I could see she was trying not to smile at the last part.

"I spent so long waiting for you. I don't want to throw you away, Scarlett. I'd never want that." I shook my head and pressed her hand to my face. "I want to keep you."

TWENTY THREE

SCARLETT

W hen I got up this morning after spending the night with Francis, I'd decided to take the bull by the horns and deal with Drake. Perhaps I should have just told him to go fuck himself, but I didn't want to be at odds with him. He used to be my best friend. And I wanted that Drake back. I wanted his smiles, his laughter, and his joy. He had to be in there somewhere, locked underneath his icy exterior. I was going to find him no matter what it took. Giving up on him would only make me unhappy. I'd already had enough of that to last a lifetime. The last ten years had been miserable for me. I was drawn back to this place with these men who had been my world for over half my life until I was stolen away. Drake was a huge part of my past. And if I was honest with myself, I wanted him to be in my future.

Drake stared at me after he'd told me he wanted to keep me. His indigo eyes weren't emotionless for once. They were full of need… for me.

"I accept your apology, but it doesn't mean I've forgiven you. I haven't forgiven any of you and I won't until I know the full truth."

"Do you want me to tell you now?"

I shook my head. There was a reason I'd brought him up here, away from anyone else. It was the place I'd first discovered he had a lot more going on behind his mask. And now I remembered him. It was even more significant. He'd been learning to play the guitar since we'd been kids and I was the only one he'd allowed to listen to him practise even when he sucked.

I felt safe with him up here, like he wouldn't harm me on this roof. Not the way he had done when we'd got into the stupid fight over the football match and he'd fucked me as a punishment. Now I wanted to change the last memory I had of when we'd been intimate. I needed to. If we were ever going to move forward, I wanted to wipe the slate clean. Well, not completely, but at least when it came to sex with him. It might be crazy to desire all four of the men who'd been my best friends as kids, but I didn't care. This was my life, and I was going to do what I wanted with it now I was no longer locked away.

"No," I whispered, taking my hand from his face and pushing him back against the armchair. "I don't want to talk right now."

I climbed up into the chair with him, straddling his lap and running my hands up his chest, along his neck and into his dark hair. His indigo eyes flickered with heat, but he didn't move to touch me.

"What do you want?"

My hands went to his face, forcing his head back so I could look him in the eyes from my position.

"I meant what I said about helping you relax." My hands drifted from his face to his chest, my fingers working to undo the rest of the buttons of his shirt. "But this isn't just for you..." I ran my fingertips along his exposed skin. "It's for me too." My hands went lower, sinking between us until I wrapped my fingers around his dick. "I want this." I watched his expression and the way his mouth twitched. "And I'm going to take it... because you know what, Drake?"

"What?"

"It's mine."

He let out a puff of air but didn't say a word. I leant closer to him until I was an inch from his mouth.

"I want to erase what happened before. I need you to touch me, kiss me, fuck me until I overdose on you. Can you give me that?"

His response was to run his hands up my chest and grip my shoulders. The gesture made me feel small in his grasp. And I needed it. I liked how he was so much bigger than me. How his hands dwarfed mine.

"I can," he murmured before he caught my mouth with his.

His kiss wasn't brutal or savage. It was soft and full of need like he wanted to drown in me, but he was holding back. Always in control. I planned to make him lose it but in a good way this time. My hand curled tighter around his cock, stroking it through his clothes. I could feel it swell under my fingers, reminding me of how thick he was. That extra girth was going to feel so damn good when he was inside me. When he was fucking me.

"Drake," I whimpered in his mouth, desperate for him already.

His hands moved along my shoulders and found the zip at the back of my dress. He tugged it down, exposing my hot skin to the air. When his fingers slid over it, I arched into his touch. He tugged the dress off my shoulders, forcing me to release him to slide it down so it pooled at my waist. Releasing my mouth, he stared at my bra-clad tits. Then he was pulling down the cups and sucking one in his hot mouth, such a contrast to his cold nature.

I couldn't wait any longer. The ache was all too real, almost violent. It pulsed and writhed, wanting to take, claim and conquer.

"Please."

"What do you want?"

His mouth pressed to my skin, delivering hot, wet kisses to the flesh.

"You inside me."

Drake's hands went to the skirt of my dress, pushing it up higher. He looked between us when he realised I wasn't wearing any underwear.

"Bad girl," he muttered before undoing his trousers and tugging out his hard cock. "You sat having lunch with me and Fletcher like this, didn't you?"

His hand clamped around my hip, drawing me lower until the tip met my wet pussy.

"Yes," I hissed when he dragged it through my folds.

"Fuck," he grunted before shoving me down on him.

I let out a harsh pant at the thick intrusion. My hands went to his shoulders, holding onto him as I sunk lower, taking every inch of his beautiful dick. My eyes locked onto those indigo blue ones when my body was flush with his.

"Tell me you want this. This is what you need, right?"

Those long fingers of his tightened around me.

"I *need* to punish you."

The raw agony of his voice made me shiver.

"Then do it with your dick. Make me feel it."

Next thing I knew, he'd stood up with me in his arms, still impaled on him, and strode towards the sofa. He pressed me down on it, planting his knees on the soft material and leaning over me. My mouth was claimed before he fucked me with intense strokes that had me arching into him. My feet dug into the fabric, lifting my hips up to give him a better angle. His hand wrapped around one of them, holding me in place. The way he was pounding into me was almost too much, but I didn't want him to stop. I needed this version of him, the one who lost control and drowned in his desire to have me.

"Fuck," he groaned into my mouth. "Fuck, Little Nyx."

I almost froze hearing the nickname from his lips. The one he'd given to me. Then I turned my face from his and buried it in his neck. Tears started pricking behind my eyes, making me want to sob on his chest from the relief of knowing he still saw me as the girl he'd once known in some small way.

"It's not enough," he murmured in my ear. "You feel so good, but it's not fucking enough."

I was about to ask what he meant when his hand left my hip and curled around my behind, brushing between the crease of my cheeks. Then I knew what he wanted. And at that point, I was willing to give him anything, so he'd keep fucking me. I didn't care how. I just wanted his cock inside me.

"There's lube in my handbag," I whispered. Prescott had put it in there, telling me I never knew when I might have need of it. "And if you're going to fuck me there, I want you to look in my eyes as you do it."

Drake was the only one who hadn't taken me that way. I wanted to see his expression. To see if it made him betray his emotions. His feelings. To witness his reaction to sliding his dick up inside me.

He pulled away and twisted, reaching over to my bag. I didn't care if he saw what was in it as he rooted around for the tube. He threw my handbag back down after he'd extracted it, along with my pack of wipes, and looked at me.

"Get on your hands and knees so I can fuck you whilst I prepare you."

The demand in his voice had me scrambling to obey, tugging my dress off my hips in the process and unsnapping my bra. Drake pulled the rest of his clothes off, leaving him utterly bare. I couldn't help looking at him in all his naked glory. The trail of dark hair from his navel to his cock made my mouth water. Those big hands of his circled my hips before he pressed inside me again, making me moan in response. The slight smirk on his face had me biting my lip. He liked how I reacted to his dick inside me.

He released my hips, picking up the tube and squirting the liquid onto his fingers. I moved my hips back into him, fucking myself on his cock while he stroked those wet fingers along my hole. I whimpered when he pressed one inside me, even though he was gentle. Didn't stop me from working myself on his dick while he opened me up to him.

He took his time as if he didn't want to rush this. Seeing him devote his full attention to me was a heady experience. Drake had once called us toxic, but I think we were merely drunk off each other. Drowning in our need to be as close as possible. And fighting against it because we both knew it was dangerous to want each other this much.

When I was practically squirming on his dick and fingers after he'd inserted three, he pulled away from me, taking a seat on the sofa and proceeding to coat his dick, still slick with my arousal in lube.

"Come here."

While I turned around and crawled into his lap, he used one of my wipes to clean off the excess from his fingers. He held his dick for me as I positioned myself, then his eyes were on mine, followed by his hand wrapping around my jaw. Mine went to his shoulders, so I had an anchor.

"You want me to look at you, hmm?" he murmured. "Here I am, take it the fuck in."

I bit my lip as he breached me, the stretch almost too much for me to handle even with his preparation. But it was worth it because the way his lips parted had me mesmerised. His indigo eyes were almost black pools of lust and desire. Drake wasn't hiding his emotions behind a mask. I could see them plain as day on his face. He desired me to the point of insanity.

Slowly but surely, I took him until he was deep inside me. I watched every twitch of his face, the way he stared at me, how his teeth ran over his bottom lip as I clenched around his cock. He was so damn handsome like this, it almost hurt to keep his gaze.

"I want to make you bleed. I want to see crimson blood all over your skin, the colour of your fucking name, scarlet red."

I shuddered at his words.

"I want you to," I whispered, rocking my hips into his and making him groan out loud, his hand wrapping around my behind. His fingers dug into my skin as if my agreeing to it was the best news he'd ever had.

"What if I bathed you in the blood of my enemies?"

"Do it."

"Fuck."

Drake pulled me into him and kissed me. It reminded me of the night he'd found me talking to Stuart and he kissed me with such savagery, I almost melted on the spot. He claimed my mouth like it was his for the taking and no one else could have it. Then he pulled me off him, flipped me over onto my front, and covered my body with his. He drove back inside me, making me yelp as his hands held mine down. His breath was hot on my ear with his thrusts, making me writhe beneath him.

"You're going to come on my cock. I'm going to fuck this tight little hole until you scream. That's your punishment for telling Fletch you're my girlfriend, causing my mother to have a go at me and for winding me the fuck up."

And what a punishment it was. The way his body slammed into mine, making me feel every single inch of his thick cock. When he dug his hand under me and stroked my clit while continuing to hold me down with his other hand and body. The pleasure and pain from how hard he fucked me. All of it had me teetering on the edge. My toes curled as my body pressed against his and I exploded, crying his name with tears leaking out of my eyes.

He followed soon after me, groaning his release in my ear. Then he was pressing kisses on my wet cheeks and nuzzling my face.

"Don't let me push you away," he whispered. "Promise you won't let me."

My heart fucking burnt with his words. They were laced with pain, like the thought of it killed him inside.

"Okay."

"That's not good enough. Promise. Me."

"How can I make promises to you when you're not giving me anything in return?"

He let out a sigh and kissed my cheek again before resting his forehead against my hair.

"Do you remember when we were kids, and you forced me to pinkie promise I wouldn't leave you as long as I lived?"

"Yes."

"That's the reason I never gave up when we were trying to find you. The others wanted to, but I couldn't break my promise. I won't leave you, Scarlett, but as you have probably noticed, I'm not good at relationships."

I tried not to smile.

"No, you suck when it comes to me."

"I don't know how to act around you."

"Well, that's a lie. You certainly know how to act when your dick is inside me and when you want to punish me."

"That's not what I meant."

I shifted, wanting to look at him. He pulled out of me and allowed me to roll over to face him. He had his hands planted on either side of my head as he stared down at me.

"No? You sure you weren't fishing for compliments about your sexual prowess?"

He didn't look remotely impressed by my question.

"My sexual prowess?"

I reached up and stroked his face.

"Mmm."

"I don't need you to compliment me on it when I just made you scream my name."

Well, that told me. The way he smirked had me raising my eyebrow.

"Fine, I promise I won't let you push me away. Happy now?"

He leant closer until our lips were almost touching.

"No, I'm not happy with you for forcing me to play hooky from work. I think I might have to punish you again."

He pressed a kiss to my lips before trailing them down my body until he was in between my legs. He wrapped both of his hands around my thighs and spread them wide.

"What do you think, Scarlett? Should I punish this pussy with my tongue?"

I squirmed because I couldn't think of anything better.

"Yes, sir."

"Good."

It wasn't quite a 'good girl', but it was almost. He'd told West he would only say it when I'd earned it. I liked their praise as much as the way they degraded me in different ways. And I wondered what it would take to get Drake to praise me the way I wanted him to. If I had to make him lose control again and again... well, it wasn't too much of a chore now, was it?

TWENTY FOUR

DRAKE

Scarlett tasted like fucking magic. I could drown in this pussy and it would never be enough. I don't know what it was about her, or maybe I did. Maybe I hated the fact West knew I'd wanted Scarlett longer than I was ever willing to admit. Maybe I was just so fucked up about it, I kept taking it out on her and it wasn't fair. While I'd apologised to her, it didn't feel like enough. I wanted her friendship back, but I needed her... heart.

Well, at least you finally admitted it to yourself.

Internally shaking myself, I concentrated on circling her clit with slow strokes and listening to her moans every time I hit a sensitive spot. Fuck, did I love being between her legs. While she might have driven me crazy today and made trouble with my family, I couldn't deny I needed this. Her. She was so fucking important to me on an intrinsic level. Being without her for ten years had twisted all of us in dark, depraved ways, but with me? It had altered things on a fundamental level. I remembered when I used to be open and free. The way she'd always bring out the best in me. And now she was bringing out the worst. I was letting my long-buried emotions eat me up inside. She was caught in the crossfire.

It didn't have to be this way. I could change it. Make it better between us so she'd bring out the best parts of me again.

"Drake," she whimpered. "Please, please, I need more."

Slipping my hand from around her thigh, I buried three fingers in her pussy, making her buck from the intrusion. I angled them to rub over the right spot, knowing how to make her dizzy with pleasure.

"Fuck, yes, there, right... there."

I almost smiled against her body, but instead, I circled her clit harder. She writhed and moaned, her hand going to my head and pushing me into her pussy. I wasn't going to tell her to stop. Not when she was close. I could feel the stirrings of her orgasm building inside her. Her pussy was so wet around my fingers.

"Drake!"

Her fist slammed down on the sofa. Then she was coming, her hips bucking into my face with each pulse. Watching her fall apart with her climax was always the most beautiful sight to behold. I didn't want to hurt her any longer. All I craved was this. Giving this woman everything. And yet, despite my wants, I knew it wasn't possible. Not with all the secrets. Not when she had asked us not to tell her what happened to her mother. It fucked me up inside, knowing she was going to have to deal with that pain soon enough.

"No more. I can't take any more."

She pushed my head away, her body going limp beneath me. I sat up on my knees, withdrawing my fingers from her. Scarlett put her hand over her face, hiding her afterglow from view. Deciding maybe she needed a minute, I grabbed the wet wipes and cleaned myself up. Then, without saying a word, I did the same for her. Scarlett watched me from underneath her arm. I didn't care about the mess. Wasn't anything I hadn't dealt with before. I just needed to show her I cared. That I would try my best to look after her, even when I struggled with my own fucking demons.

I got up and dumped the wipes in the bin before returning to her. Scarlett almost protested when I shifted her to lie down behind her body and wrap mine around her back. She let out a soft sigh, stroking her fingers down my arm with a gentle touch.

"That didn't feel much like a punishment," she said after a minute.

I rested my head on hers.

"Maybe I don't want to punish you today." I nuzzled her hair. "Maybe I'm tired of fighting with you too."

"Why didn't you tell your mum I'm back?"

Scarlett was far too perceptive, but I didn't hate it. In fact, I needed her to ask me those questions. I needed her to push me. It was the only way we'd fight through this discord between us. I was well aware of my faults. My inability to communicate my feelings. And how I needed this woman to break the cycle.

"Because then I would have to explain where you've been. It's the same reason Pres hasn't told Rosie and Francis hasn't told Eliza and Jasper. West is estranged from Henry and

227

Cynthia, but you can ask him about it." I stroked her bare stomach. "Not to mention I'd have to tell her about all five of us and what we are."

"And what are we?"

"Well, I'm pretty sure you made that clear to Fletch earlier." She chuckled.

"That was to provoke a reaction out of you."

"It worked, but it doesn't make it any less... true."

"So what? You're agreeing that you're my boyfriend then, huh?"

I let out a breath before pressing my face harder against her hair, breathing in her cinnamon scent. Being hers was all I'd ever wanted. Ever since I'd been a kid. The five of us were drawn to each other in a way none of us understood at first. It was only when we found out from our parents where we'd been born and when, did we realise the insane coincidence. For a long time, I'd been okay with fate having a hand in bringing us together. Then Scarlett was ripped away from us and it began to feel like a curse. Like something none of us could ever escape.

"I don't know what we are, Scarlett. It's complicated with all five of us, isn't it? None of us are asking you to choose, but as for labelling it... well, I don't know."

She nodded and fell silent as if the weight of what I said had settled over her. I hugged her closer, wanting this moment of peace between us.

"I take it your parents got a divorce."

My breath came out in a whoosh.

"Yeah, they did."

At the time of Scarlett's accident, my parents had been going through their issues. Mum found out Oscar had cheated on her with Mona Sinclair, a woman ten years my father's junior.

"What happened?"

"Oscar married Mona after the divorce went through and I got stuck with a whole new family, including Fletch. The only people I speak to are him and Mum, though he's skating on thin ice right now."

She turned to look at me, forcing me to raise my head.

"He doesn't seem very upset about Tonya."

"I don't think Fletch cares much about his kids. They're more assets to him. Things he can use rather than people. Besides, Tonya was an accident he wished never existed."

Scarlett eyed me for a long moment, then turned fully in my arms, pressing her naked body against mine. She was so warm and real. Her closeness melted my icy exterior. It made me want to spill everything to her.

"Why did he want to see you today?"

"To tell me Oscar wanted to see me."

"And you don't want to see him?"

I shook my head before brushing her hair out of her face. Before I could move my hand back to her waist, she nuzzled it with her nose and closed her eyes, as if savouring my touch.

"No. He treated Mum like shit and me too during the divorce. Afterwards, too. He was... cruel. He called my mother a bitch who no longer gave him what he needed and said it served me right that you disappeared because I was ungrateful for everything they'd given me. All because I couldn't be nice to his new wife. I wouldn't call her mum or give her the time of day. I was almost eighteen then. I wasn't going to call a new woman who tore my family apart along with my father, Mum. She will never deserve that title from me. And I won't forgive him for everything he's said and done. It doesn't matter if he's sorry. He's not worth my time. He's not worth anything."

It was the first time I'd admitted it to anyone out loud. I'd not even told Francis exactly what Oscar had said to me about Scarlett. It had been the final straw for me. The one that had me telling him to go fuck himself.

Scarlett opened her eyes. They were shining with unshed tears, making my heart lurch.

"I'm sorry."

"Why are you sorry? You're not to blame."

"Because I wasn't there to help you."

"Scarlett…"

She shook her head and shifted closer, brushing her mouth against mine.

"No, you needed me and I wasn't there. I'm sorry I wasn't there for all of you. I know it's not my fault. It's not like I meant to disappear, but I'm sorry all the same."

To shut me up, she kissed me. It was full of pain and sorrow like she understood why I was hurting inside. Why her kidnapping had left us fractured and incomplete.

"You don't need to be sorry," I whispered against her lips when she drew back slightly. "It's me who should be. I never meant to cause you pain. There's so much you don't understand and I don't know how to tell you."

She pressed her hand to my cheek.

"I know. I... I can't right now. It's too much. I've only just remembered all of you. That was hard enough. You never asked me where I went, but I stayed in a hotel. I barely got out of bed, couldn't stop crying and experiencing those memories all over again. It was agony, but I needed it. My past isn't just mine... it's ours and I forgot it all. I lost everything. I don't want to lose you again."

She blinked and took a breath.

"Is the person I knew still in there, Drake? Or did the world break you like it did me?"

I gave her a smile, or at least the best one I could muster.

"Maybe... you'll have to find him. I don't think anyone but you can."

"I'll try." Her hand left my face and skimmed down my chest until it met my heart. "At least I have hope. Before today, I didn't know if I could see a way out of this mess between us. Thank you for trying with me."

"Even if I'm a stubborn dick?"

She grinned.

"Oh no, especially because you're stubborn, unyielding and entirely the most difficult man I've ever encountered."

"Is that so?"

"Mmm, but I happen to like your dick, so that goes a long way to making up for your other less than redeeming qualities."

For the first time in a very long time, I couldn't help the laughter bubbling up inside of me. I let it out, my chest rumbling with the noise. Scarlett stared at me for a long moment before her smile grew wider. I couldn't stop. It was as if the floodgates from the past ten years had opened and I was purging the pain of it through my laughter. Scarlett held me the whole time, letting me work it out of my system.

When it finally subsided, I stroked her face and smiled at her.

"I knew he was in there somewhere," she murmured before pressing a kiss to my chest and nuzzling her face into it.

And I buried my face in her hair, finally allowing myself to admit I needed her more than I needed air.

"Only for you, Little Nyx. Always."

TWENTY FIVE

WEST

I'd just handed Penn a beer when the door to the stairwell opened, revealing a rather dishevelled looking Drake with his tie in one hand and Scarlett's in the other. His hair was all mussed, and he definitely had a post-coital glow about him. Scarlett was looking up at him with a smug smile on her face like it had been her intention to make Drake lose his hard edges and force him to relax a little.

Prescott walked out of the kitchen, stopping when he spied the two of them. His eyebrow shot up.

"Well, I was wondering where you'd got to."

I watched Drake's expression harden, then Scarlett prodded him in the ribs. He glanced at her with a frown.

"No scowling or getting annoyed at them," she told him as she pulled him further into the room. "You'll undo all my hard work."

"Your hard work? I think you'll find I did the heavy lifting."

The way she blushed and shoved him had me wondering if she'd forgiven him for what he said to her. If he'd actually apologised. I fucking hoped he had after my words to him.

Her attention turned to the rest of us a moment later, after she stopped blushing up a storm.

"Oh, hello, Penn," she said, her voice tight as if seeing him again brought back memories of what happened on Monday.

It made me run my tongue over my teeth, imagining her bent over Penn's tattoo chair, offering herself up for her punishment. If I wasn't sure she'd tell me to go fuck myself, I would have snatched her up, taken her to my room and fucked the living daylights out of her. Fuck the discussion we needed to have and the reason Penn was here.

"Evening, Scarlett," Penn replied with a smirk before he lifted his beer to his lips. "Nice to see you again, though I'm sure you'll be happy to hear there won't be any blood involved."

Scarlett made a show of looking around.

"What? No dead bodies today? Damn, I was so looking forward to dealing with another one with you."

He laughed and gave her a wink.

"I thought we should meet under better circumstances."

"Not sure I'd call these better circumstances," Francis said as he turned away from where he was staring out of the window.

Scarlett dropped Drake's hand and went over to Francis, wrapping her arms around his neck and giving him a smile.

"Can I make them better for you?"

"Always."

She went up on her tiptoes and kissed him. I struggled to stop from wanting to rip her away from him. It had nothing to do with jealousy, more I wanted her so fucking much, it hurt. Now she knew who I was, it made it harder for me not to want to fall back into the relationship we had before. Only I knew it wasn't possible. We would never be the West and Scarlett we had been. And it decimated me on the inside.

"What did you do to Drake?" he asked in a low voice when she dropped back to her feet.

"I helped him relax."

His eyebrow raised, but Scarlett skipped away from him, clearly in a good mood and not inclined to give any details. Drake took a seat on the sofa across from Penn while Prescott caught Scarlett up in his arms when she tried to go into the kitchen.

"Don't I get a kiss, little lamb?"

She gave him a rather enthusiastic one. Penn watched this with amusement in his eyes.

"So, it's all of you then, is it?" he asked in a low voice.

"All of us, what?"

"With her."

I shrugged and sat down next to him. Not like it bothered me. I'd said as much to Drake and Prescott. Ten years of us longing for her had made staying away from Scarlett an impossibility for all of us. Desire was a potent drug and one none of us were immune to. Only now, desire had morphed into more. So much fucking more.

"So what?"

"I can see why. She's fit as fuck, man."

I smacked him around the back of the head.

"Don't talk about her like that."

The fucker had the audacity to smirk and give me a wink.

"Someone's touchy."

I leant closer to him.

"She's *mine* and if you keep flirting with her, I will knock your teeth out. Don't think I haven't noticed."

"Yours, eh? And theirs too?"

If he thought I was going to deny their claim to Scarlett, he was barking up the wrong tree.

"Yeah, that's fucking right."

Penn and I went way back, but I'd never told him about Scarlett. Well, not properly anyway. I didn't talk about her to anyone but Prescott, Francis, and Drake. Even then, it wasn't about my true feelings. Opening up wasn't easy for me. It never had been. Not after she'd been ripped out of my life and I'd been ostracised further by my parents.

"If you could stop winding West up and actually get to the point," Drake interrupted, giving me a hard look.

"Excuse me for putting this fuck in his place when it comes to our woman," I said. "Not like you'd do it."

"I'm sure Scarlett is capable of telling him she's not interested if that's the case."

"Oh, so you'd be fine with Penn joining our little gang bang then?"

Drake's scowl worsened.

"I did not say that."

"No? You sure about that, Drake? You don't want to watch her get railed by him?"

"No, I fucking don't. I'm not Prescott, who will literally watch anyone fuck if he can. And I'm not going to pass her around like she's some toy for all and fucking sundry to use. She belongs to us." He pointed at Penn. "He is not allowed to touch her. And if he does, I will help you knock his teeth out."

I noticed Prescott and Scarlett watching us. Him with amusement and her with wide eyes, as if hearing Drake stake his claim on her, was unexpected. Perhaps I'd deliberately pushed Drake's buttons to get him to admit it in front of her. The fucker needed to stop being so closed off when it came to her. I knew it was the kettle calling the pot black, but whatever. At least I was aware of the fucked up nature of my and Scarlett's relationship. He was content to be a dick about it.

Francis snorted as he came over to sit down next to Drake.

"Well, if we're quite done with this whole 'who is Scarlett allowed to fuck' business, I think we should get on with the real reason Penn is here."

"I think I should decide who I'm allowed to fuck," Scarlett muttered as Prescott pulled her over and sat on the free sofa with her.

Penn dug something out of his pocket and slapped it on the coffee table. Scarlett's eyes widened, and the blood drained from her face when he lifted his hand off it. There sat the little issue Drake had spoken to him about before we'd left his house on Monday to deal with Tonya's body. Drake had told me about it when we were cleaning up the blood.

"I knew you took it from me," Scarlett said to Drake a moment later.

He sat there, looking between her and the memory stick he'd given Penn yesterday. I had to give my Fixer friend credit. He worked fast.

"Do you want to tell us what's on it, Scarlett? Or should we ask Penn?"

"He didn't really say, other than it would get him the information he needed if I plugged it into one of your computers. And before you ask, I didn't."

Drake turned to Penn.

"Can you confirm that?"

Penn sat back, his legs wide as if he was completely at ease with the four of us, despite the fact Drake and I had threatened to knock his teeth out and gave him a smile. He rested his arm along the back of the sofa.

"If she had, your whole system would be fucked."

Drake's eyes narrowed.

"Explain."

"Well, my techy guy said it would have ripped through your firewall and brought everything to a standstill. Whoever gave that to her wanted to fuck with you."

"Fuck." Drake turned his attention back to Scarlett. "What else did he tell you to do with it?"

"Bring it back to him when I was done," she replied, staring at the memory stick in horror. "He said he wanted information, not that he wanted to destroy your systems."

"Maybe now you'll see why you shouldn't trust him."

"Who said I ever did?"

Drake crossed his arms over his chest and frowned.

"He's going to expect you to have used it, and that's a problem."

Given none of us had directly brought up who we were talking about, I was assuming Drake wasn't prepared to tell Penn the truth. Probably wise, even though he would keep his mouth shut. We didn't need anyone else finding out about our connection to Stuart Carver.

Scarlett looked at Drake.

"You don't want him to know that I remembered."

"No. Has he contacted you?"

She shook her head.

"My phone is still off because you know who is tracking it. You said you'd deal with it."

Drake stood up and wandered over to the shelves hiding the war room. He picked up a box from there and brought it with him, placing it down on the table in front of Scarlett.

"I should have given this to you yesterday."

He took a seat, rubbing his face with his hand. The box contained a new phone for her.

"What do you want me to do with my phone?"

"You're going to turn it back on and keep it on you."

"Why?"

"If you keep it off any longer, he's going to get suspicious and it will only lead to trouble."

"But he's tracking me."

"I know." Drake pointed at the new phone. "And so will I."

That made her scowl.

"I don't want to be tracked by anyone!"

"I don't care. How are we meant to protect you if we can't find you?"

Scarlett stood up and paced away.

"So I'm still a pawn then, am I? Stuck between you and him? It's what I've been this whole time. A pawn in your games." She turned back to us. "I won't do it any longer. I'm not going to sit here and let you dictate everything to me." She pointed at her chest. "I am just as much in this fucked up situation as you are. If I go back to him with the stick and tell him I haven't done what he asked... I can't do that. I won't."

Before Drake could ask what she meant, Penn waved a hand at the stick.

"I forgot to say, we've already handled that little issue. You don't need to worry about it not looking like it hasn't been run. It fucked the laptop we originally plugged it into. If you want me to plant fake information on it, I can do that."

"Can you do it now?" Drake asked.

"If I call my man, we can have it done before the evening is over."

"Do it."

Penn stood, snatching up the memory stick in the process and walking away into the kitchen to make the call.

"I just told you I'm not doing it. I'm not taking that thing to him," Scarlett said.

"You don't have a choice."

The way her expression dropped and pain flashed across her features made my chest hurt.

"You don't understand. I can't. He'll..." she faltered and put her hand to her mouth.

"No, I don't, so why don't you enlighten us, Scarlett? Why don't you tell us why you're so afraid of him?"

She took a step back, shaking her head profusely.

"No."

"No?"

"I won't tell you a thing. I don't trust you."

With that, she turned, ran across the room and up the stairs, disappearing from sight.

"Well done, Drake," Prescott said with a scowl. "What happened to not confronting her directly about it?"

"I didn't think she would react like that."

I stood up.

"You poke at her wounds, she's going to lash out," I muttered before I walked towards the stairs.

"Where the fuck are you going?" Drake asked.

"To smoke a joint."

"We aren't done."

"Oh, yes, we fucking are. You don't need me to deal with that thing."

What I didn't tell him was I planned to find our girl and deal with the situation myself. Maybe it would be better if Francis or Prescott spoke to her, but I didn't care. If we needed her to go back to that fuck with this stick to keep him off our backs for a little while longer, then I would make her do it. She might not trust us with the truth of what happened to her in the Carver household quite yet, but I could persuade her to do the right thing. All I needed was to give our girl a little incentive. And I knew exactly how.

TWENTY SIX

WEST

I found her in Francis' room, sitting on his sofa by the window, staring out at the darkening skyline with her head resting on her knees. The lights were off, but she was illuminated by the city lights. She didn't look upset, but an air of melancholia surrounded her. Francis would have a fit if I lit up in his room, but I didn't care. I tugged my joint from my pocket along with my lighter and fired up. Then I walked into the room. Scarlett didn't look up, even when I sat down next to her.

"Here," I said, holding the white stick out to her.

"I don't want it," she whispered.

"Want something else?"

"I don't know."

"Then have this."

She shifted so she could take it from me and put it to her lips. I watched her take a long drag, filling her lungs with the sweet-smelling smoke before blowing it out. She rested her head back on her legs, holding the joint between her fingers.

"I feel like it's always two steps forward and a hundred steps back with him."

"Drake?"

She took another drag. The wisps of smoke coiled out of her lips a minute later.

"Mmm."

I leant back against the cushions.

"He has his issues."

"All of you have issues."

I shrugged and stroked her arm.

"You don't seem to mind Pres and Frankie's."

She sighed and handed me the joint.

"Their issues aren't tied up with me. They don't act like any of this is my fault. I didn't ask to be stolen from my life because of what you four did... and I know you did it for me, but it doesn't make me feel any better about it. Doesn't make it any less fucked up."

I took a drag and continued stroking her skin. She wasn't pushing me away, so I assumed she didn't mind.

"I'm conflicted," she admitted a moment later. "I don't know what the right thing to do is any longer. Nothing feels okay or like I'm on the right side of things. And I'm tired. I'm so fucking tired... and unhappy. Everyone wants something from me. If I keep giving up pieces of myself to them, I won't have anything left."

Her eyes met mine. There was so much pain in them. Too much.

"I ache inside. Everything I knew before is gone. I wanted so badly to know who I was and now... now I wish I didn't because the truth has made everything so much worse."

I handed her back the joint and stood up, striding over to Francis' bedside table to pick up an empty glass he'd left on there. Walking back towards her, I sat down and she tapped the joint into the glass before taking a drag.

"Do you hate me for forcing you to remember?"

She shook her head.

"I don't hate you, West. I just don't understand you any longer."

"I'll take that."

Her eyes narrowed.

"Why?"

Shifting closer, I ran my fingers through her light brown hair, the silky texture making me want to wrap it in my fist. I refrained from acting on the urge.

"Hate will only bring you more pain, little Scar. I don't want that for you."

"I thought you enjoyed hurting me."

I smiled.

"Hurting you to give you pleasure isn't the same thing, and you know it."

She rested her head back on her knees and gave me the joint. I took it and inhaled. As the smoke curled out of my mouth, she touched my fingers where they were tangled in her hair.

"Why did you come after me?"

"As opposed to Pres or Frankie?"

She nodded.

"To give you this." I waved the joint. "And to talk to you."

She lifted her head from her legs and stretched them out.

"About what?"

"You won't like it."

"Then I don't want to know."

I took one final drag before stubbing the end of the joint out in the glass and setting it aside. Then I reached out and wrapped my fingers around her throat. She let out a small sigh of pleasure as if this was something she desired wholeheartedly.

"I need you to take the memory stick to Stuart."

"Not you as well."

"This isn't about what I want, little Scar. It's about what's best for everyone, including you."

"Since when did you care about what's best for other people?"

My fingers tightened around her neck.

"I don't, but those three are my family and so are you. I won't let the cunt who stole you destroy what we have."

She wrapped her small hand around mine.

"What we have is purgatory."

"I'd rather live in purgatory with you than the hell I experienced without you."

Her eyes turned sad.

"West…"

I didn't want to talk about my feelings right now. Nor the pain of being without her. It wasn't why I'd come up here.

I dug my other hand into my pocket and slid out my knife. Flicking it open, I ran the flat side of the blade along her cheek. She didn't flinch, but her expression turned wary.

"If you agree to take the memory stick to Stuart, I'll give you something in return."

She looked at the blade, then back at me.

"You'll give me something of your own free will? Huh... somehow I'm not convinced."

"Put your hand out."

She did as I asked. I flipped the knife around in my hand and placed the handle in hers.

"You gave me this."

I let go of her neck to stroke along the fabric of her dress where I'd carved into her skin. It was healing up nicely and wasn't causing her further discomfort.

"I'll let you carve into me."

Her hand didn't close around the blade. She stared at me with no small amount of shock, her eyes widening to saucers.

"You'll what?"

"I belong to you, little Scar. I'll let you mark me the way I did you."

I continued to stroke the scar I'd given her, wanting to reassure her. Wanting to tell her it was okay, I would take it without complaint. I liked pain. And I'd wear her brand with pride.

"I don't understand."

I folded her fingers around the handle of my knife.

"What's there not to understand? You agree to do what Drake asks. You get to give me a scar like I gave you. My body is yours to mark where you please."

"You're serious."

"Why wouldn't I be? This isn't a trick. I've given you my knife."

Scarlett looked down at it. This had been my plan since the moment I realised she wasn't going to agree to do what Drake was asking for. An incentive for her to do what we needed her to. I wanted it too. Needed it from her. It would reassure me Scarlett wasn't lost to me completely.

"I don't know if I can."

"Which part?"

"Both."

My hand went to her hair, fisting it between my fingers. I pulled her closer by it.

"You can. You're my little warrior. You killed for me. You can do this too."

My beautiful girl swallowed.

"Why do you believe in me so much?"

Because I love you.

"You're the queen of this castle, Scar. You just have to take your crown."

"I don't feel like a queen or a warrior. I feel like a coward."

I took her hand with the knife in it and brought it up to my neck. She watched me. I could feel her fingers trembling beneath mine. The blade pressed to my skin, but not hard enough to break it.

"Remember what I said about fear? It feeds you, makes you stronger."

"How can you say that when you're not afraid of anything?"

I used her hand to drag the blade across my throat. It scraped my skin, making me lick my bottom lip.

"I'm afraid of one thing in this world."

"What's that?"

248

Pulling her hand away, I lowered it to my chest, making her place the blade flat against it, right where my heart lay beating for her.

"That you'll break your promise to me."

Her brow furrowed for a moment.

"Which one?"

Scarlett had promised me several things over the years. There was only one I cared about. The only one that would be the death of me.

Forever. You promised me forever.

"I'll leave it to you to work it out."

She gave me a look, but I wasn't going to budge on it.

"That's not fair."

"I don't play fair."

Scarlett let out a huff before she pulled her hand out of mine and looked at my knife.

"I want to carve my name in the same place I have yours," she whispered.

My heart swelled.

"Are you going to do what's necessary?"

She nodded, biting her lip.

"Use your words. Make me a promise and you can do it right now."

Her eyes flicked up to mine.

"Not sure Frankie would appreciate us potentially getting blood on his sofa."

I stood up and put my hand out. She placed her free hand in it, allowing me to tug her to her feet.

"Bathroom then."

"Can we do it in your room?"

I smiled. Of course, she'd want to do it in the place where I cut into her.

"Promise me first."

"I promise I'll take the memory stick to Stuart like Drake wants."

I stroked her cheek.

"Good girl."

Scarlett blushed as I led her out of the room, along the hallway, and into mine. My hands went to my shirt, undoing the buttons before I tugged it off and let it fall to the floor. I sat on the bed and waited for her.

Scarlett approached me with hesitant steps.

"You're going to take care of it for me, aren't you?"

She nodded as she reached me. Her palm flattened against my chest, pressing into my skin.

"Lie back."

I did as she asked, watching her climb on the bed and straddle my waist. Then she leant over me, tracing a line across my collarbone with the tip of the knife.

"You have to be precise and make it deep enough so it scars," I said when she didn't move to cut me.

"I'm nervous."

I latched onto her thigh with one of my hands.

"I've got you, little Scar, you can do this."

"I'll hurt you though."

"I want you to. I'm not scared of a little pain, remember? I can take it."

She let out a breath, then set the tip just below my collarbone. The sharp pain radiating outwards as she dragged the blade across my skin made me grit my teeth. She was careful and meticulous as she spelt out the word, branding me for life the way she'd inked herself on my heart.

Scar.

My chest swelled with pride seeing it there as blood welled out of the cuts, leaving crimson drops across my skin.

"Is it okay?" she whispered, staring at the word she'd carved into me.

I placed my free hand over hers where it rested next to the cuts she'd made.

"It's perfect."

"West—"

"Shh, I'm fine."

And I was. It fucking stung, but it was nothing I hadn't experienced before. Besides, having someone pummel your face in was worse. I could take a few cuts without wincing and complaining.

"Go get a cloth from the bathroom to clean up the blood, yeah? You said you'd look after it. That's the deal."

She didn't move. Her eyes were fixed on my mouth. Fuck. It was all I could do to stop myself from tangling my hand in her hair, pulling her closer and crashing her lips to mine. Scarlett had to do it. She had to take it from me because I couldn't give it to her. There was so much holding me back.

This guilt inside me over her accident and the years without her ate me up. Letting her scar me was my way of helping repair the breach between us. The one that was so fucking deep, I couldn't see the bottom.

Reaching up, I cupped her cheek and stroked her face with my thumb.

"Little Scar."

251

"I don't know how to fix us," she whispered. "There are so many things we need to talk about but I'm scared if we go down that road... we'll break each other."

My chest fucking hurt and not because of the cuts she'd made, but her words.

"I'm already broken, there's nothing you could do to make it worse except leave me."

A tear leaked out of her eye.

"You're not broken."

I shook my head.

"There's so much you don't know. And now isn't the time to discuss it."

She rubbed my chest and gave me a nod. As much as I wanted to keep her in here with me, for us to lay it all out on the table, there were more pressing matters at hand.

Scarlett slipped off me and went into the bathroom, bringing back a damp cloth with her. She sat next to me and cleaned the cuts she'd made. I didn't make a sound, no matter the stinging pain. It reminded me I was alive, and I had her right here. It was worth it.

When the blood clotted finally, I sat up. Scarlett had gone back into the bathroom to rinse the cloth out. Standing up, I snatched my shirt off the floor and put it back on, not bothering to button it up properly.

Scarlett took my hand when she came out and led me towards the door so we could return to the others. It was time we made a plan for her to go back to the man who'd stolen us from her.

TWENTY SEVEN

SCARLETT

I swallowed hard, clutching my handbag strap between my fingers as I walked into the stadium. It was late on Saturday night, right after the game had finished. And I'd agreed to meet Stuart to hand over the memory stick.

It wasn't something I wanted to do, but I didn't exactly have a choice. I'd made a promise to West. Not to mention it was our only option. While I didn't know the whole truth yet, it was imperative I didn't give Stuart any reason to suspect I'd remembered.

I had no idea if Mason had told him I'd gone looking for my mother. Nor what Mason thought about Tonya turning up dead. No doubt he would have known it was the boys, no matter how the body had been staged. He'd sent her after me.

The police had visited the office yesterday, but it was merely to confirm Tonya's whereabouts on Monday and what they knew. They hadn't questioned me as I wasn't in the office at the time. It made it clear while Mason knew, he hadn't said a word about it. It would only bring more questions than answers, anyway. Like, why was he tracking my phone and why Tonya was at my mother's old flat. Not sure he wanted to get wrapped up in a murder investigation. Although, finding out he was the Met Police Commissioner's son put a whole new spin on things.

I had a lot of questions for Mason, but I knew contacting him would only put me in danger. And to be honest, after all the revelations about him, I wasn't sure I could face the man without wanting to hurt him for lying to me. For being complicit in my disappearance. For allowing Stuart to hurt me the way he had. For everything.

I should want to hurt the Horsemen for their lies, but we shared a history I couldn't erase. Our relationship was complicated. And I didn't want to lose them again. Not now we'd found our way back to each other. The thing about families, even the ones you choose, was you didn't abandon them when things got tough. The boys had never stopped searching for me. And I couldn't help my feelings towards them. How my heart wanted them no matter how much they'd hurt me or done things I still didn't understand.

After getting directions from the guy at the reception desk, I made my way upstairs to Stuart's office. I was glad he hadn't asked me to go back to the estate. It was one place I wanted to avoid. It would only leave me vulnerable and weak, flooded with the awful memories I had of the place. The only time I'd felt free there was when I'd been allowed to ride my horses. Since Chocolate had died, I'd lost some of my love for it, but perhaps when this was all over, I could try again. If this was ever going to be over. I had no idea what the boys planned to do about Stuart. They didn't know how truly monstrous the man was. I don't know why I couldn't trust them with the truth of what happened while I was locked away. Drudging up those events would only cause me pain. And I wasn't willing to when they hadn't given me all of their truths.

Stuart's door was open, so I knocked on the frame. He sat behind his desk, his eyes fixed on the window outside where the dark football pitch lay, the lights having been turned off for the night. He turned his attention to me a moment later.

"Ah, Scarlett, there you are."

I stepped in and shut the door behind me, knowing he'd want this to be private.

"Hello, Dad."

The word made my stomach roil in protest but keeping up appearances was far too important.

"Come, give your old man a hug, eh?"

I didn't want him to touch me, yet my feet carried me over and I leant over his chair, allowing him to embrace me as I pressed a kiss to his cheek. The fact he was being nice to me set me on edge, but I tried not to show it. Nice Stuart was better than mean Stuart, who would hurt me for not being good enough. Who said awful things to me. Who made me feel small and insignificant. I couldn't allow him to do that to me again. Not when Francis and Prescott had been building me up. Not when the real Scarlett was back and whole. And yet being in Stuart's presence only made me feel like insignificant Scarlett who could do no right in his eyes.

Only my abuser has the power to make me feel like I'm nothing and no one.

"How have you been?" he asked when he released me and I leant back against his desk, planting my hands on the edge.

"Okay, I suppose. Not easy living with four people you hate."

Stuart gave me a bright smile.

"I imagine not, but you have your freedom for now, isn't that what you wanted?"

The casual way he said it had me curling my fingers around the edge of the desk. Stuart did not do casual questions. There was always an ulterior motive behind them.

"I just wanted to experience the world a little more is all."

"Indeed. Now, have you got what I need?"

I nodded, releasing the table to dig my hand into my bag and extract the memory stick. My fingers shook as I gave it to him. While Penn had reassured me they'd made sure Stuart would never know it hadn't ripped through Fortuity's firewall, I was nervous all the same. The things they'd had to do to stage this made me wonder about the lengths they'd gone to when trying to find me. I imagined they weren't pretty.

Stuart turned to his laptop and plugged it in.

"Are they enjoying the little surprise I left them with?"

I rubbed the back of my neck. This was the exact question I'd been dreading. And I didn't need him looking at the stick right now. Sweat beaded at my hairline, but I tried to smile.

What if this goes wrong? I'm the one whose arse is on the line here!

"They aren't exactly happy their data has been exposed to hackers."

Fake data. It had all been faked. And if Stuart found out… I dreaded to think what would happen.

"Do they suspect you?"

"Not that I'm aware. They think someone must have infiltrated their system outside of the company at the moment."

"Good. Just what I like to hear. I was beginning to think you wouldn't come through for me, Scarlett, but perhaps… you aren't so useless after all."

His words hit their target. They stung in the worst way possible.

You shouldn't let this man have power over you.

He did. He had too much. My fear kept me silent about his abuse. West kept telling me fear made me stronger, but I didn't know if I believed that. While the boys terrified me, it wasn't in the same way as Stuart. I wasn't scared they'd beat me and leave me chained up. With Stuart, I had no idea how much he'd hurt me and how far he'd go. If I would end up with a split lip or a bruised torso. Not all the scars on my body were from my accident. Some of them were from him. And the emotional scars had jagged edges. They left me feeling broken and alone.

You're not alone any longer. You have Prescott, Francis, Drake and West. You have your family back.

But they weren't the family I'd known. They were different versions of themselves. Darker, meaner and a hundred times more deadly.

The room was silent as Stuart looked over the data he'd brought up on his screen. For a minute, I had no idea what he thought, but then he sat back and smiled.

"Your mother and I have been talking."

"Oh?"

"We think it's time you came home and let us deal with the rest."

My blood froze.

"What?"

"It's been months, Scarlett, and this is all you've produced. One measly task. And you couldn't even do that right."

I swallowed, my hands bunching my t-shirt at the sides.

"What do you mean? I did what you asked."

Stuart shook his head and met my eyes. The harsh note to them had me wanting to run, but my feet were glued to the floor.

"This isn't what I wanted at all. I can't do shit with what's on here. And it's not really surprising when you send a girl who is liable to fall under the sway of four rather charming but monstrous men."

He rose from his chair, making me swallow.

"W-w-what?"

The evil smile he gave me was unnerving. I should have run when I had the chance. He reached out and gripped my hair, tugging me closer. My scalp burnt where he was holding onto it. I didn't try to pry him off. It would be useless. I wasn't strong enough. My limbs shook, and I wanted to cry. This was exactly what I'd feared the most.

"They got to you, didn't they? You think I don't know?"

"I don't know what you're talking about."

"Oh yes, you do, Scarlett. Carrying on with him right in front of my fucking eyes at the game last week."

Fuck. I knew Frankie kissing me would come back to bite me.

"Sleeping with the enemy is not what I told you to do. Is it just one of them? Or have you spread your legs for them all like some wanton fucking whore? You make me sick."

Tears pricked behind my eyes. There was so much safety in that word for me with Francis, but Stuart had gone and made it feel dirty and shameful.

"I... I..."

Words failed me as he tightened his fist around my hair. This wasn't pain for pleasure. This was cruelty for the sake of it.

"That's why you wanted to go live with them so you could fuck them, isn't it?"

I shook my head, my hands useless at my side as my body shook.

Is he going to hit me? Is he going to throw me to the ground and kick me? Tell me I'm a waste of space?

"You stupid little slut."

He shoved me away from him, causing me to slam back into his desk. It hurt, but not as much as I knew he could inflict with his fists.

"Those bastards thought they were so fucking clever, didn't they? They sent you here to burn. They don't care about you at all. You're just a warm hole for them to fuck when they please, aren't you? That's all you're fucking good for."

If I didn't move, I was going to meet the rough end of his wrath. I would go home with bruises I couldn't hide from the boys. That's if Stuart even let me go back to them. Right now, that wasn't looking like it would happen.

Run, Scarlett, just fucking run.

I'd worn my trainers. I could get away from him if my body would fucking well cooperate. Edging along the desk, I tried not to make any sudden movements. He was glaring at me so hard, I thought the vein in his template might pop.

"I didn't keep you away from the opposite sex to have you fall at the feet of the first fucking man to show you attention."

"Then why did you?"

He laughed. The sound echoed around the room, making my skin prickle.

"Because, Scarlett, when this is all over and those fuckers are dead and buried, you're a very special reward for someone. And he's waited a very long time to have you."

I'd reached the edge of his desk now, but I paused, the implications of what he'd just said making me ill.

What the fuck? He promised to give me to someone? That's fucked up. I'm not his to give away. I'm my own person. I always have been.

He couldn't just give me to some man who wanted me. I wouldn't let him. I wasn't so fucking broken down by his abuse that I'd ever willingly go along with this. But I didn't have to be willing. He would do it anyway. That's the type of man Stuart Carver was.

And then it dawned on me exactly who he was talking about. My world tilted upside down. Rage filled my veins. There was no fucking way on earth I would ever allow it to happen.

"I'm not a possession you can hand off to him like a trophy," I spat.

He laughed harder.

"Oh, dear girl, that's where you're wrong. I own you."

TWENTY EIGHT

SCARLETT

If I had any doubts Stuart Carver was evil, I didn't any longer. This man had kidnapped me and held me captive for ten years. He'd told me lie after lie after lie, beaten me until I was bloody and broken me down to nothing to force me into doing his bidding. He'd dangled freedom in front of my eyes and now… now he was making it very clear he never intended to let me go. He was going to give me away to another man when this was all said and done.

"No! No, you don't!" I shouted in his face before I turned and ran towards the door.

I wasn't fast enough. He was on me in a flash, gripping my hair and dragging me back against his chest. It hurt so fucking much, but I wasn't going to let the pain stop me. I struggled against him as he wrapped an arm around my chest, pinning me to him. My legs kicked out and my hands clawed his sleeves. He grunted when I elbowed his side.

"Let go!"

He slammed a hand over my mouth and leant over my shoulder, his disgusting hot breath dusting across my ear. I tried to scream, but the sound was muffled.

"You think you can escape, do you?" He chuckled. "It's adorable, really. You will never escape, Scarlett. I don't give a shit what happens to you when this is over. When I've given you away. All I want is for those bastards to die for what they've done, but first, they're going to admit they killed my boys. They're going to tell me where they are."

I kept trying to wriggle away from him, but he didn't budge. He didn't know I remembered. He didn't know I knew where his sons were buried. The twins. I remembered the way Ray and Ryan had treated everyone around them like they were playthings. Their own personal toys. And no fucking wonder their father was the same. We were all pawns. All of us. Cogs in his wheelhouse. He would use and abuse everyone stupid enough to cross his path until they were nothing left but a shell of themselves.

I tried to respond, but his hand across my mouth made it impossible.

"You're a stupid, stupid girl. You shouldn't have come back here and you know it. This was a test to see if you really were fucking them or not. You see, Mason told me the real reason you ran from him. He told me you'd admitted to spreading your legs for them. That was your plan to get them to trust you. Pity for you men like them don't care about the women they fuck. I know all about their proclivities. How they've cultivated a certain image of themselves but if people saw what they do in the shadows?" He spat on the floor next to me. "They wouldn't revere them."

I shivered at his words, scared of what would come out of his mouth next. What he would tell me about the men I'd grown up with. Whether I'd believe him was another matter, but I couldn't help dreading it all the same.

"Do you know what happened to the last woman they shared between them?"

I shook my head.

"They almost killed her. One could call it a sex game gone wrong. They almost broke her arm, and she overdosed on the cocktail of drugs they gave her. But she's not the first. You're just one girl in a long line of whores they've shared between them. And if I didn't make it clear, not all of them were as lucky as the last one. They don't like it when their secrets come out. You didn't take my warning about them seriously. They will kill anyone who gets in their way without hesitation, and I mean anyone. They aren't nice men. They're monsters."

I didn't know what the fuck to make of what he was saying, but he lowered his hand from my mouth. He wanted to hear what I had to say about it.

"You're a monster too," I ground out.

The way he belly-laughed at my statement made my skin crawl. As if having his hands on me wasn't doing that already.

Stuart didn't know I'd watched West kill. I stood there and let it happen. And I'd felt a sick sense of justice when he placed Tonya's bloody heart in my palm. Like her death was justified because she'd hurt me. What kind of person did that make me? One just as fucked up as the four men I'd grown up with. The Four Horsemen. And me? I was their Little Nyx. The personification of the night.

The man behind me had no idea I'd looked into the Horsemen's eyes and realised I didn't care how dark, twisted and fucked up they were. They were mine. And I was theirs.

"Perhaps I am. You ran from one cage straight into another. When they find out you're there to destroy them, they'll want you dead too."

They didn't want me dead. The boys wanted me back. They'd waited ten years for me. But Stuart didn't know I knew. He was saying this to scare me. He must know how the boys felt about me. How they would stop at nothing to keep me by their sides now I was back with them.

"If you've promised me to Mason, then shouldn't you be keeping me alive?"

"That's his job. If he wants you, he has to keep them from destroying you."

I should have known better than to expect Stuart to care about my well-being. The only reason he'd kept me alive this long was so he could use me against the boys. That much was now clear. The missing pieces of the puzzle were slotting into place, but there were still blanks for me. Things I didn't understand.

I wasn't going to get answers by staying here. I needed to get as far away from Stuart as possible and never look back. In order to do that, I had to get out of his grip and not reveal a single damn thing about how much I knew. If he realised I had remembered, I would be in worse fucking trouble than I was now. He wouldn't have a reason to keep me around. And he would hand me off to Mason like a fucking prize pony.

I will not let that happen.

Throughout the past couple of months, my loyalties had shifted. And when I'd regained my memories, it had cemented them. No matter how angry I was with the boys, no matter how many lies they'd told me, I was loyal to them. It wasn't blind or misplaced, but the deep-seated knowledge we couldn't escape each other even if we tried. It wasn't only fate or destiny, it was need, desire and, dare I say it, love. The familial type of love that was quickly turning into the desperate, all-consuming love you couldn't fight against.

I loved Prescott. And I had fallen in love with Francis, although I hadn't told him. When I was younger, I'd been deeply in love with West. The kind of love you couldn't forget or move beyond. The truth was, I didn't want to. I wanted to fix things between us, even though they were broken, damaged, and bruised. Then there was Drake. I had no idea how I felt about him, only I wanted to repair the breach between us too. I wanted to keep him as much as he wanted to keep me. If only he could show me more glimpses of the boy I'd known, then maybe we could find our way out of this toxic mess between us.

It didn't matter. I was bound to them, regardless. Bound to follow them into the dark. And to remain with them until the end.

"You know, he told me he's going to punish you for fucking them. He's going to make you feel the pain for being such a dirty little slut, selling yourself to them like a prized whore. It's nothing less than you deserve. Silly, silly girl. It wouldn't surprise me if he kept you in a fucking cage for all the care and appreciation you've given him by whoring yourself out."

I shuddered, hating the way his words cut into me. They made me feel so small. And dirty. They were tearing me to shreds and making me wonder if he wasn't right. If sleeping with four men did make me worthless.

Don't let him get to you. Don't allow his venom to sink into your veins.

It was so fucking difficult not to let those words into my psyche. I didn't want this man to have any power over me, but he did. He fucking did. And I hated him for it.

It was now or never. I had to get away from him before he destroyed me. Before he ruined what I had with my boys for me.

"Go fuck yourself," I hissed.

Then I redoubled my efforts to escape him, letting a scream rip from my throat. His hand went to my mouth again, stealing away the loud noise that might bring attention to us.

"You stupid little bitch."

I didn't let it stop me. My foot raised up, and I brought it down hard on his, making him grunt. My body shifted and moved against his as I tried to get him to loosen his grip. His hand tightened around my mouth. So I did what any girl would do in my position. I opened my mouth and bit him. He yelped, but I bit down harder, wanting to draw blood.

He pulled his hand from me before I could. Then I was elbowing him with both arms, hitting his ribs and wherever else I could get to. His grip loosened as he grunted against the impact. I used it to my advantage, pushing my hands up under his arm to give me more room. I ducked out from underneath his grasp the next moment, shoving him away from me. He stumbled backwards, but then he was coming at me. I was ready for him. My knee came up. I hit him right in the fucking balls. He let out a horrifying sound of pain, his hands going to his groin.

I didn't take any further chances. My legs carried me to the door, my hands grasping the handle and ripping it open. It smacked back against the wall, but I didn't stop. I ran down the corridor, knowing if I didn't keep going, he would come after me.

"Scarlett," he roared, the sound echoing along the hallway.

My legs carried me faster until I hit the stairwell. Slamming open the door, I took the stairs two at a time. The flights passed in a blur. The only goal I had was to get out of this building. To get away from Stuart. To never look back.

When I hit the ground floor, I flew out of the door into the reception area. The man behind the desk looked startled, but I ignored him as I ran for the door.

"Miss! Miss!" I could hear him calling after me.

I pushed the doors open and ran for my fucking life away from the stadium. In the next street over, a car was idling by the pavement. I tore open the door and jumped into it. I slammed it shut behind me and turned to the driver.

"Drive. Now!"

Drake looked at me with a raised eyebrow before his face fell when he truly took me in.

"What's wrong?"

"Fucking drive, Drake. Get me the fuck away from here."

I didn't care if I was screaming at him, nor how my arms were flailing as I gesticulated for him to go.

"What happened?"

"Drive the fucking car or so help me I will pull you out of that seat and drive it myself, even though I don't know how."

"Jesus, okay."

He gave me one last look of concern before he set off. I reached over and put my seat belt on, shoving my handbag into the footwell. I had no idea how I'd managed to keep it on me, but I didn't give two flying fucks. My heart was racing out of control, my breathing was utterly erratic, and I couldn't stop shaking.

He reached over and rubbed my thigh to get my attention, even as his eyes remained on the road.

"Are you okay?"

"Do I fucking look okay?"

"No."

"Then don't ask me stupid questions."

"Scarlett—"

"No! Take me the fuck back to Fortuity and don't fucking talk to me."

Voicing aloud what Stuart had said and done was impossible. And the fact they'd made me do this had my stomach in fucking knots. They'd sent me back to the man who had terrorised me for years. They didn't know because I didn't trust them with that information.

"I'll take you home, but you need to tell me what happened."

I glared at him despite the fact I was coming apart at the seams. Stuart might not have given me physical scars, but he'd dug the knife in anyway. He made me feel wrong, dirty... sullied. His words had punched a hole in my gut. I wanted to cry, scream, and curse at him. I wanted to curl up in a ball and fade away.

"Scarlett."

"If you say one more fucking word, I'll never let you touch me again. You hear me? Never."

Drake retracted his hand like I'd stung him. I didn't want to talk to him. I didn't want to talk to anyone. I was falling to pieces and nothing could stop it. Nothing could help me... could it?

I didn't want Stuart to have this power over me any longer. I wanted to take it back. Make it my own again. And there was only one person in this world capable of giving me those things, of showing me words like slut, bitch and prized whore didn't make me worthless. Who could degrade me to make me feel powerful.

It wasn't Drake. It wasn't Prescott. And even though Francis had made me feel safe with his use of little whore, it wasn't him either. No... the boy I'd grown up with. The one I'd loved most of my life. He was the only one who could make me feel like I was the queen he said I was. Like I was his little warrior.

What I needed more than anything was West. And I needed him right now.

The journey home was filled with a thick air of tension as I slowly disintegrated inside. The longer it took, the worse my panic became. My chest was so fucking tight I could hardly take in air. By the time we reached Fortuity, I was at my wit's end. I tore out of the car the moment it stopped, grabbing my bag and running towards the lift. My hand went to the button, pressing it several times in my desperation to get upstairs.

Drake didn't say a word as he came to a standstill next to me, but I could feel his gaze on me. Concern bled out of him. I didn't have the energy or wherewithal to deal with him. My only goal was to get to West. It was the only thing I could do.

I bundled into the lift as soon as it arrived and keyed in the code for the penthouse. Drake walked in and stood on the opposite side. He'd insisted on taking me to the stadium. He didn't trust Francis after the last time. I hadn't objected, but I was beginning to wish he'd let someone else take me.

Time passed so slowly as the lift rose up to the penthouse. I rubbed my arms, trying not to let my legs buckle as I waited. They were some of the worst minutes of my life being stuck in this fucking box with a man I craved and yet wanted to be away from at the same time.

I practically ran out of the lift when it arrived on the penthouse floor, but I was caught by Prescott a moment later. He held onto my arm and looked at me with worry spread across his features.

"Sweetness?"

"Let go of me," I barked at him, trying to pull away from his grasp.

"What's going on?"

"I need… I need…"

I couldn't get my words out even as I tried to back away.

"She's been like this since she got in the car," Drake said, waving a hand at me.

"What's wrong, little lamb?"

I looked around the room, not answering his question, searching for the person I needed, but he wasn't there.

"Where's West?"

"He's upstairs."

My eyes went to Prescott, who was looking even more concerned by the second.

"I need him, please. I *need* him."

Prescott let go of me then as if realising I wasn't going to talk. I shoved my handbag at him before running towards the stairs. I didn't care what the other three thought right now. It was all I could do to scramble up the steps and race down the hallway towards West's room.

When I got there, I tried the handle before hammering my fists on the door, desperation bleeding out of me with each strike.

Please, West, please open the door. Please… I need you. Only you can fix me.

TWENTY NINE

WEST

The pounding on my door had me frowning. I'd come upstairs a while ago, not wanting to deal with Prescott and Francis pacing the fucking living room. They were worried about Scarlett going to see Stuart. Admittedly, I didn't like the idea of her going back to him, but I knew it had to happen. We didn't have any other choice if we were to keep him from realising Scarlett had remembered the past.

I hadn't bothered to turn the lights on when I got up here. Instead, stripping down to my boxers and lying in bed as I watched the city lights below. There was a sense of peace being up here alone in the dark. Just me and the night's sky spread out before me. My fingers stroked across the scars she'd given me, leaving me content with the knowledge Scarlett knew I belonged to her.

I was considering lighting up a joint when the hammering started. I hauled myself out of bed and walked over to the door, prepared to give one of them hell for the racket. Unlocking it, I ripped it open. Scarlett tumbled into the room, falling against my chest and wrapping her arms around me.

"Scar?"

I shut the door as she clung to me, feeling her chest heaving with each one of her breaths. Having her come to me was unexpected, to say the least. The way she was letting out these soft whimpers of pain like she was falling apart had me wondering what the hell happened.

"Hey, hey, what's going on?"

I wrapped an arm around her, but she struggled against me. Then she was falling to her knees and nuzzling her face into my crotch. My hand went to her hair, intending to drag her away from me until she spoke, her voice coming out all needy and panicked.

"I need you."

"You need me?"

She looked up at me. I couldn't see her eyes in the dark, but I could tell she was in a bad way. Whatever had happened between her and Stuart, it wasn't good. It couldn't have been between her and Drake. She would have gone to Prescott or Francis if that were the case.

"I need you to... to... to degrade me."

That had me freezing on the spot.

She wants me to do what?

"Please, please degrade me, West. I need it. I can't cope with... with all these feelings inside me. I need you to take it away. Please... please... fix me."

The desperate notes of her voice were like knives digging into my skin. Her pain filled the space between us, making me ache for her. I wrapped my hand around the back of her head, stroking her scalp with my fingertips.

"How would you like me to degrade you, little Scar?"

We had to be clear about what she was asking for. It's not like I would deny her this, but I wanted to know exactly what she expected me to do. What she wanted.

"I have… I have all these horrible things in my head. I need… I need you to replace them. Break me… break me down until I'm nothing but a mess of pleasure, pain and everything in between. Break me to fix me."

I fisted her hair, pulling it taut until she winced and let out a little sound of pain.

"As my little Scar wishes."

I wasn't going to ask any further questions. This woman was *mine*. She had been mine from the moment our eyes met twenty-one years ago. And I was going to give her what she needed.

She didn't have time to protest as I dragged her towards my bed by her hair. Her hands went to mine, but I didn't let go. No, I stopped and squatted down on my haunches, forcing her to meet my eyes. There was fear in those hazel-green orbs. I smiled and tightened my hand around her hair to the point where I was almost tearing it out of her scalp.

"Tonight you are one thing and one thing only… *mine*. You better get it through that pretty little head of yours, otherwise, you and I are going to have a problem. Do you understand?"

She nodded, her face pulled back into a grimace. Little exhales left her lips in quick succession as if her fear was making it impossible for her to speak.

"Good girl… although, I don't think you are a good girl. That word doesn't belong to you."

She whimpered in response.

"No, you're a bad one. A dirty little girl who craves things she shouldn't."

Her hands reached out to me, but I batted them away with my other hand.

"Oh no, you don't get to touch me. You haven't earnt the fucking right."

Oh, but the way a tear fell from her cheek had me smiling.

"That's right, cry all you fucking like. Beg and plead with me, but it won't get you very far. Dirty little bitches like you don't deserve rewards. They deserve to be used like the whores they are."

She let out a choked pant at my words.

So, you want me to call you names, do you, Scar?

"Is that what you are, Scarlett? A slut who wants nothing more than to get fucked six ways from Sunday and beg for more? So fucking wanton. So needy. I bet your little pussy is dripping for me right now. She's begging to get abused."

She shook her head.

"Such a little liar."

I stood, pulling her with me by her hair. She yelped, but I didn't care. No, I threw her down on the bed face first and shoved my knee into her back, pinning her there.

"Don't you worry, you nasty little slut. I'm going to use every one of your holes for my pleasure. You won't be able to walk straight when I'm done with you. And you're going to love every second of it even as you beg me to stop. Even when you're crying and gasping for fucking air. I'll keep using you until you're nothing but fucking dust."

Reaching out, I ripped open the drawer of my bedside table and extracted a pair of handcuffs. She struggled weakly against me as I gathered up her wrists behind her back. I locked her in place before shoving my knee between her legs and rubbing it against her jean-clad pussy. She gasped with the friction.

"See this here? It's fucking mine. It belongs to my cock."

"West."

"No use begging me, slut. I'm not going to grant you mercy."

A sob erupted from her mouth. It didn't stop me from leaning into her further, making her whimper and yelp with the way her jeans were digging into her sensitive skin. She could cry all she wanted. This is what she'd asked for. There was nothing she could say to stop me.

I'm going to break her.

Moving away from her, I went over to my drawer and extracted a tube of lube along with a rather imposing looking dildo, throwing them on the bed. My knife rested on top of the bedside table. I picked it up, flicking it open and running the tip of the blade along my finger.

"Are you fond of the clothes you're wearing, my little fucktoy?"

"N-n-no."

"Good."

I knelt at her feet and tugged off her trainers. I wasn't going to ruin them as I'd bought them for her. It made me smile to see her wearing them. Her socks came next. Then I peeled her jeans from her legs, exposing her lace-clad behind to me. I pulled those off her too, then I rubbed them against her wet pussy, gathering up her arousal with them. Dumping her knickers next to her, I used my knife to cut down the back of her cardigan and t-shirt, shredding both pieces of clothing. I ripped them off her body and threw the ruined fabric away before using my knife to cut her bra off her body.

I left my girl naked apart from the cuffs around her wrists and she lay there all the while, sobbing her heart out but not telling me to stop. She didn't utter a word of protest. I ran the tip of my knife down her spine, making her shiver and her skin rise with goosebumps.

"Are you scared, slut? Are you afraid of what I'm going to do to you?"

"Y-y-yes."

I laughed, stroking the flat side of the knife along her behind. Then I dipped it between her legs, gathering up her arousal on the blade.

"Open your mouth and stick out your tongue."

Hesitantly, she did as I asked. I brought the knife up and set it on her tongue.

"Lick."

She ran her tongue along the blade.

"That's it, taste yourself. Only dirty little sluts get turned on by monsters. You know that's what I am. A fucking monster. Your very own villain."

Picking up her arousal drenched knickers, I removed the blade and stuffed those in her mouth instead. Her muffled noise of protest only made me chuckle.

"Don't worry, I'm going to feed you my cum later, whore. You'll have to swallow all of it or I'll make it worse for you."

I slapped a hand across her behind, making her jolt and whimper.

"Mmm, look at this." I pulled open her cheeks, staring down at her beautiful little holes. "So ripe for fucking, aren't you? I'm going to make you feel it, little Scar. Feel each and every inch of me inside you. Fuck you so hard, you sob from the pain, but you won't be able to tell me to stop, will you? Not with your mouth full."

Her answering muffled cry was all I needed. My hands went to my boxers, tugging them off to leave me as bare as she was. I ran a hand along my cock, stroking the hot, throbbing flesh. Fuck, I was so ready to be inside her.

Taking both her legs, I shoved her further up the bed so she was swaying there, resting on her shoulders as her arms were cuffed behind her back. I knelt on the bed behind her and slid my arm underneath hers, holding onto her shoulder. With my other hand, I notched the head of my dick at her entrance, rubbing her arousal all over it. She whined, pushing herself against me.

"My needy little slut wants dick, doesn't she? She wants my cock so fucking badly, she'll let me do anything to her."

Her answer was to rub my dick with her pussy, shifting those hips to entice me to fuck her.

"Are you going to fuck yourself on my cock, huh? Is that what you want?"

She shook her head, moaning into her makeshift gag. I chuckled, running my cock over her entrance, but not quite dipping it inside her.

"No? Do you want me to fuck you?"

She moaned again.

"That's right. You want me to use you until you're a panting, sobbing, whimpering mess. You want me to make you feel so much fucking shame for being the dirty little slut you are, don't you?"

Her hips bucked. I tightened my grip on her shoulder, forcing her arms up to restrain her further.

"No. You're going to stay still and take it like a good little bitch. That's how I'm going to fuck you. Like you're a bitch in heat."

My free hand wrapped around her hip and I shoved my cock deep inside her, making her cry out through her gag. I pushed deeper until I was flush with her body, feeling her pulse and strain around me.

"Look at that needy little pussy taking me so fucking well. So she should. She's mine. Made for my cock."

I pulled back and slammed inside her again. Then I released her hip, sliding my other arm between hers and gripping her other shoulder. I fucked Scarlett with deep, brutal strokes, using her shoulders as leverage to allow me to give it to her with zero restraint. She cried through her gag, tears streaming down her cheeks, but it didn't stop me. If anything, it only made me give it to her that much harder. I knew it was hurting her, but she wanted the pain. She craved it. She wanted to be broken into tiny little pieces.

"That's it, bitch. Take my cock. Take it until you bleed for me. Scream, cry and beg. No one is going to hear you. No one is coming to your fucking rescue. I'm going to destroy you."

THIRTY

SCARLETT

It hurt. God, it fucking hurt. I screamed into the gag, trying to struggle against him, but the way he had me restrained made it impossible. The way he was fucking me was brutal, savage, and merciless. But it felt so good too. It felt so fucking right. It was exactly what I needed. What I craved.

My muscles strained with the cuffs on my wrists and his arms between them and my back, holding my shoulders down while he slammed into me. No matter how hard the others had fucked and used me, nothing could prepare me for the way he did it. None of our previous encounters were in any way shape or form as violent as this.

More tears flowed down my cheeks. I was helpless against West. Utterly at his mercy, not that he had any for me. I'd told him to break me. My mind was fighting against the inevitable even so. It was protesting at the way he spoke to me. The way he hammered into me. The pain was overwhelming. The pleasure too. They were two opposing forces trying to tear me into pieces. And I wanted them to.

Please destroy me. Ruin me for good. I need it so fucking bad.

I couldn't tell him because my mouth was full. I could taste myself on my underwear. Taste my need in the fabric. And it only made me greedier. Made me want him so badly, I was coming undone with it.

"You think this is everything, do you, slut? I'm not even halfway fucking done with you," he growled at me.

West sounded more like an animal than a man at this point. His voice was gruff and full of menace. He wanted me scared. And I was utterly terrified. I had no idea what he was going to do to me next.

Abruptly, he pulled away from me, releasing my arms. I slumped down on my shoulders, shifting my arms against my back. They ached from the strain, but there wasn't much I could do about it.

My eyes followed his hands grasping something next to us on the bed. Two things. A tube of lube and a sex toy. I swallowed against my gag. It was a rather large dildo. Was he going to put that inside me? And if so... where?

West popped the cap of the lube and slathered it all over the thing, making it look even more imposing. He was smiling to himself, making me think he was about to stick that thing somewhere it might hurt if he didn't prepare me for it first.

"Do you see this, little Scar?"

I whimpered. I wanted this. I needed him to break me, but fuck was I afraid of it too.

"Sluts like you want more than just one cock in you. You crave it. And don't forget, I've seen the way you come when you're impaled on two dicks so you can't tell me you don't love it."

He shifted behind me again and placed the head of the dildo at my pussy, rubbing up and down. Then he slid the tip inside me. I almost let out a sigh of relief, but then I felt cool gel falling on my skin from above. West was holding the tube above us and dribbling it between my cheeks.

Oh, fuck!

He dropped the tube on the bed, pulling the dildo away and resting it on my behind. Then he was feeding me his cock again, stretching my pussy out for him. His fingers went to my other hole, rubbing the lube in. The wicked glint in his eye made me nervous, especially when he slid his finger inside me, pushing the lube in.

"That's right, slut. I'm going to slide this in you, make you take every fucking inch whilst I pound this pussy."

I made a noise behind the gag, but he merely chuckled.

"You can try to tell me you don't want it, my dirty little bitch, but I know you do."

Another finger joined the first, stretching me out for that fucking thing. I was relieved he was giving me some preparation, but I knew it would hurt even so. He wanted me to feel the pain. And I couldn't deny I needed it.

Break me. Please fucking break me, West.

After only a minute, he withdrew his fingers and then the toy was there, pressing against me. I tried to move away from him, but he slapped my behind so hard, I yelped.

"Don't you fucking dare, whore. I told you to stay fucking still."

Then he leant over me, fisting my hair and pulling my head back. He grazed his teeth over my ear, then he bit the lobe.

"You are mine and if I want you to take this fake cock up your arse whilst I fuck your pussy, you will. I will remind you of who you belong to with each fucking stroke."

He pressed it forward, forcing it to breach me. Fuck, it burnt on the way in, but I wanted it. The pain was breaking me into tiny pieces. My mind was fracturing with the physical strain. With his words. With everything. The sheer girth of this thing was far more than I'd ever taken before. There was nothing I could do about it. I couldn't run away. I could barely scream around the gag.

West released my hair and straightened, his eyes going straight to where he was pressing the dildo up inside me.

"Fuck, look at that. It's stretching you out so fucking wide. Mmm, what a sight you are. Crying and panting, tasting yourself with every breath you take whilst I fuck you silly."

And with that, he forced it deeper. I cried harder, trying to scream, but it came out all muffled. West groaned at the noises I was making. At the way he was stretching me, making me so much fucking tighter for him. I was in delirious pain. It was so fucking pleasurable, driving me to a state of liberation unlike anything else I'd experienced. I was so close to losing it completely. Allowing it to drown me.

"What's that? You want me to fuck you harder? You want it to hurt?"

I was stuck. I could only shift my arms on my back. He wrapped his fist around the middle of the cuffs and held them down, stopping me from moving any further. He let out a low growl of annoyance.

"What the fuck did I tell you, whore? Huh? I warned you not to fucking move."

Another shove of the dildo and it was so far up inside me, I thought I might pass out. West held it there, forcing me to take what he'd given me. He released my cuffs and then he was slapping me, spanking my behind with rapid strokes I could hardly keep up with. I screamed against the gag, but he didn't stop. He kept going until I was broken. A sobbing, panting mess of shame because I liked this. I wanted this man to do this even as my mind rebelled against it.

With one hand, he held the dildo inside me. The other wrapped around my hip. And then he fucked me with long, deep strokes, making me howl behind the gag. It was to the point of being far too much. I cracked and shattered under his savagery. My mind went somewhere else. Somewhere words couldn't hurt me any longer. A state of delirium where nothing felt real, but I could feel it happening to my body. I could feel him wrecking me like I'd asked for. And fuck, it was everything.

Every. Single. Fucking. Thing.

West let go of my hip and reached around me, his fingers rubbing over my clit. And that was it. I lost it. I trembled, struggled and strained, but he kept stroking me, driving me higher until I was at my wit's end. And then I was coming so hard it drove through my entire body like a fiery inferno razing its way along my skin, burning away all the horrific things Stuart had said to me. Making it impossible for them to hurt me any longer.

My climax ruined me completely. And West was the wielding force of my destruction.

My body slumped on the bed when I came down. If it wasn't for him holding me, my knees would have given out. He hadn't stopped fucking me through my climax, and he was still giving it to me just as hard now. I was done, but he wasn't. He was still using me for his pleasure.

I whimpered against the gag, wrung out from the pleasure and pain. Broken in two by the boy I'd grown up with. The one I still loved no matter the distance and years between us. Even though West wasn't that boy any longer, my feelings hadn't disappeared or lessened. But we had so much separating us. Too much to talk about.

Those words would wait. They'd stay inside my heart while I was still so fucked up about our relationship with each other.

West released me a moment later, ripping the dildo from me and throwing it down. Then he was pushing me over onto my back. He straddled my chest and tore out the gag from my mouth. I choked and coughed, but I wasn't allowed to recover. The man leant over me and shoved his cock between my now vacant lips. He fucked my face, staring down at me with such an intense expression, I thought I might combust. Those beautiful amber eyes were full of violence.

"That's it, I'm going to paint your fucking mouth with my cum, you dirty little bitch."

He groaned the next moment, erupting inside me. His taste mixed in with mine, a heady cocktail of pleasure seeping across my tongue. Evidence of how hard we'd climaxed with each other.

He pulled his cock from my mouth when he was spent and wrapped his hand around my throat.

"Swallow."

I did as he asked. He could feel my throat working, and it made him smile. Then I was sucking in air, trying to regain my equilibrium as it had been thrown into the abyss. West stroked my throat with his thumb, making me shiver.

"What a good little slut you've been."

I couldn't answer him. My throat was raw from crying and screaming.

He shifted off me and turned me on my side, unlocking the cuffs and throwing them away from us. Then he took one of my arms and rubbed it down before doing the same to the other. The next thing I knew, he'd picked me up from the bed and carried me into his bathroom. He set me down in the bath, put the plug in, and turned on the taps. I lay there, unable to move as the water filled around me. He pressed a kiss to my forehead and left me there while he went back into the bedroom.

I stared at the water flowing from the taps. My mind drifted. I wasn't sure what was up or down any longer. All I knew was I felt wrecked beyond belief.

West returned a moment later, dumping the sex toy in the sink before he climbed into the bath behind me. He held me against his chest after he'd turned off the taps. He stroked my skin, soothing me with each touch.

"You were such a good girl, little Scar," he murmured in my ear. "Such a good girl for me."

My hand wrapped around his wrist, holding it to my chest. He nuzzled my hair.

"I know, you can't talk yet and it's okay. I'll take care of you, my perfect little warrior. You did so well."

His praise made my heart tighten in my chest. It took my broken pieces and started to knit them back together.

"I'm so proud of you, little Scar. So fucking proud."

I turned my face into him, wanting him closer. Needing him to engulf me. He would repair me. He'd make me better. I'd known coming to him was my only option. It had been my only way out of the mess Stuart had left me in. West gave me the one thing I needed more than anything else. A safe place to break into tiny little pieces. He'd ruined me. And now... he would put me back together.

"That's my good girl," he whispered. "My little Scar."

I was his. His girl. His forever. And he was mine too.

THIRTY ONE

PRESCOTT

West trailed his hand along the bannister as he walked down the stairs, the morning sun glowing around his light brown hair like he was some kind of fucking king. At least, that's what his expression bore. One of satisfaction and confidence. Like he'd spent the night revelling in his basest desires. I, on the other hand, had spent the whole night worrying about Scarlett. The panicked way she'd told me she needed West was like a punch to the fucking gut. Not because she needed him but seeing her in that state tugged at my heartstrings. Made me want to soothe her, but I couldn't. Not when she'd been so desperate to find West.

"Where's Scarlett?" Drake asked, giving West a dark look.

"Asleep," he replied as he walked across the room, barely sparing our friend a glance.

"Is she okay?" I interjected, unable to hold my tongue. "Did you ask what happened with Stuart?"

West's eyes went to me as he reached the kitchen. For a moment, he merely scrutinised me. Then he went over to the fridge and pulled the door open.

"I didn't ask her. She wasn't in a fit state to talk about it."

"But how is she?"

West took the milk out of the fridge, shutting the door and setting it on the counter. He stared down at it with a furrow between his brows.

"I don't know how to answer that, Pres."

My stomach hit the floor. The last thing I expected was for his cocky, confident self to disappear the moment I questioned him about Scarlett.

"What do you mean?"

"When I was done giving her what she asked for, she was spaced out, content, but so fucking spaced out. I took care of her and all, you know, but she didn't speak. Then she conked out when I put her to bed and hasn't surfaced since. I didn't want to leave her, but she needs to eat when she wakes up, so I came down to make her something. I asked Frankie to watch her."

I had wondered where Francis had got to. He'd not been down this morning. And irrational jealousy surged inside me. He'd asked Francis rather than me. Then I remembered Scarlett felt a certain sort of safety with him she didn't have with the rest of us. Rubbing the back of my neck, I turned away and looked out the window.

What the fuck is wrong with you?

Insecurity is what I was feeling. It was fucked up and ridiculous, but there we were. I was messed up, no matter how hard I tried to hide it. Messed up because my father had flitted in and out of my life whenever it suited him, leaving me feeling as though I was just something he picked up when he was bored.

Fuck you, Ezra Ellis. Fuck you for making me feel like I wasn't worthy of your attention. Fuck you for abandoning me. Fuck you for everything.

I wasn't unaware of why I felt this way, but it was horrifying all the same. That I would ever feel jealousy or insecurity when it came to Scarlett. I knew she loved me. Knew she needed me. Something about this relationship between the four of us and her was tearing at the edges.

"What did she want?" Drake asked.

"I don't think you want to know the answer to that question."

I turned around in time to see Drake give West a questioning look.

"Try me."

"What she wanted is between me and her, Drake. I didn't ask you what you and her did up on the roof on Thursday. And don't you dare fucking ask her either. I know what you're like. You'd punish her to get it out of her."

"Are you lot fighting again?" came Francis' voice.

All of us looked to the stairs where he was standing at the top of them. Next to him stood Scarlett, her hazel-green eyes narrowed and her hair a wild mess of curls down her back. Her gaze went straight to West, who looked at her with something akin to adoration, but West didn't do adoring. He did brutal and vicious.

The two of them walked down the stairs. Francis had his hand on her lower back as if she needed steadying. She left him to walk into the kitchen. West didn't say a word as she approached him. Her hands went to his chest. She stared up at him for a long moment.

"I didn't get to say it last night, so I will now," she said, her voice quiet and full of appreciation. "Thank you."

He reached up and stroked her hair.

"There's nothing in this world I wouldn't give you, little Scar. Nothing."

She nibbled her bottom lip. There was one thing I knew he refused to give her. A kiss. And I wondered if she'd comment on it.

Scarlett leant forward and rested her face against his chest, pressing her ear to his heart. She rubbed her fingers along his pec as if she needed to feel him and know he was real. Then she placed a kiss over his t-shirt on his heart before pulling away. West did nothing other than watch her as she turned and spied me standing near the windows.

Her feet carried her in my direction, her eyes full of apology. I didn't know what she had to be sorry for. If anyone had to apologise, it should be me for having these fucked up feelings about what happened last night. For the way she'd begged me to let her go.

The moment she reached me, I took her hand and brought it to my lips, kissing the heel of her palm.

"Pres…"

"Are you okay?" I whispered into her skin. "That's all I care about."

She stepped closer and frowned.

"Stop it."

I dropped her hand.

"Stop what?"

"Being so selfless. What's wrong? And don't tell me it's nothing. I know you, Pres. I can see it in your eyes."

My chest got tight. Scarlett had been the only one I'd ever opened up to about my father in the past. And now she was looking at me like she knew exactly what I was thinking.

"I need to know you're okay first, little lamb."

She let out a sigh as if I was frustrating the fuck out of her. "I'm fine."

I looked around, finding the others staring at us. It made my skin itch. Thinking too hard about Ezra always did.

"Are you?"

"Yes. West took care of me. Now, will you please tell me what's going on with you?"

"Not with an audience."

She took my hand.

"Okay, let's go somewhere else then."

"You are going to sit at the table and eat breakfast, Scar," came West's voice from the kitchen. "You can talk to him after that."

Scarlett didn't look back at West. Instead, she dragged me over to the table and sat down, making me sit next to her. Her thumb rubbed up and down my hand like she knew I needed soothing. Such an observant little lamb. And I should have known better. Scarlett remembered me. She knew what I was like and there were things about me that had never changed despite the years separating us.

"You're doing what he said," I murmured.

"I need to eat," she responded with a shrug.

"You seem… different."

I couldn't explain it, but something had shifted in her since last night.

She looked at me with a resigned expression on her face.

"I feel different."

"What happened?"

Her eyes clouded over.

"All you need to know is he…" she faltered as West came over with a mug of tea for her.

"He?"

West set the mug down and eyed her as if he wanted to hear her answer too. She picked it up and sipped at it.

"Stuart doesn't know I know about the past. He… he threatened to take me back to the estate and told me some things that scared me, so I ran before he could keep me there."

She gripped my hand tighter.

"What things?"

Scarlett turned her head and caught Drake's eyes across the room where he was sitting on the sofa.

"How many women have you shared before… me?"

The question made me look at the others even though it hadn't been directed at me. Why would she be asking unless Stuart had told her about it? Was this what she meant by things that scared her?

"Eight," Drake replied.

"How many of them are alive?"

Francis flinched. Her question had clearly made him think of Chelsea.

"Five."

"Did you kill them?"

Drake leant forward, resting his arms on his knees.

"Yes."

"Why?"

"They didn't keep their mouths shut. And judging your questions, another one has ignored the NDA she signed."

Scarlett's expression was impassive, making me nervous. It was Drake who had wielded the axe, but we were complicit in the entire affair. He'd made them all look like suicides. It was how we got away with it.

"We didn't mistreat them if that's what you want to know. They were paid for their services. They knew what they were getting into. People can be fickle when money is involved."

She took another sip of her tea.

"He said you almost killed the last one."

Francis went deathly pale.

"Chelsea talked," West muttered, his expression turning grim.

Fuck, just what we needed. Another one spilling the beans. I thought we vetted them better.

There was one after Chelsea. Rina Gregory. We'd stopped seeing her before the first night we'd shared Scarlett. She'd gone back to Canada with the money we'd paid her, so there was no chance of her talking.

Drake rubbed his chin and eyed Scarlett for a long moment before he extracted his phone from his pocket.

"Don't," Francis said with a desperate note in his voice. "You promised."

Drake looked at him.

"She broke the rules, Francis."

"Let me fix it. I need to fix it."

The way Drake scowled made me flinch.

"No, you won't do what needs to be done. I don't trust you with her."

Scarlett put her hand on West's arm.

"Who is Chelsea?" she whispered.

"Not my story to tell, little Scar. You need to ask Frankie."

Her eyes went to him and Drake, the two of them still arguing over the whole Chelsea situation. If she talked to Stuart, fuck knows who else had done. We needed to clean up this mess, starting with her.

"I'll do what's fucking necessary," Francis said. "I'll fix this shit, okay? It's my mess. I should be the one to handle it."

"He's right, you know," West said, turning away from us to look at Drake. "Demons have a way of gnawing at us when we don't exorcise them ourselves. Let him deal with his."

It made me think of my own demon. My father. And how I had never rid myself of the legacy of abandonment he'd left behind.

"Fine," Drake conceded after a moment. "Do it tonight and no fucking excuses."

Francis gave him a nod before he sat down and looked out of the window as if he was contemplating the fact he had to kill tonight. We all knew what he meant by 'fix it'. How he had to make the problem go away... permanently.

You talk, you die. That was the rule.

West left the table and went back into the kitchen to finish making Scarlett breakfast.

"What else did Stuart tell you?" Drake asked as he turned back to Scarlett.

"He promised me to Mason when this is all over."

Scarlett's voice was flat and void of emotion. But me? The horrifying knowledge howled inside me like a fucking storm raging in my soul.

"No," I ground out. "Fuck no."

"Pres—" Drake started.

I slammed my free hand on the table.

"No. She doesn't fucking know about his sick obsession with her. This just makes it worse. I am not keeping it from her."

Scarlett looked at me, her eyes widening.

"What? His obsession with me? What are you talking about?"

"He's wanted you since you were a teenager. He used to watch you when he picked up the twins from school like a creepy fucking stalker. We never told you about it because you didn't know who he was. But we knew. We saw him."

"The twins?"

I shook my head. There was too much she didn't know. And we couldn't keep the truth from her any longer.

"Mason was their friend. Like we told you, his father is best mates with Stuart. None of this was random. It's all connected, sweetness, all of it."

THIRTY TWO

SCARLETT

Prescott looked incensed as he talked about Mason. After all the revelations involving him, I'd lost all interest in being anywhere near the man. He wasn't who I thought at all. Neither were the four men in front of me, but I understood them more now I remembered who they were.

"Mason was Ray and Ryan's friend? Is that why he hates you so much? Because they grew up with their fathers being best friends?" I asked.

Prescott nodded.

"That and you. He hates us because of our relationship with you."

It made me sick to think about him staring at me when I'd been younger and me having no clue.

"And his father?"

"We're pretty sure he's dirty. We just can't prove it. He was the one who questioned us when the twins went missing. Then he became the commissioner years later. We can't touch him for obvious reasons. And his association with Stuart makes it difficult for us too."

I hadn't asked them why they hadn't come to get me when they found out where I was. Guess I was about to find out.

"Stuart has too many friends in high places," Drake said, rising from the sofa and coming closer to the dining table. "We were four nineteen-year-olds with nothing when we found out he had you. We didn't know where he'd taken you or what your life was like, only that, one day, we would get you back somehow."

It took me a second to put his words into perspective.

"You couldn't get to me… even though you wanted to."

Prescott squeezed my hand.

"No."

"Then why did you do all that shit to me when I did come back?"

Drake looked away.

"You were here to ruin us. We knew we couldn't trust you, especially when you didn't remember us. And we were going to use your connection to Stuart to ruin him after we…"

He rubbed his fingers on his chest, like the words physically hurt him to say.

"After you what?"

"Broke you down enough so you'd do what we wanted instead of what he asked you to do."

The words hung in the air. I didn't know how to react to it. I'd kept calm this whole time, needing to process everything they were revealing to me.

"You wanted to break me?"

"Yes... and trust me, I'm aware of how fucked up it sounds, given our history with each other. We all knew it was a risk we had to take. Stuart is obsessed with finding out the truth. He'll never stop coming after us unless we put a stop to him."

My heart had never ached this much. The organ protested so vehemently in my chest. It was as if someone had their fist around it, squeezing the life out of me. Not just because of what Drake said about wanting to break me. He was right about Stuart. He would never stop coming after them. Never stop wanting the truth. Never stop plotting their destruction.

My fingers went to my chest, rubbing it even though it wouldn't stop the pain. I could barely even feel Prescott's hand wrapped around my other one. It was all I could do to focus on not screaming at the four of them about how fucked up all of this was.

"He wants you dead, but not before you admit you killed his sons," I managed to get out. "He needs that first."

I wanted to tell them Stuart had called me a wanton whore for being with them, but the words caught in my throat. Even though West had broken me down last night and put me back together with such tender care and affection, I still couldn't say it. Still couldn't tell them the truth about Stuart and his treatment. I don't know what was holding me back. Perhaps it was the fact the four of them had planned to use me in their own revenge plot. They were going to use me as a pawn, just like Stuart had.

West walked over with a plate and set it down in front of me. I looked up at him. Into those amber eyes I'd loved most of my life. At the man who'd given me comfort and love. Who always stayed by my side, no matter what happened or the things we did. And I needed him. Fuck, did I need him. I wanted his comfort more than anything else.

My heart still recognises you. It still belongs to you.

I was up and out of my chair, ripping my hand from Prescott's before I wrapped myself around West, pressing my face into his chest. Breathing him in felt like coming home. For a moment, I could pretend he was the boy I'd known all those years ago. Feel his heart hammering in his chest and know it belonged to me.

He stroked my hair and leant closer, nuzzling his face into it as if he couldn't help himself, either.

"Little Scar?"

"I need you," I whispered into his t-shirt.

It wasn't a lie. West called me his little warrior, but sometimes I didn't feel very brave. Right now, I was trying so hard to hold it all together. To not cry over the fact my best friends had wanted to break me. They were going to use me for their own means, and I wasn't okay with it.

"You need to eat."

I nodded against his chest. I was running on empty at this point.

West sat down in my vacated chair, setting me in his lap and tipping my face up to his. He stroked my cheek with his thumb. Then he turned me to face the table and placed the knife and fork in my hands. For the next five minutes, no one said anything as I ate the eggs, bacon, and toast he'd made for me. When I was done, I leant back against West's chest and he wrapped his arms around me.

"Better?" he murmured in my ear.

With something in my stomach, I didn't feel so weak. And having him at my back made me feel... braver. That's what the boys had always done for me. They raised me up, so I wasn't scared to be me.

"A little."

"Even queens need someone to lean on when everything gets dark."

I shouldn't be surprised at his perceptiveness. At how he knew what I needed.

"You're not just someone to me though."

"I know."

It was like an unspoken agreement between us. We didn't need to say it. Open that can of worms between us when I was already dealing with everything else.

I turned to Drake, who was leaning against the table.

"What changed?"

His brow furrowed for a long moment.

"You."

"Me?"

"You changed everything."

West stroked my stomach, making me shift in his lap.

"Does that mean when you drugged me, it wasn't part of your plans to break me?"

None of us had said it out loud before, but facts were facts. They had drugged and fucked me together.

"No. It wasn't. That came... after."

"After what?"

"After we all realised we wanted you as a woman more than we wanted to use you," Prescott said. "We played it off as being a part of our plans, but that's not the truth. I think we can all admit it."

When no one disagreed with Prescott's statement, I looked down at the table. I'm not sure it made what they'd done any better. How could any of this be okay? Then again, I wasn't expecting anything else. They'd changed in the past ten years. Become darker versions of themselves. Men with a moral compass that didn't fit society's standards, only their own. And in a lot of ways, I couldn't fault the way they were. I was just as fucked up inside. I hadn't ever been a good girl who did as she was told. I'd always been reckless. And I was my own person. No one else got to tell me how to be or what was right or wrong. I'd forgotten that version of Scarlett, but I knew her now. I was more than aware of who I'd been and who I'd become.

"And making me kill that guy?"

"Like we told you at the time. Loyalty and something to hold over you. It wasn't a part of our original plans, but it served our purposes in trying to break you. Except it didn't break you, little Scar, it made you stronger," West said, continuing to stroke my stomach.

It had broken me, but Francis put me back together that night. He made it all okay. And I'd be forever grateful to him for it. My safe place was in his arms with him calling me his little whore. Stuart hadn't taken it from me last night. I wouldn't let him steal these four men away from me again. I couldn't.

"Only because Frankie made sure I didn't fall apart," I murmured.

Francis was still sat on the sofa, staring out of the window. I wanted to go to him because I knew he was suffering on the inside. However, our conversation about the truth wasn't done yet.

"He's good like that," West whispered. "You've always needed him to keep you safe."

I turned to look at him.

"Is that why you're okay with this? Because you know I need them?"

"Yes."

He said it so matter of fact like it was obvious he would give me what I needed. I didn't know what to say. It was something the old West would have done. Maybe the boy West hadn't died the night of my accident. It was traumatic for me. And it must have been so for him too. My mind had protected me. But what had it done to him? It was a conversation for another day when things weren't so... precarious.

I turned back to Drake.

"Okay, so this plan... it's changed now?"

He gave me a sharp nod.

"Then what's next?"

Drake shifted, dropping his hand and curling around the edge of the table.

"You're not... angry?"

"Oh, trust me, I'm not happy, but me having a go at all of you is not going to get us anywhere. It's not going to change what happened. I want to focus on the future... and how you're going to make it up to me."

He didn't respond to me immediately. The furrow in his brow made me want to smooth it away. Yes, Drake and I had a tumultuous relationship, but it didn't change the fact I cared about him. Didn't erase our friendship nor our past.

I leant forward, reaching out and running my fingers over his hand. Drake looked down at where I was touching him. His indigo eyes held a fuck ton of emotion in them for once. He let me see his pain. It leaked out of him, battering me with its intensity.

"I'm sorry for hurting you," he all but whispered.

He turned his hand over, allowing me to stroke his palm instead. I ran my fingers over his calloused tips.

"I need to know what else Stuart said to you last night."

I didn't look away from him, even though thinking about Stuart made me want to run.

"The memory stick was just a ploy… a test to see if I'd do what he asked of me. And he knows it didn't work. I don't think it was meant to. He thinks you got to me because Mason told him I'm sleeping with all of you. I think that's why he told me about the other women. And before you ask, no, I'm not upset about it. I needed to know the truth from your side of it rather than his."

Drake gripped my hand in his, reassuring me he understood.

"He said you'd want me dead when you found out I was here to destroy you. He doesn't realise I know. And he told me it was Mason's job to keep me alive if he wants me… that Mason plans to punish me for being with all of you when this is over."

It was all I could tell them. The abuse Stuart had hurled at me wasn't worth repeating.

"You being dead is the last thing we'd ever want, Scarlett."

"I know. I'm not worried about that. I don't want to go back to him again. I can't. So whatever your plans are, it can't be that."

I didn't care what they were going to do to him. Staying away from Stuart and Mason was my priority. The things I'd learnt about the two of them made my skin crawl. And the fact Stuart had put his hands on me last night. I couldn't go back to that. Back to my abuser. Never again would I allow him to get to me.

"Are you going to tell us what he's done to you?"

I looked away. I should tell them. And yet I didn't want it to make a difference to what they were planning on doing to Stuart. I needed to know what they intended first. I needed to make sure I could trust them to keep me safe. None of them had yet earned my forgiveness.

"I'm not ready to talk about it. And I want to know what you intend to do about him."

"We haven't decided yet."

My eyes went to Drake again.

"What do you mean?"

"Everything has changed since you remembered us. But I suppose one thing hasn't…"

"That is?"

He gave me a smile.

"We want Stuart dead."

THIRTY THREE

PRESCOTT

Scarlett stared up at Drake with a frown. She'd been awfully calm about everything, even though I could see the emotional strain all this was having on her. I wasn't sure what was holding her back from telling us about her life with Stuart. And I planned to find out, but not yet. She clearly needed a little more time.

"I should have expected that," she muttered and shook her head.

She slid her hand from Drake's and sat back against West's chest. I wanted her in my lap, needing me that way. This jealousy shit needed to fuck right off.

"I guess what happened last night changes things," she said after a moment.

Drake gave her a sharp nod. The fact Stuart had played with her mind pissed me off. I wanted to wring his neck. Judging by the state she'd been in when she got back, there was more to the story than what she'd told us.

"Well, in that case... whatever plans you make, I don't want to be left out of them. I'm not a pawn, nor will I allow you to continue using me like one. You left me out of your plans once and look where it got us." She waved a hand around. "And if you want me to trust you... and forgive you, then you're going to start treating me like the fucking equal I am. Is that understood?"

West rested his chin on her shoulder.

"There's my little warrior," he murmured before pressing a kiss to her neck.

I watched Scarlett shiver in his embrace, but her gaze didn't leave Drake's. While we'd always been a democracy, she knew as well as I did, he was the sticking point in this situation. I could see the cogs turning in Drake's mind. Always processing all outcomes before he made a response. It was his way. Totally anal if you asked me, but I was the 'forge ahead without thinking' one of our group. And I had no issues with including Scarlett in our plans going forward. We were a team, after all. Bound together by fate, need, and desire.

It was plain and simple. We needed her. And she needed us.

"Yes," Drake said simply after a full minute had ticked by. "Good."

Then Scarlett's attention drifted from Drake towards Francis. He looked like he wanted to be sick. I knew the Chelsea situation weighed heavily on him. It was time he put it to bed once and for all.

"Frankie," she called softly.

At the sound of her voice, he turned his head, and she beckoned him over with her fingers. It took a few moments before he rose from the sofa and made his way over to us. He stood next to Scarlett, who hadn't got up from West's lap. She took his hand and pressed a kiss to his knuckles. He let out a long breath.

"Sit with me?" she murmured, pressing his hand to her cheek.

The way his grey eyes broke in front of us made me aware of just how much Francis was holding onto inside. Scarlett hadn't mentioned if they'd exchanged those three little words with each other yet, but it was clear by the way they looked at each other, both of them had fallen in love.

He stroked her cheek with his thumb before he shifted away, taking the chair from the end of the table where Drake was leaning and placing it next to Scarlett and West. Then he sat down and leant over, placing his head in Scarlett's lap. Her fingers went to his hair, stroking the strands like she was soothing a lost child. His hand curled around her thigh in a rather possessive manner.

"We need to talk about a couple of things," she said a moment later, still caressing Francis' head. "This relationship between the five of us... I don't want it to end, but I need you to know I'm not okay with how things have gone down. Especially not the way you drugged me. Both times you've... shared me, they've been under fucked up circumstances."

I couldn't blame her for it. She had been under the influence of Ecstasy last time we'd fucked her together.

"So, this time it's going to be on my terms. I decide what happens and when. You're all going to earn my forgiveness by doing what I tell you to."

None of us said a word. I had a feeling I knew what she was going to ask of us given the conversation that had occurred between us when I'd fucked her up against my window the day West and Drake brought her home.

She looked between us before taking a breath.

"I want it to happen tomorrow night." Her eyes went to me. "And I want Pres to be in control of what happens. I want him to tell you how to fuck me whilst he watches us."

I shifted in my seat, the thought of it arousing me way more than was appropriate right now.

"You want to put Prescott in charge?" Drake said through his teeth.

"Yes. Is that going to be a problem?"

Scarlett's voice was almost sickly sweet. I put a hand to my mouth to stop myself from snorting.

"It's fine with me," Francis said without moving from his spot in Scarlett's lap. Her fingers were tangled in his locks. "I'll do whatever you want, Scar. I just want you. That's all I care about."

"I'm in," West said, nuzzling Scarlett's neck. "But don't you fucking tell me to do something you know I won't, Pres."

He was warning me not to order him to kiss her. And quite frankly, I had zero plans of forcing him into dealing with his shit with Scarlett. It was between them. She'd address it when she felt the time was right.

"You have my word," I replied, giving him a wink.

He eyed me with suspicion for a moment but turned back to Scarlett when he realised I wasn't joking. She was still looking at Drake, waiting to see what he would say.

"Fine, tomorrow night," he finally said, crossing his arms over his chest.

"Are you sure?" Scarlett asked, with a twinkle in her hazel-green eyes.

I could tell she was thoroughly winding Drake up with her behaviour. His hands flexed on his arms and he looked tense. He couldn't do a damn thing about it. She wasn't going to let him punish her. Not when we were meant to be earning her forgiveness.

"Yes."

She clapped her hands together.

"Good. I look forward to it."

She turned my way and gave me a bright smile.

"We need to talk."

Her hands went back to Francis' hair.

"I know, little lamb."

She gave me a nod before she leant closer to Francis, stroking his hair back from his forehead.

"I need to speak to Pres now," she whispered.

His hand around her thigh tightened.

"We can talk later," I volunteered, knowing she would likely say no.

It's not like I wanted to have a conversation about my stupid jealousy and my father, even though I knew it had to happen.

"It's okay," Francis said with a long sigh. "I'll be fine."

He sat up, forcing Scarlett to drop her hands from him. She slid out of West's lap, taking a step closer to Francis. Leaning down, she cupped his face with her hands and pressed her mouth to his. He clutched her t-shirt in his fists as she kissed him. Before she pulled away, she pressed kisses down his jaw and nuzzled his face with her nose.

"Later, okay?"

He nodded, letting go of her t-shirt and looking away. Scarlett had a furrow between her brows as she stepped back and indicated with her hand I should follow her. I got up and walked with her up the stairs to my room. Scarlett lowered herself into my armchair when we got there, leaving me to stand by the window. I placed my hand on it, staring out at the skyline.

"I'm jealous of the fact you went to West last night."

There was no point in beating around the bush. Scarlett deserved my honesty after everything between us.

"I have no right to feel that way. He gives you things I can't, and I promise that's okay, but you have to understand, seeing you so distressed hurt my fucking heart, little lamb. And the way you ran from me…"

I rubbed my chest with my free hand.

"I'm sorry."

"No, don't do that, Scarlett, don't apologise. This is my shit. It's not your fault you needed him."

I felt her presence behind me a minute later. Her hands splayed out over my back before her face pressed into the centre of it.

"I always need you, Pres, always. I just… West… you know, I…"

"You loved him first."

Her fingers dug into my skin. I hadn't been able to keep the bitterness out of my voice.

"It's not that. I mean, yes, I did love him first, I still… love him, but it's not the reason I needed him last night."

I shouldn't ask her. I shouldn't fucking ask her.

"Why did you?"

She turned her face, pressing her cheek into my back as her hands curled around my shoulders, the nails digging into the fabric of my t-shirt.

"I trusted him to break me."

My breath caught in my throat.

"Break you?" I choked out.

"I needed him to degrade me without safe words or reassurances that I could stop it at any time. It had to be him. West knows me in a way no one else does and I'm not going to apologise for that." She gripped me tighter, the sharp prick of her nails almost piercing my skin through my t-shirt. "You know I love you. I fucking love you to death. God, Prescott, you have no idea of the depths of my feelings. I ache for you. My heart hurts with loving you. And I can't help that I love them too, okay? I can't… but it doesn't change my feelings for you. It never will."

Her words ripped my fucking soul right out of my chest. I loved her to death too. I loved her so much it was like I couldn't breathe without her. Scarlett was the one person in this world who had the power to tear me to shreds, but I trusted her not to. I trusted her with my life.

"Promise you'll never abandon me, sweetness. I need you to promise."

And there it was. The truth of the matter.

She let go of my shoulders, instead, wrapping her hands around my waist and encouraging me to turn around. There were tears in her eyes as she came into view. I leant back against the window. Hating myself for this conversation. Hating the understanding in her eyes. She knew. She fucking well knew.

Reaching up, she cupped my face with her small hand.

"I promise I will never abandon you, Prescott Ellis. I will never leave you in the dark. I will never walk away from what's between us. You have my word, my heart, and my soul. I love you."

"Little lamb," I whispered, pressing my face into her hand. "This is about Ezra."

I nodded.

"Oh, Pres."

She dropped her hand from my face, only to go up on her tiptoes and wrap her body around mine. Her hands went to my neck, cupping the back of it.

"He doesn't deserve you. Never has. Never will. You are so much more than he will ever know. Look at what you've done with your life. This place you've built with the others. You don't need his approval or his praise, okay? I'm proud of you and I'm sure Rosie is too. He does not get to take away from your achievements."

Fuck, how I craved those words from her lips. The ones having the power to heal the hole in my heart my father left behind when he abandoned me. I hadn't seen him in years, but there was still an invisible Ezra sized scar etched onto my skin.

"You still have his number on your phone, don't you."

It wasn't a question. It was a statement of fact.

"Yes," I whispered into her hair as I pressed my face to it.

"I want you to erase it when you're ready to let go of the pain he's inflicted on you. When he's no longer tied to your self-worth."

"Okay."

I wasn't yet, but I had Scarlett now. She'd help me.

"Good."

She released me, her eyes still shining with unshed tears as she dropped back to her feet.

"I know you can, Pres," she told me as she took my hand and pressed a kiss to the heel of my palm. "You can do anything you set your mind to. I believe in you."

"I love you, little lamb, so fucking much."

She smiled, making me reach up and wipe the pad of my thumb under her eye, catching the tear falling from her lashes.

"And I know you love them. I want you to love them... they need you as much as I do. We all need each other."

She brushed her fingers over my chest.

"You know, I like it when you're all jealous and possessive of me. I shouldn't but I do."

I bit my lip.

"Is that so?"

She nodded, fisting my t-shirt between her fingers and tugged me against her.

"Yeah, because I'm rather jealous and possessive of you too."

I leant closer to her.

"Trust me, sweetness, I'm aware."

She grinned before I kissed her, melting into her embrace and knowing it would be okay. As long as we communicated and didn't let stupid shit get in the way, we'd navigate this together. Me and my little lamb were meant to be. And I wouldn't let anything break us apart again.

THIRTY FOUR

FRANCIS

As I raised my gloved hand to knock at her front door, I realised it was long past time I dealt with this entire situation. Deep down, I'd always known it would come to this. I knew what she was like. The way she held grudges. How she allowed shit to fester in her soul.

Chelsea McDonald was twisted in a way I recognised. In a way I knew intimately. It was the same sickness torturing me. And it's why we'd become friends.

The sound of my rapping on the wooden door rang in my ears with its finality. It would be the very last time I came here. And the last time I would ever allow my feelings for someone to blind me to the reality of who they were.

Did I want to do this?

No.

Did I have to?

Yes.

The door opened as I dropped my hand, revealing a tall girl with dark hair and olive skin. Her brown eyes were narrowed and her posture stiff.

"Hello, Francis," Chelsea said, her voice dripping with disgust. "What brings you to this neck of the woods?"

Chelsea lived in Knightsbridge in a house paid for by Daddy. The fucked up part of all this was she didn't need the money. She was a bored, over-privileged twenty-two-year-old woman who had more possessions than sense.

I understood Chelsea McDonald. I recognised the parts of her that yearned for acceptance and not to live in the shadow of other people. I shared them with her. The difference between me and Chelsea was I'd actually cared, whereas I was a means to a fucking end for her.

"I think you know why I'm here."

For a moment I thought she would slam the door in my face, but she sighed and stepped back, allowing me to walk into the house where this would all come to an end. She shut the door behind me and led me into the living room.

"Do you want a drink?" she asked, ever the perfect hostess her mother had taught her to be.

"No, thank you."

"Well, I do."

I followed her into the kitchen, watching her open the fridge and extract a bottle of wine. She got a glass out of the cupboard, popped the cork and poured the white liquid. As she sipped at it, she leant against the counter and levelled her gaze on me.

"I didn't expect you to come. I thought it would be Drake. That's what he told me… he would be the one to end it if it ever came to it. Doesn't really surprise me. The big stoic one with the blood kink being my executioner."

She shook her head.

"But not you, Francis. You're not the type."

I dug my hands in my pockets. She had no idea. I'd kept the monster hidden from almost everyone in my life. I didn't want to keep him from Scarlett any longer. And only when I put this to rest would I be able to show her the truth.

"You know, it's funny you say that, Chels... me not being the type."

Her doe eyes searched mine.

"What's funny about it?"

"You're acting like you know everything about me."

"Don't I? I remember you liked to talk... a lot. Especially about her."

Her voice soured on the word 'her'. Yes, I'd talked about Scarlett, but I'd never told her who my girl was. I'd never given Chelsea a name nor the full story. It was more about the loss of my best friend all those years ago. How it tore me up inside. Those were the things I'd told her. Not Scarlett's secrets. And certainly not mine.

"We're not here to talk about her."

She sipped at her wine.

"No? You sure about that? You don't wish to atone for your sins one last time?"

I shrugged.

"I have nothing to atone for, Chelsea. It's you who thinks everyone has something they're hiding. Some kind of darkness staining their souls with corruption."

There was only one regret I had. Causing this woman physical pain because of my own distracted mind. But I didn't need atonement. I needed to end this for good. To put my demon to rest.

Perhaps before Scarlett came back into my life, I would have said otherwise. Now Chelsea had betrayed all of us to Stuart Carver, my need to apologise had all but evaporated. I may have been emotional when I told Drake I needed to do this earlier, but now I was resolute. Especially given the petulance in Chelsea's voice. The way she was looking at me like she could wind me back around her little finger. It was a pity she didn't know the real me. She had no fucking clue.

"Yeah right. Last time we saw each other, you couldn't stop apologising for what you did."

"I see the spoiled little princess is still front and centre."

She put her glass down on the counter and scowled.

"What's that supposed to mean?"

"You want me to apologise because you like the attention. It has nothing to do with me or what I need."

Her mouth thinned. My emotions had been all over the place on the way over here but seeing her had brought it home to me. She didn't give a shit about anyone but herself. I was merely someone she liked to toy with.

"You're not even sorry you're here to kill me?"

"You knew what the price of talking was, Chelsea. Don't put this on me. And I'm not here to kill you. You're going to do that to yourself."

"Excuse me?"

I smiled at her, extracting my hands from my pockets and spreading them.

"Did you think I would finish you off myself?"

"Isn't that why you've come?"

"That's not how we operate. Not when it comes to people like you."

"People like me?"

Did she not know? She came from money. While she might be the youngest of five, she was still spoilt as fuck. All of this shit had been her acting out because the rest of her siblings were always more successful than her. Always achieved more than her. Made her parents proud. Chelsea was the disappointment of the family. The one who could never do anything right. The girl who spent her parent's money on frivolous activities. The one her parents didn't think would amount to much.

At first, I sympathised with her plight. It wasn't like my parents had ever made me feel like I was second best to anyone, given I was an only child. However, I was the quieter one out of me, Prescott, Drake, and West. The one in the shadow of their popularity. It was stupid because they'd never made me feel that way. I was the one who didn't think highly of myself, and it showed.

In that respect, I was the same as Chelsea. Always second best. And yet… I wasn't bitter about it in the way she was. I didn't act out like a fucking child because I didn't get my way. No, I took my shit and dealt with it. I made something of myself off my own back.

I didn't have sympathy for the woman in front of me any longer.

"Yes, you have everything you could have ever wanted, Chels, but the one thing you don't have is a fucking clue about what it's like to really struggle."

She pursed her lips and didn't respond to me for a long minute.

"If you're not here to kill me, then why the fuck did you turn up on my doorstep?"

"I mean, if you want to get technical, I am here to make sure you die. But as for who pulls the trigger? Well, that would be you."

She scoffed.

"You expect me to kill myself?"

I shrugged.

"Pretty much."

"Fuck you, Francis."

I took a step towards her.

"I'm sorry I hurt you, Chelsea. It wasn't my intention. But you talked... and to Stuart Carver, of all people. If it had been anyone else, we may have let it slide, but no, you had to talk to the one person who has a vendetta against us. So, yes, you are going to kill yourself because it's the least you can do for me after the shitstorm you've caused."

"The least I can do for you?"

"That's right."

She tried to lunge for me, but I sidestepped her and shook my head.

"Don't make this harder than it has to be."

I wasn't about to leave my DNA anywhere in this fucking place. In fact, I planned to make this as clean as possible, but if she was going to resist, then I would just have to make sure it looked like she'd done it all herself.

"You're a bastard. All of you are," she seethed, staring at me with no small amount of irritation.

"And yet you still let us pay to fuck you in ways that would make your mother blush."

"Screw you!"

She tried to come for me again, but I was wise to her shit. I grabbed hold of her arms and wrestled them behind her back. When she tried to stamp on my foot, I turned her around and directed her out of the kitchen towards the stairs.

"Get the fuck off me!"

"I told you not to make it hard on yourself, Chels. It didn't have to be this way."

I picked her up when she struggled and carried her up the stairs. She weighed nothing, so clearly hadn't been taking care of herself since we last saw each other. Unsurprising really. Probably decided she would fake an illness to spite her parents.

She kicked out and screamed at me the whole way up, but I ignored her. It wasn't anything I hadn't heard before. When I got to her bedroom, I dumped her on her bed, held her down and took my bag off. From it, I extracted a rope I'd fashioned into a noose earlier. While it might be extremely fucked up for me to decide this was how she would die, I didn't care. Ropes were my thing. And knowing I snuffed out her fucking life by choking it out of her, well, that was just a bonus.

"Now, I'm going to need you to write a little note to Mummy and Daddy, telling them all your fucking woes and how you can't live in the world any longer."

"If you think I'm going to—"

"I think you're going to do as I say, because you know if I don't finish you off, then Drake will. And he won't be so fucking nice about it."

She shut her mouth then, staring up at me with no small amount of fear in her eyes. I wasn't playing around. Chelsea had talked. She'd fucked things up for me and, more importantly, for Scarlett. If she hadn't said a fucking word, then Stuart wouldn't have been able to tell Scarlett about this shit. It's not like we would have kept it from our woman, but it was our story to tell, not his.

"Go write the note. Now."

She got off the bed and stalked over to her dresser while I prepared the rest of the things I needed. Walking out of the room, I went over to the stairs and looked down at the lobby. Then I knelt down and looped the rope around the railings, tying it off so it was secure. I went downstairs and found a chair from the dining room, placing it underneath the hanging rope.

Chelsea walked out of her bedroom and looked at me from over the railings. Her eyes went to the rope and the noose. She paled a moment later.

"Are you serious?"

"About what exactly?"

She waved at my setup.

"You want me to fucking hang myself?"

I shrugged.

"Yes."

"That's sick."

"It's no less than you deserve for talking. Now come down here with your note."

She stomped down the stairs, making it very clear she was a little sour puss over the whole situation. I didn't pity her fate. If you fucked with my family, I wouldn't hesitate to do what was necessary. Drake thought I wouldn't go through with it. But what he didn't realise was I had one huge fucking incentive.

I was protecting Scarlett.

Not because it was the right thing to, but because I fucking well loved her.

"Give it to me," I demanded when she got to the bottom of the stairs.

She shoved it into my hands. I read it over, shaking my head at the overdramatic nature of it. But it was Chelsea all over.

"Get on the chair."

I left her to do it while I set the note on the side table next to a vase of white roses. Picking one out of the vase, I placed it by the note. Then I walked over to the woman I had come to despise for her actions.

"Put the noose over your head."

"Who is going to believe I did this myself?" she asked, her voice full of annoyance.

I smiled.

"Only everyone who knows you have a flair for the dramatic, Chels."

She grabbed the rope and slipped it over her head, letting it settle around her neck.

"Now, pull it tight or you're going to have a rather painful death."

I didn't tell her she would die in agony, regardless. Didn't seem to be any point.

Her hands tightened the noose, then she looked at me. For the first time, I saw regret in her expression.

"Are you really going to make me do this?"

"I'm not making you do anything. You're doing this to yourself, remember?"

"Fuck you."

I decided I'd had enough and kicked out the chair from under her. Crossing my arms over my chest, I heard the rope snap into place and saw her hands go to it. I watched her struggle as the rope began to choke her, pressing down on her windpipe. Her legs flailed. She started gasping for air and trying to reach for me.

I did nothing, merely waited for the life to drain from her eyes. Witnessed her choking, strangled by the noose until her legs stopped kicking and her arms dropped to her sides. Her head lolled the next moment.

Uncrossing my arms and I walked closer, observing her to make sure she was dead. Chelsea wasn't breathing. Her chest had gone utterly still. It was done. I'd protected my family.

I went upstairs and collected my bag, keeping things exactly the way they were so as not to leave a trace of my presence. There were other details I attended to, like pouring out the rest of her wine, so it looked like she'd had her last glass before the end. Then I walked out of her house, shutting the door behind me, and eyed the street. No one was about as I walked down the steps from her house.

It was time I returned home to my family now I'd handled that little threat.

It would be on the news soon. Chelsea McDonald, the youngest daughter of Winston McDonald, the owner of McDonald hotels, would be found dead in her house from a suicide. It would be sad, of course, but I didn't give two shits any longer. There was nothing to tie me back to her, but it sent a fucking message to Stuart Carver.

You fuck with us. We'll fuck with you right back.

And I was going to make sure that fucker paid a heavy price for his interference in our lives.

We're going to come for you, Stuart. You better fucking watch yourself

THIRTY FIVE

FRANCIS

When I got back to the penthouse, I found Drake waiting for me. He asked me if it was done, and I nodded before making my way upstairs. I didn't feel like telling him what happened. It wasn't relevant, anyway. As long as the job was done, it didn't matter how I'd gone about killing her. Besides, if I hadn't been able to go through with it, I would have texted him earlier.

I opened the door to my bedroom, stepped in and shut it behind me, letting out a sigh. There were no regrets in my heart over killing Chelsea. She deserved her fate after she'd betrayed us. I was merely weary from dealing with so much over the past couple of months.

As I turned towards my bed, I stopped dead in my tracks. Scarlett sat cross-legged up against the headboard, her long wavy hair up in a messy bun with a rather tight tank top and a tiny pair of shorts on. The sight of her made my mouth go dry.

"Hey," she said, her voice soft.

I hadn't expected her to be here when I got back. And the fact she was... it gave me a weird feeling in my chest. Like my heart was trying to escape. The cadence of it had me wanting to rub my chest to stop it from being so fucking loud.

Without thinking about it any further, I walked over to the bed, kicked off my shoes and crawled onto it. I lay down and put my head in her lap. My fingers went to her thigh, stroking her soft skin as if to remind me this woman was mine.

"Do you want to talk about it?" she asked, her hands going to my hair.

I'd never enjoyed having it stroked before her, but her small hands playing with the strands calmed me. It was her. Scarlett quieted my soul.

"Are you sure you want to know what I did?"

Her hands didn't stop stroking.

"I'm not scared of you or what you're capable of, Frankie, nor will it change anything between us."

My fingers moved higher, stroking along the hem of her shorts.

"I made a girl kill herself."

"Chelsea."

I nodded. She'd heard us talk about Chelsea earlier. It was time I told Scarlett the truth about my relationship with the girl whose life I just helped end.

"Chelsea was, I guess, special to me, but in a really fucked up sense. She came from money. Her father owns a chain of hotels. Youngest of five and always in their shadow. Her demons... I understood them. And she understood mine."

My fingers dipped underneath her shorts, running along the seam of her underwear. Scarlett's breath hitched. I needed to touch her. It grounded me.

"Prescott met her in a club over a year ago. He brought her back here, and we shared her that night. We didn't pay her, but it soon became clear she was okay with our…"

"Your sexual desires."

I stroked my fingers across her pussy, still hidden by her underwear, making her jolt.

"Yes. And so we set out an arrangement with her like we did with the others. She signed an NDA. We were very clear about the terms. She knew what would happen if she talked."

I let out a sigh. Chelsea had used us like we'd used her. Our play sessions were an escape. A way to get out of her own head and indulge in something twisted.

"At first, she was like the others who came before her. She would visit us, we'd play, and she'd go home with money in hand. Then she started to linger afterwards. The others ignored her, but I let her hang around. Allowed her to ask me things. Then we started having sessions with just the two of us… and sometimes we talked afterwards."

I wished I'd never started talking to her. Sometimes you did things when you were desperate for a connection. When you longed for someone you'd lost.

"I told her about you. I mean, not in any real detail, but that I'd lost a girl who was special to me. And the closer it got to us being able to set the bait, to encourage Stuart to send you after us… the more I needed a connection to something… someone."

My chest ached all over again. I shifted in her lap, turning my head to look up at her. Scarlett's eyes were on me. They weren't full of disgust or anger but understanding.

Fuck. She looks just like she did when we were younger.

Scarlett always had that way about her. The one making you want to spill all your secrets because you knew she'd take your hand and tell you it was okay. Tell you she understood what you were going through. She was the one person who had never failed to reassure me.

"What I really wanted was you, but I couldn't have you."

Her hand left my hair, her fingers going to my cheek and stroking it instead. I wanted to kiss her. To drown in her.

I love you, Scarlett Nyx.

It was high time I admitted it to myself. I'd fallen in love with her. And there was no reason for me to be scared she couldn't feel the same way. Not when she looked at me like I was everything she needed.

"Then it happened... the thing that fucked everything up between me and her."

I looked away from my girl and stared out the window instead. I could see the night's sky from where I was. It was beautiful, but not quite as stunning as Scarlett herself.

"There's something I haven't told you about my desires."

Scarlett moved her hand from my cheek to rest it on my shoulder.

"I want... I want to wrap you in metal chains, to make them so tight it almost hurts with the strain of being bound by them. I want it so fucking badly sometimes, it makes me crazy, but... but I fucked up with Chelsea and now I'm scared to use them on anyone else."

She let out a breath, then kept stroking my hair with her other hand.

"What happened?"

"The day we found out you'd applied for a job, I had a session with her. And I was so fucking distracted by the thought of seeing you again, by knowing all of our efforts had finally paid off... I made the chains too tight. I started the session with her, but I wasn't really in the room. And when I twisted her a certain way, it pulled on her arm to the point where I almost dislocated her shoulder, almost broke her entire arm. She was screaming and crying about the pain. I thought it was a part of the game at first, but it became clear it wasn't and I unchained her immediately."

I swallowed, feeling bile rising in the back of my throat. The whole thing made me feel ill. It was crazy because I killed without remorse several times. Guess when it came to sexual games, it was different for me. They were about pleasure not snuffing out a life.

"She went crazy at me, telling me I was insane and this was all sick... that she only did it to make me happy. Then she ran out. I didn't know what the fuck to do. It messed me up, you know, seeing her like that... having her hurl all this abuse at me like I was some kind of sick deviant who got off on keeping women chained up against their will, which is the opposite of what I want."

Sighing, I turned my face into her lap, not wanting to look at the sky any longer.

"It hurt because I thought she understood me, but no, she just cared about herself and her own sick need to get back at her parents. It's why she was seeing us in the first place. She knew her parents would hate it. Then West had to go make it all worse by giving her pills to help with the pain and she overdosed on them."

Scarlett squeezed my shoulder, but I didn't look up at her.

"The next time I saw her, a few days later, she told us all to go fuck ourselves and she never wanted anything to do with us again. Drake warned her what would happen if she talked, but she told him she wouldn't say a word if we stayed away. So we did. I hadn't seen her until tonight... and knowing she'd told Stuart. How it must have sounded to you coming from him... well, I couldn't forgive her for it. I told you once I would kill anyone who hurt you. Her actions caused you harm. I made her pay the price for talking."

I lapsed into silence when I'd got it all out of my system. There wasn't anything else I could tell Scarlett unless she wanted details. I imagined she wasn't interested in knowing everything that had gone down.

For a long time, neither of us said a word. I relaxed into her touch, feeling the weight of the burden lifting off me. I'd held onto this pain for so long. Telling Scarlett felt cathartic. Admitting the truth to her... helped me in ways I'd never imagined possible.

"Do you feel better now it's over?" she whispered, her fingers burying deeper into my hair and stroking across my scalp.

"Yes."

"Are you tired?"

"A little."

"Then I'll help you get ready for bed."

I was about to tell her there was no need, but she leant down and pressed her lips to my forehead.

"Let me take care of you, Frankie, I want to."

How on earth could I deny her? I'd spent my whole life looking after everyone else. Making sure they didn't fuck up beyond belief. And I was tired. So fucking tired.

"Okay."

She encouraged me to get up and go into the bathroom to brush my teeth. When I came out, she'd turned out the lights, leaving her illuminated by the city below us. Scarlett sat at the end of the bed as I approached her. Her fingers went to my belt, undoing it before she unzipped my jeans. I allowed her to pull them off me, taking my socks with them. Her hands curled around my hips, drawing me between her legs.

"What happened was an accident, Frankie. You didn't mean to hurt her." She pressed her face to my stomach, nuzzling it with her nose. "I know you would never hurt anyone like that during sex on purpose. You're the kindest, most compassionate man I know." Pulling back, she stared up at me. "It's okay to make mistakes. It doesn't change who you are. And who you are is beautiful in my eyes."

My heart was on fucking fire. My hand went to her cheek. I needed to touch her. To feel her.

"I watch you because I can't help myself. You're a fallen god, carved from the heavens and made to be mine. That's how I see you."

Her fingers went to the hem of my t-shirt, pushing it up my chest. I let go of her hair to tug it off, dropping it on the floor and allowing her to see me. Her hands ran up my abs, tracing lines along the grooves and edges.

"You are perfect. I never want you to feel like you aren't everything I need. You're not second best, Frankie. You belong at the top of the podium. And I will worship you until the day we fade from this world."

I stroked her face, not wanting to say a word in case it broke this moment between us.

"Thank you for protecting me. For protecting our family tonight. I appreciate everything you've done and everything you do for me. Let me show you how much."

THIRTY SIX

SCARLETT

Staring up at Francis, I couldn't help but feel for the things he'd been through. The pain he'd had to experience without me in his life. I wished I could take it away for him. My heart blazed with it. The need to make him feel better. To let him know he was king in my soul alongside his three best friends. It wasn't a matter of one being favoured over the other. I had enough room for all of them to take up equal places.

My fingers went to his boxers, tugging them down his legs. Francis didn't stop me. He kept staring at me with those silvery-grey eyes I adored so much. The way they changed with his emotions, like two storm clouds rolling in the distance.

There was a desperate need inside me to care for him. To look after Francis the way he did me. He deserved to be worshipped like the fallen god he was.

I didn't care that he'd helped a girl to her grave tonight. Nor that he'd made a mistake with her before I'd come back into his life. It didn't matter to me he was a killer. I was one too. Francis could burn the world to the ground and I would still fall at his feet. I would do it for all of them. And it's exactly what I did. I slipped off the bed and knelt at his feet, running my hands up along his hips.

"I belong here," I murmured, leaning closer to press a kiss to his happy trail, "at your feet."

He sucked in a breath, his hand going to the back of my head and cupping it. My hand went to his cock, stroking it with my fingertips in a teasing motion. The way it twitched under my caress had me wrapping my hand around it. I pressed more kisses to him, making my way closer to it with my mouth. He started to harden, the blood rushing down to his cock as his arousal grew.

"Do you want your little whore to worship you? Show you how much she appreciates you?"

"Yes," he choked out on a shaky breath, his fingers tightening around the back of my head.

I licked my way down his length, feeling his dick jump against my tongue. He groaned like he was a man starving for my touch. It sent a tingle rushing down my spine. He'd gone down on me so many times, but I wanted him in my mouth. I wanted his cock to choke me, starve me of oxygen because it was like Francis told me last time we'd been intimate. He was my horseman. The one who liked to deprive me of orgasms until I was a panting, begging mess.

Famine.

"Tell me what you want, Frankie. Tell me how to make you feel good."

340

My fingers enclosed around his shaft, stroking while my mouth went to the tip, my tongue flicking out to curl around his crown.

"Wrap your lips around me."

I did as he asked, sucking him between my lips and swirling my tongue around him. He let out a soft sigh as his fingers stroked along my scalp.

"Good girl."

I hummed against his skin. Knowing I was making him happy filled the space inside me that craved their praise. It went hand in hand with when they degraded me. I liked it a little too much.

"Take me deeper, little whore. Use your tongue… show me how much you want my cock in your mouth."

My free hand curled tighter around his hip. I took him deeper until he hit the back of my mouth. My tongue curled around him and I used my other hand to stroke what I couldn't fit. There was a certain kind of power in having a cock in your mouth, knowing you could make the man it was attached to lose himself in you, in the pleasure you were giving him. Even when he rammed his cock down your throat and made it hard for you to breathe, you were still in control. You had him at your mercy.

I sucked him, making sure to get his dick nice and wet with each slide of my mouth along his shaft. The soft exhales he made and the way he held my head told me how much he wanted this. How much he needed me.

I love you, Francis Beaufort. I love you so much, it hurts my whole damn soul.

My hand slid from his cock to his balls, cupping them and stroking along the skin. He grunted, pressing his hips into me, forcing his cock to slide into my throat as I swallowed.

"Fuck, little whore, that's it."

With my mouth full, I couldn't tell him how much I needed this too. How I wanted to give him everything. Lay myself down and offer my body, my heart and my soul up as a sacrifice. All I could do was keep sucking him. Keep showing him I wanted him this way.

Francis and I had shared so many intimacies, but this was different. He was letting me have control when usually he was the one tying me down. And I loved him even more for it.

He went deeper, making me choke on his length. The way his silver eyes glowed as he stared down at me had my pulse spiking. My nails dug into his skin, but I didn't pull away. I wanted to give him all of me. Every single part.

"You're such a good little whore for me."

I pulled back slightly, slipping him from my throat before I hummed. The groan escaping his lips had me stroking him again with my fingers, wanting to work him up until he exploded. His fingers speared into the bun I'd put my hair in, keeping a hold of me so I wouldn't go anywhere. Didn't he know I had no intentions of leaving? I wanted to give him this.

"You feel so good. So fucking right. Fuck, Scar, I want to tie you up so fucking bad."

His cock popped out of my mouth as I shifted my head back. My tongue ran up his shaft, glistening with my spit.

"Do you want to see the way the metal chains leave indents on my skin?" I asked, cupping his balls again as I continued to run my tongue up and down his dick.

"Fuck, yes I do. I have these small ones to wrap around your chest. They'll look so beautiful against your skin."

"I want that, Frankie. It makes me feel beautiful when you stare at the indents. When you mark me with your ownership."

His resulting groan as I licked his balls made me smile against his skin. Then I sucked him into my mouth again, bathing the head of his cock with my tongue.

Honestly, the thought of him chaining me up turned me on far more than I expected it to. I loved the ropes. This didn't feel that different, only it would put more strain on me. Being at his mercy, feeling the fear, made me wet as hell. It drove me to crave darker, more depraved sex. The next time I asked Prescott to chase me, I wanted it to be dirtier... perhaps when it was raining so we'd get muddy while he fucked me until I cried.

First, I wanted Francis to wrap me up in his chains and make me see stars. He needed it. It was clear this was important to him, especially given he was scared to do it now. I trusted him with my life. I knew he wouldn't hurt me. I wanted to restore his faith in himself.

Francis had fixed me. I was going to fix him right back.

I slid my mouth down his shaft, enjoying the way his hips moved to meet me and his hand in my hair, encouraging me further.

"Fuck, harder, suck me harder."

Doing as he asked, I hollowed out my cheeks and gave him more suction. His head tipped back with his groan.

"What did I do to deserve you?" he muttered.

I wanted to tell him he didn't do a single thing. Francis was someone I could drown in, no matter what.

Working what I couldn't fit in my mouth with my hand, I went faster, wanting him to come. I needed it so fucking bad. My pussy throbbed, but I ignored it. This was about him. Making my man feel good. Soothing him. Bringing him a sense of peace.

He let out a strangled sort of moan before his head dropped down. The piercing look in his grey eyes almost had me stopping in my tracks, but his other hand wrapped around my head and he shoved his dick down my throat without warning. I gagged around it, the sound echoing around the room.

"Fuck," he grunted before erupting, spilling his cum down my throat.

I could do nothing but let him, holding myself there until he was spent, and he pulled out of my mouth. Choking a little, I swallowed. Francis stroked my hair in a gentle motion, reassuring me I was okay. I leant my face against his thigh, still clutching his hip. Letting him go felt like effort.

"Good girl," he murmured. "My good little whore."

I nuzzled his skin, practically preening for his praise. There was a deep-seated need inside me. One that desperately craved the words from their lips. The ones telling me I'd pleased them.

After a moment, I pulled away and shifted back towards the bed, climbing onto it. I took Francis' hand and encouraged him to get in bed. He pulled back the covers and got settled underneath them. I crawled up the bed, reaching out to grab the glass I'd left on the bedside table and taking a sip. Then I straddled his hips and leant over him, bringing my mouth to his. Francis kissed me, his lips melding with mine before his tongue probed the seam. It wasn't desperate and all-consuming, but reassuring and sweet.

"Take your clothes off," he ordered when he pulled away. "I want to feel you all over me as I fall asleep."

I pulled them off, wanting to give him exactly what he'd asked for. Sliding under the sheets next to him, I curled up against his side, loving the way he wrapped an arm around me, holding me to him. My hand brushed over his chest, coming to rest on his heart as I laid my head in the crook of his shoulder.

For a long minute, we were silent, then I kissed his skin and rubbed his chest.

"Frankie."

"Mmm?"

"Look at me."

He reached over and stroked my cheek, looking down at me with those beautiful eyes of his.

"I need you to know I trust you implicitly. You're not going to hurt me. It'll be you and me in the moment, okay? Nothing but you and me."

He shifted, turning on his side so our chests were pressed together and our mouths were breathing the same air. If I wasn't aware of how much I adored this man before, I certainly was now. He was my sun, stars, moon and sky. I couldn't imagine my life without the place of safety he provided me.

"You have no idea what that means to me, Scar... what you mean to me."

"I think I do."

He smiled, his lips brushing against mine.

"Should I bring the ropes out tomorrow, for... you know?"

He winked, which made me grin.

"For Drake?"

"Mmm.

"Yes… yes, you definitely should."

"Consider it done."

He kissed me again before settling back against the pillows and closing his eyes. I reached up and ran my fingers through his hair.

"I'm beginning to think you have a fetish for my hair," he murmured.

"I like that you stopped gelling it."

"I only did that for you… I noticed how much you like playing with it."

Could I love him more? Probably, but my heart was so damn full right then.

I leant closer, rubbing my nose along his cheek, which only made him smile.

"Open your eyes."

He did it slowly, meeting mine with an intense gaze. I almost got lost in those silver depths, but I had something to say to him. My hand slid down and cupped his cheek.

"Maybe now isn't the time to admit this, but I can't keep it locked away any longer."

His lips parted, but he didn't make a sound.

"I love you."

Before he could actually respond, I pressed a kiss to his lips, wanting to cement my words with it.

"I love you," I whispered, kissing him again. "I need you to know I can't live without you and I love you."

His arms tightened around me, his tongue slipping into my mouth to deepen the kiss. His body rubbed against mine, the friction making me ache. When he released my mouth, he flipped me onto my back, pressing between my legs and rocking his hips into mine. He pinned my hands by my head, leaning closer to run his tongue along my jaw to my ear.

"I can't live without you either," he murmured. "And I'm going to show you how much by fucking you until you scream my name, claw my back and beg for more."

I shook underneath him, trembling with the need for him to make good on his threat.

"Please," I whispered, feeling his dick hard against me. "Sucking your cock made me so wet."

It didn't matter if he hadn't said it back. I had to get the words out. To reassure Francis, he was in my heart for life. Because I really did love this man to death.

"Then it's time I took care of this pussy so my little whore doesn't go without."

His hand slid between us, notching his cock to me, and with one thrust of his hips, he drove home. He made good on his threat to fuck me until I screamed his name in ecstasy and bliss. When we lay together afterwards, I whispered how much I loved him all over again until his breathing evened out and he drifted off. He'd been through a lot today. Knowing I could help alleviate his worries and pain somewhat allowed me to fall asleep without a single care in the world.

But the world was waiting for us. Waiting to sink its claws so deep and pull apart the pocket of peace we'd forged. And it was only a matter of time before it came knocking on our door to wreak havoc on us again.

THIRTY SEVEN

SCARLETT

I walked into the play space with my head held high. The only stitch of clothing I had on was a little black silk robe that fell to mid-thigh. Considering what I was about to engage in, I should have walked in naked, but I was apprehensive about it. The last time I'd been in this room, Drake had punished me. And I wanted to erase the memory. Replace it with something new. Tonight was about forgiveness and coming together as a unit. The way we were always meant to be.

Well, I wasn't sure our relationship with each other would have grown into this if I'd not been stolen from their lives. If it would have turned sexual with anyone else but West. And yet, I couldn't imagine not having them this way.

My four men were all bare as they waited for me. And they were *mine*. No one else could have them. They belonged to me and I to them. My mouth watered at the sight of their perfect, hard, naked bodies. I was an incredibly lucky woman.

Prescott sat in an armchair facing the end of the bed while the other three were sitting in front of him. They were all waiting for me.

I'd had a very long discussion with Prescott about the dos and don'ts of this evening after we got upstairs when we were done with work for the day. This was about me, after all, and what I wanted and needed. I'd already prepared myself in every way I could before I came in here. I didn't want anything getting in the way of pleasure.

Walking over to Prescott, I laid my hand on his shoulder. His blue eyes met mine as he turned his head up towards me. The smile he gave me set my heart on fire.

"Hello, little lamb. Are you ready to begin?"

I leant down and pressed a kiss to his forehead, stroking his cheek in the process. It would be a while before he got to touch me, so I savoured his skin on mine.

"Yes," I whispered in his ear. "Knowing you're going to be watching has me wet already."

I pulled away before he could respond, straightened and dropped my robe. The way four sets of eyes darkened as they roamed over me made me feel powerful. It reassured me I was in charge. In control.

I stepped towards the bed, keeping Prescott at my back. My hand drifted to the biggest scar on my stomach from the surgery to bolt my pelvis back together. At some point, I would need to have a conversation about what it meant to me to have lost the ability to have children, but not now. Not when this was about forgiveness. About carving out a small pocket of time for the five of us to come back together now so many of our secrets were behind us.

"Francis, go sit up against the headboard," Prescott said.

He did as Prescott asked, shifting up the bed until his back was to the headboard. Francis' silver eyes glinted in the low light with such wickedness, I was hard-pressed to stay where I was.

"Our little lamb told me she's wet. I want you to check, Drake."

I stepped closer to Drake, who wrapped his hand around my hip and tugged me closer.

"Slide your fingers between her legs."

Drake held onto my hip with one hand, staring up at me with those terrifyingly beautiful indigo eyes of his. He ran his other hand up my inner thigh and delved between my lips, letting out a little exhale when he met my wetness.

"She's soaking," he murmured.

"Is she? Are you sure? I think you need to inspect further... with your mouth."

Drake took one of my legs, pushing it up over his shoulder and forcing me up on my tiptoes to match his height. He held onto me as he buried his face in my pussy, his tongue seeking out my wet hole. My hands went to his head to steady myself as he licked me. I let out a strangled moan of pleasure.

"Does she taste good?" came Prescott's voice.

"She tastes like a wet dream," Drake said, pulling back slightly to look up at me again. "And she's ready for cock."

The deep rumble of his voice sent shivers down my spine.

"Good. Go sit on Francis' dick, little lamb. Show him how much you appreciate him getting so hard for you."

Drake released me, setting my leg back down on the ground. I stroked his hair before I crawled on the bed towards

Francis. He already had his hand wrapped around the base of his cock, so I could slide right down on it when I reached him. We both groaned in unison at the intrusion. He wrapped his hands around my hips and encouraged me to ride him.

"Lean forward, let us see you fuck him."

The demand from Prescott had me shifting the angle of my hips so the rest of them could see the way Francis' dick slid in and out of my pussy.

"I think that pretty mouth of hers is a little too empty. How about you go fill it for her, West."

I turned at the sound of Prescott's latest request, finding West moving towards us. He stood, wrapping his hand around the back of my head, and tipped it up to meet his eyes.

"Open, little Scar."

My mouth dropped open, and he didn't hesitate to slip his cock inside it. I curled my tongue around the tip, feeling him throb against it. Humming around it, I took his dick deeper, wanting him to give me the whole damn thing. I loved his dick so much. The things he did with it made my insides clench. Francis' hands tightened on my hips as he let out a grunt.

"That's it, fuck her mouth. Don't be gentle," Prescott ordered, "make her feel it."

West shunted his hips forward, burying his cock halfway down my damn throat in one brutal thrust. I gagged, my hand going to his thigh as my other curled around Francis' shoulder. West pulled back and shoved his way in again, doing exactly as Prescott said. He fucked my mouth without mercy. And I was drowning in the pleasure of it.

"You're looking a little forlorn there, Drake... how about you go fill her last little hole? I know she's prepped herself well for us."

I could tell by the sound of Prescott's voice, he was enjoying this a little too much. I wanted to look around and see if his hand was wrapped around his dick, but West had his hand in my hair now, fisting it between his fingers to keep me still.

I felt Drake rather than saw him when he moved to sit up on his knees behind my back. The pop of a cap signalled he was about to fill me up real fucking good. One of the things I'd done before coming in here was to stretch myself out for them and lube up so they could fuck me any way they wished. Well, any way Prescott ordered them to.

Drake wrapped a hand around my shoulder before pressing the head of his dick to my hole.

"Bear down," he murmured in my ear, his breath fluttering across it.

I did as he said, stilling my movements to make it easier for him to enter me. I yelped around West's cock as Drake slid inside me, the stretch making me dig my nails into Francis' shoulder. He let out a little grunt but didn't tell me to let go. I couldn't help it, Drake was thick. Combined with Francis in my pussy, it was a lot to take at once.

"Such a good little lamb, taking them all so well. Go slow with her, hmm? She needs a minute."

Drake was careful as he slid deeper, allowing me time to adjust to him.

"Fuck," he grunted in my ear.

I'd asked Prescott for this. Told him I wanted the three of them in me at once, but he got to pick who went where. There were other requests I had. He would oblige me in the order he saw fit. I hoped he would let me watch him stroke himself while the others fucked me. The thought of him watching turned me on. This time I was in my right mind, so I wanted to experience it all. Every single part with a clear head.

When Drake was finally seated inside me, I moaned around West's dick. He'd stopped fucking my mouth so hard while I was adjusting to the others' dicks. Drake pulled out a little way and thrust back in. Then he and Francis were making me rock back and forth on the two of them.

"None of you are allowed to come yet," Prescott's voice cut through our little foursome. "Well, except our little lamb. She gets to come as much as she likes."

"Are you serious?" Drake ground out.

"Yes. This is about her pleasure, remember? We're earning her forgiveness."

"Jesus. First, I get West ordering me around and now you," Drake muttered.

West snorted, shoving his dick deeper in my mouth.

"You can't tell me you didn't enjoy me forcing her to suck your dick, not to mention all the blood."

I couldn't make a comment, considering my mouth was full, but I was amused by their little discussion. Especially Drake's reaction. He needed to lighten up.

"Wait, you actually allowed West to tell you what to do?" Francis asked.

"It was his punishment for her," Drake said, his voice sounding all defensive. "I wasn't going to interfere with that. And he's right. I did enjoy it."

"Then quit grumbling about me telling you what to do," Prescott said. "Also shut up and fuck her, you're ruining my show."

The three of them shut up and concentrated on giving it to me. The fullness was unlike anything else I'd ever experienced. As they ground harder into me, I squirmed on their cocks while West continued to ram his down my throat, leaving me lightheaded from the lack of oxygen. He must have sensed it was too much for me, as he pulled out enough to let me breathe properly. Stroking my jaw, he stared down at me with heat flaring in those amber depths.

"Look at you, little Scar, being such a good slut for us."

"West!" Drake interjected.

"She likes it, don't you, Scar? You're our good little slut."

I moaned around his cock. I more than just liked it, I loved the way he degraded me. We'd crossed over a line the night Stuart had threatened me and I'd gone to West. He'd broken me down while still making me feel like a queen in his eyes. His little warrior. It's what I felt like when he called me his slut. I reclaimed the word as my own. And I wasn't the least bit ashamed of it.

"Mmm, she does like being our whore," Francis agreed, his hand leaving my hip and digging between us, seeking out my clit.

"Our dirty slut is loving being filled by three dicks. I can see it in your eyes, little Scar. You want us to use and abuse you."

I moaned again.

I want it so badly. Please use me.

This was exactly how I imagined being with them while Prescott told them how to fuck me. And it felt so good. Even better now it was on my terms. It was me who had initiated it. I wasn't on anything. It wasn't for some fucked up game. It was because I wanted it. We wanted it. We needed this together.

And as Francis stroked me while I got fucked by the three of them, I found myself unable to hold back. My body shook as I cried out around West's cock. The waves of my orgasm rushed through me, leaving me boneless and limber. It was almost too much, but I didn't try to pull away from them. I didn't ask them to stop because I trusted Prescott to know how much I could handle. He knew what I needed, not only because I'd told him, but he knew my body like the back of his hand.

When I came down to earth, I leant back against Drake, feeling him wrap his arm around me to keep me upright. The three of them stilled and West slid his cock from my mouth, letting me pant, sucking in breath after breath.

"I would call you good boys, but you might deck me for that," Prescott said.

I snorted while I felt Drake let out a low sound of annoyance.

"Now, it's time to switch it up a little. West, you sit in the middle of the bed. Francis, you tie Scarlett's hands above her head. Make her ride West."

It hadn't escaped my notice that West's preference was to fuck me from behind. And I had specifically asked Prescott to address my little issue with West. I wanted to see his face. Needed to see how he came apart as he gave it to me. I wasn't going to force the kissing thing, but this... this needed to be remedied.

Once upon a time, West had made love to me when we'd been sixteen. Tonight, I wanted to see if that side of him still existed. The only way I could do it is if I could see his face. And I hoped it would go a little way to healing the breach between us. I would do anything to fix West and me.

Prescott had been right when he said I loved West first. I loved him so fucking much, I bled with it. And somehow I had to find a way to reconcile the man he was now with the boy he'd been when we were kids.

THIRTY EIGHT

WEST

I did as Prescott told me, sitting in the middle of the bed. Unlike Drake, I wasn't going to complain about being ordered around, considering I knew all of this was Scarlett's doing. She wanted this. She and Prescott had spent an hour talking before dinner, going over the details. And I was trying to make her happy by not being combative. There was no point when this would be enjoyable for all of us.

Things between Scarlett and me had started to improve, but I knew we had to have a long conversation about the past. It was a black cloud hanging over the two of us, making it impossible to move forward in the way we both wanted.

Drake slid out of Scarlett and sat against the headboard. She got off Francis and came closer to me. I was on my knees and she made no bones about sitting in my lap, facing me. Her hand went between us, stroking along my cock before she rubbed it against her pussy. I stared at her, aware this was the first time we'd be facing each other when she was in her right mind. The last time we'd all fucked her together, she'd sat in my lap, but she was high on E, so it wasn't the same.

Scarlett lowered herself down on me, making me grunt as my cock was encased in her hot, wet little pussy. She had her other hand on my shoulder to steady herself. My hands went to her hips, wanting to keep her upright.

Francis got up, picking up the ropes he'd left on the bed and came over to us. He gathered up both Scarlett's hands, binding her wrists together and attaching the rope to the metal ring above us. Her arms were raised up in the air, leaving her at our mercy.

"Are you going to fuck me?" she whispered as her eyes met mine.

Our faces were so close together, within kissing distance, and it fucked with me. I couldn't look away from her. My hand slid from her hip, up her chest, until I met the scars I'd given her. I stroked them, then wrapped my hand around her neck, holding her in place.

"Is that what you want? For me to fuck you real good, my dirty little slut?"

"Yes," she breathed, her eyes going to the word she'd carved into my skin. The cuts were still healing, but I was proud as fuck of it. Of her name on my skin.

The rest of them knew about it, but tonight was the first time they'd seen the word in the flesh since Scarlett cut into me. And none of them said a word about it. It's like they finally understood why me and Scarlett needed this. They were our unspoken feelings displayed on our skin.

"We better ask Pres if I can give it to you then."

It took her a long moment before she broke eye contact with me to look over at Prescott, almost as if she was reluctant to. We sat side on to his position. My eyes went to him too, finding the guy with his hand around his dick, watching us with lust-filled eyes. I almost rolled mine. Typical Prescott getting off on watching us. I couldn't deny it was hot, but I wasn't into voyeurism the way he was.

"I think she needs gagging, don't you, West?" Prescott said, with a twinkle in his eyes.

My dick twitched at the reminder of how hard I'd fucked her while she moaned through her arousal drenched knickers. It was the hottest sex I'd had in my entire life. And I craved more of it with her.

"Fuck yes, she does."

"There's one in the drawer."

He waved a hand towards the drawers we kept next to the bed. Francis moved over to grab it, pulling it out and bringing it back over. He fit the ball-gag in Scarlett's mouth, securing it behind her head.

"Now you can fuck her and make sure to draw it out... make her want to beg to come even though she can't."

I gripped her hip tighter and thrust up, making her take all of me. She moaned around the gag as I did it again.

"And our edging king can help you along there. Touch her, Francis. Make her crazy whilst he fucks her."

Francis knelt behind Scarlett and ran his fingers up her back while I continued to give it to her, my fingers tightening around her neck. Then I shifted back on my knees, changing the angle to give Francis better access to her body. The ropes around her wrists kept her from moving too far with me. He leant his chin on her shoulder. His hands cupped her breasts, caressing them.

"This is what you want, little whore?" he murmured in her ear.

I stroked her neck with my thumb, making her tremble while Francis pinched her nipples. Scarlett moaned around the gag, drool pooling at her lips. He gripped them harder. She bucked, her pussy clenching around my cock with the movement. I grunted and gave it to her harder in response, my hand around her hip almost bruising with my grip on it.

Francis let go of one of her breasts, ran his hand lower to meet her clit, and stroked it in the most gentle and teasing manner I'd ever seen. She wriggled in our grasp, trying to encourage him to go faster, but he was deliberately keeping her on the edge. Her unintelligible noises behind the gag had me grinning.

"Look at that. Our little slut is so needy. She wants to come so badly, but we're not going to let you quite yet."

I watched her cheeks flush with embarrassment at my words even as she tried to rock against my cock while I fucked her. My fingers around her neck tightened to the point where she started almost choking around the gag.

"Your blushes are so fucking cute. Pity we all know how much of a desperate slut for cock you are."

"Jesus," I heard Prescott mutter. My eyes darted to him, finding his eyes fixed on the way Francis and I were playing Scarlett's body. I smirked before looking at Drake, who was also similarly fixated on us, his pupils completely blown, hiding away the indigo of his eyes.

Francis stroked her harder, making Scarlett squirm in her restraints. Not that she could go very far since she was sandwiched between us. I loosened my hold around her neck so she could breathe properly again. Tears ran down her cheeks as her chin dripped with drool.

Fuck, you're beautiful like this, little Scar.

"West, you have permission to come in her. But not before you two make her come," Prescott said a moment later, waving a hand at the three of us.

I redoubled my efforts to give it to her, making Scarlett yelp behind the gag. Francis pinched her nipple while he stroked her clit and kissed her shoulder.

Scarlett's eyes went to me. I could see the need in those hazel-green depths I loved so fucking much. The want. And I had a sneaking suspicion she'd asked Prescott to make this happen. To have me fuck her in a position where she could see me fall apart. Despite the fact, we were surrounded by the others and Francis was touching her, I couldn't help feeling as though the two of us were lost in our own bubble. It was the way those little whimpers behind her gag sounded like she was desperate to tell me how much she needed me.

"It's okay, little Scar," I whispered. "I've got you. Let go."

My fingers stroked down her throat, reassuring her I was right there fucking her the way she deserved. More tears slid down her cheeks, but I knew they weren't ones of pain. They were a cathartic release for her like she could finally embrace the side of herself that craved this kind of sex. The dark side of her little soul was on fire and it burnt for me. It burnt for all of us.

Her muffled cry signalled her climax right before she clenched around my cock. Her body bucked between me and Francis, making me growl in response. I was so close as she came, needing to fall apart with her, but something deep down made me wait, made me want her full attention on me when it happened.

The moment her body stilled, my hand left her throat, gripping both her hips as Francis pulled away. Then I fucked her harder, using her hips as leverage to give it to her without mercy. Her eyes remained on me.

"Take the gag out of her mouth," I demanded, not even caring what Prescott had to say about it.

Francis must have seen the determination in my eyes because he did as I said. Scarlett sucked in air before her tongue darted out of her mouth, licking up her dripping spit.

"I want you to come for me," she whispered. "Please."

Her words set me off. My cock erupted, making me let out a grunt, but my eyes remained on hers. I let her see what she did to me. I let her watch me come apart for her. And all I could see was her adoration reflected back at me. It reminded me of the day we'd lost our virginity to each other. The day we'd declared our love. It felt so fucking right to be with her like this. And then it was over all too soon as I slowed the thrust of my hips until we both were sitting there staring at each other, unable to look away.

Fuck, I love you, Scar. I love you so much it hurts to breathe. You are my world.

Perhaps the others realised this moment was significant, as none of them said a word. I reached up, cupping her cheek in my palm.

"My perfect little Scar," I whispered, drawing closer so I could wrap my arms around her and hold her close.

She let out a soft sigh as I buried my face in her neck and kissed her skin. We stayed like that, locked together until I softened and she shifted against me.

"Let her down," Prescott said.

Francis immediately started untying her, letting Scarlett drop her arms to my shoulders. She crawled off me, but not before planting a kiss on my cheek.

My attention went back to Prescott who had a rather devious smirk on his face. I wondered what the hell he had up his sleeve next. His eyes were on Drake, leading me to think what happened next was going to cause a ruckus.

"Give her the rope."

Francis handed Scarlett the rope he'd used to tie her up with. She tested the weight before giving Prescott a smile.

"A little birdy told me you've been practising knots, little lamb. I think it's time you showed us your skills." He pointed at Drake. "Tie him to the wall."

Drake's eyes widened, and he sat up straighter.

"What the fuck, Prescott? No."

"Excuse me? No is not allowed in this room."

Scarlett moved closer to Drake, ignoring his refusal as Prescott had given her a command.

"I don't give a shit. I'm not letting her tie me up."

"Drake," Scarlett's soft voice sounded, "don't you want to make me happy?"

That made him freeze in place. She crawled into his lap, laying the rope down on her legs. Then she was reaching up and stroking her fingers through his hair.

"I think you need to let me have control for once," she continued. "I want to find my Drake in there. And I promise I'll make it good for you."

He let out a breath. I could see the conflict in his eyes. He wanted to please Scarlett but giving up control was a big deal to him. I could understand his reluctance. However, he and Scarlett had to find a way to overcome the shit between them. And perhaps this was exactly what both of them needed.

"You really want this?"

"Yes, please... sir."

For a long moment, we all held our breath, wondering which way this would go. Then Drake raised his hands and put his wrists out to her in supplication. And that was a miracle in itself.

THIRTY NINE

PRESCOTT

I watched Scarlett take hold of Drake's hands and press a kiss to each of the insides of his wrists. Unable to stay in the chair any longer, I got up and moved to the bed in time to watch her pick the rope up and bind his wrists. The little furrow of concentration in her brow was so fucking cute. This woman. She was fucking everything. And getting to do this with her was a whole experience in and of itself. It wasn't like the other times I'd watched, not when she and I were in control of everything.

"Where's your knife?" I murmured to West, who was sitting next to me.

"On top of the drawers."

"Get it for me."

West shifted off the bed, eyeing me with a curious expression. Scarlett was busy tying Drake's hands to the ring above him. He looked distinctly unimpressed by proceedings, but he had no idea what I had planned for him next.

"Is this okay?" Scarlett said, turning her attention to Francis.

He moved closer and reached up, checking over the knots she'd made. He gave her a smile and stroked her hair when he was done.

"They're very good, little whore."

She leant closer to him. Francis took her cue and kissed her, letting their mouths meld together for a long moment. She was smiling and glassy-eyed when he released her. Then he moved back and sat next to me. He'd get his reward in a little while, but for now, it was Drake's turn.

Scarlett ran her hands down Drake's chest, giving him a smile. She reached out and grabbed the lube sitting on the shelf next to them. Then she squirted it out on her hand and coated Drake in it. He let out a harsh exhale at the way she was touching his cock. After wiping her hand when she was done, she leant towards Drake, pressing a kiss to his lips. Scarlett pulled back, her eyes full of mischief before she palmed his dick again and positioned herself over it, right where he'd taken her before. He grunted when she sunk down onto it. She arched her back, holding onto his shoulder to steady herself until she was fully impaled by him.

West was twirling the knife between his fingers, watching them with a raised eyebrow next to the bed.

"Give her the knife," I said.

West knelt on the bed and passed the knife to Scarlett. He sat down and watched her flip it open before she ran her finger along the blade. Drake's eyes fixed on the metal. I could see the cogs turning in his brain before heat flared in his expression.

"Cut yourself, little lamb, let him see you bleed for him."

She put her palm out and set the tip to the edge of her hand before she sliced downwards. It wasn't too deep, but she winced with the action. Red liquid pooled in the cut she'd made. She handed the blade back to West when she was done.

"Fuck," Drake hissed.

Without being prompted to, Scarlett took her bloodied palm and pressed it against her breast, rubbing the blood over it. She did the same with the other one. Then she pressed her palm to Drake's face, streaking blood across it before she offered her hand to his mouth.

"Do you want to taste me?" she murmured as she rocked her hips into him, giving them the friction they both clearly needed.

Drake didn't answer her. His tongue darted out and drew a line up her bloodied palm. She let out a little gasp. The way he groaned made her press her hand against his face so he could continue to lick at her wound. This could be considered incredibly fucked up, but it was Drake all over. This was his thing. He liked blood. And I certainly wasn't going to judge him for it.

Her other hand went to his chest. She moved up and down, riding him. They were watching each other intently until Drake closed his eyes and nuzzled his face into her hand.

"This is what you wanted to give me?" he asked in a low voice.

"Yes," she replied with a nod. "I wanted to show you I'm okay with it."

He opened his eyes and stared at her for a long moment.

"Kiss me."

She cupped his face and leant closer, pressing her mouth to his. Her hips moved faster as their tongues tangled with each other in a heated kiss. I'd never seen Drake attack a woman's mouth the way he was doing to her. He strained against the restraints, trying to get closer to her. It was so unlike the man we'd all come to know. The cold-hearted and emotionless Drake, who'd closed himself off from the world. No, this was Drake from before Scarlett's accident coming back to life in a small, but very significant way.

"Fuck, you're going to make me come."

"That's the idea," she murmured before kissing him again.

I wasn't going to tell her no. In fact, I needed to see it. Watch the indomitable Drake fall apart for a woman. For our woman.

"Well, fuck," Francis muttered next to me. "Never thought I'd see the day."

"Did you doubt her?" I murmured back.

"No, but... it's Drake."

I grinned, but my attention was fully on the scene in front of us. Scarlett was moving faster now, her forehead pressed to Drake's as she fucked him. There was nothing he could do but let her set the pace. Let her have full control over him.

"Come for me," Scarlett ordered, increasing her movements and digging her other hand into his hair. "Do it. Come inside me."

His harsh pant was the only warning she got. I watched him close his eyes and his body jerked with the impact of his climax. Scarlett pressed her mouth to his again, kissing him through it until he stilled.

Scarlett pulled back, giving him a gentle smile when he opened his eyes. She stroked his face when he smiled back. Drake never smiled unless he was with us. I gave them another moment before I decided it was time to move this along.

"West, can you please clean up Scarlett's hand and chest? Francis, let Drake go. When you're done, come over here with her. I'm done watching."

The two of them immediately got started on the tasks I'd given them. Scarlett sat in West's lap while he cleaned her up and wrapped her hand. He cleaned her chest of blood with a wipe before cleaning her up a little below too, considering she'd had two of them come inside her. Francis let Drake go, then came back to sit by me, waiting for Scarlett. Drake didn't move. I had a feeling he wanted to savour what just happened.

Scarlett came over to us when West was finished.

"How would you like me?" she asked with a tilt of her head.

"Sit on Francis."

She crawled into Francis' lap and took him in her arms, sinking down on his still hard cock. He let out a grunt, his hands going to her hips. West chucked me over the lube. I slathered my cock in it, setting the tube down and settling myself behind her back. Scarlett encouraged Francis to lie back against the covers and leant forward, allowing me better access. I gripped her cheek and spread her for me, notching my dick to her tight little entrance. Pressing against her, I felt resistance for a moment before I slid inside. She let out a little groan of pleasure. Scarlett was becoming quite adept at taking two of us at once. In fact, I was pretty sure she enjoyed it more than we did, the corrupt little thing she was.

"Fuck me, Pres," she hissed. "Please, fuck me."

I gripped her shoulder and pulled her upright, flattening her against my chest and pushing into her.

"Is this what you want, my little lamb? You want my cock?"

"Yes, yes, yes."

I thrust up, going ever deeper inside her.

"You want us both, don't you?"

The whine from her lips was her only answer. Pulling back, I did as she asked and fucked her.

"Watching you is so fucking hot, you know. Makes me so hard for you," I whispered in her ear as Francis began to fuck her too, his movements slower than mine. "You're stunning. The most beautiful creature I've ever seen. You're like a goddess, especially when they fuck you with no mercy. Watching you in all your regal glory is the best sight in the whole damn fucking world. You're our queen, sweetness."

"Pres, quit being so perfect."

I let her go then, grinning as I pushed her forward and gripped her hips. Francis moved his hands down to her thighs to allow me to fuck her harder. She pressed her body to Francis' and took his lips in a long, lingering kiss. Her hands curled around his shoulders, holding on for dear life while I took her, driving her and Francis ever higher.

"Harder, give me more," she whimpered a minute later. "I need to feel it tomorrow."

I pulled her up again and encouraged Francis to sit up too. The three of us held onto each other, our bodies moving together in unison to give her what she needed. Francis buried his face in her neck as I gripped his side to give us both more leverage. His hand was around me, bracketing Scarlett between us.

"Fuck," she cried out. "Yes, like that. Fuck!"

The way she was bucking against us had me hard-pressed not to come. I'd watched them this entire time, becoming more and more aroused by the sight of naked bodies pressed together in ecstasy. It wasn't just anyone, though. It was her and my best friends. That was all I wanted for the rest of my life. Us and her. I'd never wanted anything more.

"Come for us, little whore," Francis ground out. "Let us feel you."

"Frankie," she whined.

"Do it. Come. Now."

She ground against him a moment longer, then she was crying out and clamping down so hard on the two of us, my orgasm burst forward without warning. I let out a low grunt, erupting inside her. She clenched harder and then I could feel Francis throbbing through the thin wall separating us. His groan let me know he was unable to hold back, either. We shuddered against each other, never wanting it to end. It was a moment I didn't think I would ever forget.

This whole night had changed something between us. The way they'd allowed Scarlett control of the situation through me was a turning point. It showed the five of us wanted to make this work even though we had so many dangerous waters to navigate before we'd be free. And we needed to cement our bond this way. It felt natural for it to happen like this.

I let go first, pulling out of Scarlett and sitting back on my hands, panting wildly. Scarlett didn't move off Francis straight away. Her hands went to his hair, and she pulled him back to stare into his eyes. Unspoken words passed between them before she kissed him. Releasing him, she pressed her mouth to his ear. I couldn't be sure of what she whispered to him, but it sounded very much like "I love you."

Scarlett slid off him and came to me, curling herself around my body and holding me tight against her. I watched Francis' expression. He seemed to be reeling from what had passed between them. Then he shook himself and schooled his features.

"Thank you," Scarlett said, "all of you... I needed this."

I stroked her hair.

"You're welcome, little lamb."

"Take me to bed, Pres. I want to stay with you."

"You going to let me clean you up first?"

She nodded before letting me go. Before we left, Scarlett hugged the others and kissed Drake and Francis, saying goodnight to each of them. She took my hand and let me lead her out of the room, back to mine. We went into my bathroom. I set her on the counter before cleaning her up thoroughly. Then I did the same to myself.

The two of us got into bed after I dressed her in a sleep shirt and shorts. I'd pulled boxers on, as they were what I usually slept in. Scarlett curled up on my chest, her hair brushing across my skin.

"Did you just tell Francis you love him?" I asked, unable to help myself.

"Yes, but it wasn't the first time... that was last night. He hasn't said it back yet, but I'm not worried. I know he loves me."

"You sound awfully sure of yourself."

She raised her head and looked at me.

"Frankie needs something before he can admit it to me. And I'm okay with that."

I stroked her hair back from her face.

"And what's that?"

"To chain me up so he can erase what happened with Chelsea."

I smiled.

"Well, aren't you a perceptive little thing. I take it he told you what happened."

She leant her chin on her fist where it was resting on my chest.

"He's been hurting over it for a long time. And I want to make it better for him. He deserves that, especially after the way he's taken care of me."

If I hadn't been aware of it before, it was very clear now. We all needed Scarlett. She was the missing part of us. The light in the darkness. Except our girl was just as dark as we were. She just shone with it in a different way.

"You're exactly what all of us need, you know that? Our perfect girl."

She blushed but didn't look away.

"I forgive you, Pres… I forgive you for everything. I don't want to live in the past any longer. Our future is what's important." She flattened her palm on my chest where my heart lay. "And I want it with you and them. We belong together."

My heart burnt with her words.

"I don't think I deserve you."

Not after everything we've done to you even though you've forgiven me.

"Too bad you don't have a choice in deciding what you deserve. That's up to me. And I've decided we're going to make it through this with each other. So you just have to deal with it."

Then she clapped three times, turning out the lights and laid her head back on my chest. I didn't have a response for her, so I kissed the top of her head and closed my eyes.

"Goodnight, my king," she whispered against my skin.

"Sleep well, my little lamb."

And tomorrow, we would start on that journey to the future she wanted... I hoped.

FORTY

SCARLETT

As my phone rang in my hand, the sound blaring in my ears, I knew I couldn't hide from this forever. A part of me had known it wouldn't be the last I heard of Stuart after I kicked him in the balls and ran. Perhaps the boys would have told me not to answer it, but I didn't want to run or hide from this. If the boys wanted Stuart dead, then we had to face this head-on. We had to move against him. It meant taking this risk and having a conversation with the man who'd stolen the last ten years of my life from me.

I brought the phone up to my ear and sat down on the sofa. The boys were still asleep, but I woke up early and slipped from bed. Prescott had been flat out on his back, the morning sun dappling his face. I stared at his handsome features, memorising every last one. The love I had for him was unfathomable. I didn't know it was possible to love one person so much, let alone four. The truth was... I was in love with

Prescott, West, Francis, and Drake. No matter what they'd done in the past, I couldn't help the way I felt about them.

Last night had meant everything to me. It changed things between the five of us. It went a long way towards showing me they were willing to do anything for me. Their giving up control had given me more confidence in myself. I wasn't weak. And I wasn't going to allow Stuart to make me feel that way ever again.

"Hello, Stuart," I said, pressing to accept the call. "You took your time."

I had expected him to be on my case straight away, but clearly, he'd taken some time to think about what he was going to do about me.

I heard him scoff before he answered.

"Perhaps you're just not that important, Scarlett."

I pressed my lips together. He was trying to put me on the back foot. Of course he was. I shouldn't have expected anything less.

"What's more important to you than destroying the Horsemen?"

"That ridiculous nickname. Honestly, I would have expected better than for you to fall for that malarkey. Then again, you've always been a disappointment, haven't you?"

Don't let him affect you. Don't do it.

"What do you want?"

"I know you're hiding in that ivory tower of theirs so I won't come after you."

I hadn't left the building since I'd run from him. Not even to go out and get Drake lunch. Instead, I'd made it here. In fact, I did it for all of us. The boys had decided they weren't going to replace Tonya, and I'd work for all of them. It wasn't exactly taxing considering I'd learnt their routines in the time I'd been here.

"You've always needed someone else to protect you, haven't you, Scarlett? It's pathetic really, that you've been so blinded to their charms."

"I haven't been blinded to anything except doing what you wanted me to. But that's what I get for being locked away in a prison for ten years, isn't it?"

"Do you think they're not going to throw you away the moment you're no longer useful?"

I gritted my teeth, clenching my fist in my lap.

"No. They aren't."

They care about me. They were and still are my best friends, but we're more now. So much more.

I was tired of hearing him railing against them. Tired of him acting like he was better than my four men. Stuart wasn't any better. Who kidnaps a sixteen-year-old girl from a hospital on a hunch she might know something about his sons' disappearance, then keeps her captive? It was just plain fucked up on so many levels.

You could say the same about the four boys who killed for you.

I could and I would, but somehow, it was different. They'd done it to protect me. Stuart wanted to hurt me and the boys. He didn't care about me at all.

"Your delusions are going to get you killed."

It was my turn to scoff.

"The only person who wouldn't care if I died is you."

"After your little stunt on Saturday, I should kill you. You're worthless to me now, Scarlett. Absolutely worthless. I would say you're their perfect little whore who will only give them heirs, but you can't even do that, can you? No, you're fucking damaged goods now."

My throat constricted with his words. I put my hand to it. Of all the things he could throw at me, that was the very worst. I'd never got over it. Never. While I might have buried my emotions regarding the fact the accident had stolen my ability to have children, he knew where to hit me the hardest.

"Shut up," I whispered.

My mind registered the sound of footsteps, but I didn't look up. My eyes were fixed on the floor. His words hurt me so fucking much. They made me feel broken. Like I really was damaged goods after the accident.

"Such a pity, isn't it? The only other thing you'd be good for and you can't even do that. I suppose they'll just have to wear you out until they get bored with you, won't they?"

You're not worthless because you can't have kids. You're just not.

The surgery they'd performed to bolt my pelvis back together had left me with damaged fallopian tubes. There was too much scarring. If they hadn't performed it, I would have never been able to walk again, but losing my ability to conceive was a heavy price to pay. I hadn't even had a choice in the matter, either. All of it happened while I'd been unconscious. It had to have been my mother who told them to save my life. Told them to do whatever was necessary to allow me to walk again. But I didn't know that for sure.

"Shut up," I said, a little louder this time.

"You never really had much value, that's why you felt the need to whore yourself out to them."

Something inside me snapped. Enough was enough. He'd been my abuser and my worst nightmare for far too long. I wasn't going to stand for it any longer.

I jumped up from the sofa, my hand balled at my side, and my whole body flooded with rage.

"Shut up! Just shut the fuck up. I'm not worthless. I'm not a whore and I'm not fucking damaged goods. I'm not going to sit here and listen to your shit any longer. I'm fucking done. You don't control me anymore, Stuart. I will never forgive you for all the shit you put me through. Never, you hear me? Fucking never. I hate you. I fucking well hate everything about you and your fucking wife. You are both liars."

I'd practically screamed it down the phone to him, not even caring when I looked up and found four sets of eyes on me. There was no going back now. Prescott, West, Francis and Drake had heard every word of my diatribe against Stuart.

"What did you just say to me?"

It was as if the red mist had settled over me the same way it had done when I'd stabbed a man to death. I wanted to rip Stuart's face off.

"You fucking heard me. I hate you. I am never doing anything you say again. In fact, you can go fuck yourself."

"You little bitch. If you think I'm going to stand for this, you are out of your fucking mind."

"I don't give a fuck any longer. You kidnapped me and kept me locked up like a fucking prisoner, tried to brainwash me, beat me and locked me in a cold fucking cell when I did anything you didn't like and made me feel like I was nothing. So go fuck yourself. I hope you fucking die."

I could hear him suck in a breath like he couldn't believe I would say such things to him.

"What?"

"You heard me. I know the truth, Stuart. I fucking know you kidnapped me and held me captive for ten years."

For a long moment, there was silence on the other end of the phone. My chest heaved with the anger coursing through my veins. My eyes were fixed on the four men of my past. I'd admitted so many things in the space of a few minutes. And I had no idea what they felt about me telling Stuart I knew the truth.

"So, it's come to this, has it? You remember who they are." He let out a little chuckle. "Did you know that's what I wanted? For you to remember them and what they did so you could tell me the truth. But I think you have no intention of doing that, do you?"

I would never tell him what Prescott, West, Francis and Drake had done to his twin sons. It was a secret I'd take to the grave.

"No."

"Then listen very closely, Scarlett. Your days are numbered. I'm going to come for you and you won't survive it. None of you will, but I'm going to start with you. They stole my sons from me. Keeping you for ten years wasn't enough. I will end you permanently. Only then will they understand what they've done."

I didn't want to listen to him any longer. I couldn't. Not when he'd threatened my life. And the lives of my men. Without even ending the call, I threw the phone halfway across the room, letting out a roar of fury. Then I was running towards it where it had landed on the floor near the dining table. I stared down at it, hating the very sight of that damn phone and the man on the other end of it.

"Go to hell, you piece of shit!" I screamed before I picked up a chair.

I slammed down the leg of it on the phone again and again.

"I hate you. I fucking hate you."

The phone was a mess of bent plastic and metal by the time I was done with it. The screen was practically annihilated. I panted and realised I'd started crying as tears slid down my cheeks. Setting the chair down next to the demolished phone, my chest caved in and before I knew it, my legs buckled. My knees slammed into the wooden floor and horrifying sobs erupted from my mouth.

"I hate him. I hate him so much."

Pain, hatred, and fury raced through me. I couldn't deal with all the emotions driving through my system. It hurt so fucking bad. My chest constricted and my whole body shook with the violence of them. It ruptured my very being and splintered it into a thousand pieces. The person who'd abused me had threatened to kill me. And not just me, he was going to kill the men I'd fallen in love with too. I couldn't take it. I couldn't.

A pair of arms wrapped around me from behind. And that warm body pressed into me, pulling me back into their lap. I kept crying, my hands grasping their forearms. Through my tears, I could see tattoos across them.

West.

He didn't say a word, merely held me to him while I broke down. The horrors of the last ten years washed over me, drowning me in the memories of everything Stuart had done to me. All the beatings. All the name-calling and taunting. Everything.

"I hate him," I sobbed, my tears blurring my vision entirely.

"I know, little Scar," West murmured in my ear. "Do you remember what I told you?"

I choked back another sob.

"You'll kill anyone who's hurt me because I'm yours."

"So what am I going to do?"

"Kill him for me."

"That's right. We're all going to end his life for you."

And while it shouldn't have made me feel better, it did. Knowing they were going to rid the world of Stuart for me had my broken pieces stitching back together. They'd killed for me once before. They were going to do it again. And this time... I would help them.

FORTY ONE

DRAKE

My hands were balled into fists at my sides. While I was sure Scarlett had been through hell and back, hearing the truth of what Stuart had done to her was far worse than I'd ever imagined. He'd beat her. Fucking beat her. A girl who almost died. He made her life worse.

Francis, Prescott and I stood helplessly as West held onto our girl. Her pain bled from her pores. Her sobs echoed around my skull. And I couldn't take it.

I need to make it better for her. I have to.

Before I knew what I was doing, I'd walked over to them, undid my suit jacket button and knelt between West and Scarlett's spread legs. I took her face in my hands, tipping it up towards me. The tears falling from her beautiful eyes almost decimated me. She'd been in so much pain for so long. I couldn't begin to fathom the depths of it.

"One of you get me some tissues," I said to Francis and Prescott before levelling my gaze back on our girl.

She blinked as a little sob fell from her lips. I stroked her wet face with my thumb, wanting to show her I was here. Fuck knows I was terrible at comforting people. To be honest, both West and I were, but we were trying. Both of us had to try for her. Perhaps we should have left this to Prescott and Francis, but I didn't give a fuck. I couldn't stand by and watch her fall apart. My chest ached with a need to make the pain go away for her.

Leaning forward, I pressed a kiss to her forehead.

"I promise I'll make it hurt when he dies," I whispered. "I'll make him suffer for everything he's done to you."

"Drake," she whimpered.

"You'll never have to go through that again, Scarlett, not as long as I'm still breathing. I'll be your executioner. Let me do that for you. Let me make this right."

For a moment, she said nothing. I pressed more kisses to her face, desperately wanting her to know I would do anything to fix her broken soul. I'd fucked up so much with Scarlett. This was the one thing I was good at. Ending people's lives. And I'd do it for her in a heartbeat.

"You don't even know everything he did."

"Will you tell us?"

She nodded slowly. I don't know what Stuart said to make her break like this, but I was determined she wouldn't suffer at his hands or his words any longer.

"He... he threatened to kill me. He said he's coming for me. And all of you, but he's going to take me first so you can suffer like he has."

I sucked in a breath. There was no fucking way we would let Stuart get hold of her.

"That's not happening, you hear me? We won't let him have you. We'll keep you safe."

"I know you will. I trust you... all of you."

Her admission made my heart ache. All this time she'd kept saying we didn't have her trust, but now... now we'd proven we would do anything for her. She was going to trust us with her truth, and it meant everything.

"Will you let West take you over to the sofa?"

She nodded again, a fresh set of tears spilling down her cheeks. Even crying with red eyes and a blotchy face, Scarlett was still the most stunning woman I'd ever beheld. It was her inner beauty. She shone like a fucking beacon, guiding us to her, keeping us captive under her gaze. And I no longer wanted to fight the pull. I wanted to drown in it. Drown in her.

"Good girl," I murmured without thinking about it.

She let out a shuddering breath, then let go of one of West's arms to grab hold of me. Her fingers speared into my hair, dragging me even closer until her damp lips brushed mine.

"You have no idea how long I've waited to hear that from you," she murmured, pressing her mouth against mine.

Her kiss was urgent, like all of her feelings were pouring out of her with it. The longing, the need, the lust. And it was over all too quickly. She sat back against West's chest, closing her eyes and putting her fingers to her lips. Her other hand dropped from my hair, allowing me to stand up and straighten my clothes out.

West didn't immediately get up with her, seemingly content to let her decide when she was ready. Prescott had brought over the tissues, but I waved them away towards the sofa. We could clean her up there. He and Francis walked over to them and sat down. I followed them and tried not to allow my rage out. The anger built inside me like a ticking time bomb, just waiting for me to unleash it. It was directed solely at Stuart. What Scarlett had said to him on the phone was only the tip of the iceberg.

West finally helped Scarlett up. She wrapped her arms around him and whispered something none of us could hear. He nuzzled her hair before taking her hand and bringing her over to the rest of us. I expected her to sit with him, but she crawled into my lap instead. Francis handed me the tissue box. Pulling a few out, I took a hold of her chin and cleaned her face with them. She was still dressed in a sleep shirt and shorts, so hadn't got ready for the day yet.

Dumping the sodden tissues on the coffee table, I sat back and let Scarlett lean against me. Her hand tucked under my suit jacket and her head rested on my shoulder. I kept an arm around her while my other hand went to her bare thigh, stroking her soft skin with my fingertips.

"It didn't start immediately," she said, loud enough for all of us to hear. "After I woke up from my coma, they told me they were my adopted parents... but they always got upset if I tried to ask them about my biological ones."

Her fingers rubbed along my chest like she was worrying at it. It reminded me of every time she was nervous and she'd rub something between her fingers in her agitation.

"It took me months of rehab to learn to walk again. They got me a speech therapist to help me learn to speak again too. It was gruelling, but I was determined not to let what happened to me destroy my entire life." She sighed, her body deflating with the sound. "I guess it started when I was eighteen or nineteen. I can't really remember. I mean, the first time he got angry with me, that is. Like truly angry, to the point where I was sure he would hit me. I asked if I could leave the estate. I was tired of being cooped up and not allowed to go anywhere."

She shifted in my lap. No doubt the memories were painful for her to recall.

"He went ballistic, shouting and raging about how it was dangerous for me to leave. I didn't understand it at the time, but he scared me so much, I didn't ask again. A year later, I tried to run away. I just wanted to see something else, something new. I took my horse, Chocolate, and we rode for miles. It was so freeing... but then Mason found me and brought me back to the estate."

She stopped, turning her face into my neck and letting out a shuddering breath.

"Stuart hit me in the face repeatedly, leaving me with a swollen black eye. He shoved me down and kicked me in the ribs for good measure. Then he threw me into a room with no windows. It was just bare concrete walls and floor. The only thing I had was a bucket. That was it. He left me there for a week. His staff fed me and gave me water. It was the only time I saw anyone. He finally let me out when I agreed to apologise... and things were never the same again. I can't count the number of times he beat me up and threw me in there for stupid reasons. Like every time I woke up screaming from a nightmare... that's why I taught myself not to make a sound, so he wouldn't have a reason to put me in the cell."

Scarlett fell silent. My hand tightened around her thigh with my fury. How fucking dare he treat her that way. Like she was an animal, less than fucking human. I couldn't call myself a good man. But this? This was going too far. I maimed, tortured, and killed those who deserved it. Stuart hurt my girl for no good fucking reason.

I pressed my face to the top of her head, trying to push down the anger inside me. No fucking way I would take it out on her. She didn't deserve it. All I wanted to do was cherish Scarlett. To give her everything she needed. To make up for everything I'd done to her.

"No one stopped him," she said after a few minutes had gone by. "Not Phoebe and not Mason. The only other people I was allowed to interact with were his staff, and they turned a blind eye to it. I suppose he pays them enough to keep silent. After I tried to escape, he refused to let me go riding by myself and he upped his security. I never attempted it again after that, but it didn't stop the beatings. It didn't stop his rage. He... he made me feel worthless like I was nothing. His words hurt me worse than his fists. I knew I could recover from the beatings, but the things he said... they were worse."

She pulled her head from my neck, sitting up and meeting my eyes for the first time since she'd started talking.

"When he dangled the chance of freedom in front of me, I took it. I had to... the thought of staying locked up on the estate made me die a little inside." She let out a breath. "I'm so sorry for everything. For doing the things he told me to. For wanting to hurt all of you. I didn't know... I didn't... I'm... I'm sorry."

I let go of her thigh to reach up and cup her face.

"There is nothing for you to be sorry for, Scarlett. Nothing at all," I told her, trying to keep my voice even. "We didn't help matters either. This mess... it's our fault, not yours."

She shook her head.

"I don't blame any of you for what happened that night... you were protecting me. And my fall was an accident. I decided to come after you. I'm just as responsible for everything that went on as all of you are. Placing blame isn't going to get us anywhere. It's not going to change what happened. I just want... I want to move on."

My eyes went to West when she said it. His amber eyes were full of pain, like her saying what happened was an accident drove the knife in further. He blamed himself for being unable to save her, but none of us ever had.

"But there is one thing I have to talk about... I have to say."

I dropped my hand from her face, wondering what it was.

"The reason Stuart upset me so much on the phone was... was because he told me I was damaged goods." She looked down at her lap. "Because I can't... I can't have..."

She seemed to visibly steel herself.

"I can't have children of my own."

Scarlett had no idea we knew about it. We knew her life-saving surgeries had robbed her of her fertility. And I didn't want to say anything right then. Not when she'd been through too much today already.

"I hate that he uses it against me. It digs at the wound the whole thing left inside me. I know it doesn't make me any less of a woman, but it still hurts."

"You know we will never see you any differently because of that, don't you?" I said when she volunteered nothing further.

A tear slid down her cheek.

"I... I wasn't sure what you would think."

I looked at the others. All we'd ever needed in life was each other. Nothing else was necessary.

"I won't speak for anyone else, but I don't need that from you. I just need you, Scarlett. Only you. The rest doesn't fucking matter."

She looked up at me then.

"Are you sure?"

I stroked her cheek with my thumb, brushing away the wetness.

"Yes, but if you need to talk about it more, we're all here for you."

She shook her head.

"I'm... I'm not ready."

"When you're ready then."

She took my hand from her face and pressed a kiss to my palm. Her hand was still bandaged. The way she'd cut herself for me last night only made me fall deeper for this woman. She was so willing to accept the things we needed. And I wanted to give her the same courtesy in return.

"You can stay up here today, okay? I don't want you to come down to work. We'll manage without you."

"Thank you," she whispered.

"And I meant what I said. I will be your executioner. You just tell me who and I will end them for you."

Scarlett said nothing, but she gave me a sad smile. Then she slid out of my lap and went to Prescott. He enfolded her in his arms and kissed her hair.

"I love you for you, little lamb," he told her. "You're perfect to me."

"I love you too," she whispered before she let him go and crawled over to Francis, burying herself in his chest next.

He stroked her back and murmured something in her ear that I couldn't hear. She gave him a nod and rose to her feet. Her attention went to West then. He'd sat silently through this whole thing. She went over to him and dropped to her knees at his feet. Scarlett took a hold of both his hands and looked up at him.

"Will you stay with me... please?"

West was notorious for taking random days off during the week. I didn't care in all honesty. West was good at what he did. It wasn't so much he slacked off. When he was at work, he was laser-focused. He got things done in less time than most people because of it, so I never got on his case about his lack of attendance.

"As you wish, my little Scar."

I imagined those two were in for quite the conversation when the rest of us left to go downstairs for the day. All of us needed a discussion about what we were going to do regarding Stuart, but it could wait a day for her to recover. I didn't think Stuart would try anything straight away. Besides, she was safe in our penthouse. We wouldn't allow anyone to get to her here. No matter what, the four of us would protect our girl with our lives, just as we had done ten years ago when we ended the lives of Stuart's twin sons. Nothing would stop us from ending him and putting this whole thing to rest so we could get on with our lives without the threat of Stuart fucking Carver hanging over our heads. Nothing at all.

FORTY TWO

WEST

When the other three left to go downstairs after the five of us had breakfast, Scarlett sat next to me on the sofa and took one of my hands. She ran her fingers down the skull on the back of it. Then she took my other hand, touching the tip of her forefinger to the Gemini symbol on mine.

"This is for the twins… isn't it?"

"Yes," I replied, eyeing her warily.

She wanted to talk, that much was clear, but whether or not it was about us, I didn't know. Last time she'd told me if we talked about our relationship and the past, it might break us. Did she still feel that way? Or did she want to repair the breach ten years had left in its wake?

"Will you tell me about the rest?"

I took her hand and made her point to the next finger.

"The teardrop is for the girl we killed when she accidentally came upon us torturing someone for information about you."

I directed her hand to the next one. "Five for the men I killed when we were searching for you. And the sword is for the last man who gave us the missing piece to the puzzle of where they were keeping you."

"That's ten people, including Tonya."

I shrugged. I hadn't yet decided about how I would honour her death in ink, but when I did, I'd take Scarlett with me to Penn's place to get it done. She should be there with me.

Penn Harlow didn't tattoo just anyone. He had to like you for him to be willing to get his tattoo gun out. And Penn didn't like many people in this world. He did say he'd be more than willing to ink up my girl if she was ever that way inclined. Scarlett had made quite the impression on him. He'd told me the woman who stole my heart had to be a special kind of crazy and Scarlett was definitely that. I'd laughed, but I guess it was true. She was special. And a little fucked up.

"Those are the ones that died by my hand, Scar. It doesn't include the ones I tortured and Drake ended. I might like violence, but he likes death... he's fucking ruthless. There's a reason he told you he'd be your executioner."

She shivered and looked away.

"I don't know how I feel about that."

"That he'd kill for you?"

She shook her head as she slid her fingers in between mine.

"No. I shouldn't be okay with the fact you all would kill for me... but I am."

"Then what's the problem?"

"Is it my fault he's like that? I mean, he told me about Oscar and what happened, but I can't help feeling like I bound him to a promise and this is the result."

I frowned and stroked the back of her hand with my free one.

"What promise?"

"I think we were like eight or nine and I made him pinkie promise he would never leave me. He told me it's what made him never give up on me. He didn't want to break his promise."

Drake took his word seriously, but even so, a promise they made when they were that young? I was beginning to think I should have paid attention to Drake and his feelings for her a lot sooner.

"You didn't turn him into the person he is, little Scar. He did that all on his own. People react to pain in their own way. It's his coping mechanism. To shut down his emotions. You aren't responsible for it."

She looked at me then, a multitude of emotions flickering in her hazel-green depths.

"Is it wrong of me to miss the way we were? And I'm not talking about Drake. I miss us. I miss... you."

"No, it's not wrong."

It could never be wrong. I missed us too. The closeness. Our connection. The way she calmed my warring soul and how I made her reckless. Everything about her and me was beautiful and fucking tragic at the same time.

"What happened after I disappeared? What happened to you?"

There was only one way this conversation was going to go. And that was to give her the undiluted truth.

"I lost myself without you. It broke me. I became… cruel and violent. It was as if all the goodness had been ripped away and left me with nothingness."

The way tears brimmed in her eyes at my words had me pressing on. None of this was her fault. Not really.

"I blamed myself for not being able to save you. It consumed me. My… guilt. And the longer it took to find out where you went, the worse I got. It's like nothing mattered any longer. I did fucked up shit, didn't care about anything or anyone. I turned into someone no one recognised."

My fingers tightened around hers, not wanting her to go anywhere.

"Henry and Cynthia couldn't deal with me the way I was. They did try to get me help, but when I was…" I faltered and looked down at our hands.

You have to tell her.

There was no way out of this. She needed to know.

"I was diagnosed with an antisocial personality disorder when I was eighteen and they disowned me for it. The last time I saw them in person was the day they kicked me out. And I'd prefer to keep it that way. You know what Henry was like. He just got worse."

Scarlett let go of my hand, only to cup my face with both of hers. She tilted my face up, so I'd meet her eyes.

"Do you think that makes you broken?"

"Doesn't it?"

"No."

I didn't know if I believed her. Anyone who found out about my issues thought I was broken. They thought I wasn't right in the head. Well, the boys never treated me like I was a fuck up, but they were different. We were each other's family. Everyone else? They plain fucking sucked with their judgemental attitudes.

"I don't think you're broken, West. I would never think that about you despite all the shit that's happened since I came back." She dropped a hand from my face to her collarbone. "Even this doesn't make me think any less of you."

"But you told me I'm not your West any longer. I'm not the person you... you..."

I couldn't say it. I couldn't bring myself to.

"Do you think I would have come to you after the shit Stuart said to me if I didn't still want you?"

I swallowed. She had done that. I'd not hesitated to give her what she asked. In fact, it had changed things between us. Made me feel as though she trusted me a little more than she had done before. And now I knew she liked degradation, I made no bones about doing it in front of the others. Scarlett wasn't ashamed of her kinks, even if me calling her my little slut made her blush.

"You never told me what he said that night."

She sighed and stroked my cheek.

"He said many things about me being a whore and a slut for opening my legs for all four of you, but that's not the point. You were who I felt safe with after it happened. You helped me. I trusted you to break me and fix me again afterwards. I still need you so fucking much."

My heart ached like someone had wrapped a fist around it and squeezed. It was her tiny one, taking my breath away and stealing my ability to keep my feelings a secret any longer.

"I need you too."

There was no one on this earth I needed more than Scarlett. She was my one.

"Do you think we can ever get back to where we used to be?"

I ran my fingers along her bare thigh.

"I don't know... but I want to, or at least, to be in a place where we're okay."

Before I could stop her, she let go of me and crawled into my lap, straddling my thighs and wrapping her arms around my neck. I put my arms around her, feeling her soft, warm body pressed to mine. It calmed the part of me that craved destruction and violence. Put me on a more even kilter. She was my balm.

"I don't want you to feel guilty over the accident, West. I don't blame you for it. It was an impossible situation."

My arms tightened around her.

"I didn't save you," I whispered, "and you almost died, Scar. You almost fucking died... and—"

"It wasn't your fault. Please stop blaming yourself for something you had no control over."

"But you can't..."

She pulled back and looked at me as my hand drifted from her back to her stomach.

"I know I can't, but it's still not your fault."

The sadness in her eyes cut me.

"Do you want them, Scar? Tell me the truth. I need to know I didn't ruin everything for you."

Her hands went to my hair, stroking through the strands and brushing against my scalp.

"It's a moot point. It doesn't matter if I do or not. I can't."

"I don't care. I need to know."

I kept my hand on her stomach. Her worth had nothing to do with her ability to conceive. She was perfect in my eyes, no matter what.

"When you can't have something, your idea of the future changes. It might take me time to deal with my feelings on the matter, but it doesn't change the facts. I don't need children, West. I need you, Drake, Frankie and Pres. We are a family."

She pulled me closer by my hair, resting her forehead against mine.

"You ruined nothing. And if we're ever going to get past this, you need to forgive yourself."

How fucking true were her words. I wasn't blind to the fact.

"I don't know how."

"I'll help you… but you have to let me."

My hand slid up from her stomach to grip her throat. I stroked my thumb down her pulse point. She sighed into my touch.

"Don't you know I'd do anything for you, little Scar?"

"Even burn down the world?"

"Especially that."

She smiled and shook her head against mine.

"I don't want you to burn the world. Just make it safe for us to be together as a family."

It's not like I wouldn't have done it before, but now she'd specifically tasked me with it. Make it safe for us. It meant destroying everything and everyone who threatened us. I had two people front and centre on our kill list.

Mason and Stuart.

I would quite happily off Phoebe as well, but she wasn't as important as the other two. If I put Mason's father on that list, no doubt Drake would tell me why it wasn't an option. We would have to find another way to get him off our case, especially when we wanted to kill his son and his best friend. Those were things we'd have to discuss, but not today. Not when Scarlett had been through too much already.

"As you wish."

She turned in my lap and rested her head on my shoulder. A little noise of contentment sounded in her throat. All I could think about was how she'd cuddle up to me when we were younger at every available opportunity. And how it felt so right to have her in my arms now.

"Tired?"

"Yeah," she sighed, nuzzling my chest.

Her affectionate gestures were something I hadn't been expecting. Hell, I didn't know she would be so okay with my diagnosis, either. It's not like I went around telling people about it, but this was Scarlett. She had a right to know the truth.

"Should I take you to bed?"

"Only if you're in it with me."

I pressed my face to the top of her head.

"I wouldn't want to be anywhere else."

I picked her up off the sofa with me and carried her upstairs to my room. Pulling back the covers, I set her down on the bed and tucked her in. I undid the top few buttons of my shirt and sat down next to her. She reached out and placed her hand on my thigh after I dragged my laptop off my bedside table.

Just because I wasn't going downstairs, didn't mean I wasn't going to work while Scarlett was sleeping.

I stroked her hair, watching her close her eyes and drift off. When I was sure she was asleep, I leant down and pressed a kiss to her forehead.

"I love you," I whispered.

Prescott had told me I needed to say it out loud. After my conversation with Scarlett, I couldn't help but utter the words, even though she couldn't hear me. It was a start. A steppingstone towards a better future with her. And I just hoped I would learn to forgive myself with her help so I could tell her when she was awake.

FORTY THREE

FRANCIS

My fingers brushed over the various chains I'd laid out on the bed in our play space. I had been concerned about doing this tonight when Scarlett had been through an emotional upheaval earlier. Prescott had assured me it would be exactly what she needed. And according to West, she'd spent half the day asleep, and the rest curled up on his chest while they watched a film together. My girl was well-rested and wanted me to give her an experience she wouldn't soon forget. I was so fucking ready for this, even if I was nervous too.

I heard a noise from behind me and turned around to find Scarlett closing the door behind her. Swallowing, I watched her approach me. She didn't have a stitch of clothing on her body. It was all I could do not to grab her, pin her down and do deviant things to her body. I clenched a fist to attempt to keep my cool.

"Hello, my little whore, are you ready for our game?" I asked when she stood before me.

The way she shuddered at my words had me fighting a smile. It was even harder not to when she knelt at my feet and bowed her head.

"Yes."

She'd braided her hair as I requested so it wouldn't be in the way or get caught up in the chains. My hand went to it, fisting it and forcing her head back. Those hazel-green eyes told me she was truly submitting. She would do anything I said.

"What's your safe word, Scar?"

"Red."

"Good girl."

I wanted her to know she could stop this at any time. It was important after the disaster that was Chelsea. But I wasn't going to think about her. It was time I put my demons to rest.

"Get on the bed."

I let go of her hair and she obeyed my command, crawling onto it, dodging past the chains and kneeling in the middle right where I wanted her. My hands went to the smaller chains, picking them up before I walked around to the side of the bed and knelt on it. I wrapped the small chains around her torso. They were set out a little like a harness and wrapped around her breasts, highlighting them on her chest. Then I put a leather collar around her throat. It had several metal rings around it.

Taking both her arms, I pushed them behind her back and attached metal cuffs to her biceps. They were joined in between by a metal bar. I secured another set around her forearms, then I cuffed her wrists together too. Through loops around each of the cuffs, I ran chains up from her wrists to her neck.

The next chain I attached was one to the front of her collar. It would act as my leash and a way for me to hold on to her if necessary.

"Is this too tight?" I asked, needing to reassure myself I hadn't hurt her.

"I'm fine, Frankie," she murmured, giving me a nod.

"Do you trust me?"

"Always."

Picking up a small silk item from the bed, I set the blindfold over her eyes. Scarlett let out a shuddering breath. Perhaps she was scared of what would happen next because the last time we'd blindfolded her, it had been when we'd taken her for the first time. I wasn't going to hurt her, though. I was going to drive her wild.

Carefully, I encouraged her to lie on her stomach. Then I cuffed her ankles, attaching a chain to each. I secured those chains to her collar, forcing her to bend up in a rather unnatural position, although I gave her a little leeway, so it wasn't too uncomfortable.

I stepped back and looked her over. She was so fucking beautiful it almost hurt to see her this way.

She would heal me. Set me free from all my fucking pain. This woman was my everything.

"You are... words can't describe how I feel right now. Is it okay for you?"

She couldn't move with the way I'd chained her up.

"I... I like it," she responded a moment later, "being bound by you... it makes me feel safe and free."

I let out a long breath, relieved she wasn't in pain or averse to this. Kneeling on the bed again, I ran my fingers up her calves, making her shudder in response. I intended to stroke her body around the chains until she was begging me to touch her pussy. My fingers went to the backs of her thighs, gently running along her skin.

"Frankie," she panted.

She could hear me, but she couldn't see. I was going to use it to my advantage. Shifting around to her side, I stroked her elbow right below where I'd secured the cuffs. Then my fingers went to her shoulder. My touch was so soft, it was likely tickling her. While I could use a crop or something else to do this, I preferred my hands on her. Skin on skin contact. With each stroke of my fingers, her breathing got heavier, like she was anticipating my every move.

Leaning closer, I pressed a kiss to her shoulder and made my way down her arm until I reached the first cuff. Scarlett squirmed as much as she could against her restraints.

"Oh god!"

"I'm not your god."

"No… no, you're not."

I kissed between her shoulder blades right between where her arms were bent back.

"What am I, little whore?"

I ran my fingers down her side, making her jerk.

"Frankie, please."

"I won't touch you where you want me to until you say it."

My fingers reached the curve of her arse. I brushed my fingers along her cheek. Scarlett let out a low whine.

"My horseman."

I moved lower until I was between her legs. Then I kissed my way down the inside of her calf towards her thigh.

"Which one, little whore?"

She tried to shift in her restraints. I kissed down her thigh, nearing her pussy, but not quite reaching it.

"Tell me if you want my tongue on your clit."

I blew on her pussy, making her tremble.

"Fuck," she cried out. "Please!"

"You know how to make this torture end."

I stroked her thighs, brushing my thumbs close to her pussy, teasing her with my touch. Perhaps it's what she wanted, for me to torture her like this. My hand slid up her cheek and grabbed hold of the chains attached to the cuffs on her wrists, pulling on them to put pressure on her throat.

"Or do you like it when I tease you, hmm?" I tugged harder. "I can see how wet you are, whore. You like this."

"No, no, I don't."

I chuckled and blew on her pussy again.

"A little liar as well as a whore. Such a bad girl."

"Frankie," she choked out. "Please touch me."

I tutted and smacked her across her behind, making her jolt again.

"Bad girls don't get rewards, whore. You should know that by now."

When she didn't respond to me, I smacked her again and again until she let out a little cry of distress, like it was too much for her.

"Have you had enough yet?"

I stroked her cheeks, tugging on her chains again. Then my thumb dipped between them, stroking just above her tight little hole.

"Please," she whined.

"Say it and I'll make you come so fucking hard."

Her pants got louder as I kept stroking her. My hand drifted from her behind, closer to her pussy. Closer to where she wanted me, but she hadn't said it. She hadn't given me what I'd asked for. I was desperate to hear it from her lips. This was me embracing who I was inside. Letting go of the past and forging ahead with the future. And I needed her to unbind the last chain wrapped around my heart.

"Frankie!"

I pulled even harder on her chains.

"That's not it, whore. I'm your fucking horseman. Tell me which one I am. Say it out loud."

I held the chains in place, almost choking her with them.

"God, please, Frankie, I need you. I need you so fucking bad."

"Say. It."

"Famine! Fuck, you're my Famine."

Releasing my hold on her chains, I spread her with both my hands, and then my tongue was between her legs, sliding between her folds and seeking out her clit. She moaned loudly when my tongue flicked over it. I shoved two fingers inside her pussy the next moment, making her squirm. There was no mercy to the way I pumped them inside her as I sucked her clit into my mouth. I wanted her to come hard before I fucked her. And when I did press inside her with my cock, I would deprive her of this all over again.

"Please, oh god, oh... oh, fuck."

I didn't say a word, kept fucking her with my fingers and tonguing her until she was gasping for air. And when she was on the precipice, I removed my tongue, leaving her hanging. She let out a pained whine as her body strained against her bindings.

"Did you think I was going to make it easy?" I murmured, pressing a kiss to her pussy as I continued to slide my fingers in and out of it.

I watched her shake her head.

"Mmm, are you going to be a good girl for me, little whore?"

"Yes, yes, I am. I promise."

Removing my fingers from her pussy, I stroked her clit with one. She let out a little sigh followed by a low moan when I spread her cheeks again with my other hand and tongued her little tight hole.

"Oh, oh, Frankie, fuck."

Her encouragement had me continuing since she was clearly enjoying the sensation. I rubbed her clit harder, making her body shake. Then I speared her pussy with two fingers. I ducked my head underneath my hand so I could tongue her clit again. This time, I didn't pull away when she was close. No, I sucked her clit into my mouth and ran my teeth over it.

"Shit, fuck, oh, oh, Frankie!"

She exploded, her pussy clenching hard around my fingers as she bucked in her chains. They rattled with her movements, making my cock throb in anticipation. I wasn't sure I could wait any longer. I needed inside her. Wanted to see her face as I thrust into her pussy over and over. I needed her to know how, even though I was the one tying her up, she was the one in control of my fucking heart. She owned every inch of me. And I would do everything in my power to be her safe space for the rest of our lives.

When her body stopped shaking, I shifted back, releasing her entirely as I sat up on my knees. Then I reached out, unchaining her legs from her neck so she could relax. She laid her head down on the bed as I lowered her legs. I released the chains, joining her collar to her arm cuffs and removed the cuffs from her ankles. I didn't need those any longer.

I flipped Scarlett over onto her back, my eyes roaming over the small chains clinging to her body. They'd left such delicious little marks all over her. I ran my hands down her chest, flicking her nipples and making her whimper in response.

"Are you ready for more, little whore?"

She nodded, biting down on her lip. I leant over her and licked her nipple.

"Use your words."

"I want more, please."

Biting down on her nipple, she arched into me as best she could, with her arms still bound behind her.

"Tell me exactly what you desire."

She planted her feet into the covers and pushed her hips up into me. Even though she couldn't see, she could feel me there. And there was no clearer sign of what she needed from me than this.

"I want you to fuck me."

I ran my hand down her stomach and dipped my fingers between her legs.

"How hard?"

"Make it hurt."

I almost groaned at her words.

Such a kinky little whore.

"And what do you want me to fuck you with?"

My fingers slid inside her wet little pussy, making her shift against the intrusion.

"Your cock. I want your cock so fucking badly. Please, please fuck me. Show me I'm your little whore, please."

How could I deny my sweet but fiery woman when she asked me so fucking nicely for it? When she told me exactly what she wanted.

"Please, don't deny me any longer... please, Famine... please fuck me."

FORTY FOUR

FRANCIS

I released Scarlett and shifted off the bed. My fingers went to my clothes, pulling them off until I was bare. There was nothing else I wanted more right now than to feel her wrapped around me. She'd done so beautifully. Having her fully restrained by chains was something I never imagined she'd allow. Scarlett surprised me at every turn. And yet I shouldn't have been. My girl had a reckless streak. Always willing to try new things, no matter the danger. Such a curious little thing. Needing to go one step further than anyone else.

I knelt back on the bed and ran my hands up her legs. She made a little sound of pleasure under her breath, clearly waiting for me to do more.

"I like denying you," I murmured, gripping her hips and pulling her up into my lap. "Seeing you all worked up is the highlight of my day."

Her pant in response was due to me rubbing my cock along her folds.

"Is this what you want, little whore? You want me to give you my dick?"

"Please."

"So fucking needy, aren't you?"

"Frankie, please."

She shifted her hips, rubbing against me. I dipped the tip into her pussy, making her moan from the small intrusion. Giving her a couple of shallow thrusts to tease her, my girl arched up, trying to take more.

"No wonder West started calling you a slut when you're so fucking desperate for dick."

I slid deeper, trying not to groan at the delicious sensations engulfing my cock.

"Only for you, Drake, Pres and West."

I settled my hand across her hip, sliding my thumb to her clit and rubbing gently.

"I should fucking hope so. You're ours."

She arched up into my touch.

"You're mine too. No one else is allowed to touch you."

I raised an eyebrow. Not that she could see.

"No? What would you do if they did?"

The way her lip curled up into a snarl had me thrusting deeper.

"Rip their fucking face off."

The vehemence in her voice had me rubbing her clit harder. I'd threatened violence to anyone who touched her, so for her to do the same? It made the emotions inside me expand. Made me fall ever deeper in love with this woman. The owner of my soul.

"Well, remind me never to get on your bad side."

One final thrust had me impaling her completely. I held myself there for a long moment, adoring the way she rippled around my cock. Then I let go of her hip to wrap my fist around the chain attached to her neck, tugging her up until she was seated in my lap. I held on and stroked my other hand down her body, pressing the small chains into her skin.

"I wouldn't hurt you, Frankie... I love you."

I shuddered at her words. Yes, she'd said it before and I believed her, but every time she told me how she felt, my heart ached with a longing to say it back.

My hand went to her blindfold, pulling it from her head. She blinked a few times before her eyes adjusted and focused on me. I ran my thumb along her bottom lip, rocking my hips into her to keep the friction between us.

"Do you?"

If I let go of the chain, she would flop back down on the bed, but I didn't want that. I needed her close. To be honest, I wanted her arms around me. It was so unlike me, with my need to restrain and bind who I was with. Scarlett was different. She was the balm to my burning soul.

"More than anything."

My hand slid behind her head, cupping the back of it so I could move her closer. Scarlett watched me with such an open expression of love, I was hard-pressed to keep my fucking cool. In fact, I was losing it. And I didn't care.

"Thank you for giving me your heart," I whispered, my voice growing hoarse.

Then I was pulling her off me and flipping her onto her stomach. My hands fumbled with my need to uncuff her. One by one, they came off, and I discarded them on the bed.

Scarlett stretched her arms out, but I didn't give her much time to do it. I turned her back over and pulled her into my lap again, sinking her down on me. I took her hands and placed them on me, wanting her touch so fucking much, it almost hurt.

Her brow was furrowed when I looked at her.

"What's wrong?"

I undid the collar from around her neck and threw it away. Then I cupped her face with one hand, stroking her jaw.

"Nothing."

"Why did you take them off?"

How to answer that… how to begin to explain… fuck. I just need you, Scar.

I shifted and laid her down with me, covering her body with mine while remaining deep inside her.

"Frankie?"

"I… I need you to hold me."

The way her expression grew soft had my heart slamming against my ribcage. She wrapped both her arms around me and slid her legs over mine, holding me close. A part of me felt complete with her pressed against me this way.

"Like this?"

I nodded, resting my forehead against hers. Her hands stroked along my skin. I trembled under her touch, feeling so fucking vulnerable and exposed as she stared up at me.

"I'd do anything for you," she murmured. "All you need to do is ask."

"I know, Scar… I know… I'm just…"

"Just what?"

"Scared," I whispered.

"Of what?"

"The way I feel about you."

Being in love with her wasn't terrifying, it was the depth and level of my devotion to this woman. The way she completed me. How she never judged or made me feel like I wasn't her everything, despite the fact she cared for three other people the same way.

I would die for you, Scarlett Nyx. I would lay down my life in place of yours.

"Why?"

"Because… because I'm so in love with you, it hurts to look at you and feel these things. To know I would give up everything to be near you. I love you, Scar. Loving you is like breathing fucking air. I can't live without it."

I moved inside her, needing to drown in her after I'd admitted the truth.

"I need you. I've always needed you and it's only now I realise how much."

My mouth found hers, kissing her deeply until we were both breathless. She moved back against me, angling her hips to give me more access. I planted a hand next to her head, rising up a little to get better leverage.

"You have me," she told me before kissing me again. "You always have me. Forever. I promise. I love you. I love you. I love you." She punctuated each one with a kiss. "You're the safest place I'll ever have. I belong with you."

I buried my face in her neck, pressing harder against her while I continued to pound her deliciously wet pussy. The relief I felt inside me at finally being able to tell her I loved her was making me all the more desperate to come inside her. To claim what was mine.

"Harder," she moaned beneath me.

My free hand wrapped around her hip, gripping her to angle her upwards, giving me access to fuck her deeper and give her more. She pressed her feet into the covers to help me, matching me thrust for thrust.

"Fuck, Scar," I groaned against her skin.

One of her hands clutched my back while the other slid between us so she could stroke herself. I only continued my rhythm, wanting to make sure she reached the edge too. Needing to feel her as she came.

"I'm going to... fuck, Frankie, I'm..."

Her words set her off, making her clench hard around me. I choked out a breath, sinking deeper inside her to feel the waves of her climax washing over her body. Then I fell too, feeling it drown me. Her. She was the wielding force behind the eruption. I slammed into her again and again, wanting it never to end. Wanting her this way forever.

"Scar," I whispered, "I love you. I love you so much."

I didn't care that I hadn't kept her chained up the whole time. This feeling. This moment. It was worth it. Worth everything. I didn't need anything else but me and her together. Scarlett did the fucking impossible and set my demons free. My whole soul felt lighter from the experience of being with her like this. From showing her my true self. And giving her my heart.

The comedown was slow and winding, neither of us wanting to let go of each other. I kissed her up her jaw and met her mouth. Scarlett's hands speared into my hair, pulling me closer. We kissed, tongues curling around each other like they belonged this way. Then I finally released her, pulling away and laying down beside her on my back. She curled up against my side, stroking my stomach in slow circles.

"Was that everything you needed?" she asked after a long moment of silence.

I turned my head to look at her.

"Why wouldn't it be?"

"I guess I just want to know that it helped with... you know."

Reaching over, I ran my finger down her cheek.

"It did."

She pressed a kiss to my collarbone.

"But that's not the only reason I wanted to chain you up. I wanted you, Scar. You are who I need."

Her smile made my chest squeeze.

"Don't worry, you made it very clear how much you wanted me. All that teasing and making me wait only made me come harder."

I snorted and stroked her shoulder.

"That's the idea. Maybe next time I'll make you wait longer. Or... perhaps I'll get one of the others to help me tease you."

Her eyes widened.

"Who?"

I tipped her chin up with my fingers.

"That's for me to know and for you to find out."

She pouted.

"That's not fair."

"I'm not a fair guy when it comes to you in my bed."

I kissed her gently to soften my words. There were a few ideas knocking around in my head. I knew she liked to be spanked, so perhaps I would enlist Drake's help next time. He wouldn't object to punishing her with his palms while she was chained up and helpless. I had to shove the thought away before it made my dick hard again.

We lay together for a few more minutes before I sat up and helped her out of the rest of the chains. The indents all over her body were beautiful. I stared at them for a long time before I picked her up and carried her out of the room. I'd tidy the place up tomorrow. We went along the hallway to my bedroom and I set her down in my bathroom. We cleaned up together, making sure to be thorough.

She stood by my wardrobes a few minutes later looking over her clothes while I lounged on the bed in my boxers.

"You not coming to bed?" I asked when she slid her fingers over a blouse.

"I'm not tired if I'm honest."

"No? Planning on staying up late like Drake always does?"

She turned her head towards me and frowned.

"What do you mean?"

I probably shouldn't have said anything if he hadn't told her, but Drake wasn't big on giving up his secrets. And given I couldn't get him to take his fucking sleeping pills, maybe she could.

"Drake is a bit of an insomniac. That's why he had the rooftop garden built. He plays up there at night so he doesn't disturb the rest of us."

"He has insomnia? So that's why he's awake at weird hours."

"Mmm. And he refuses to medicate it because he's a stubborn bastard who overthinks all the damn time."

She smiled.

"I've never met anyone more stubborn than him... except perhaps West, but he's more determined than stubborn."

Determined was one word to describe West. He was single-mindedly hell-bent on a path of destruction. And in all honesty, I couldn't blame him. Life hadn't been kind to any of us, but especially not him.

"Well, perhaps you can talk some sense into him. He let you tie him up, so maybe he'll listen to you about this."

She laughed and shook her head. Then she pulled out a little floaty black dress, sliding it over her body without putting anything on underneath it. She came over to the bed and leant over me, pressing a kiss to my lips.

"You don't mind if I go speak to him about it? I'll be back, I promise."

"Of course not. Go deal with my idiot best friend. I'll be waiting."

She smiled and kissed me again.

"I love you, Frankie."

I stroked her cheek.

"I love you too, my little whore."

She visibly shivered before she pulled away. I picked up the book I'd left on my bedside table and tucked myself under the covers. If Scarlett could help Drake with his little problem, then I had no issues with her disappearing for an hour or so. I looked forward to her return. Falling asleep with her in my arms after declaring my love would be a perfect end to this evening.

I'd be forever grateful to my girl for helping set me free from my past and reassuring me we would remain together for the rest of our lives.

FORTY FIVE

SCARLETT

M y feet carried me up the stairs towards the roof. I slipped on a pair of sandals before I came up here. They were soft on the concrete floor as I made my way towards Drake's glass structure. He hadn't been anywhere in the penthouse, not that I'd checked his bedroom. I'd never been in there before and I wasn't sure if or when Drake intended to allow me access to his private space.

Drake sat in his armchair reading on his tablet. His hair was messy like he'd run his hands through it several times. He'd changed out of his suit into a plain white t-shirt and dark jeans. His feet were bare as usual.

Drake looked up when I approached, his brow furrowing as he took me in.

"What are you doing up here?"

"Well, hello to you too. Did you turn into Mr Grumpy between now and dinner?"

He scowled at my words.

"No."

"Am I not allowed up here?"

He rubbed his cheek.

"You are."

"Then what's the problem?"

I stopped next to his feet, looking down at the supposedly not grumpy and very stubborn man who drove me crazy at times with his cold-heartedness. We were working on that. On getting him to open up to me completely.

"There isn't one. I was merely asking why you are here."

"I wanted to see you."

He looked stumped.

"Oh."

"May I?"

I waved at his lap. He set his tablet down on the arm of the chair. I slid into his waiting lap and stroked his chest.

"Is something bothering you, Drake?"

"Other than the obvious, no."

My fingers left his chest and curled into his hair instead, stroking his scalp. Drake's lip twitched at the contact, telling me he liked it even if he wasn't willing to admit it.

"Are you sure? I can help you if it is."

He gave me a suspicious look. I didn't want to come out and straight-up tell him Francis had disclosed his insomnia to me. Then again, I wasn't sure how else to broach the subject. Drake wasn't exactly the most forthcoming person. It's not as if I'd forgotten what happened with Stuart earlier but being with West all day and then Francis this evening had made me feel better. I was less anxious about Stuart's threats. The boys would protect me. I was safe here with them.

"I'm fine, Scarlett."

I leant closer, pressing my lips to his jaw.

"I don't think you are. In fact, I think I know what you need to help you feel better."

He didn't stop my advances.

"What's that?"

"To punish me for making you let me tie you up."

He let out a breath. Then his hand fisted my braid, and he pulled me away from him. Those indigo eyes became hard.

"That's only one of the things I want to punish that bratty little mouth for."

I smiled at him. It only made his demeanour that much more terrifying. And my pussy throbbed in anticipation. Yes, Francis had thoroughly fucked me and made me feel on top of the world, but it didn't stop me from reacting to Drake this way. Fear made me wet.

Over the past few days, mine and Drake's relationship had turned over a new leaf. If I was ever going to get him to keep opening up to me, then I needed to push him harder.

"This mouth?" I licked my lips.

"Yes. Get on your knees."

He didn't let go of my braid as I slid off the chair, instead, leaning forward with me. His other hand curled around my jaw, gripping it in an iron hold. It hadn't taken much for me to provoke him into punishing me. And I was rather pleased with myself for getting him on board so quickly.

"You're going to put this bratty mouth to good use rather than taunting me with it. Do you understand?"

"Yes, sir."

"Good. Now get my cock out and suck it. You better make it good or I'll be very disappointed in you, Scarlett."

I shivered with his words. The deepness of his commanding voice had me trying not to rub my legs together.

"Yes, sir."

He released me and sat back, putting his arms on either side of the chair. I leant forward and undid his jeans, stroking my hand along his length. It jerked under my touch. He was already hard. I tried not to smile. This turned him on. And I couldn't any longer deny I liked it when he ordered me to do his bidding. I liked it when he punished me. And I liked it when he made me afraid of what he'd do next.

When I freed him, I licked around the crown. He didn't outwardly react to it. His cold, hard stare made me shake. I wrapped my hand around the base and sucked him into my mouth. The way he watched me with a rather impassive expression as I took more had me wanting to put my hand under the skirt of my dress. I wouldn't. No doubt if I started touching myself, he would put me across his knee.

You want that.

I tried to shove the thought away, but it blared in my head.

Do it. Provoke him into spanking you. You want it. You want him to do it then fuck you with that cold expression of fury on his face.

What was getting into me? Was I turning into the brat he kept telling me I was? Did it even matter when I craved this? It had been far too long since he'd seriously punished me. After what happened in the playroom between us, things had been shaky. Now I'd accepted I liked the way he treated me, how he would teach me a lesson for misbehaving, I wanted us to get back to that. And what better way to start than deliberately taunting him.

Smiling around his dick, I slid my other hand under my skirt. His eyes registered the movement almost immediately. Then they blazed with annoyance. I'd hit the mark.

"I didn't say you could touch yourself, Scarlett."

I popped off his dick.

"I can't help it, sir, sucking you off makes me so wet."

He didn't need to say a word for me to know he was even more turned on by me disobeying him than he wanted to admit.

"Such a brat," he muttered, then leant forward, grabbing my braid again and hauling me into his lap. He lay me across his spread legs and ran his hand along my behind. The next thing I knew, he'd flipped up my skirt and found me knicker-less.

"Have you been walking around with a bare pussy again, Scarlett?"

"Yes, sir."

"So brazen. I see I'm going to have to teach you why that's inappropriate."

"Don't you like knowing you can fuck me at any time?"

I heard him stifle a groan. He did like it but he wasn't going to admit it.

His palm came down hard on my behind, making me jerk in his lap.

"I expect you to wear underwear at work. If I find you without, I will put you over my knee and punish you until you're crying. Then I'll leave your bare little pussy unfulfilled for an entire day until you've learnt to keep yourself in check."

I shuddered as he continued to spank me, each slap harder than the ones before.

"And before you think about coming up with a loophole, I'll inform the others they're not allowed to touch you either. It won't just be a punishment for you, it'll be for them too."

I whined under the strain of the pain radiating from my backside. Not to mention what he'd just threatened.

"Yes... sir," I choked out as the slaps kept coming.

This spanking he was giving me felt like a long time coming. It had been building between us ever since we'd established this new branch of our relationship. I desperately wanted to tell him how much I needed it. How I desired the pain he dished out. How it made me wet and achy for his thick cock inside me.

When I thought I couldn't take it any longer, he stilled, rubbing his hand over my cheek. The movement aggravated my sore, abused skin. I whimpered, shifting in his lap. His cock was still out. I could feel it digging into my stomach.

"Get on your hands and knees facing away from me."

The command had me scrambling to obey. I crawled onto the floor and presented myself to him. I didn't look back, but I felt him kneel behind me. Both of his hands landed on my cheeks, making me wince. Then his cock was nudging my entrance, sliding back and forth across it.

"Is this what you want, Scarlett?"

"Please, sir. Please fuck me."

Drake could probably see all of the impressions on my skin Francis' cuffs and chains had left when he shoved my dress further up my body, but he didn't comment on it. His hands were back on my backside, kneading the sore flesh. I bit my lip, trying to hold still while he punished me all over again with the movement. It was made worse by the way he thrust against my pussy, the head of his dick knocking against my clit repeatedly.

"Fuck, Drake! Fuck me, please."

I earnt another slap across my raw behind. Calling him Drake had been the wrong thing to say, but I didn't care. I wanted him more than I gave a shit about being punished.

"Please," I all but cried.

And finally, Drake gave me the relief I so desperately craved. He sunk his dick inside me. I let out a harsh pant. The wetness of my pussy allowed him to slide inside me with absolute ease. He went deeper, making my fingers curl beneath me. I winced when he gripped my behind yet again instead of my hips. He began to thrust, holding my raw skin like he wanted to further punish me. I was so over sensitised from Francis' teasing earlier and Drake's punishment, I arched my back and tried not to come instantly. Usually, I needed external stimulation, but my body was hyper-aware of every part of him that was touching me. The way his hips slapped against me with each of his thrusts, making me take him deep and hard.

"Fuck!"

If he stroked my clit right now, I would fall apart on the spot. The way he was mercilessly ramming his dick into me, pressing against the right spot with each of his strokes was a pleasure overload.

I dared to look back at him. Drake's cold and stoic expression had my heart stuttering in my chest. He was so focused on fucking me, making me feel every inch of him inside me. There was such brutality in the way he gave it to me.

Like he was doing this to punish me too. And I loved every moment no matter how much my body strained to take the unrelenting force of his body pounding into mine.

Then he adjusted his angle. It was like a fucking firework went off inside my body, sending waves of pleasure and pain up my spine. Drake hammered into my most sensitive spot like he was hell-bent on driving me into oblivion. I cried out, my hands scrabbling against the wooden floor below me.

"If you want to be a good girl, you'll come for me," he gritted out. "Come all over my cock, Scarlett."

His hand tightened around my punished skin while the other slid underneath me. All I could focus on was his words and the untold pleasure building inside me. A good girl. I could be a good girl for him. His fingers were on my clit, stroking across it without mercy. And I was fucking done. My elbows gave way as my climax rocked through me, I slid to the floor, my hips only held up by Drake's hands on me and his dick impaled in my trembling body.

I was lost to him. I never wanted us to go back to the toxic push and pull between us. All I wanted was this. Him being unrelenting in the way he fucked me after he dished out punishment. I wanted Drake to open up to me fully. For us to be a mix between how we were as friends when we were younger and how we were now in our rather tumultuous sexual relationship. I just wanted him to be... mine.

When I came down from the clouds, Drake pulled out of me and tugged me up by my braid. He spun me around on my knees and shoved me down on his dick. I opened my mouth in time for him to slide into it. A few sharp thrusts and then he was coming down my throat.

"Swallow it," he demanded in a low growl that had me shuddering.

I did as he asked the best I could with him still erupting in my mouth. When he pulled away and tucked himself back in his jeans, I swallowed hard. Tipping my head back, I looked up at him. His expression was no longer so fierce and unyielding. In fact, he looked at me with tenderness as he put his hand out to me. I let him pull me to my feet and didn't object when he wrapped an arm around me to hold me against him. My legs were still a little shaky.

"Did you come up here to provoke me?" he murmured as he ran the fingers of his free hand down my throat before curling them around the back of my neck.

"No... I came up here to talk to you, but then you seemed grumpy so I thought you might need me to help you relax and get your mind off whatever it is that's bothering you."

He let out a sigh and pressed me harder against his body.

"Apparently you know me better than I do."

"Do you have trouble sleeping?"

I decided I might as well come out and ask him about it. Drake wasn't the type to beat around the bush.

He narrowed his eyes.

"Who told you?"

"Frankie."

He let out another sigh and looked away over the city skyline.

"Yes, I do... it's like my brain doesn't stop whirling. I have a very hard time shutting off."

"Does nothing help?"

I wanted to know if there was anything I could do for him. Thinking of him up here all alone night after night made my heart ache. His loneliness was too much for me to handle. All I wanted to do was be there for him the way I had been when we'd been kids.

"A few things do. And you just gave me one of them."

I grinned.

"Oh? Sex helps, does it?"

He rolled his eyes and looked at me again.

"Yes, but it's more than that… it's you. Even though I worry about you all the time, having you here next to me makes it… better."

My hands went to his chest, sliding up it.

"I make you better?"

He nodded.

"Well, allow me to help you even more in that case."

I went up on my tiptoes and kissed him. He gathered me up against his chest, kissing me back with the intensity that was uniquely Drake. The very stubborn ice king of my heart devoured my mouth, making my toes curl and my chest ache with the way he attacked me with his tongue.

When he let me go, I dropped back down to my feet, but Drake cupped my face with both his hands.

"I'm trying," he whispered, staring at me with no small amount of affection in his eyes. "I'm really trying to let you in, little wisp."

I bit my lip, attempting to process what he'd just called me. The other three had given me pet names, but Drake having one for me was new. He was the one who came up with my Little Nyx nickname. It didn't feel quite like me any longer even though I was Scarlett Nyx. I preferred their individual names for me. They made me feel special.

"That's new," I whispered back.

He actually smiled at me.

"It's how I see you in my head. A little wisp of a woman come to drive me to distraction."

His little wisp. I can't believe that's what you call me in your head, you beautifully stubborn man.

I didn't want to press him further on it, but it made my heart hurt. Drake was trying, and it was all I could ask for.

"I'm not sure you'd be very impressed if I told you how adorable I think you are when you're being sweet."

He didn't stop smiling, but he shook his head. Leaning closer, he pressed a kiss to my forehead. It made me relax further into his body. The gesture meant everything to me. Then I tried to hold back a yawn as tiredness settled over me. I'd been thoroughly used this evening, and it was starting to hit me.

Drake chuckled as he pulled back and saw me putting my hand over my mouth.

"I think someone needs to get some sleep."

"I guess you're right."

He stroked my face and dropped his arms from around me.

"Go to bed, little wisp. We'll talk more tomorrow, hmm?"

I nodded, stroking his arm and gave him a smile. Then I turned and walked away towards the stairwell, feeling on top of the fucking world. Yes, there were a thousand things going on that were so wrong, but everything between me and the boys was good. I finally felt like we were on the right track with each other.

I practically skipped into the stairwell, completely ready to curl up in bed with Francis. My head was in the clouds as I descended the first lot of stairs. As I turned the corner to go down the next set to get to the penthouse floor, a coldness washed over me, making me shiver a little. Before I had a chance to glance around to see where it came from, I was forcibly slammed against the wall by a large solid body. I let out a yelp, surprised by the sudden movement. A hand slid over my mouth, muffling the sound.

The next thing I knew, a hood was shoved over my head and tightened around my neck after the person slid their hand from my mouth. They pressed it back over on top of the fabric, stopping me from making another sound. I struggled against them, regaining my senses.

What the fuck is happening?

Something sharp dug into my neck. I cried out against the hand over my mouth, continuing to wriggle and try to push them off me. The body was too fucking solidly built for me to do much. They held me against the wall as my movements grew sluggish. Then I knew what the fuck the sharp prick was. Whoever this was had drugged me. This was a kidnapping. I was being kidnapped yet again.

Fuck. Holy fuck. No. No! This can't be happening! It can't be!

I was almost desperate with my struggles but my body grew weaker until it almost gave out.

The last thing I thought about before I lost consciousness was that I should have heeded Stuart's warning about him coming for me. Perhaps the boys weren't able to keep me safe after all. And I might need to save myself before this war was over.

ACKNOWLEDGEMENTS

Thank you so much for taking the time to read this book. I really appreciate all of my readers and hope this book gave you as much joy reading it as I did writing it.

My biggest thanks for this book goes out to my amazing friend and alpha reader, Ashley. This has been quite the adventure. You and I both know this book almost broke us emotionally. The trials and tribulations these characters went through gave me such a lot of heartbreak and joy. You were there every step of the way, making sure I got my words down, helping me through the difficult patches and just being the most amazing best friend I could ever ask for. There might be an ocean between us, but that never stopped us. ILY bby! You and me for life… along with all the Daddies!

Thank you to Chrishawn for being an amazing friend and helping me get through this mammoth monster of a book. I'm so grateful to have you in my life.

Big thank you to my author bestie, Elle. We've grown so much over the years together and I'm grateful to have you in my life to share our writing woes and successes.

Thank you to my husband for being there for me no matter what and always putting up with my craziness. Love you to the stars and back.

ABOUT THE AUTHOR

Sarah writes dark, contemporary, erotic and paranormal romances. They adore all forms of steamy romance and can always be found with a book or ten on their Kindle. They love anti-heroes, alpha males and flawed characters with a little bit of darkness lurking within. Their writing buddies nicknamed Sarah: 'The Queen of Steam' for their pulse racing sex scenes which will leave you a little hot under the collar.

Born and raised in Sussex, UK near the Ashdown Forest, they grew up climbing trees and building Lego towns with their younger brother. Sarah fell in love with novels as teenager reading their aunt's historical regency romances. They have always loved the supernatural and exploring the darker side of romance and fantasy novels.

Sarah currently resides in the Scottish Highlands with their husband. Music is one of their biggest inspirations and they always have something on in the background whilst writing. They are an avid gamer and are often found hogging their husband's Xbox.